a timeless series novel

Cheyenne

book one

Lisa L Wiedmeier

Copyright © 2011 by Lisa L. Wiedmeier
Editor: Sam Dogra
Copy Editor: A-1 Editing Services, Jodi Tahsler
Front cover design by Phatpuppy Art
Back cover design by Timeless Productions

For more information on the Timeless Series visit:
http://www.lisawiedmeier.com/ www.timelessseriesnovels.com /
www.facebook.com/TimelessSeriesNovels /
http://lisawiedmeier.blogspot.com/

Edition III
ISBN-978-0-983-9052-0-2

For Glenn, Coley and Cody.

The other loves in my life.

ACKNOWLEDGMENTS

Mom, Dad, Laura, Lane, Kelli, Meagan, and extended family—For loving and supporting me through this journey.

Kayla, and Amanda—My first readers who pushed me on.

Sam—RRPS Master and diamond carver who helped me fashion Cheyenne into a true gem.

Andre, Kim, Connie, and Judy—Whose kinds words and support encouraged me to reach new heights.

Sandra, Julia, Anita and Kelli—My first book addicts.

Courtney—My first Team Callon member.

If I could have looked into the future to see what I would have become, I wouldn't have become the person I was always meant be. ~ lw

1

CHAPTER 1

The warm breeze caressed my cheeks, and I sighed. The sun was filtering through the forty-foot pines that surrounded our home, casting sunshine smiles. At least, that's what mom called them when I was young. She said the sun did this to spread its happiness throughout the forest. I smiled; she had a unique way of painting the world to a four year old.

A large glop of soap dropped on my head followed by a sprinkling of water. I fell back on my hands, and the car mitt I was using to wash the wheels of my Jeep became encrusted with gravel from my driveway. I knew who the culprit was.

"Colt, behave yourself!" I shook my head as I rose to my feet. He was being especially devious today for some reason. Our eyes locked, blue on blue. His bulky fingers were wrapped around the hose sprayer as if it were the trigger of a gun.

"Don't even think about it," I said firmly as a glint formed in his eyes. He wanted to see how far he could push my patience.

"And what if it just accidently happens, Cheyenne?" A sly grin formed on his lips.

1

"Then you will find out what payback means." I fought to provide a firm tone of reprimand. He knew as well as I did that I could probably never pay him back. But it was worth a shot. He stood and stared me down for a few long moments. He pressed the trigger on the hose and proceeded to rinse the remaining soap off the roof of my Jeep.

Looking at the mitt in my hand, I began to pluck off the gravel. Moments later, I gave up and walked alongside him, raising my mitt and watched him grin.

"You just can't keep anything clean, can you?" he asked. I rolled my eyes. He knew he was the one who caused the problem, yet felt the need to tease me—just as he teased me about everything.

"Just rinse it off for me, please. I can't wash my car with gravel." I extended my arm, and he turned the sprayer on full blast. I cringed as the rock fragments flew off, and the water coated the front of my shirt as well as my jeans.

"Oops." A hearty chuckle followed.

Calculatingly, I gradually raised my eyes to his and narrowed them. "Oops?" I questioned.

"Oops," he replied as he raised his brows, trying hard not to laugh.

I lunged for the hose. We were both laughing and wrestling for control of the trigger. I knew I was no match for him. He was enormous in comparison to my frame of five foot five. He was around six four, stocky, and should have been a football player. He should have been a lot of other things, the last of which was my best friend.

Running around the side of the Jeep, I grabbed the bucket of soapy water. He was right behind me. I managed to swing it in his direction, and the water lurched out, hitting him square in the chest.

2

I burst into loud laughter. Colt didn't slow as he lifted me from the ground and carried me to the grass in my front yard.

"Oh, you will pay for that one!" he said as he tickled me.

"Stop! You'll make me pee my pants!" I screeched.

He continued with his tickling. "I'd like to see that!"

"Colt!" I pleaded. Eventually he stopped and sat next to me, both of us catching our breaths. "I'm soaked you know," I said through my smile. He looked down and grinned.

"Yes, you are." He sighed and lowered himself to his back, and we both lay and looked up through the trees. We were lying in a patch of sunshine, and the sun heated us nicely. It had been an unusually warm spring so far. Today was the start of spring break for us. Colt had come over to help me wash my car before I left for a week-long camping trip with my parents.

"Are you sure you can't come with us?" I rolled to my side to get a better look at him. This was one of the few times we could see eye to eye. He had come on quite a few camping trips with us over the last year and a half. My adoptive parents, Gene and Alexis, loved him. Often they would invite him without even telling me.

"I would if I could, but I already told you that I'm going away for the week."

"You've said you were going away, but you haven't told me where." I began to fiddle with a blade of grass between my fingers, somewhat annoyed that he wouldn't tell me his vacation plans. What was the big deal?

"It's not important. I'll be back Sunday. You should be home by then. I'll come over as soon as I can." He picked up a small twig and tapped my blade of grass with it. "You can call or text if you have service." He was trying to ease my irritation.

"So, why is it that you're my friend again? You should be playing football and dating the head cheerleader or something, but instead you're here, tormenting me and supposedly helping wash my car." Sarcasm riddled my words. If he could be troublesome in one way, then I could be troublesome in another.

"I've been wondering about that myself." He began tapping his finger to his temple, pretending to be deep in thought. "However, that answer is probably lost in the mists of time." I wrinkled my nose at him. A lock of his blonde hair tumbled forward, and I giggled. "Let's see, I'm your friend because we get along so well, for starters. You're not like any typical girl I've been around...hmm, as for football, I already told you I've had too many concussions, so I can't play anymore. And as for the head cheerleader," he snorted. "Who needs that headache?" He tilted his chin down. "Does that work for you?"

"I suppose that will have to do," I rolled my eyes.

He soared over me, as he began his tickling assault again. "Stop!" I bellowed with little success. He eventually relented and helped me to my feet. The afternoon had waned, and we began cleaning up the mess. I took the bucket and the cleaning mitt to the front porch while Colt wound up the hose.

"You have to get going, don't you?" I frowned slightly as my long blonde hair drifted in the breeze, disrupting my sight of Colt. I tucked it behind my ears.

"Yeah, I have a flight to catch." He sounded disappointed. "Your parents are due home about six, right?"

"Yeah. My dad's plane came in about an hour ago. They were supposed to stop and get my mom a new cell phone and talk to them about the service up here. It's been hit or miss lately. The error code comes up as network problems." I paused as I looked out into the forest surrounding our home. My eyes caught sight of a dark shadow. It moved so quickly that, had I blinked, I would have missed it. I stared, trying to determine if it was real. I was getting a small headache, so maybe it was just a dark blotch in my vision.

"Cheyenne?" Colt said quietly, bringing my attention back to our conversation as his fingers touched my arm.

I looked up. "After that they'll be home. Thanks to your help, I already have the camping gear lined up in the hallway. They wanted to leave tonight."

Colt glanced at his watch, his gaze reflecting his reluctance to depart. For being just my friend, he was a little on the protective side. I guessed it's a guy thing.

I wasn't quite sure how I had gotten so lucky to have Colt as a friend. He had begun hanging out with me at the start of my junior year. Looking a little bewildered, he said he was lost when he came into the first class. He asked for my help, and though I was surprised he asked me, I complied. We found out that we had all the same classes together. At the time I thought it was strange, but I figured there are only so many combinations. He was easy to get along with, and I found myself hoping we'd become friends. Pretty soon, we were always together, and after he met my parents, they started inviting him to join us all the time.

"Come on," I took hold of his arm. "You need to go. I'll be fine." I walked with him to his motorcycle. He had been excited to have it out recently with the nicer weather. The balmy afternoon was unusual for us, living in a mountainous region of northern Idaho. The spring temperatures were warmer than expected, but I wasn't complaining. Colt mounted his bike, and I stood a few feet away as he started it.

"You know, for someone who's had too many concussions, you really should be wearing a helmet."

He didn't reply, but just grinned, and I shook my head. I stepped closer to remove the few leaves I saw stuck in his tousled hair. He very slowly and intentionally gave me a hug. I inhaled slightly, his musky scent filling my head as his arms tightened. It's not that it was unlike him to hug me good-bye; however, the way he did it set my senses on high alert. He drew back and placed a warm kiss on my cheek, near my ear, lingering as his breath caused my pulse to beat faster.

"Miss you already, Cheyenne."

I swallowed and stepped back. "Same here," I replied in a choked voice, and I swore that I heard him chuckle under his breath.

"I'll see you next Sunday." He smiled as he revved the engine.

I watched as he rode down our long gravel driveway and disappeared into the surrounding pine trees lining the highway. I wasn't sure what to make of it all—his hug and lingering touch.

The breeze touched my skin again and caused the hair on the back of my neck to stand on end, but it wasn't from being cold. I turned and looked into the forest surrounding my home, trying to shake off the feeling that someone was watching me, a shadow constantly looming—like the shadow I thought I saw earlier. I always felt safe when Colt or my parents were around, but when they were gone, it was a different story. I didn't dare tell them. I didn't need them to think I was paranoid.

I quickly entered the house.

Colt was not only my best friend; he was pretty much my only friend. We had moved a lot over the years, and this was the longest we had stayed in any one location—Sagle, Idaho. It was going on three years. Relocating so much made it difficult to get close enough to anyone. I always had it in the back of my mind that I shouldn't invest too much energy, as we wouldn't be around. Colt and I were due to graduate in May, but my parents had been acting weird again. This was usually the sign of an impending move.

Plopping down on the couch in the living room, I stared at the sleeping bags, camp stove and miscellaneous equipment. Even though it was my spring break, my parents had outvoted me, and we were going camping again. It's not that I really minded going camping, but I would rather have spent spring break in a tropical location for a change. I wanted a great tan. I wanted the sun to give my hair more blonde streaks. I wanted to brag to Colt about my skin being darker than his when I came back. Torture and tease him, just a little, as he always did to me. I smiled. We always had fun together. He always knew how to brighten my day.

My parents were excited about this trip. They had been planning it for months, and the warm weather was a bonus. It didn't matter what the weather conditions were, though; they were not intimidated by storms in the least. I can't say I felt the same way. My parents were excited to get away, to have time to talk, they said. They had mentioned there was something they wanted to discuss with me. My mom wouldn't give me any hints, but she said that I was finally old enough to know and to understand whatever the big secret was. I was an only child. My parents had adopted me as an infant, as they were unable to have children of their own. Did it have to do with my birth parents? I wondered.

My phone vibrated. It was my mom. "We're running late. Be home soon," the text read.

I replied, "K. See you soon." I hit the send button and "network error" displayed. Argh! What a pain this was becoming! Apparently, they hadn't stopped to get it fixed yet. I would have called, but when my phone gave that display, nothing would go through. We didn't have a land line anymore, only cell phones.

My stomach growled. I glanced at the clock, and it was after five thirty. Grabbing a yogurt and bottle of water from the kitchen, I rummaged through the pantry for some granola bars. I ate my snack and waited patiently for them to arrive.

Seven o'clock rolled around, and they still weren't home. I was starting to grow anxious. Because we lived on the outskirts of town, the airport was at least an hour and a half away. It took me over half an hour to get to school. I began pacing. Another fifteen minutes passed, and I picked up my phone again to text both my mom and dad.

"Where are you? You said late, but how late?" I hit send, and there was no error message this time. I fiddled with my ring as I waited. My mom was usually really quick with her replies—she never kept me hanging. Five minutes passed and nothing. I dialed her number. Thankfully it rang, but it went straight to her voicemail.

"Mom, where are you? I'm getting really worried. Call me." I hung up and immediately dialed my dad's number. It also went to his voicemail. "Dad, what's going on? I thought you would already be home. Please call me. I just want to make sure everything is alright." I pressed end and waited.

My heart began to thump as I waited. Something wasn't right, and I felt it down to my bones. The computer! I ran to my laptop and immediately began searching the internet for any recent news. My imagination was running out of control. I tried to convince myself that they were just delayed because of some road construction, or maybe there was an accident on the highway and they weren't able to get around it. If I was having network errors, then what was there to say they weren't also? Maybe they were in a bad zone and couldn't receive my texts or voicemail. They would be calling any minute. I was sure of it.

The internet and television provided no information. My shaking hand hit the off button on the remote. I glanced at the clock hanging above the antique desk in the corner of the living room. It was now ten p.m. My head jerked to the sound of tires on the gravel drive and then a car door closing. Relief washed over me, and I headed towards the front door.

Pulling it open, I saw the last person I would have been expecting.

"Cheyenne Wilson?" a warm, deep voice said as the man stepped up on the porch and into the light. It was the local sheriff. I had met him a couple times with my parents while in town.

"Yes?" I held onto the doorframe to steady myself.

"I don't know if you remember me, but I'm Sheriff Taylor."

"Yes," I replied with a shaky voice. "I remember you."

Hesitating, he took a step closer. His brow was creased and his jaw tight. His fingers were white from pressing so hard on the hat he held in both of his hands.

"May I come in?" he asked. "I need to talk with you."

Blinking, my breaths grew heavier. It couldn't be good news. "S-sure," I replied and stepped further into the hall. I swallowed. "Watch your step. My parents and I are going camping this week. I have all the gear out in the hallway." I tried to remain calm as I said it, tried to distract myself from thinking about the real reason he had come.

Nodding, he walked into the living room. I slowly closed the door and followed. He had turned towards me and was waiting.

"Can we sit?" he suggested.

Numbly, I walked to the couch, and he sat on the coffee table in front of me. "W-what's going on?" Suddenly I was trembling in dread.

"Cheyenne," he said softly, as he set his hat on the table next to him. "I'm afraid I have some bad news for you."

Everything froze in place when he said those words. I didn't move. I didn't breathe. I didn't blink or swallow.

"There was a terrible accident, and your parents, Gene and Alexis, were involved." He hesitated as his hazel eyes searched mine. "I'm sorry. They didn't survive."

The tears began to stream down my cheeks. All I could hear was the ringing in my ears along with the words "they didn't survive."

"Cheyenne?" His face grew concerned, and his hands locked on my arms. My parents were gone—gone! They were in an accident, and they didn't survive! I should have gone with them. Why did my mom insist on me staying at home? I should have been there with them. Why didn't I tell them that I loved them before they left? I had said it when I was little, but it had been years since I told them...said those three words. I love you. For some reason, we just stopped saying it. My heart was cracking, and the pressure was pushing me down. I felt my eyes roll to the back of my head, and I tumbled over.

I felt so numb.

A cool washcloth touched my forehead, and I came back to my senses with a deep breath. The sheriff was speaking quietly on his phone. "Joni, I think you need to come by the Wilsons' place. Cheyenne passed out when I told her. I'd feel better if you came. I'm not sure what to do for her." He paused. "Okay, see you in a few."

Forcing my eyelids to open, I watched him bend down in front of me. "Cheyenne, my wife Joni is coming. She's a nurse, and I want her to check you out. She'll be here shortly. I need you to just stay still and rest. I'll be right back. I'm going to get you a glass of water."

I nodded and closed my eyes. I heard him moving around in the kitchen. Quickly returning, he placed the water on the table before me. Vaguely aware of his presence, I stared out the small window as he paced the floor. This had to be a mistake. My parents would be arriving soon, and they'd clear this whole mess up.

"Cheyenne?" the sheriff's rough voice said, but I didn't reply as he leaned down again and touched my arm. It was an effort to keep breathing.

Headlights broke the darkness—Joni had arrived. The sheriff went to open the door, and his wife made a direct beeline for me. She asked me a few questions as I drank some water. I managed to compose myself enough to answer. Moving to the couch beside me, she sat holding my hand as Sheriff Taylor began contemplating his next move.

"You're alone out here, is that right?" He was pacing the floor as his stubby hand began running through his thinning brown hair.

"Yes."

He took a deep breath. "I'd like you to consider coming into town with us until we can locate some additional family for you."

Now, I was the one who took a deep breath. As much as I appreciated his concern, I just wanted to be alone until I could process that this was real. "I don't have any other family. Gene and Alexis were my adoptive parents. My birth parents were killed when I was young." I was surprised by my answer, as I had managed to say

11

the words in a fairly calm, level tone.

The sheriff blinked and exchanged a glance with Joni as she squeezed my fingers. "I'm sorry, I didn't know you were adopted," she said tenderly.

"It's alright; it's not like we announce it. I don't remember my birth parents."

"What about any aunts, uncles? Are there any grandparents that you know about?"

"My parents didn't have any family left. It was just the three of us."

The sheriff's eyes saddened. He was hesitating and didn't know what to say.

"I'm eighteen, and technically I don't require a guardian, but I'll call my friend, if that will make you feel better," I said firmly. "Right now, I would really like to be alone, if you don't mind." I needed to get them out of the house. I may have given them the impression that I was tough, but on the inside, I was crumbling away with every passing moment.

"I'd really like for you to come with us regardless. I don't think it would be..."

I cut him off as I stood, touching his arm. "I'll be fine. Please, I really don't want to leave my house right now. I'll let you know if I need anything."

We stood and stared at one another. A few tense moments passed before he relented. "I'll be back out tomorrow to check on you." He took Joni's arm and led her to the door, only to turn around as he reached the hallway. "Do you promise you'll call that friend of yours?"

"Yes. I'll call him as soon as you leave."

"Will he be able to come over?"

"I don't know, but I'll call."

"Who?" His chin lifted and his jaw firmed as he called me on my lie.

"Colt O'Shea; he's a friend from school."

"Colt O'Shea," he repeated, pulling the face from his memory. "The tall blonde kid?"

"Yes." I would contact Colt as soon as they left, but I didn't know how soon he would be able to come. I was assuming he was already on his way out of town.

The sheriff nodded and took Joni's arm again as they walked towards the front door. "I'll be back out tomorrow afternoon. Call me if you need anything." I nodded. He had left his business card on the table.

Standing in the doorway, I watched them enter their separate cars and drive down the long driveway. My strength faded with every passing second. I closed the door and bolted it behind me. I collapsed to the floor, my hand still holding the doorknob at an awkward angle, and began to sob. My heart was aching and every part of my being was crying out—screaming for my parents to return to me. All the words I should have said, all the love I should have shown. The three words that I would forever regret not saying...*I love you.*

My world was crashing down around me, and the weight of the situation was crushing me. I was alone now—I had no one else. Such a short amount of time I had with them, only eighteen years.

I stared unseeing at the equipment that was cluttering the small hall. I don't know how long I sat there, but the torrent of tears finally subsided. My cheek was resting on the cold hard wood flooring, and my phone was still sitting on the end table by the couch. We were supposed to leave tonight...I would never have another minute with them, and never share another conversation.

Crawling to the end table, I picked up the phone. I knew I would not be able to compose myself enough to talk to Colt so I would have to send him a text. "My parents were in an accident; they're never coming home." I hit send and waited. My heart sunk into further despair as the network error message displayed across my screen. I dropped the phone and began to weep anew.

I managed to drag myself to my bed; the night was long and a never-ending deluge of tears and emotions flowed through me. The crying came in uncontrollable bouts, but somehow sleep found me and took away the pain. It was only temporary, as when I woke in the morning I realized it wasn't a dream. It was real. My parents were gone from my life—forever.

CHAPTER 2

I fumbled my way through the following day by texting and trying to e-mail Colt unsuccessfully. The phone kept giving me network errors, and the internet was down as well. I vaguely remembered seeing a notice around from the phone company, saying they would be working on issues, and it may cause temporary outages. The same company provided the cell phone and internet. I was in no condition to drive to town and try a different method. I wanted to contact the sheriff, but I knew that if I did, he would become aware of my solitude. He would somehow force me to stay with him and his wife, and that wouldn't work for me. I was better off at my own home. I didn't need anyone hovering, constantly asking if I was alright.

Sheriff Taylor and Joni arrived in the late afternoon and brought me lunch. I managed to keep my emotions under control with great restraint as I spent the afternoon with them. We ended up at the kitchen table.

"Cheyenne," the sheriff's voice held such sympathy. "We need to talk about burial arrangements. I can drive you into town on

Monday, and we can go to the funeral home."

I nodded. I knew this part was coming. Never once in my life did I ever think about burying my parents, and now I had to go to the funeral home on Monday.

"Did you get ahold of Colt?" Joni questioned, as she squeezed my hand.

"I've been texting him. He'll get here as soon as he can." It was the truth, though not the whole truth.

The chair squeaked across the kitchen floor as Sheriff Taylor rose. "Joni," he said softly as he glanced at her and then back at me. "We're going to leave now, Cheyenne. You call me if you need anything, okay?" Once again, I nodded and followed them to the door. "I'll be by around ten a.m."

Standing in the doorway, I watched as they drove away, once more wondering how I managed to avoid them forcing me to come to their home. They mentioned it once, but I touched his arm and told him I would be fine, and the sheriff didn't push it anymore.

I turned toward the entry, my eyes lingering on the forest, when I saw it—another dark misty shadow clinging to the trees. A shaky breath left my lips, and I blinked, fighting to clear my vision. I froze, staring at the unmoving object. Without warning, the hair on the nape of my neck began to rise. I closed my eyes briefly. I was imagining things again, imagining that someone was watching me. I shook it off and went back into the house, bolting the door behind me. I went into the kitchen to double-check that the back door was bolted also. I rewet the washcloth and headed straight for the couch. Lying down, I placed the wet cloth over my swollen lids as I rested. My head ached again, and my vision was blurring slightly. I would try texting Colt again soon. He'd reply and everything would be better...it had to be.

The sheriff returned Monday morning and drove me to the funeral parlor. He helped with the decisions that needed to be made. I decided on cremation. Neither the gentlemen assisting us or the sheriff would come right out and say that it was a wise choice, but I understood that not much of my parents' bodies remained. They would have the urn ready for me by the end of the week.

I tried texting Colt again while in town and finally one message sent. I waited in earnest for a reply; none came. I longed for his presence. I needed him so desperately and had no way to tell him.

The week passed quietly with frequent visits from the sheriff and his wife. I managed to drive into town and collect my parent's remains. I knew what I wanted to do and where I wanted to go. Once home, I hiked the familiar trail that we had taken so many times alone. It was quiet and peaceful as I passed through the trees. We had walked this path many times in the last three years. This home was by far my favorite of all the locations we had lived.

As I crested the small ravine, I looked down into the landscape below. This was my mother's favorite spot. During the summer months, there would be a large patch of wildflowers growing off the side of the hill. I closed my eyes and replayed my memories of my parents. My mom would always bring a bouquet home with us afterwards. She said it was because she wanted the scent to remain fresh in her mind.

I climbed down into the area where the flowers would grow, and sprinkled their ashes. Tears wet my lashes, as I thought of all the fond moments that we would never share again. I choked down the feelings that I would never be able to express and mourned the time that I would never spend with them. I sighed and set the small wooden urn down in the dirt. My eyes closed, as I let the tears continue to fall. They fell until I had no more to give.

Time passed slowly, but it did pass. On Friday, exactly one week to the day my parents died, I was staring at the camping equipment still in the hallway. I hadn't touched it. I knew they were gone, but I think deep down I still had hope they would just show up and we would leave. I needed to have things ready if they came. That's why I left the items there. I just couldn't move them—not yet.

My head was beginning to get that familiar ache. I had been getting frequent headaches lately, and sometimes they were so bad that I was barely able to do much else but lie in a dark room. My parents and Colt knew about them, and they were concerned. I tried to hide it most of the time so they wouldn't worry. I was sure this headache was just from all the crying I had done over the past week.

Sunday morning arrived, and the throbbing in my head was even worse. Rounding the corner from the stairs, I tripped on a sleeping bag. I landed on the floor and sat there. My parents weren't coming home, and the overwhelming emotions were building inside again. I had to get rid of these things. Every time I looked at them, it reminded me my mom and dad were gone. I rose to my feet and began dragging the items to the basement stairs through the pain of my pounding skull. Opening the door, I started tossing everything down. Each piece that I threw crushed my already broken heart more.

The stove crashed open as it hit the basement floor. I threw the pots and lantern down after it; glass shattered. The box of utility items went next. The tent and all its parts smashed into the growing mess. The backpacks and then the sleeping bags were next. Standing numbly at the top of the stairs, I didn't scream or cry.

I was alone.

I couldn't do much else as I leaned against the doorframe and finally collapsed onto the floor. I knew Colt was supposed to be back today. I consoled myself with the fact that he would come over as soon as he could.

Sometime later, there was a familiar knock on the front door. I didn't move. A key turned in the lock, and the door opened. Colt knew where the hidden key was located on the porch, and he had used it.

"Cheyenne?" his concerned voice rang out. His heavy footsteps stopped in the living room. "Cheyenne, where are you?" I didn't answer as his pounding feet ran up the stairs.

"Cheyenne!" his voice was growing more panicked as he ran back down the steps. He moved into the kitchen and stopped. He found me sitting at the top of the stairs with my back turned to him.

"When did you get back?" my cracking voice asked.

"This morning," he replied sorrowfully as he moved closer. He squatted and turned me around.

"I've missed you," I whispered as my head hung low.

He lifted his fingers to my chin and tilted it up. I looked up into his empathic eyes. "I just now received your text and voicemail messages," he explained. "I'm so sorry."

"You're here now." Colt didn't hesitate. He drew his strong, secure arms around me, and I latched on to him as if there was no tomorrow. He lifted me and carried me to the living room, where we sat on the couch. The flood of tears returned. I had worked so hard for the last week to keep my emotions under control around Sheriff Taylor and Joni. Now that Colt was here, it was like a dam had burst. I wanted to tell him how alone I felt, how my sobs echoed through the silent house, but I didn't. I just sat in silence and took comfort in the arms that held me.

Eventually, the tears slowed, and I realized just how much my head was aching. It was like a stampede of horses were loose and pounding the ground with their deafening rhythm.

"I'm sorry, Colt. I didn't mean to ruin your shirt," I said in a muffled tone. My face was pressed into his shoulder, which was now stained with smeared remnants of mascara.

He drew back and tilted my chin up, wiping the remaining tears away with his thumbs. My eyelids were so swollen that I could hardly open them. "How about you lie down for a while? You're not looking so good. When was the last time you ate or drank anything?"

"Yesterday," I replied, as I closed my eyes. "My head is hurting something awful."

He released a deep sigh. "Wait here, while I make you something to eat and drink. I'll bring some aspirin for your head, too."

After he rustled around in the kitchen for a time, he returned with a tray of sandwiches. I ate part of one, drank some water, and took the medicine. He gently pressed my shoulder down as I was now lying with my head across his lap. He started to run his fingers through my hair. It didn't take long before I fell into a deep sleep.

I woke in a panic. It was Monday morning, and the sun was up— we were going to be late for school. I tried to sit up, only to have his large hand gently push me back down. I looked up in desperation.

"It's okay," he said quietly. "I've already called about today. The school knows what's going on; Sheriff Taylor told them. Apparently, they've been trying to contact you. You can go back when you're ready."

I knew that no matter how much time they gave me, I would never be ready. How could I?

The weeks began to blur together, but not a moment passed without thoughts of my parents. I missed them desperately. Colt was a constant figure at my side. It had been over five weeks since my parents' deaths, and he had been staying in the extra bedroom. It brought me comfort knowing that he was close, but I knew that he couldn't stay in my house with me indefinitely. We had discussed it, and tonight was his last night staying over. I was going to have to be on my own. I had never met his parents, and he never mentioned them. We never went to his house; only mine. I didn't even know if they cared that he'd been staying with me this whole time. It seemed strange, but I hadn't thought to ask.

"Cheyenne, you know I don't mind staying." Colt's blue eyes were soft and compassionate as he reached for my hand across the kitchen table. I was trying to complete some assignments for school. I had been given extra time due to the circumstances, but I really needed to make some effort.

Quickly averting my eyes, I tried to focus once more before I lost my willpower. I drew my hand back. "I know, but it's time. Besides, you hang off the bed in the spare room. I'm sure you're looking forward to sleeping in your own bed."

He sighed. "It's not that bad here."

I snorted. "Yes, it is. I've seen you." I immediately cringed. I didn't want him to know that I had been in his room while he slept. A couple of times I had awakened in the early morning hours after a bad dream and crept down the hall to see him. I just needed the comfort of knowing he was there.

"You've seen me?" his voice raised an octave in surprise, but I could see the humor behind his pretend shock. I had just given him the ammunition to tease me. Turning away, I tried to figure out how to get out of this one. "So, how many times have you watched me sleep?" he asked.

I tried to change the subject. "I have a project that's due for my art class. I need a subject to draw. Do you mind posing for me?" I flipped the pages of the book in my lap.

"I don't know," he pondered. "Will I be awake or sleeping?"

"I want to do one outside and then one inside. The outside pose will be you sitting on a rock or something. The one inside will be more natural, relaxed. You can watch TV or read a book or something," I said nervously.

"I see. Maybe I'll take a nap." I looked up to see a devious grin spreading across his lips. Those lips...I shouldn't be thinking about those lips. Ever since the day he kissed my cheek and hugged me before he left on his motorcycle, something had changed. The fact he was around even more wasn't helping. Suddenly, I was starting to feel like I wanted more from our relationship. He was always there for me, and I didn't want to live without him.

Of course, I had always known Colt was striking. I saw the girls at school ogle over him. I just never gave the idea of him being interested in me a second thought. I wasn't a knock out. I was just average, not someone he would pursue, at least that's what I had thought.

I blinked and then nodded. "Fine then. Later this afternoon."

Rising from his chair, he squeezed my arm. "While you finish here, I'm going to tackle the mess at the bottom of the basement stairs." He paused, as once again his face softened. "You don't need to deal with it; I'll take care of it for you."

I felt the tears wanting to come, but I held them back. "Thank you," I whispered. I watched as his long stride took him to the basement door and he quickly descended the stairs.

I heard the clanging of the camp stove and pots as he cleaned up the mess I'd made of the camping equipment. I couldn't deal with the memories it brought up, so I took my books and went to the living room. I put my iPod in and tried to think of other things. I managed briefly to keep my mind off my parents; however, I didn't manage to keep my thoughts off Colt.

He was the closest friend I'd ever had. I had purposely built up a barrier around myself, so I didn't get hurt when I moved so often. Somehow, he managed to break down that wall, and I let him into my life and heart. I had opened up to him, telling him secrets that I had never told anyone else. I told him why I didn't have many friends. I told him that most times I felt out of place at school, and he understood. It was like he knew what I was thinking. He was attuned to what I needed most.

I didn't ask him to stay with me at the house; he just did. I never asked him to start driving me to school, but I accepted it. Now that my parents were gone, I realized how much I relied on him. It was as if he desperately wanted to help take care of me. He was just a friend, though. That's what friends do for each other, right? I was starting to confuse those lines, and I didn't want to say anything if he wasn't confusing those lines too. I was so deep in thought that I jumped when he touched my shoulder.

He chuckled. "Are you ready for me to strike a pose?"

"Yeah, sorry. I must have had my music up too loud." Rising, I gathered up my charcoals for drawing and followed him out the front door.

"Where to?" He towered before me. Glancing around the house, I then went to the side yard. There were pieces of sunshine breaking through the trees by the decorative grasses. I sighed.

"Over here," I said quietly and pointed where I wanted him to sit. I took a number of steps back and rested myself against a large boulder. I looked up and saw Colt pretending to pose and then quickly changing positions. It made me smile, and he knew it. "Like this," I said. I deposited my art supplies on the ground and stepped closer, squatting before him to rearrange his arms, legs, and head. "That's better." I toppled forward, leaning a little into his shoulder before I regained my balance. His firm hands helped steady me, but not before I heard him inhale as he turned his face into my neck.

"Have I ever told you how good you smell?" he asked.

I took a few steps back. His face was soft and sincere. He wasn't teasing.

"Thank you," I managed to mumble as I went back to the rock. I fumbled with the charcoal between my fingers and didn't look up. I flipped my sketchpad open and froze as I gazed at him. His icy blues locked on mine, and it took every effort within me to begin my drawing.

I tried to put down on paper what was before me, the shape of his face, how angular his jaw was, and the perfect placement of his eyes. A gentle breeze blew, causing a wisp of his blonde hair to fall across his forehead. I had a sudden urge to push it back with my fingers. I needed to move on; I had a drawing to finish. I didn't need to get caught up in this emotion—it was just a wisp of hair. *Keep your mind focused,* I told myself. *Focus...*

As I traced the outline of his broad shoulders, the image began to emerge on paper. Colt's t-shirt was snug across his chest. He shifted slightly, and I watched his muscles flex. I tried to refocus. He had his legs stretched out before him, long and well defined. The weather was warm, and his shorts revealed more than enough of his tanned legs. His skin was already golden from the sun.

"You know," Colt said playfully, "you're going to have to start working on your tan. I've already got you beat for color so far." He winked, and I fought to remain focused on my work, at least as best as I could under the circumstances.

"Yeah, well some of us go to school and work on homework." I knew Colt was with me every day and in almost every class. However, he never seemed to work on homework like I did. "I don't have the luxury of lying around in the sun all day."

He chuckled and I continued. We both knew that I was only a shade or two lighter and would soon pass him if I worked on it.

I wiggled my bare toes in the warmth of the sun. The grass was soft and inviting; I slid down further to sit. The pine trees swayed slightly as the breeze picked up. I brushed the hair away from my lashes, as it tickled my nose and cheek. I looked up and saw the dark storm clouds approaching. I sighed and added my finishing touches.

"Okay, you're done for now. We can wait until later to do the inside pose." I closed my sketchbook and saw Colt's outstretched hand. He helped pull me up, and we entered the house just before the rain hit.

The winds began to blow, and the rain pelted the ground as we made it to the cover of the porch.

"We can do it now," he offered as he opened the door and we walked in. He turned, lifting his fingers to my cheek. My heart lurched to a stop. The way he was looking at me stopped me cold. "You have black charcoal all over your cheek and nose, Cheyenne." He used his thumb to brush it away.

"Thanks," I muttered and waited until he was done.

"Where do you want me?" He grinned.

"On the couch. You can watch TV or read or whatever you want to do. I'm going to sit on the stairs." I sat on the wooden landing. Plopping down into the couch, Colt picked up a magazine and began reading. At least he wasn't staring at me. The winds slowed, but a light rain continued.

I sketched out his features and the surrounding area. I tried to do it as quickly as possible, and even though I didn't want to study him as intently as I had outside, my heart fluttered. I finished and walked towards him. He extended his hand and took the book.

"Let's see what you've done."

I was by no means an artist. I could draw a passable portrait but the second half of the assignment was to create a more modern piece.

"Is this what you think I look like?" he cackled. "Cause if so, I'll be scheduling some plastic surgery."

I yanked the book away from his hands. His eyes danced with mischief. "It's abstract," I said in annoyance. "It's not supposed to be perfect. Besides, I never said I was an artist. I only took the class because I needed the credits."

"Well, it's a good thing, because if you had paid for the course, I would tell you that you needed to ask for a refund," his laughter was growing and soon, so was mine.

"You're horrible!"

"I know," he said as he grabbed for my arms and hugged me. He gave me a peck on the cheek. "I got you laughing though."

I sighed. "Yes, you did...thank you."

CHAPTER 3

Without my approval, life without my parents continued, and soon graduation was upon us. I really didn't want to attend. I had no one to invite, and that fact itself brought up painful thoughts too easily. Colt had managed to get me there, but I was still protesting.

"Colt, I don't want to go," I said with determination.

"You'll be fine," he replied gently. "They're letting me walk with you so you're not alone."

"I don't want to be the only one whose name is called and it remains silent. I have no family in the crowd to clap and cheer like they do for everyone else. Besides, who really needs to see me get my diploma? Anyone who was important in my life can't be here." I stared at the freshly waxed gym floor. It was becoming easier not to cry.

"Maybe I want to see you walk. Maybe you're doing this for me, instead of you." I made the mistake of looking up, and I saw the firm resolve in his baby blue eyes. I knew I wouldn't get out of it. "Do it for me, Cheyenne. It's important." I had no choice but to give in.

I lowered my head again. "Just don't expect me to go to any

parties." I knew he had received several invitations; I only received them because of my acquaintance with him.

"Thank you," I said quietly. He drew me into a hug, and I found security in the warmth of his strong arms.

After graduation, Colt forced me to follow him around as we found our friends and wished them luck. They took the time to ask me about my future plans, and I tried to answer as best I could, but I really hadn't thought that far ahead. I was supposed to be traveling with my parents, but then the accident happened. I was merely surviving, and the thought of leaving and going someplace where Colt wouldn't be around was unsettling. I was trying to distance myself, but it wasn't easy.

Colt walked me to the car and placed his arm around my shoulder, making me feel slight and small. "How about if I take you out to dinner? We could catch a movie afterwards," he thoughtfully asked, knowing what an especially hard day I'd had.

"I appreciate the offer, but I think that I need to go home and be alone."

Sympathy creased his brow. "I understand. If you change your mind, call me."

"I will," I promised.

As I drove home, my thoughts turned to Colt. The way he made me smile, bringing happiness to my day. He would catch me twirling my ring on my index finger and running my fingers over the etched design. Most times, he would stop me by putting his hand over mine and running his finger over it instead. He would urge me to vent my feelings and try to calm me when I got worked up. We both knew he couldn't solve all my problems—there was nothing he could do to bring my parents back—but his comfort helped take the edge off and make each day bearable.

The wind blew my hair around, and immediately I thought of my mom. She loved my long, blonde, wavy hair. She said it looked like the sun kissed it during the summer months. I would get naturally lighter highlights running from my crown to the tips. She told me the curls and waves made her think of finger curls. That was what they used to call it when she was a child. It made me smile.

I came home to an empty house, but the solitude was what I wanted. It was what I needed. So much had changed, and I needed to sort through my feelings. Colt had done an excellent job of not letting me be alone and not letting my thoughts wander too far. It was time to face them; school was over, and I wouldn't have that distraction anymore. I had to deal with the new reality of my life head on. I needed to move forward.

Sitting in the living room, I stared at the piano. My parents loved to hear me play. I cherished my music—I needed to play to release my never-ending stream of thoughts. I pushed myself up, and sat on the bench with my hands shaking as I looked at the keyboard.

I gazed at the ring on my right index finger. It was the ring my mom had given me when I was about six years old. I always wore it. It was funny, I realized only now, that it had never been resized. It remained on the same hand and same finger and yet continued to fit perfectly.

I allowed my thumb to drift over it, feeling each curve and every etched symbol. Closing my eyes, I let my music begin to fill my mind. It was never anything else but what I created, at the moment I needed it. My music would take me to my happy place, a safe place. It would help me find some peace.

The music flowed softly, and I allowed it to glide over my heart. I caressed each shattered piece with the love that I knew my parents had for me. In my mind, I saw the notes mingle in the air. They were flowing over my thoughts as I began to replay the memories of my life with my mom and dad. As I played, I realized my friendship with Colt was somehow intertwined.

I had never known my biological parents; they had died when I was born. It was something we never talked about, but I had always wondered about them. My adoptive parents loved me and cared for me as if I was their own. They were devoted, kind, and thoughtful. They always kept a watchful eye out, overprotective like most parents probably are.

We lived a simple life and had modest homes. Most of them were located outside the city limits in a surrounding mountain community. I had always assumed this was because my parents were outdoor lovers. We spent most of our free time hiking, climbing, and exploring the wilderness areas. My dad always said it was wise that we know how to manage in the wilderness on our own. He taught me to use the stars, sun, and moon as my compass. He showed me the different varieties of plants that were edible, his best method for fishing, how to start a fire, and how to build a shelter. Really, he taught me how to survive just about anything that could or would come my way.

I allowed these memories to linger in my thoughts as I played the piano, morphing each song into the next. They weren't anyone else's melodies; they were my own. They came from deep within. I continued to play, thinking of what my life had become and the weeks that had followed their loss. I only finished playing when I knew my music had completely filled me to overflowing. My heart finally felt settled with the emotions. It had been such an overwhelming day. I needed to move on, and I needed to be strong.

"Don't like the way your bedroom looks, Cheyenne?" Colt asked. He was leaning against my doorframe with his arms crossed, looking a little mystified.

I was completely distraught over not being able to find a small pink and white jewelry box. I had been ripping my room apart, and my clothes were tossed aside and the dresser drawers were on the floor. I was frantically digging through my closet at that moment.

"I can't find it. I need to find it," I panted as I continued to tunnel through my shoes. My heart began racing as the anxiety kicked in.

Colt moved in closer, but remained standing in the closet behind me. "What can't you find?"

Looking up, panic-stricken, I replied, "The box. My jewelry box." My heart began pounding even faster, as the realization set in. It was gone. Colt immediately squatted in front of me, taking my arms in his hand. He lifted me from the floor, his eyes searching mine.

"Is this important?"

The tears that had become less frequent over the months came spilling out. "Yes. It was the jewelry box my mom gave me when I was six. It was a gift, and it held my ring at one time. I just need it...I just need it, Colt."

"What does it look like?"

"It's small, with pink and white material over it. The top has some scratches and a dent in the lower left corner where I dropped it once," I replied through the tears.

His words held such empathy, "Let me help you look for it. Where was the last place you had it?"

"It was on my dresser...and now it's gone." Colt released his hold as we exited the closet.

"We'll find it. I'm sure it's here some place."

We searched the entire house but couldn't find it. I didn't understand how it could go missing, but as I thought about it, I realized I hadn't even noticed it was gone until now. I had no idea when it had disappeared. As I pondered it further, I came to the realization that other things were missing as well. What was the possibility that someone had come into the house and taken things? It made no sense, but where else would they have disappeared to?

I was sitting out on the front porch of my home. It was official. This was now my home and not my parents'. It had been willed to me, and it was already paid in full. I had a home, but I didn't know what that would mean for my future.

A summer breeze wafted in the air, stirring the large ancient pine trees and causing the scent of fresh-cut grass to drift in the air and tease my nose. Colt had come over earlier in the morning and helped me mow. It was a daunting task, considering the size of the yard. The manicured lawn was small, but the meadows surrounding the house hadn't been done yet. It took a couple of hours to complete the job. Luckily, I only had to do them twice a year, once in the spring, which I had missed, and once in the fall.

My mind drifted back to my circumstances. What was I going to do? Where was I going to go? I was fortunate to have my parents set me up so well for my future. I had no financial worries. It was as if they knew someday I would have to stand on my own. We had talked in general about their deaths, and I knew they had a will in case something happened. I just never thought it would happen like this—an auto accident when they were so young instead of having our whole lives until they grew old.

The house had been paid off, and after the accident, I had received insurance money for the truck. I also received a substantial payout from their life insurance policies and when I went to the bank, I found out they had opened several accounts in my name. They all showed large dollar amounts in their balances.

I watched from a distance as the mail truck deposited the envelopes in the box. My damp hair was cooling as it fluttered in the air, and I began the long stroll down the gravel drive. The patches of sunshine breaking through the trees kissed my skin as I passed under their canopy.

After closing the mailbox and flipping through the letters, I glanced up towards the house, into the dark forest. Instantly, the hairs on my neck stood on end.

I inhaled a shaky breath.

Something unmistakable large lingered in the shadows beyond the house.

"It's nothing," I mumbled, trying to convince myself. I stared for a few moments more. I was just seeing things. My mind played tricks on me before. As a child, I had told my dad about the shadows, but he dismissed them as figments of my imagination. *It was just my imagination; that's all.* I walked back to the house, and sighed in relief when the door shut behind me.

I wasn't paying much attention as I tossed the mail onto the desk, but then an odd envelope caught my eye. It was addressed to Cheyenne Wilson, and seemed to be from a bank, but not one I recognized. I picked it up. Hesitating for a moment, I ran my finger under the back flap. Another account? How many were set up for me? And why? It was strange. Why would my parents have so many? Were they trying not to draw attention to themselves? Hiding something? I pulled the paper from the envelope. It wasn't a checking account statement. It was a billing statement for a safety deposit box. The renewal payment was due in a couple of weeks and would be pulled from the account listed below, which appeared to be yet another savings account.

I didn't remember my parents saying anything about a safety deposit box, especially at a small bank in Helena, Montana. I didn't recall ever seeing a key, but I rummaged through the desk drawers looking for one anyway. Was there something I had somehow missed? What was in the safe deposit box? Why was it in my name? Pulling out the third drawer of the desk and running my hand through the papers, I searched for some sort of clue. I felt something strange on the bottom. There was a slight bump.

I pulled the drawer completely out, dumping the contents on the floor. My fingers ran across it again; yes, it was there, and it wasn't my imagination. It seemed to be a small but deliberate imperfection of the drawer lining. I looked for a corner to pull away; I held it up to the light while gently finding the top and bottom sections. My nail caught an edge, and I delicately pulled it from the drawer bottom. A picture fell out.

It was a photograph of my parents and I at the Helena Cathedral. I fought to keep the tears at bay.

We were at a Christmas Mass in Montana. I remembered it well, because it was such an exquisite cathedral, with majestic twin spires rising from the foundation. I could still picture the stained glass windows sparkling from the light reflecting off them. The marble statues adorning the room. The white marble altar. The scent of incense in the air combined with the carved oak pews, and the music meandering through the halls from the organ.

I pressed the photo to my chest. What I wouldn't have done to have a hug from my parents right now.

My daydream ended quickly as I realized the oddity of having a picture hidden in a drawer. Why had it been left there?

The picture dropped from my fingers and fell to the floor. I stared.

A note was on the back.

The note read: *The key to your future is hidden in the past. Don't let what is stained deceive you. Music is your guide. GA*

GA...my parents' initials. What were they trying to tell me?

I read through the note once more. The key to my future is hidden in the past. Don't let what is stained deceive you. Music is your guide.

My mind whirled around the possibilities. What did these have in common?

I pressed my fingers to my head and plopped down into the couch. I hated riddles, had no patience for them whatsoever...but one thing was obvious. I was meant to find this note. Somehow, I just had to figure out what it meant.

CHAPTER 4

Colt arrived before I was ready for him. I had spent so much time on the photograph and note that the afternoon had flown by. I was hesitant telling him about my recent discovery. I didn't know what my parents had hidden from me. I also got the impression he didn't want me to go far from home. And if this was where I thought the mystery was leading me, I was going to be traveling to Montana researching a safety deposit box.

Colt glanced at the mess on the floor by the desk in the living room. "Doing some spring cleaning, Cheyenne?" he asked.

"Sorta. The drawer was stuck, and when I pulled it out, all the papers scattered to the floor. I was trying to put them away and got sidetracked." It wasn't the complete truth, but close enough.

"I see," he replied as he bent down to help me pick everything up. Sliding the drawer back in its place, he tested it to make sure it would operate smoothly. He glanced at me, as if I was hiding something, but said nothing.

"Are you hungry? I could make you some dinner," I offered, trying to change the subject. I stuffed the remaining items in the drawer and closed it. He had taken a step back to get out of my way, and was staring down at me.

"I'm good. Have you eaten yet?" he replied casually.

"No, but I'm not hungry at the moment." I quickly needed to think of a diversion. "Thank you, by the way, for helping me with the yard this morning."

"You're welcome, but you already thanked me a couple of times."

"Oh," I replied and turned towards the couch, knocking over the pile of DVDs that were sitting near the TV. Dang! If he didn't suspect I was hiding something before, he would know now for sure from my clumsy behavior. He could always tell something was going on. "You want to watch a movie?" I asked, as I began rummaging through the movie pile.

"Sure," his deep voice made my nervousness even more pronounced, as he dropped into the couch and waited. He knew me too well; he didn't buy what I was telling him. I put a movie in and sat in the chair, as far away from him as I could get. I don't know what we watched. I was trying to keep my distance, trying to come up with a way not to tell him. I began twisting my ring with my thumb as I thought it out.

The movie ended too soon for my liking, and Colt bided his time until he had me cornered in the kitchen. There was only one way in or out of the room, and he was standing in the doorway blocking it.

"So, what's going on?" he demanded.

"Nothing," I replied a little too quickly and cringed at my own guilt.

"Nothing?" he answered with a reproving tone.

I didn't reply.

He leaned in the doorway, crossing his arms. I knew he did it deliberately to make his arm muscle bulge beneath his clingy t-shirt. He grinned at me with a twinkle in his blue eyes. He was only a friend, but when he would produce that crooked grin...My face was a dead giveaway for my feelings! I spun around and started digging through the cupboard to hide my blush.

"What's this?" he asked.

I glanced his way and frowned. I'd left the newly found picture clipped on the fridge.

"Um, just a picture I came across while cleaning."

"You found it in the drawers?"

I blinked.

He flipped it over and read the note on the back.

"It's nothing important," I said.

He nodded and then added. "If it's nothing important, then why's there a note on the back?"

I was trying to ignore him as I moved to the pantry in the corner and began clanking cans and boxes around. It took him three steps to cross the kitchen floor and trap me in the pantry. I didn't turn around. I could feel him behind me, blocking the exit, while he stood in the doorway. I knew at some point I was going to have to turn and face him, and he would probably get the information he wanted. I wasn't good at lying to him.

Slowly turning, I realized that he had leaned down and his face was only inches from mine. I jumped. He laughed. Angry at his reaction, I pushed at his rock-hard biceps. They didn't budge. I sighed and flashed him an exasperated expression, while I made an effort to duck under his arm. This time, he caught me by my arms and twisted me around to face him again. Two steps and he had me pinned against the kitchen wall, his musky scent inching dangerously close. I kept my gaze locked on the floor. He moved his hand off one of my arms and cupped his fingers under my chin, gently pulling my face up to meet his eyes. I closed mine, fearful of what I would expose. He patiently waited for me to open them as he kept hold of my chin. I could sense he was smiling. He knew he would get it out of me.

Slowly lifting my eyes to meet his stare, it was just as I thought. He had the biggest grin plastered over his face. He knew that he had won. My gaze wandered from his blonde hair down his face to his lips; he could be very distracting sometimes, especially when I wasn't sure of his actions anymore. I could maybe tell him part of the truth, but I couldn't let him know everything. I didn't even know everything yet.

"I have to go out of town for a few days and take care of family business," I said, matter of fact.

"Is that it? You seem more distracted than just going out of town for 'family business' would imply." There was a deeper questioning to his tone.

"Nope. That's it. I just didn't want you to worry about me, so I wasn't going to tell you until I came back. Sometimes, you can be a little overprotective," I snapped back, slightly miffed that he could make me so confused.

He was still cupping my face lightly with his fingers and grinning while he gazed down. The problem was that I could stare into his eyes for a long time—they were warm and inviting. I kind of liked the way that he was holding me at the moment. I knew my face had softened. I could see the same emotions mirrored in his. A shiver ran through my body. He felt it too and chuckled under his breath. He had been torturing me with his touch for months now, but he kept me constantly guessing because he never made a move.

Moving his fingers from my chin, his thumb gently caressed my cheek, stopping at the back of my neck.

I stopped breathing.

He ran his hand down my throat, pausing at my neckline. I was still staring into his eyes, but his expression seemed to have changed. It was more protective. He took a step forward and pressed me up against the wall. His right hand moved back up my shoulder, briefly stroking my neck, and then down my arm again to plant itself on my waist. My heart was fluttering at this point. I wasn't quite sure what was happening, and I couldn't do anything to stop it—I didn't want to. My arms were limp at my sides.

His voice was soft and serious. "Is overprotective a bad thing?" he asked, in a deep gravely voice.

"No," I whispered back.

He stared for a few long moments and a flicker of some deeper emotion flashed into his eyes only to be pushed back. He could have very easily leaned down and kissed me, right then. I wouldn't have done anything to stop him. My breath had returned and was becoming more labored as I looked at his chest, not knowing what to expect or what I wanted. His warm lips touched my forehead in a tender kiss. He let out a big sigh and stepped back, releasing me from his touch.

"Just call me when you get back."

I inhaled and looked up to see that he was walking toward the front door. His good-bye had almost sounded unconcerned, which was strange, considering the protective way he had been acting since my parents' death. I barely heard the door open and close, and then he was gone. I stood in the kitchen for quite awhile. My heart was still beating too fast. What just happened? I had no answer. I hadn't seen that coming. I gradually made my way upstairs, but I didn't sleep well that night. I was too distracted, replaying the evening's events in my mind. Nothing had actually happened, but I couldn't help but wonder. Would he have gone further and kissed me? Just recalling the look on his face made me blush. Just what was he planning for me? For us? Where did that leave us now...friends or more than friends?

As I was packing, I wondered if Colt would suddenly show up and offer to tag along. I had told him I wanted to go alone, but I wouldn't have protested too much if he came. I realized that I had unconsciously been trying to distance myself from him. Used to being alone and losing all the people I knew, I guess I was trying to make the inevitable separation easier for me when the time came. I was sure Colt would eventually go off to college or something, although he never mentioned his future plans to me. I never asked—maybe I didn't want to know the answer. I was on my own now, and I needed to be strong. It was what my parents would have wanted me to do—live.

Carefully placing the spare key on the ledge above the porch, I headed towards the Jeep, only turning to look back once. I was only going to be gone a week or two, but leaving the place that was featured in so many of my good memories of my parents still hurt. I turned on my GPS system and locked in my coordinates. I was on my way, sure this new destination would hold some answers for me about my parents. They had hidden something, and I needed to find out what. I wasn't going to let them down.

I drove down the long driveway slowly, listening to the wheels crunch on the gravel and turned onto the road. I would need to head through town, and I was convinced that Sheriff Taylor would see me somehow and flag me down if I left without telling him. Since that grave night, he had made it a habit to visit me every couple of weeks. He wanted to ensure that I was taken care of, but he seemed satisfied when he knew Colt was with me.

I stopped at his office, knowing that I would need to be quick about this, just let him know I was leaving town for a few weeks so he didn't worry. I was a little taken back as I entered the office at the nonchalant expression his face produced...it was as if he expected me.

"Well, hello, Cheyenne," he said. "I was about to make a trip out to your house today and talk to you about a few things..." he trailed off, seeming preoccupied with the piece of paper in his hand.

I was a little stunned. It wasn't time for him to make another visit to the house. He had just come last week. "Talk to me about what?" I asked apprehensively.

"Well." His attention drifted to me again. "I've been wanting to talk to you about staying out at your house alone. I've been troubled."

"Oh, well, I don't think you need to worry about it right now. I was actually here to tell you that I am leaving town today, as a matter of fact."

"I see. May I ask where you're heading?" His brows creased with fatherly worry.

"Montana. I've been doing some research on a few accounts that my parents held. I need to make a trip to close them." I didn't feel the need to elaborate any further. He didn't immediately reply. His jaw tightened, and he seemed to hesitate over his next words. "I wanted to let you know that I've been concerned about recent activities around your home. I've noticed some strange occurrences while you weren't around. I'll have the deputies run by about once a week to keep an eye on things." He ran his fingers through his brown hair, pushing his perfect part off-center slightly. "Not many folks drive out towards your place unless they're heading there for a reason. I don't like you being so isolated."

I didn't know what to say. Actually, I did; it would explain the weird feelings that I would get and the chills when I would look into the forest—the shadows. I had been telling myself that it was my imagination, but perhaps it wasn't just me. "What kind of strange occurrences?" I warily asked, not sure I really wanted to know.

He once again hesitated, debating whether or not to tell me. "Just strange things," he hedged. I could tell he was hiding something. He obviously didn't want to scare me any further; I was sure that fear was now clearly written all over my face.

"Thank you," I muttered. My head was spinning. I would have to be careful. It wasn't just my overreaction because I was alone so often—it was real. What were they looking for? I hadn't found anything of much value...nothing to unlock a great mystery at the house—except the picture and riddle. Did the safety deposit box have something to do with it?

"I would really like you to keep in touch with us," the sheriff interrupted my reverie. "Just in case I come across anything new." I jerked my head up and brought my attention back to him.

"Sure, let me give you a cell number where I can be reached." I quickly jotted down my new number on the pad of paper on his desk. Colt had bought me a new phone, and I had changed carrier services. He wanted to ensure that I could make a phone call when needed, especially after what happened the night my parents died.

"Are you okay?" the sheriff asked, touching my arm. I looked up, slightly distracted.

"I'm good. Just a lot on my mind. I need to get going now. I have a long drive ahead of me. Please tell Joni thank you for me."

"I will. Take care now." I could feel his gaze on my back as I walked to the front entrance.

The breeze should have been refreshing, but it wasn't. I sat in the Wrangler briefly, trying to calm myself before I left town. I was seriously considering calling Colt and asking him to come, but I just couldn't do it. I didn't know what I was going to find, and I surely didn't need to drag anyone else into it if I was being watched or followed. I also needed to learn to handle things on my own. I wanted him to be around, but there were no guarantees in life—I was living proof.

I sighed. I was going to miss Colt. I knew I had made it like I would only be gone a couple of days, but I suspected that once I was in Montana, I would want to stay for longer. Maybe figure out why my parents had come here in the first place, and opened a safety deposit box for me, why not in Sagle?

I debated with myself about calling him. I didn't want him angry or hurt that I'd deceived him, and that's what finally won me over. Dialing his number, I hoped he wouldn't answer. It would be easier to leave a message. Luck was on my side; my call went straight to his voice mail.

"Hey, Colt, it's Cheyenne. I just wanted to let you know that I wasn't completely honest with you last night. I gave you the impression that I'd only be gone a few days, but actually I may be gone a few weeks. I'll call you when I can or when I get back. Please don't be angry. This is something I have to take care of on my own." I hesitated a moment before continuing. "I do like the fact that you're protective of me, and I hope I didn't hurt your feelings last night when I said it. I'll talk to you soon."

I'd have to deal with him when I returned. My feelings seemed to be all mixed up. I had too many other things to concentrate on, and I needed to focus.

As I drove out of town, the windows were down, and the wind blew loose strands of hair around my face. Thoughts of my parents were on my mind, and as the miles disappeared beneath my tires, I let my mind wander. A strong sense of regret weighed down my heart. I should have expressed my gratitude more...I just always expected them to be around for me.

I had changed over the months. I was stronger and now felt like I could handle my new life alone. With all my parents had left me, I felt like I had a destiny, a purpose to fulfill. What that purpose was, I was sure to find out soon. Without risk there was no reward, I would take this on and drive forward to whatever fate lay ahead.

The wind whistling through the car wasn't loud enough to block out my thunderous thoughts. I reached into my backpack and pulled out my iPod, set it in its cradle, and soon music was streaming through my speakers. After a few songs, I realized it actually made my heartache worse. It was becoming increasingly difficult to drive with tears running down my cheeks. I turned off the iPod.

Suffering in silence seemed better, at least for now.

CHAPTER 5

After spending a paranoid night at a sketchy hotel in a small town en route, I arrived in Helena in the afternoon. It was clear and bright, not a cloud in the sky, perfect weather for late June. The air was warm on my skin, and it felt comforting. The weather matched my optimistic mood. I decided to take a small detour before heading to the bank; an iced coffee was sounding pretty good at the moment.

I ordered my favorite drink; vanilla iced blended coffee with whipped cream and caramel sauce on top. The whipped cream and caramel sauce were the best. Usually when no one was watching, I'd lick the inside of the lid to get every last drop of the addictive syrup. Once, my dad caught me doing this and started laughing. I'd gotten caramel plastered over my nose. If Colt had ever seen me do this, I would never live it down. Glancing around, I indulged shamelessly and grinned.

Thoughts of my parents caused me to sigh, and I pulled out the photograph with the riddle. I'd been trying to decipher their message with little success.

My fingers traced the outline of them and I smiled at the memory.

I was only twelve at the time and didn't understand why we'd traveled here for that Christmas, there were a lot of things that had remained a mystery and only now I was questioning why.

I wanted to visit the cathedral while in town. I glanced at my watch, I had plenty of time before the bank would close.

Too much time had passed since I had visited the cathedral. The massive size and beauty were just as overwhelming as I remembered, and my fingers tightened around the handrail as I glanced up at the rising towers. I was so tiny in comparison, so insignificant in their presence. I made my way up the concrete steps to the entrance.

I walked toward the two columns flanking the solid carved oak door, and I couldn't help but think it should have been the entrance to a castle housing royalty.

I stopped in my tracks. On the cathedral door was a sign announcing its closure. It was under renovations. Disappointment hit me hard; I should've done research first before showing up. All I wanted to do was walk inside again... I glanced around, no one was in sight. I pushed on the door and it opened.

My soft-soled shoes were quiet as I passed over the threshold. The angels and saints sparkled down at me from the stained-glass windows, and I basked beneath a torrent of colors.

Moments later I was met with a blockade of construction walls.

Determination took over and I wound my way through the corridor to the main sanctuary thankful it was empty as I peered around the corner. The hand-carved pews were a vivid mahogany, so smoothly polished they beckoned to be sat on. Chandeliers with gold leafing flickered in the dim light. For a long time I just stood and stared at so much beauty and peace surrounding me. It had been a rough number of months and taking a moment for myself was just what I needed.

Checking over my shoulder to make sure I was alone, I walked into the foyer again. I found a sign showing a picture of what the new remodel would look like. The organ would have a new home...

Pulling the picture from my pocket, I flipped it over and read the riddle once again. My mind narrowing in on two phrases...

...Your future is hidden in the past. Music is your guide.

I pushed my fingers to my head, rubbing my temple gently. I was still so unsure what my parents were trying to tell me. Why couldn't I figure this out? What was I even doing here?

The cathedral was closed; I shouldn't have even come inside. But reliving the memories seemed like the right decision at the time.

I sighed and suddenly had the familiar unnerving feeling of being watched. The hair on the back of my neck rose, but after glancing around, I saw nothing. I opened the construction door with my heart pounding in my chest, afraid of being caught snooping without permission. But I just had to have a peek at the organ. I remembered my dad lifting me to the bench and allowing me to press the keys. This was a memory trip after all...

Walking down the corridor, I came across the gallery door housing the organ. The photograph inside my pocket seemed to tingle against my leg. I pulled it out, steeling myself.

The key to your future is hidden in the past. Don't let what is stained deceive you. Music is your guide. GA

I exhaled loudly. Why wouldn't this riddle leave me alone? Every step I took always led me back to it. But it still didn't make any sense. Why would my parents hide a key? Why would they have never mentioned anything about it? Wouldn't they have given me some clues over the years? And what was the key for? I shook my head. I was so going to look the fool if I got caught.

I stared at the organ, my mind still so jumbled.

My fingers traced the top panel and I stared at the keyboard before me. My heart was longing for my dad to be here and I sat on the bench my hands hovering over the keyboard.

Did I dare try and play? What if I was heard? I was already trespassing...

Heart racing, I pressed random notes. Nothing happened. Odd... Frowning, I tapped my fingers on the bench. Maybe they were refurbishing the old organ.

Determination sent in and I pressed the notes G and A together in memory of my parents, only this time a I heard a small click from the lower panel.

I ducked under the keyboard, searching for the source of the noise. There was a loose section in the lower left corner of the panel.

I gently pried the piece of ancient wood away. The hidden compartment contained a small box. As calmly as I could, I reached inside and opened the lid. My breath caught...a key! It looked like a key to a safe deposit box. Could it be?

How could I have not seen this clue before? I sighed. It was because my parents knew my memories would lead me here.

A shuffling noise echoed nearby, causing me to panic. Hurriedly, I placed the key in my front pocket and closed the small compartment. The noise was coming closer, and as I crouched under the console, a very real fear gripped me. *Was I about to be caught?* The shadows were lengthening as the sun retreated for the day, which worked to my advantage. If I could stay away from the light, nobody would see me.

The door creaked open, and my pulse began to thunder. Was someone looking for me? Did they see me come into the gallery? I leaned forward, desperate to take calming breaths. Blood rumbled in my ears, and for a moment I wasn't sure whether the loud noises I was hearing were in my head or real.

The door suddenly closed as quietly as it had opened. I sat waiting for my heart to slow before I could move a muscle. I pulled myself up and then hesitated while my sweaty fingers gripped the doorknob. *What if they came back?* Long moments passed as I pressed my ear to the door. Whoever had been peering in was now gone. Opening the door, I slid through, glancing left and right. I all but ran to the main entrance, my eyes darting about. I allowed a small smile of triumph. I'd done it! My parents would be proud of me.

I should have been paying closer attention, but I was too caught up in my momentary victory. When I rounded the corner, I hit what seemed like a brick wall. My nose pulsed with pain, and the wind was pushed from my lungs. I rebounded onto the floor, banging my head on the tiles. What just happened? I looked up, dazed, as I struggled to catch my breath. My hand unconsciously rose to my head.

"I'm so sorry. Are you okay?" a deep voice asked.

Suddenly I couldn't speak and it wasn't just from being caught. I didn't know what to say. I felt so immature and childish. My eyes were too busy drinking this stranger in. Scruffy brown hair reached to the nape of his neck. The faintest hint of stubble shadowed his square jaw, and he had beautifully tanned skin and the most brilliant hazel eyes I'd ever seen.

I shook off my astonishment. I needed to focus. The twinge in my

51

head suddenly roared to life.

"Are you alright?" the man asked again, this time with more worry as his fingers stretched out, offering to help me up. "Can you get up?"

I took his hand, hesitating as I fought to regain control of my wits. "Yes," I said faintly. "I'm sorry. I didn't see you there." I blinked a couple of times, fighting back the blazing pain as I bit my lower lip. How was I going to get out of this one?

"No problem," he replied. He grasped my elbow as he held me steady for a few passing moments. His hand was warm, strong, and rough against my skin. I took in his towering frame; he was so tall and so handsome.

"Are you in a hurry?" There was worry as he eyed me. "You came running down the corridor. Is everything okay?" He scanned the hall behind us, as if he were expecting someone chasing me.

I opened my mouth to answer, but it turned to a grimace as the headache decided to up the volume. I couldn't even come up with a lousy excuse... His voice was becoming like a stampede in my ears. I needed to get back to the Jeep and lie down.

"Um, yes, I'm fine," I answered his second question first, trying to buy myself time. He thought I was in a hurry, why? He noticed I had been running and looked to see if he saw anyone. Was someone there? Did he or someone else open the gallery door? I tried to gather my thoughts together. "I'm sorry, I shouldn't have come in here."

"Oh," He nodded.

"I've got to go." The words nervously rolled from my tongue. I stared at the marble tile. "I'm sorry. If you'll excuse me, I'll be on my way." I scooted around him and made my exit of the cathedral. I was in no condition to carry on a conversation, especially after the embarrassment I had already caused myself. I didn't glance back.

I needed the refuge of my Jeep to escape my humiliation. As I hurried toward it, my eyes caught sight of a sandstone-colored pick-up truck parked at the far end of the parking lot. The windows were darkly tinted, but it was the height of the vehicle that caused me to stare. It was eerily familiar. In fact, it looked almost exactly like my dad's truck. I tried to rationalize my déjà vu away: this really shouldn't be too odd; it's a mountain town. They need cars with four-wheel drive to get around during the winter months. I was really becoming paranoid!

I climbed in my Jeep with keys still in hand. It was warm outside, and I didn't want to close the door yet—I needed the fresh air. As I sat, I began to feel the trauma of the day overwhelm me. During my drive here, I had been stressing about what the riddle meant. Why did my parents hide the picture? I also couldn't keep my mind off the safety deposit box, and why it was kept a secret. What did it contain that my parents' thought only I should know?

I was getting another one of my migraines. The majority of the time they came on slowly and I was able to manage them. Before my parents died, they were concerned, but we never visited a doctor. After my parent's death, my headaches had seemed to evolve into something worse; black spots were now blurring my vision when they came.

I closed my eyes as the throbbing in my skull began to deepen. How was I going to drive like this? I hadn't even gotten a motel room yet; I'd just have to find the closest one and hope it was clean.

I let my head lightly rest on the seat. I was hoping if I just sat and waited it out for a little while, it would subside enough to drive. The keys dropped into my lap, and I placed my fingers on the side of my temples, massaging them gently. I attempted to lift my head slightly and open my eyes, but I winced as I felt enormous pressure on my skull. I felt like it could explode at any moment. What was happening to me? I'd never had one this bad before.

The distant hum of cars on the road echoed as I sat in the parking lot. Suddenly a warm touch on my left forearm caused me to yelp. I tried to pull free, but the hand didn't move.

"Are you okay?" It was the man I had run into at the cathedral. He must have followed me.

"You don't look so good; you must have run into me harder than I thought..." he trailed off. "Do you need some help?"

I couldn't open my heavy lids; the immense pain in my head was overwhelming. I could barely spit out the words. "No...I'm fine." I tried to pull my arm back again.

I knew I wouldn't be fine. I was totally incapable of doing anything at that moment except sitting there. I couldn't even move. I knew I was getting to the point where I might pass out from the throbbing in my temples. Why was this stranger so interested in helping me?

"Please let go of me." For the third time, I struggled to pull my arm back and forced myself upright.

"I don't think that's a good idea."

It happened so fast I couldn't react. I felt his grip tighten, so strong it surely left imprints on my wrist. Weakly I tried to fight back, but it was no use. Even if I was at full strength, I'd have been no match for him.

His hands slid around my back and grabbed my waist. Then I was tugged into the air, away from the driver's seat, and lifted into his chest. He moved me to the rear seat of the Wrangler. The sensation of movement made me nauseous, and I moaned softly, praying I wouldn't be sick. I struggled to flip open my eyes only to see blurry black spots; I closed them again.

I fought to release myself from the stranger's grasp, but he only held on tighter. I struggled to use my legs to thrash around, but he must have seen it coming because he quickly moved and locked them down. I attempted to open my mouth in protest when his hand reached for my face.

"It's okay. I'm not going to hurt you," he said sympathetically. You have to calm down and quit struggling. I don't want to hurt you."

"You're scaring her," another voice rumbled and my mind became even fuzzier.

"We're going to take you someplace safe..."

Other low grumbling voices reached my ears, but it was too difficult to find out who they belonged to. Suddenly my body fell limp, and everything faded to black.

I woke to the sensation of someone running their fingers through my hair, gently brushing my temples and forehead as they passed over them, jarred me into awareness. I was lying in bed. The touch seemed familiar. I must be dreaming that I was at home, Colt sitting next to me.

I heard the whine of a machine. My fuzzy brain told me I wasn't dreaming. Where was I? My body went rigid, and the hands stopped moving.

"Cheyenne, it's okay. You're safe."

That voice! It was the sweetest sounding voice I could imagine. It was Colt! I tried to pry my eyes open, but they were so heavy. I tried to sit up, and he cupped his fingers around my cheek, making sure not to jostle me. A sympathetic grin rose on his lips.

"It's okay, just stay still," he said.

"Colt, you're here..." My voice was filled with relief.

"Of course I'm here," Colt said. "I drove as fast as I could."

I'm in the hospital? A sharp pain grew between my eyes and I pinched my eyes closed. Did the hospital call him? He was the only contact in my phone... A door opened and footsteps neared.

"Cheyenne?" a voice said. "Can you open your eyes for me?"

My lashes fluttered. A woman in a white coat was leaning over me with a small flashlight.

"I'm Dr. Dawson. You're in the hospital, you've had an accident."

I stared at Colt for a moment and thought back. The last thing I remember was that I was possibly being kidnapped...

"What happened?" I muttered, my head hurting and fuzzy.

"It seems you had a fall, you've got a good sized bump on the back of your head. Are you hurting anywhere else?"

"No, I don't think so..." A wave of nausea ran through me and I sank to the bed. "Just feel a bit sick."

"Understandable," Dr. Dawson said. "But we've given you some medicine, it should kick in soon." She fingered her stethoscope. "Do you remember what happened?"

I lowered my head. I didn't want to admit I'd been snooping around a cathedral without permission.

"Sort of," I said. "I was rushing, ran into someone and hit my head. Must've hit it harder than I thought."

"Well, since you were unconscious when you came in, we did a head scan. The good news is that we didn't find anything on it."

"So can I go?"

Dr. Dawson sighed.

"We would prefer to keep you in for twenty-four hours just to observe you."

I grumbled. So much for making a quick trip to the cathedral.

"However," she continued on, "Your friend Colt has offered to care for you. He told us about your situation at home. I'm sorry for your loss."

I sighed. Just another reminder I was all alone.

"You've really had me worried," Colt said.

My head rolled towards him. "I'm sorry you had to come all this way."

"Don't be stupid. Of course I'd come for you. I'd always come for you." He leaned in closer and gently kissed my forehead. "You're safe now."

"Thank you."

"Is this what you want?" Dr. Dawson asked.

I nodded.

She flipped her chart open and scribbled on a paper. "I'm going to discharge you and send you home with some tablets. I'll have the prescriptions filled and you can be out of here early afternoon."

"Thank you."

She smiled and left the room.

"I'm sorry, Cheyenne," Colt said. "She..."

"It's alright, Colt."

"I'm gonna take care of you. You're coming home with me."

I faintly smiled. I'd never been to his house before...

By early afternoon my medications were ready and Colt assisted me to my Jeep.

"You have keys to my Jeep?"

He nodded. "The spare pair your parents gave me."

"Oh," I replied slightly suspicious on how he'd gotten here without his truck. But that was a thought for another time as I was a little disappointed; I'd have to make another trip later to find out what was in the safety deposit box. I needed to be well first and the safety deposit key was now missing again. Chances were it got knocked out of my pocket when... A shiver raked me. When whoever was trying to help and scared the crap out of me.

"Don't be too surprised by what you find at my place," Colt said.

I nodded and reclined my seat. My eyes closed and I let the rhythm of the car sway me into a light slumber.

The car had stopped moving and my eyes opened. Colt exited the Jeep and was walking around to my side. He opened the door and I tilted my head in curiosity. I surely hadn't been sleeping that long...

"Where are we?" This didn't look like anyplace near my house. The trees were denser and Colt's truck was nearby.

"Home," he replied and helped me out.

"We're in Idaho?"

"No, Montana."

I stopped. "Why?"

"It's my home."

"You have a home in Montana?"

He smiled and pulled me along. "Don't worry, you're safe now."

I took in my surroundings. His home was a cabin in the middle of the woods. The only sounds I heard were birds chirping.

He helped me up the stairs and held the door.

I was surprised at the beauty that lay before me as we entered the great room. Two of the three walls were covered from floor to ceiling in windows, exposing the scenery outside. The main interior wall beside the bedrooms held a massive stone fireplace. The third wall made up the kitchen. The vaulted ceiling held massive wood beams running the length of the room. The hand-carved wood flooring was stained in a dark walnut finish.

The main sitting area contained a large wool rug anchoring the furniture into a cozy sitting area. The far corner of the room was equipped with a grand piano, positioned in such a way to allow a spectacular view of the forest from any angle.

I was buzzing with curiosity as I turned to Colt. He simply shrugged, and sat me down on the couch while he dropped the medicine bottles, and my safety deposit key on the coffee table. I noticed a sandwich and a soda had been placed on it as well. Draping an arm around my shoulder, Colt tapped the plate.

"I bet you're famished. Eat up."

I nodded, grabbed the plate and placed it in my lap, but didn't eat. Who'd made a sandwich and where did he find the key?

So much for hiding it from him...

"How's your head feeling? You really scared us, you know."

"Us?"

He tapped the plate again, and I took a small bite, watching his reaction, as he straightened his shirt, not keen on answering me just yet. I took yet another small bite, awaiting his reply. His cool gaze settled on me.

"Us, as in Callon, Daniel and myself."

"Callon and Daniel?"

"I was concerned for you, and they came to help."

"Who are Callon and Daniel?"

"They're like...family."

I pressed my hand to my forehead, which was starting to throb again. Colt hadn't mentioned them before. In fact, he'd never mentioned anything about himself. For years he'd stuck by my side, and yet I was only just starting to realize how much he'd kept from me. How much I didn't query.

It made me wonder about a few other things as well. I'd overheard the nurses talking about Colt being there so soon after I'd arrived.

"How did you get to the hospital so fast?" It shouldn't have been possible, given that he was supposed to be in Idaho. And I didn't know I was going to find trouble in Helena. Yet Colt seemed to have seen everything from the beginning. As if he'd set out a plan to follow me...

I shrugged his arm off, suddenly uncomfortable. Colt had known me for so long. It was only natural he'd pick up on my thoughts and be better at gauging what I was feeling. But to predict exactly where I'd go?

Colt looked hurt as he withdrew his arm.

"So," he said, avoiding the question, "are you feeling better or not?"

I stared back at him with uncertainty. I felt like I hardly knew the man sitting in front of me. "I'll answer you when you answer me."

"Your well-being is more important at the moment."

He wasn't going to answer, and I didn't want him to know that I was still in pain. "Better." It wasn't a complete lie. I was better than sixteen hours ago, but my head still hurt.

I set the plate down on the coffee table, and Colt handed me the soda. Taking a small drink to satisfy him, I turned and faced him head-on. This time he was going to answer my questions—no more games.

As I was about to speak, two men walked into the room. Both were watching me closely. I recognized one of them. He was the one I met at the cathedral, the one I ran into, the one who'd yanked me out of my car and held me in the backseat.

My heart started to pound in apprehension as he moved closer. Colt placed his hand on mine, and I leaned into his shoulder. Uneasily, I inhaled. Colt gave the two men a quick glance and they stopped their advance.

"This is Callon, and this is Daniel." He gestured to each.

Now I knew the mysterious stranger's name, *Callon*. Daniel was the smallest of the trio. He had the same tanned skin, but his hair was jet black, and it swooped at his brows to frame his face.

"Hello, Cheyenne," Daniel said. His dark blue eyes were soft, and his boyish face welcoming.

Callon said nothing as he walked over and sat directly in front of me on the coffee table. He exchanged a glance with Colt, and tilted his head. I blinked. Did I just miss something? There was a lot more to that gaze than met the eye. I turned toward Colt, my eyebrow raised in question. He gave me an awkward smile.

"Colt told us he was bringing you home. How are you feeling?" Callon questioned.

"Better," I replied nervously.

He picked up the medicine bottles on the coffee table, inspecting them, before putting them back down.

"I'm confused," I said while staring at Callon. "You were at the cathedral..."

"I like old architecture," he replied gruffly.

I blinked.

"Are you always rough with a woman the first time you meet

61

her?"

He raised a brow. "You needed assistance."

"Well, wasn't it lucky you were there to help me?" My eyes met Colt's. "And, Colt, you arrived so fast at the hospital you must've been driving a jet." My eyes narrowed. "You knew I was at the cathedral. So why were you following me?"

I pulled away from Colt's arms, and Callon moved back to perch on the table. It was my turn to make them feel a little uncomfortable now.

CHAPTER 6

"What I'd really like are some answers. I'm not so dumb to think you just suddenly appeared at the right place at the right time. Yes, I had a debilitating headache, but I could've made it to a hotel. I appreciate the 'rescue', but it seems to me that this was a little more planned than you're making out," I said, not bothering to hide my irritation.

Colt and Daniel shifted in their seats, uncertain how to answer. Daniel began fiddling with the pillow on the couch nervously. I was directing my question at Colt, but it was Callon who answered, with some hesitancy.

"You're right. This was a thought-out plan."

I scowled.

"Why were you following me? Why did Colt say I'm safe now? Why wasn't I safe before?" The questions came quickly as I tried to piece things together.

"We're watching over you, and your safety is of great concern to us," Callon said.

"Why?" I wanted to know.

Callon glanced at Colt before he replied, his face softening.

"Gene and Alexis were murdered."

I immediately slid back in my seat, all of my concerns flying out of my mind as I processed this horrible information. My hand touched my throat. "Murdered?" I could barely make my lips form the word.

"Yes."

I had thought my whole life had turned upside down when my parents died, but this...this was worse. It made it even worse to know it wasn't an accident. I loved them so much. How could someone deliberately hurt them?

Colt drew his arm around me, trying to comfort me. I looked up in confusion. "Why didn't you tell me?" My thoughts ran wild. Was that why I would get weird feelings about being watched? The sheriff said strange things were going on at the house. Was it the murderer? Were they looking for me next? A shiver ran down my spine.

Colt's eyes filled with sympathy. "I didn't want to scare you. You needed to finish high school, Cheyenne. Why do you think I was around even more than before?" His fingers brushed my hair aside tenderly.

Fury burned beneath my chest, but I kept my expression guarded. He'd withheld this information from me; what else had he decided to hide from me? The weight of his question swirled in my head. "I thought it was because you wanted to be around me," I said faintly, as the realization sunk in. "I thought it was because you were my best friend."

I inhaled a shaky breath. The emotional roller coaster I'd been riding for months was rising again. It took a few moments to regain my thoughts. I didn't move as Colt's arm tightened, and I watched my fingers begin twisting the ring on my index finger. "Why were they murdered?"

"They were protecting a secret," Callon replied. He squared his jaw and looked me in the eye. *"You."*

I shook my head. This couldn't be true. "Me? A secret? I don't understand." I looked up, wide-eyed.

"You won't understand yet, but you're very special. When the time is right, we'll explain. You need to trust us."

"Trust you?" I turned to Colt. His cool eyes seemed unsure. "How can I trust someone who's been deceiving me?" His face softened, and I looked away. How could I have spent so much time with him and not suspected he had an ulterior motive? As much as I wanted to give these three men the cold shoulder, I couldn't. They held all the answers. The trio sat silently as they awaited my next question. "Do you know who murdered them?" I was assuming they would know, since they said *I* was the secret. Colt and Callon exchanged uncomfortable glances, and finally Colt nodded. I studied their silent communication. What was up with them?

"A very dangerous man." Callon's jaw was rigid. He shifted in his seat, crossing his arms, and it was clear he wouldn't tell me more.

"So, let me get this straight." I closed my eyes briefly and shifted forward in my seat, away from Colt's embrace. My fingers massaged both of my temples. "Colt and my parents have been protecting me because I'm a secret. A secret you say I won't understand right now, but in time you'll tell me." I paused, thinking again. "My parents were murdered by a very dangerous man because of this secret, *me*. You've been helping Colt protect me, but I was never told. I've been kept in the dark." My temper flared. "And you expect me to trust you?"

"Yes." Callon's voice was cold, irritated that I hadn't accepted his order without question.

"How long?" My eyes narrowed as I lifted my head towards Callon, my hands falling to my side in tight fists.

"How long what?"

Was he doing this just to aggravate me? "How long have you been watching me?"

"A while."

What a pathetic, unclear answer! Figures. "More than two years?" Colt had been with me for that long, and only now did I see why he never talked about his parents. He had to be older than he'd let on. He didn't live with his parents, and my parents never brought up the topic. They had to have known.

"Yes," Callon confirmed.

I continued, a mixture of anger and anxiety rising. "Did you know my parents?"

"Yes." Callon's reply was so devoid of emotion it bothered me. I was just a job...

"You were working with them?"

"Yes."

I turned and looked at Colt again, desperately trying to maintain my composure. "So over the last two years, you've been around protecting me. My parents invited you along on trips and dinners so you could be close." These were the facts. My lips began to tremble, as anger boiled in my chest. "I shared secrets and feelings with you that no one else knew, and for what? So you could pretend to know me? Figure things out about me for your job? Deceive and lie to me? You screwed with my feelings, made me confused...just for the fun of it?!"

Something inside me gave way, and the tears began to stream

down my cheeks. All these months he'd played with my heart, with every touch, every word. "How could you!"

Colt extended his arm to touch my shoulder. I knew he was trying to comfort me. After all, that's what he was good at; that's what he'd been doing for the last two years. Making sure I was safe and had a shoulder to cry on. I should've seen it sooner, all those long walks in the woods, going to movies, just hanging out together. He was pretending to be my friend. My *best* friend. I pulled away and rose from the couch.

"Cheyenne." Colt reached for my hand, but I stepped out of reach.

I didn't want to hear anything more. Not now. I was wounded; a piece of my heart suddenly torn apart. I was just a job for him. The friendship, the feelings I had for him, all a lie. He wasn't who I thought he was. It was just too complicated to process now.

Sniffling and wiping the tears from my cheeks, I stopped just inside the hallway. I didn't turn around. "Callon, am I allowed to leave?"

"No." His tone was softer, as if to apologize for his gruffness before.

"So I'm being held against my will?"

"It's for your own safety," he said but that didn't make me feel better.

"I see."

Daniel suddenly appeared at my side with my bag in hand. It was if he knew I was looking for an escape. We continued down the hallway to a bedroom. He departed leaving my bag near the door while I stood in the far corner, staring out into the forest through the open windows, my thoughts pooling together. I'd been hospitalized, followed, tricked and lied to, and now I was with people I didn't know, who were curbing my liberties. Since when had Colt or Callon become my dad? How had this spiraled downhill so quickly?

Dusk arrived, and with it a chill in the air, which made me shiver. I wrapped my arms around my chest, but I couldn't ease the pain of my aching heart. Another loss in my life. Colt was the one who pulled me through my parents' death. I'd thought losing my parents was the worst pain imaginable, but losing Colt—my strength, my friend—I was hurting more than I thought possible. Who could pull me through the loss of my best friend?

I didn't bother to close the bedroom door; I didn't think it mattered at this point. I was being watched; I wasn't allowed to leave. A door wouldn't stop them. I was a bird in a cage, wings clipped.

Heavy footsteps stopped at the doorway. I continued to stare out the window. They continued until they were directly behind; it was Colt. His breath touched my head; the heat from his body warmed my back. More tears spilled, and I gritted my teeth to stifle my sobs. He was hesitating. We stood like this for what seemed forever before he finally broke the silence.

"Cheyenne, I'm so sorry." His voice was soft, gentle, sincere. "I didn't mean to hurt you. I want you to know it's not like that for me. It never has been. Each and every moment I've spent with you has been a blessing, and with each passing moment I've loved you more and more."

He loves me? I inhaled a shaky breath. I didn't want to hear this now. Not when my heart was being pulled in all directions.

"I'm not with you because it's my job; I'm with you because I couldn't live with myself if anything ever happened to you. When you told me you were leaving town, I wanted to tell you to stay. I didn't want to let you out of my sight. When Gene and Alexis died, you came to me to find comfort." His hands hovered at my sides, not touching me, but longing to.

"I've wanted to give you so much more than just comfort. I've wanted to give you my love, my heart, my soul. I've been waiting to tell you this; I wanted to tell you this in the kitchen the night before you left. Please forgive me. I never meant to hurt you this way."

I kept quiet, mulling over his confession. So I hadn't been wrong that night in the kitchen. That protective look in his eyes, those emotions he pushed back...he loved me! What was I supposed to think? Was this just another act, an attempt to pull me back into his world?

I stood immobile for a long time. Just a half step back and I would be pressed up against him, just a half a step and his tender embrace would provide the security I wanted—needed.

I wouldn't let myself do it. I drove back all emotion and continued to stare out the window. Now I was grateful for the breeze. It cooled my flushed skin.

Colt was still standing behind me, waiting. Slowly I turned, keeping my gaze locked on the floor as I walked past. His arm stretched out to grasp me, but didn't.

It was dark outside as I crawled onto the bed and sank into the mattress. I curled up into a ball on my side and closed my eyes. The bed sagged as Colt sat down. I knew he wouldn't leave me. He didn't touch me; didn't say a single word. He just sat there, my protector. My lids grew heavy, and my head began to ache again. Exhaustion overcame me, and I quickly fell into a deep, dreamless sleep.

My lids fluttered open. It was still dark. A big yawn escaped me, and I stretched. I had slept fairly well, but was still groggy. I glanced around the room. Dawn was just beginning to break. Shades of red and orange kissed the wooden floor. Twisting, I winced. My right arm was achy.

I carefully righted myself, only to hear Colt's deep breathing. He had slept next to me on top of the comforter. I turned to see his face, which was hidden in the shadows. It was peaceful.

I sighed. Despite everything I'd learned the day before, I still liked it when he was near. He always made me feel good about myself...but was any of it real? I remembered his words last night. He said he loved me, and wanted to be with me. Could I truly believe that?

But then there was the bigger issue. Callon told me I wasn't allowed to leave, and I needed to get into the safety deposit box. I was now sure that whatever lay in wait was exclusively for me. If I were a secret Mom and Dad were protecting, then surely whatever was in there would at least throw some light on the subject.

I bit my lip, as more hurdles began to appear. How was I going to get into town? I couldn't just tell my guards about the key and box, although Colt might already know what the key was for. They hadn't been completely truthful with me, so why should I be with them? If they wanted me to trust them, they'd have to earn it.

I slid out of bed quietly, being sure I didn't disturb Colt. The last location for the key was in the great room on the table. Glancing to my right stood the nightstand...along with my medications and the key. I swiped the key off the table.

I grabbed a medicine bottle and remembered I'd woken and taken some, but I didn't recall the key on the table. At least that would explain why I felt so tired and heavy yesterday, all this medicine they'd been pumping through me was surely taking its toll. I slid the bottle back onto the nightstand.

Next I went in search of my bag. I pulled out some clothes and shoes and silently crept to the bathroom. I changed into something comfortable, something I could run or hike in. I had no intention of staying. They said I couldn't leave. Ha! They had no idea what I was capable of, especially when I was mad!

I pulled my hair back, brushed my teeth, and quietly washed my face. I returned to the bedroom to deposit my pajamas and grab some cash, along with my driver's license. Colt was still asleep.

I surveyed the windows. I would make too much noise if I climbed out one of them. I thought it best to try the front door first. If Colt was asleep, maybe the others were, too. On the way to the great room, I walked past a partially open door. It was the laundry room, and it had a large window I could crawl out of. Perfect!

I slipped in and paused, listening intently for any noises. So far, so good. Slowly, I opened the window. It slid easily in the frame, and I managed to push out the screen with little effort. It fell to the ground, and I followed. It was a little farther down than I thought, and I fell forward onto my chest. A soft grunt escaped my lips, and I wanted to kick myself. If I were any louder, they'd be on me quicker than I could blink my eyes. I took off into the forest, my heart beating rapidly beneath my ribs.

I had no idea where I was going, but once I was away, I would use the sun as my guide and find my way back into town. I was sure I could manage, after all the training my dad had given me over the years. I pressed my hand against my pocket insuring the key had remained intact. I now had the missing piece I needed. I ran with everything I had, my senses alert for anything that would try to stop me.

Suddenly something tackled me from behind, and I was smashed to the ground, two large arms wrapped around me. They locked around my sides, preventing me from getting injured. It knocked the wind out of me, and I was pinned down on my back before I had a chance to fight back.

"Don't fight me!" a voice commanded. "I don't want to hurt you!"

"Get off of me, Callon!" I screamed and began struggling.

"I'll get off when you stop fighting," he said.

I wasn't about to give up easily. I tried to push myself up, but he held me down firmly. It was still dark under the patches of dense trees, but I hoped he could see my scowl.

"Let go of me, before you make me mad!" I said through clenched teeth.

It happened so quickly I wasn't even sure what took place. Callon leaped to his feet, yanking me with him. I was thrown over his shoulder like a sack of potatoes, and he began walking back. "Put me down!" I howled. He didn't respond. I tried to push myself free, but he wouldn't relent. I wasn't going anywhere but back to the cabin.

Once inside, he dropped me on the couch, then sat on the coffee table leaning forward. I became very uneasy; he was too close to my face. I pushed back into the sofa. I could see the resolve on his face. No longer the handsome face I'd seen in the cathedral, but a frightening cold-hearted monster.

"Cheyenne," Callon said, his tone like ice. "We're here to protect you. I told you yesterday that Gene and Alexis were murdered. We're sure their killer is after you now. You can't leave." He waited a moment for his words to sink in before his eyes fixed on me. "We will stop you if you try. I'll say it again. This is for your own good; we're not going to harm you. You need to trust us."

His hands came to rest on my knees, and I thought my heart was going to leap from my chest. His touch was electric, like a spark that jolted through me into a place deep inside. The sun's rays filled the room, though I hardly noticed, as I was locked in his gaze.

"Do you understand?" he asked.

I took a breath to steady my nerves. "You can't keep me here." I couldn't hide the tremor in my voice.

"Yes, we can, and we will." Callon's tone was final. "There's a lot you don't know or understand yet. Get used to the idea of us being around. You're not going anywhere."

I didn't reply. My mind froze, unable to form coherent thoughts, as we remained entranced in each other's stare. This was going to be harder than I'd imagined; I'd never seen such determination.

Callon eventually withdrew his hands and moved away, much to my relief, but I remained seated. The rest of the day passed. I didn't say much, too consumed with contemplating my options. Callon's eyes never left me as I moved around the house. Did he expect me to run out the front door while he was watching? Night came, and Colt stayed in my room once more.

I woke early the next morning, and made my way down the hallway and into the great room. Callon was seated in a dark corner of the kitchen, arms folded across his chest. I paused before I rounded the corner. I couldn't see his face, but I knew he was staring at me. Like a panther awaiting its prey, he watched my every move. I lowered my eyes. It was a bit unnerving to know he could intimidate me this way. I didn't like it one bit.

The piano in the corner of the room overlooking the forest beckoned me. I sighed. Back home, whenever I needed to think, I'd usually go out running or sit down and play my heart out. Since running was out of the question, this was the next best thing. I proceeded to the piano, sat on the bench, and started to play.

The music was my own melody that spilled out from within. There was no way to describe the change it made in me, except that it was soothing, calming, restful.

As I played, I let the sorrow and pain pour over the notes. I hadn't played since graduation, and only now did I realize how much I'd missed it. I laid all my emotions out on the keys, visible only to those who knew how to read me.

My mom always knew when something was bothering me; she could tell by the tone of music I played and the fact I always closed my eyes to really absorb it all. The thought of her provoked my tears. The bitter saltiness ran down my cheeks, souring my lips. How I wished she were here to hear me play, how I wished I could show her how much I loved her. Never again, I vowed. Never again would I hold back my words of love.

My mind was still a jumbled mess from all the recent events. My melody continued, as my mind turned to sort through the trailing thoughts. What did I know so far? Colt had been with me, along with my parents, to watch over and protect me, to keep me a secret. Why and from whom? It made no sense. *I was never anything special.*

I lived a normal life. My parents never once made me feel different, never once said anything that would cause alarm. My mom had said they wanted to talk to me about something, something I was old enough to know. Would it have been the secret? I would never know. They were gone and could never tell me.

Callon insisted I should trust them. Trust the people who had been hiding their identities from me for years—secretly watching me as I remained unaware. I was supposed to just fall in line. This didn't work for me, at least not yet.

As I continued to play, the haze over my mind began to lift. A plan was coming to life in my head; a way I could get away from Colt, Callon, and Daniel, if even just for a little while so I could escape into town and find out what was in the safety deposit box. What I would find might reveal what my parents hadn't been able to tell me in time.

The plan was formed. I could do this. I *would* do this. I would probably pay the price later, but it would be worth it. I needed to find out who I was.

I finished my last note, let out a sigh, and looked up. I didn't realize how long I had been playing, but the sun was now streaming through the trees. I also appeared to have attracted an audience.

Callon was sitting in the chair to the right of me, his stare at ease, if a little curious. Daniel was sitting on the fireplace hearth, and Colt was on the couch. No one spoke, but their gaze tracked me as I walked toward the couch to put on my shoes.

I would have to be polite, let them think that I was more accepting of the situation, but not go overboard. I was going to become an actress, as they had been actors in my life. I would bide my time until my chance would come and I could go through with my plan. I wasn't going to speak to Colt if I could help it. I still didn't know how I felt or what I wanted. He would just have to wait until I was ready.

I needed to break the silence. I looked at Callon and politely asked, "You want me to make you some breakfast?" I was referring

75

to all of them.

"No, we're fine." Callon rose, drawing closer. "Let me show you where the pantry is." He pointed to the closed door on the kitchen wall. "There's cereal, granola bars, and such. We tried to pick out items that you might like."

I nodded and opened the pantry door, pulling out a box of cereal. He pointed to the cupboard containing the bowls and opened the silverware drawer. As I poured my cereal he stepped behind and opened the fridge, setting the milk carton before me.

Leaning against the counter, I ate breakfast quietly, avoiding visual contact as much as possible. An occasional glance revealed Colt staring nervously, and Callon's cool stare, filled with distrust. Daniel was occupied with the television, laughing from time to time. My presence didn't seem to have any effect on him. He seemed happy-go-lucky, like not much bothered him.

I washed and rinsed my bowl, pausing for a moment searching for a towel. At once a hand appeared with one. It was Callon.

"Umm, thanks." I was a little surprised; I hadn't heard him move closer.

His eyes met mine. The corners of his lips twitched, as if he wanted to smile, but it never made it. "You're welcome." He hesitated, and at last managed a smirk. "Are you better this morning?"

I raised an eyebrow. Was he trying to put me at ease or did he think I was up to something? That stare of his always left me feeling vulnerable, like he could stare right into my soul and know my most intimate thoughts.

"I'm fine." I put the bowl away and set the towel on the counter. I really wasn't in the mood to talk. I needed to be cautious if he was already picking up I was plotting something.

I lowered my head and bit my lower lip. I needed to slow down. I had thrown a novel into my pack just in case I had time to read, and now was as good a time as any. I wasn't going anywhere, today.

After retrieving my book from my backpack, I sat down in the chair in the far corner of the great room.

This new novel would be a good distraction. I could read and see how the day presented itself, what clues I could pick up on.

I unwillingly lost myself in the book while the trio moved about the house. The story was more engrossing than I'd imagined. I made myself comfortable in the chair, sitting sideways, allowing my feet to dangle off the armrest. I caught them glancing my way, uneasy. Inwardly I smiled. It felt good to be the one putting them on their guard, rather than the other way around.

Colt seemed to linger the longest, waiting for me to speak. I'd not been this silent since we'd first met; I knew it was killing him. It wasn't all that pleasant for me, either. I wasn't as angry as before, but I wasn't just going to cave and forgive him that easily. I wanted him to suffer just a little bit longer.

Callon made lunch and brought it to me. "Thank you," I said as he set it on the armrest by my head.

I turned and pulled it into my lap and proceeded to eat, wiggling my ankles in the process. I was the only one eating. Strange, since they hadn't wanted breakfast either. Maybe I had been too absorbed in my book and didn't notice them eat.

After a while, I decided to go outside and sit on the porch and read beneath the warm sun. All three were watching as I walked out the front door and found a comfortable seat on the porch.

They followed, no doubt to keep me in sight. The sunlight trickled through the trees and a charming breeze touched my skin.

"You should really find something more interesting to do than watch me read." I didn't look up from the book, fighting down a smile. They were milling around on the porch.

"Must be a good book," Callon muttered.

"Yup." Obviously, I was the first in their witness protection program, as they didn't seem to know what to do.

Daniel and Colt stepped off the porch as I glanced up. They had a football and began tossing it back and forth. I watched until Colt caught me and winked, and I immediately pulled myself back into my novel. But I could already feel the heat in my cheeks. Argh! I'd been caught staring! I listened as Callon hopped off the porch as well and they all began horsing around.

It was hard not to watch what they were doing because they were being so rowdy. I gave up reading and let my eyes wander. Daniel was annoying Colt and Callon with his antics. He moved about with a light touch to his step. It was really quite entertaining as they interacted with each other. I found myself smiling even though I didn't want to.

They joked around for most of the afternoon; I was assuming part of it was for my benefit. The day slid by quickly and soon, dusk had come. I entered the house, they followed inside, and this time Colt brought me dinner. I was still annoyed as he handed it to me.

"Thank you," I said stiffly.

"You still mad at me?" Colt questioned.

I glanced down before I answered.

"Yes."

He stood for a moment regarding me, before walking away. He had made me a grilled cheese sandwich. I scanned the room and again noticed no one else was eating except me. I frowned. I ate and then took the plate to the kitchen, washing it and putting it away.

Still a little tired from the latest headache and failed escape, I decided to head to bed early. I turned towards the trio and announced, "I'm going to bed. I'm still tired."

"You are? Do you still have your headache?" Callon shot to his feet, his brow furrowed with concern.

"No, just tired." Without any further words I departed for the bedroom. I changed, washed up briefly in the bathroom and crawled into bed. The window was open and it provided a cool breeze.

I closed my eyes. All I could do was bide my time. Weariness took hold, and I quickly drifted to sleep.

CHAPTER 7

I woke to birds chirping outside my window. It was a peaceful sound, unlike the riot inside my heart. I remained distant with Colt as I'd been processing this new situation, but was starting to get withdrawal symptoms. He was here with me, but I missed him—missed the way our relationship used to be.

It was quiet when I entered the great room. Colt saw me first and flashed a large grin, which melted a little bit of the ice I had built up as protection. He and Daniel were playing cards in the corner and Callon was reading. The moment I entered, Callon was on his feet and walking towards me.

"Are you feeling alright?" He raised his hand to touch my wrist. I backed away, confused.

"Yes, why?"

"You slept over ten hours last night." Was that warmth I was seeing in his hazel eyes? I quickly shook it off. This was *he who must be obeyed* speaking.

"I must have been tired." I shrugged, but his question made me curious. I glanced around, wondering if it would be worthwhile to probe for more information. What could it hurt? "So are you a doctor or something, Callon? Is that why you're constantly asking me questions about how I'm feeling and deem it necessary to check my pulse?"

"Yes."

My shock must have been evident, as he was smiling.

"You're a doctor?" I repeated in disbelief.

"Yes."

"Shouldn't you be at work then?" I was a little sarcastic.

"I'm on sabbatical," he calmly replied. I swore I caught his eyes twinkling with amusement.

I huffed and went into the kitchen. I bet he was really enjoying watching me play stupid. My stomach growled as I began digging in the pantry for some cereal. *He was a doctor, interesting.* At least that would explain why he'd been so interested in my medicines.

Dr. Callon had followed me and was inspecting my cereal pouring. I decided now was the time to ask. I had made some observations over the past week, and was confident I'd covered all bases. It was time to put my plan into action.

"Callon, I've noticed the three of you don't eat much, and I was wondering if I made dinner, would you eat?" I fiddled with my fingers, looking down nervously. "You won't hurt my feelings if you'd rather cook for yourself. I just want to know."

Callon studied me for a few seconds before he answered, "What did you have in mind?"

A huge smile wanted to spread across my face, but I held it back. I hadn't expected Callon to be fooled so easily. "I was thinking about making some tortellini primavera and maybe a fresh berry pie."

"Sure, we'll eat it." Though his reply was positive, I could sense he was still hesitating. He was waiting for the punch line, so to speak.

I continued. "I'm assuming since I'm not allowed to leave, I wouldn't be able to go to the store to get a few items?"

"That would be correct." He crossed his arms. His trademark stare returned, yet somehow it was different from the past week. What *exactly* was different I couldn't quite figure out.

I blinked. This was *he who must be obeyed*. Get a grip, girl. "If I make a small list, would you be willing to get some things for dinner tonight?"

"I could do that."

I turned toward Daniel, who was now edging closer to the kitchen, listening in. "Daniel?"

"Yeah?" He seemed surprised that I'd address him.

"Would you be willing to take me on a hike to find some fresh mushrooms and berries while Callon and Colt run to the store?"

Callon shifted uncomfortably, and I looked at him. Could he see through my plan? Think! I had to throw him off the scent.

"The dish tastes better with fresh ingredients, and I know the berries and mushrooms grow around here." I hoped that was enough to convince him. Callon nodded once, and I turned to hear Daniel's reply.

"Sure."

What was with the head nodding? Once again I felt like I'd missed something important. I was sure all three were questioning my requests, since they all knew about my failed escape and my unhappiness at being kept here.

Shaking it off, I walked over to the far counter and found a piece of paper and a pen. I proceeded to the pantry and started searching for the items I knew I would need, grabbing a couple Ziploc bags in the process. I jotted down a few items and turned to the fridge to assess the contents. I added a couple more items to the list and then handed it to Callon. I turned to Daniel.

"You ready?" It was now or never.

"Yup." Once again he glanced at Callon, then seemed a little more assured.

I grabbed the bags from the counter and followed Daniel out the door. I didn't turn back, smiling as we left the cabin.

I knew my way around mountain trails pretty well, and I could find directions by using the sun and stars as my guide. I also knew where to look for the mushrooms and berries. They grew plentiful in the region. Some mushrooms had to be avoided because they were poisonous, and some berries could incapacitate a person for a short period of time. My dad had taught me, and thankfully, I'd listened.

I'd chosen Daniel to accompany me, as he didn't seem to play close attention to details. He'd been the only one I'd voluntarily chatted with and even then it was at a minimum, but somehow he'd made a connection with me.

He who must be obeyed, on the other hand, would be too suspicious. Since he'd known my parents, he would be aware of what my dad had taught me over the years. And Colt knew me too well; he'd see straight through me in seconds. The tricky part now was to get Daniel talking. I was sure he would answer my questions without paying close attention to what I should or shouldn't know.

"Do you know where the berries are?" I was assuming that he probably knew the area well since we were staying at their cabin.

"Yup." His childish grin broke through, filled with warmth. "Some of the best berries are in season now. It'll take us a little while to get there." He hesitated, looking down at me. "Are you sure you're up for this?"

"I actually feel great today. That's why I wanted to cook something. I've been craving tortellini and a berry pie." I sheepishly looked down. This play-acting was coming quite naturally. "I guess I'm being selfish to make you eat what I want tonight."

He shrugged as we passed over a fallen log.

"Sounds good to me. Callon's not really a culinary genius," he chuckled.

"How often do you eat?" I had only seen them eat once since I'd been with them.

"Often enough."

Often enough? What did that mean?

"What about sleep?" I asked. I knew Colt slept, but he never went to bed at the same time I did. If I wasn't such a heavy sleeper I might have figured out a pattern already.

"Yeah, we don't need much sleep either."

I raised an eyebrow. "What makes you so different from me that you don't need to eat or sleep as much?"

He hesitated, glancing back with a contagious smile. "I'm not that different from you."

"What's that supposed to mean?"

He didn't respond. Sighing, I trudged on in silence. We stepped over decaying trees and pushed past branches, as I absorbed this new information. How strange that they didn't eat and sleep much, but he said he wasn't *that* different from me. My curiosity burned. What were they hiding?

"So Daniel, how old are you?" I would have guessed he was twenty-two.

"Old enough to race you up this hill!" He stuck his tongue out and took off running.

I didn't get my answer, but I got more than I would have if I had asked Colt or *Mr. Evasive*. I tried running after Daniel, but he was too fast. I was actually surprised how fast; it wasn't normal for someone to move like that. In fact, it didn't seem like he was running at all; he would just suddenly appear further in the forest.

I tried to catch up, but lost him through the trees. I was in good shape, but was no match for Daniel's speed. I stopped to lean up against a massive pine. That was when I spotted them. A few feet away sat a large cluster of berry bushes, and beyond that were the Wallow berries I needed. About time!

I pushed my way through the bushes to the small purple berries that clung to the forest floor. I was fortunate they resembled blueberries; my over-bearing guardians probably wouldn't be able to tell the difference.

Or so I hoped.

I didn't need huge amounts; a handful would do the job just fine. I stared down at the bluish stains on my fingers. Abruptly my chest felt tight, and I took a calming breath. I'd never done something like this before, and I wasn't sure I'd be able to pull it off. But the lure of the deposit box was too much. I had no other choice.

I carefully broke off a couple of leaves. I would need those so I wouldn't end up like the others. Speedily packing them into one of the Ziploc bags, I placed it into my side pocket. I wouldn't have much time before Daniel came back to look for me, so I anxiously started picking the safe huckleberries. Just as I finished, Daniel came tromping back, looking around for me.

"I'm over here, Daniel," I called out. "I found some berries."

He stuck his head around a tree, grinning from ear to ear. "I thought I lost you," he said.

"Actually, you did," I said, smiling as well. "Fortunately, when I stopped to catch my breath, I saw the berries. I figured you'd come back sooner or later."

Daniel laughed—a beautiful, carefree sound that warmed my heart. He had a sincere happiness about him. I had to like him. He had a knack of putting me at ease, treating me as if we'd been friends for years. Quite unlike someone else I'd become familiar with...

I shook my head. No need to cloud my day thinking about *him*.

"So, ready to look for some mushrooms?" I asked.

"Sure!"

"This time, don't go running off on me," I warned. "I'm not fast enough to keep up with you, and you wouldn't want to lose me and have to go back alone would you?"

He flashed a toothy grin, then grabbed my arm to make sure I couldn't get away. We strode on, arm in arm, until we made it to the top of the ridge. Just beyond lay a small valley, where grasses and wildflowers flowed down from the base of the trees and swayed in the breeze. A small creek meandered its way from side to side, like a snake carving a way through the undergrowth. The water glistened under the sunlight, each ripple dancing to its own song. I turned; Daniel was staring at me with a shimmer in his eye.

I proceeded into the opening, my fingers outstretched so they could touch the plants as I walked by. I leaned down further to take in the fragrances. It was such a sweet scent; it made my heart still and kept my worrisome thoughts at bay.

I looked up into the sunlight and closed my eyes, warmed by the summer rays. After a few moments I turned to find Daniel next to me. A small smile grew on my lips. He was so different than Colt and Callon. The way his black hair fell on his face, and the freckles on his nose that I hadn't seen before, made him seem younger than he was. He was so genuine, so open, and so comfortable to be around. It was as if he were my brother, a brother I'd never had, but always wanted.

I took a few more steps, found a small patch of soft grass by the creek, and sat down. I loved the gentle gushing of a creek. The trickle of a river was beautiful too, but rivers could also be loud, roaring, overpowering. A creek was gentle, relaxing. It caressed my mind; a song to ease the pains of the soul. Daniel sat nearby and I closed my eyes again, taking it all in. We both remained still for a long time, until I finally broke the tranquility.

"Thank you," I whispered. "I needed this today." How he knew I didn't care. The fact that he did warmed me on the inside. A cabin filled with cold stares from *he who must be obeyed* and not talking with Colt had taken its toll.

"You're welcome, Cheyenne. This is one of my favorite places. I was hoping you'd like it, too."

He had me there; I loved this place. But we'd been gone for too long. It was time to head back.

I only needed a handful of mushrooms, and once they were stowed away, we began the hike back. It took less time than I expected. Upon entering the cabin, both Callon and Colt were sitting in the great room, in deep discussion. Their voices hushed, and I went to the kitchen and started pulling out pans to make dinner, hoping if I ignored them they would continue talking. They had gone to the store and set the items out on the counter to make it easier. I took a calming breath. Phase two of my plan was about to begin.

I made the pie first. With the oven on, I created the piecrust. I then proceeded to make the berry filling, being careful when touching the small Wallow berries. I pulled the leaves out, rinsed them, and secretly put them into my mouth and chewed. They were vile, and the taste made me want to gag. I swallowed hard to get them down.

Mixing the special berries together with the huckleberries, I added in the remaining ingredients and poured the contents into the piecrust, quickly covering the filling with the top crust and placing it in the oven.

I glanced at the trio, as they'd remained in the great room. "Do you mind if we have an early dinner?"

Callon nodded. "Sure, that'd work for us."

"Great, I'm starving. Hope you're hungry." I grinned and returned to my work. They were still discussing something in hushed tones too quiet for me to hear. Did they suspect what was going on?

Concentrating on my task at hand, I finished making the main course in no time at all. It was only three in the afternoon, but the pie was done and the Tortellini was ready. This would give me plenty of time to make it to the bank before it closed at six. At least, I was hoping it was six and not earlier. Why hadn't I looked it up on my computer? Too late now...

I set the table, then called them over to eat. Daniel dug in without any hesitation, as if he hadn't eaten in over a week. It was amazing. I didn't even see him chew. It looked like he swallowed every bite whole. Callon and Colt ate more slowly, watching me. Hungrily, I consumed my whole plate of food.

"This is delicious, Cheyenne," Callon said with newfound appreciation.

Daniel and Colt nodded as well. "Thanks," they said in unison.

"Where'd you learn to cook?" Callon sat back in his chair and crossed his legs.

"My mom taught me. She was an excellent teacher." Fond memories of baking cookies together streamed to my mind.

"She taught you well," Callon said. "I'm impressed."

"Yeah, well, it isn't that exciting cooking for one. Too many leftovers." I looked up. "Although with the three of you, I don't have to worry about it." I gave a faint smile. "I hope you saved room for pie and ice cream."

"Can't wait," Colt replied.

It was nice knowing they really did enjoy the meal, even though I was technically poisoning them. I gathered up the plates while they sat and chatted about baseball, talking about their favorite players. Pulling four bowls out of the cupboard, I went to the freezer to get the ice cream. I carefully cut the pie and dished it into the bowls, being sure to scoop large amounts of ice cream on their servings. I slid one to each of them, returning to the counter to grab my own, and sat down again.

Once again, Daniel didn't disappoint; he started shoveling it down. Colt and Callon both hesitated until I started to eat and then they dug in. I had about twenty minutes from the time the berries went into their mouths until the side effects would kick in. The only antidotes were the leaves I'd eaten earlier. My dad had warned me to eat them at least an hour in advance to get the antitoxin into the body.

The berries paralyzed the muscles. They weren't potent enough to stop a person from breathing, swallowing, or blinking, but their arms, legs, and torso would remain immobile. The effects would only last about half an hour to an hour, depending on the dosage. I just needed to make sure the three of them were sitting on the couch or loveseat because I wouldn't be able to move them if they fell. I didn't want to hurt them, just have time to get away.

They finished the pie, and I once again gathered up the plates with their help and started cleaning. Colt neared the counter and leaned across the sink full of dishes to look at me.

"Are you still mad at me?" he asked.

"No. I'm fine," I replied, as I started washing. I really had gotten over being angry with him. I wasn't exactly thrilled about the situation, but I couldn't stay angry forever. He'd been desperately trying to make amends. Now what I'd done was probably going to make *him* mad.

"Why don't you sit down and watch the baseball game? When I finish the dishes, we can go for a walk and talk about it." I gave a quick smile to let him know it was okay and pushed my hands into the sink further, scrubbing and swirling the water around.

"Ok, we'll go for a walk then, after you're done." He repeated and slowly moved his arms around me in a hug; still unsure about how I would react. He pressed his face to mine and gave me a soft kiss on my cheek, near my ear. The butterflies in my stomach came to life. I'd missed his touch.

I listened intently as he walked away, waiting to hear the creak of the leather on the sofa when he sat.

I let out a sigh of relief. All three were watching television. Colt was on the couch, slouching across the majority of it. Daniel was in the overstuffed chair with his feet dangling off the ottoman and Callon was sitting in the corner of the loveseat. This was going better than I thought.

I finished cleaning the kitchen and walked into the bedroom to get my wallet and change into my skirt and blouse—just in case I needed to look impressive, regardless of the fact that I had the key. I didn't want to look like a slob walking into the bank. If I needed to convince a bank clerk, because I was late, I'd probably have a better chance if I was more presentable.

When I returned to the great room, the trio had a dazed look on their faces. The berries were doing their job. Their eyes followed me across the room, filled with frustration and anger, as they could do nothing to stop my upcoming escape.

Setting my backpack on the kitchen counter, I went to Daniel first. His head was in an uncomfortable position so I carefully placed both my hands on his cheeks and repositioned it so it was resting on the back of the chair. He was staring at me, more curious than anything else.

"I'm sorry, Daniel. But I have to do this. I want you to know I had a wonderful day hiking with you, and I can't thank you enough for showing me your valley." I produced a small smile. "Don't worry; this will only last about an hour." I gently brushed his dark hair from his eyes.

I turned to Colt, who was sprawled across the couch. His eyes met mine, filled with a mix of concern, helplessness, and anger. I knelt so I could get close to his face. His massive body was so still, and his arms lay limply at his side. Reaching out, I took one of his hands in mine and pulled it to my chest.

"Colt, forgive me. This is the only way I'll be able to leave. I'm not angry with you. I was hurt, but I know you meant what you said." I didn't know what else to say; I had so many emotions swimming in my head and heart right now. "I didn't want to say the wrong words and hurt you, so I've said nothing at all."

I sighed.

"You hold a special place in my heart. But I'm not sure it's the same kind of love you have or desire from me in return. You understand me, you make me laugh, you comfort me, and you make me feel safe when you wrap me in your arms. I really don't deserve someone like you. I hope you'll forgive me."

I closed my eyes and pulled his hand to my face, cupping it into my cheek while I lowered myself towards his lips. I kissed him softly, and his lips trembled at the contact. A sense of regret hung low in my stomach. I kissed him again, then carefully folded his arm to his chest and rose.

Callon was drooped in the love seat, his face clouded with irritation. He was annoyed I had gotten the better of him. I gave a sly smile as I neared. I'd won, and there was nothing *he who must be obeyed* could do about it. Victory was sweet, at least for the moment. I warned them they couldn't keep me here. They didn't think I could get away, ha!

I sat next to him, looking into his hazel eyes while I slowly placed my hand to his cheek. I couldn't help myself. After being under his thumb, it was about time he got a taste of his own medicine. Deliberately, I stroked his left cheek, letting my hand trace his neck, his shoulder, and down his arm to his fingers where I paused.

His gaze changed from irritation to something else, and I felt a corresponding reaction, although I wasn't sure if it was excitement or something deeper. I moved my hand to his left jean pocket. The key to the Jeep wasn't there.

I moved my hand over his right pants pocket. This time I found what I was searching for. I pushed my hand up under his wrist and

92

pressed my fingers into his pocket to grasp it. He knew what I wanted, but his stare distracted me. There was a passion in his eyes that set my heart fluttering. It was so deep and intense that I stopped what I was doing. Closing my eyes, I pulled the key free, struggling to keep my pulse from bounding.

Leaning forward, I bent close to his ear and whispered, "You should have never underestimated me, Callon. I was surprised at how easy it was. I'm sure you're dying to know what I did. Here's a hint: I hope you liked the berry pie. Not so much fun being held against your will now, is it?" I lightly blew warm air through my nose.

My mouth continued before my mind caught up. "Maybe one day we'll meet up again under different circumstances. That passion in your eyes, who knows where that would lead?" Oh great! I was getting cocky and stupid and wrapped up in his good looks. Step away, Cheyenne. Don't waste all your hard work.

But my body took over, moving without my consent. I caressed his ear with my lips, then lifted my head...right as my hand slipped off the couch and my lips collided with his. I quivered slightly—he felt it. I'm not sure why I said what I said or why I didn't pull away when my mouth met his, but it was too late now. It was foolish and reckless and totally unlike me, but I wasn't me, I was someone else—the secret!

It didn't matter now, this would be the last time I would see them for a while. Any attraction, conscious or subconscious, I had for Callon I would force myself to forget. He'd only looked at me twice with any warmth, but seeing his gaze now...

I took a shaky breath as our eyes met. "Good-bye."

I jumped up and ran to the kitchen counter to grab my pack.

Time to go.

I flew out the front door and dashed to the Jeep with car key in hand. It started right up. I was very grateful my dad had insisted on getting a GPS system installed. I had saved the bank address in my favorites menu. I stomped on the gas and was soon speeding down the dirt road.

It took about ten minutes to reach the main highway and then I was able to really open the engine up and rocket down the road. My heart was pounding, the adrenaline flowing, but my mind was clear.

I was back in control again.

CHAPTER 8

Time raced by. I had known my plan would work, but I was still in shock over the success. I had never done anything like this in my entire life. I could picture my dad being proud of me—I was proud of me.

I had so many questions racing through my mind, observations I'd made about the trio. I knew Colt, or at least I thought I did; however, I knew nothing about Callon except his rather bossy attitude. Even with as little conversation as Daniel and I had, I'd learned the most from him. Either he didn't know anything, was excellent at hiding the truth, or was afraid to reveal too much because of Callon.

That their presence had been kept hidden from me continued to both hurt and anger me. They'd been watching me along with Colt, although I'd never seen or caught wind of them. Why hadn't my parents told me? I inhaled a shaky breath. Probably because they knew it might frighten me, and they wanted me to have as normal a life as possible. So much for normal now...

Town was an hour away; at least, I guessed it would take that long because I was too busy screaming down the highway to notice the time. The mileage log on the GPS system said it was about one hundred and twenty-five miles; I must have been driving like a bat out of hell to get there so quickly.

Glancing at the clock, I saw it was five fifteen. The sign on the bank door said it would close at five thirty; I had just enough time to get what I needed.

I parked the car around the corner and jumped out, my heart burst into flight. Everything was falling into place.

Straightening my shirt and blouse, I made my way to the bank entrance. Once inside, I located the clerk in charge of the safety deposit box area. I was in luck; he was a young man, about twenty-five. He was scrawny and had a pale complexion. Probably hadn't had much luck with finding a girlfriend.

The sign said that access wasn't allowed into the safe deposit box area after five p.m. I put my best foot forward, and strolled over to his desk. I was going to have to really work this poor guy to get what I needed. But I was prepared to do just about anything at this point. I had to find out what lay in wait for me. I needed answers; who I was, and what else was being kept from me. *You're an actress,* I reminded myself.

Callon, Colt, and Daniel would be on their way by now. I was positive they would come into town first; that's what I would have done. I didn't tell them where I was going, but they seemed pretty adept at finding me, and they'd already found the key. Regardless, I wasn't going to make it easy for them. I had managed to get away and was fairly confident I could stay away.

"Hello, Joseph," I said in my most persuasive voice. I wanted to gag. I wasn't going to win any Oscars for this performance.

The clerk's head flipped up so fast that if it hadn't been attached at his neck it would've flown into the air.

"Uh, hello. Can I help you?"

"Well, Joseph, you don't mind if I call you Joseph, do you? That's what your nametag says, and it's such a cute name." He blushed as I poured on the charm.

"You can call me Joseph," he answered, hope in his eyes. "What can I do to help you?"

"Well, you see, Joseph," I emphasized his name on purpose, "your sign says I can't get into my safe deposit box after five, and I was hoping you could help me out. I left some important documents in my box, and I really have to have them for tonight. I tried to make it down here earlier, but got a flat tire along the way. Some really nice gentlemen stopped to help me, but it took longer than I expected." I batted my lashes. Inside I was cringing at the foolish display I was making.

He stared at me for a moment, glancing at his watch and then answered, "Bank policy says we can't allow customers into the secure area after five, but in your case, you did really try to get into the bank before the cut off time, so I'll make an exception." He gave an optimistic grin. "Do you have your key?"

"Yes," I replied, and placed it in his hand as I squeezed his fingers. I was relieved it had worked so easily.

"Please follow me."

He led the way behind the counter to open the secure door to the room. He glanced at the number, and proceeded to the right where he stopped and hopped up on the step stool, placing the key in box number 258. He then placed his master key into the adjoining lock and turned them both. The small drawer popped out and he stepped down the stool with the contents in his hands.

"This way, please."

He motioned for me to follow. We entered a private room where he set the box on the table.

"It's all yours." He smiled and walked out, closing the door behind him.

My hands were shaking. I didn't have time for nervousness; I needed to get the contents out speedily. I released the lid and slid the items in the box toward the table. A small package wrapped in a cloth with a leather strap fell out. Attached to the leather strap was a ring. But it wasn't just any ring. It was the most stunning piece of jewelry I'd ever seen.

It was a sterling silver band that held a brilliant, sparkling, blue stone. It reminded me of the rare blue diamonds I'd heard about but never seen. I touched it with my fingertips, and it threw flecks of light onto the walls. Was this what my parents wanted me to find?

A soft knock on the door made me jump. I'd have to explore the ring and package later.

"Ma'am, we're closing, and I need to ask you to come out."

I rose to my feet and swiftly opened the door. This time the clerk jumped. "Thank you so much, Joseph." I reached out and squeezed his arm. He was pleasantly surprised.

He smiled and said in a choked voice, "You're welcome. Come back anytime."

Grinning, I walked to the front entrance with my prize in hand. It was five thirty. Only fifteen minutes had passed. This would give me plenty of time to head out of town before the trio could make it.

My attention remained on the ring and wrapping on the small book as I walked around the corner. I knew approximately the distance the car was from the bank entrance and didn't bother to look up.

I didn't realize someone was walking very closely behind me, until I was at the driver's side door with my hand raised to unlock the car.

I froze.

Colt was standing there, arms crossed, but his disposition wasn't as angry as I'd thought he'd be. I stopped in my tracks, only to have two hands grasp my arms from behind. Colt shook his head and closed his eyes. How could they have found me so soon?

Colt reached over and pulled me to his side as the other hands released their grip. I turned to see Daniel standing behind me. A moment later, the same sandalwood-colored truck I saw at the cathedral pulled to a stop in front of us. Colt moved me to the side while he opened the front door, and Daniel took the key for the Jeep from my hand. In one quick motion, I was hoisted into the front seat and pushed to the middle, sandwiched between Colt and Callon.

I looked at Callon's face while he watched Colt buckle me in. He didn't look angry—in fact, he looked almost gleeful, as if he knew they'd catch me again. They both glanced at my hands and saw the book with the ring. Suddenly their expressions became alarmed, but the emotion disappeared as rapidly as it had come. *That was strange.* Moments later we started the long drive home.

My mind was whirling. I had given the three of them an extra large dose of the Wallow berries; it should have knocked them out for a least an hour. But they were here waiting for me, and I was only in the bank for fifteen minutes. It didn't add up.

Callon hadn't said anything. Memories of our parting flooded back, and I pressed my eyes shut. How could I have done something so stupid?

Cringing, I decided I would speak first to gauge their reactions. After all, I wouldn't be leaving them anytime soon. "I guess I'm in a heap of trouble, huh?" I tried to make my tone light, but it came out with a nervous laugh.

"Heaps," Colt replied, as he slid his arm around my waist. My breathing hitched a little.

"How did you recover so fast? You should've been down for at least an hour." Was what my dad had taught me wrong? Still no response. Without thinking I muttered under my breath, "Next time I'll have to try something different."

Callon flipped his head so fast that it jolted me back. "There will not be a next time, Cheyenne." His voice was cold as he spoke through clenched teeth. "If I recall, you said, 'Don't ever underestimate me.' I won't leave your side, if that's what it takes. You took advantage of the situation once, and you can be damn certain it's never going to happen again."

He who must be obeyed was rearing his ugly head and scaring the crap out of me.

Callon drew in a deep breath to calm himself.

"Colt warned me I shouldn't be too trusting of you," Callon informed me, "and he was right. I know how you manipulated that bank clerk; don't expect that to work on me. Heaps of trouble is the tip of the iceberg. You have no idea what you've got yourself into."

I blinked. It was all I could do; I had nothing to say. I'd been a fool. How did I ever think I saw a softer side to him?

I averted my eyes from Callon's anger and stared down at the book in my hands. I ran my fingers over the cloth wrapped around it and played with the ring, wondering what significance it held. Colt's hold provided a small sense of comfort from Callon's rant. I leaned my head into his shoulder, and he squeezed his fingers around my waist.

No one spoke a word the remainder of the drive to the cabin. Daniel was following behind us in my Jeep. I began wondering how mad he was at me. He'd been nothing but nice to me, and I'd repaid that kindness by using him.

Why did I care? It wasn't like we were all that close. But I'd felt so at ease with him in the meadow. I would have to apologize and earn his trust again. I told myself it seemed like I'd have plenty of time to make it up to him, at least.

We pulled onto the dirt road that led up to the cabin. The sunlight had faded, and darkness crept into the trees. We came to a stop just to the side of the outbuilding. Colt opened the door and slid me off the seat and into his arms.

He wrapped both his hands around me and pulled me close. One of them found its way to the small of my back, pushing me closer still. The other hand moved to the back of my neck as he pressed his lips to mine. I blinked.

My arms were locked against his chest, clinging to the small book; I could do nothing to stop him. He kissed me with such zeal, his lips unyielding, searching for a response. I closed my eyes.

He was pressing against my sides and my chest; it was hard to breathe. I parted my lips trying to speak, and he misunderstood, he thought I wanted more. He began kissing me with even more fervor, taking one step forward and pinning me against the truck door while his massive arms tightened about me. The ring tied to the leather strap on the book was digging into my chest. My head started spinning.

Colt finally loosened his grasp, and I sucked in air. My body trembled. Every part of my arms and chest were aching, and my neck was on fire. Colt's breathing wasn't labored at all. He knew exactly what he was doing.

He whispered in my ear, "Cheyenne, you don't know what I'm capable of; how much love, how much passion, how much strength. How I want to keep you wrapped in my arms to make you safe.

"Your life is so fragile right now. You left me helpless tonight, even if it was for a short period of time. I wouldn't have been able to live with myself if something happened to you.

"You need to know I would go to the ends of the earth for you. I could and would do anything to keep you from harm. Don't you ever make me helpless to protect you again. If you think that *heaps* of trouble is bad, you don't want to know what comes after that!"

I was still trembling in his arms, as he moved his lips down my jaw again and this time tenderly kissed my lips, one, two, and three times. I let out a sigh and kept my lids closed for a few more moments before I could peer into his baby blue eyes. He had that protective look again, like when he had me cornered in the kitchen before I left Idaho. I couldn't decide if it was romantic or possessive, but I knew he had been scared for my safety. I was still pinned up against the truck in his arms when Callon interrupted.

"Are you done now, Colt?" His voice had an edge to it I'd never heard before.

Colt released his hold, and I dropped to the ground. I was happy to be against the truck for the moment. I was able to steady myself against it. Colt made sure I didn't fall by keeping his hands under my arms for support. He moved them to his sides and turned.

"I'm done now. She's all yours." There was a grin on his face as he walked away, giving a quick wink he bounded up the steps into the cabin. I was stunned momentarily until I turned towards Callon.

Crap, now I was really in for it. Callon stared at me for a lengthy moment, studying me, contemplating what he was going to do. Panic began to bubble in my chest. Being alone with him was not on my list of top ten things to do in life. I didn't know if I should be scared, or nervous. I was stupid, and now I'd pay the price for my recklessness.

I kept my hands wrapped around the book—I didn't move an inch. He quickly cleared the distance between us and grabbed my arm. It wasn't a gentle pull, it was *I'm mad at you and you're going to get it* pull.

I stumbled alongside him as he led me into the forest. It was dark, and I couldn't see where he was taking me. My feet were tripping over stumps, and branches were scraping across my legs. My shirt caught on a branch and I heard a tearing sound. *Damn!* This was one of my favorite ones.

We were getting further and further into the forest and walking faster and faster. I was having a hard time keeping up. My upper body was already sore, Callon's grasp on my arm was tight and painful, my legs were getting scratched up, and my good shirt was torn. Scared or not, I'd had enough. I planted my feet, and yelled, "Stop! You're hurting me!"

He continued to drag me through the undergrowth until I was standing directly in front of him. He sat me down onto a fallen log abruptly. He released his grasp and took a couple of steps back, crossing his arms and leaning against a large pine tree.

The gurgle of a small creek trickled in the distance. The darkness encased us, and I couldn't see the expression on his face. I didn't know if he was angry, and I couldn't tell if I had pushed him too far.

I shouldn't have touched him the way I did. I shouldn't have said the things I said. I shouldn't have kissed him, accident or not...what had I done?

Callon's expression had changed after I kissed him. For once, it didn't frighten me; it made me wonder *what if?* What if the circumstances were different? Would he be drawn to me the way I was drawn to him? Was I teasing him, tempting him to come and find me? If that was the case, it worked, because he found me and now I was in trouble. Or was it that I enjoyed feeling some sort of momentary power over him, like the power he had over me?

We stared at each other for what seemed like an eternity. My fingers still clung tightly to the book in my lap. Turning away from his gaze, I attempted to break the invisible barrier between us. My fingers loosened and drifted across the leather strap that held the ring. I examined the ring, admiring the beauty in the small stream of moonlight that broke through the dense trees. Callon cautiously approached and sat down on the log.

I didn't look up and sighed before I spoke, "I'm not sorry for leaving. I don't like being held against my will. I didn't have any other choice."

Callon replied quietly, "You always have a choice, Cheyenne. You could've asked."

"I did, and you told me I wasn't allowed to leave."

"Yes, I did, but I didn't say you couldn't go with an escort."

"Maybe next time you should clarify," I sneered as I met his cold stare.

"Maybe next time you should ask," he growled. He waited a moment before he spoke again, only this time with more control. "Is that what you were looking for?" He pointed to the book in my lap.

"Yes."

"It was at the bank?"

I nodded.

"Is that why you manipulated the bank clerk? To get into the safe deposit box?" He raised his brows.

"Yes," I responded shamefully. How had I stooped that low?

"Poor guy. Never saw it coming, huh?" Callon's demeanor softened.

"Guess not."

"That's quite a weapon you have there. I feel sorry for the poor man you unleash it on—he won't stand a chance. I only saw a small portion you used on me today..."

I cut him off, "I didn't use that on you today. You say you would've let me go if I asked, but I don't know if I believe you. I had to take matters in my own hand."

"So you think our words and actions should agree, huh?"

"Yes?" What was he getting at?

"So, the way you touched me, the trembling in your hands and lips, they were saying something?"

Oh great, the kiss! I knew this would come up. I didn't answer. How could I? He'd cornered me, and I'd walked straight into his trap. I lowered my head as I ran my fingers over the ring. When would I learn to think before speaking?

"And the words you spoke. '*One day we'll meet up again under different circumstances. I can see the passion in your eyes. Who knows where that would lead?*'"

He quoted me almost perfectly. "You forgot *maybe*," I snapped back, trying to defend my reckless actions.

Callon ignored my comment and continued. "Who knows where

that *would* lead, not *could*. You said *would*. That *would* implies something. W*ould* is stronger than *could*. *Could* is a maybe, whereas *would* is a definite."

"And *maybe* overrides *would,* and the meaning thus changes," I shot back.

There was no anger. He was calm. He was in control again. He was making me uncomfortable and taking great satisfaction from it. "You know it was always meant to be this way. We were to meet up with Gene and Alexis; you were meant to be with us."

His words may be true, but I didn't know. My parents never told me about their plans. Somehow I knew this confusion was not what my parents wanted for me. I remained silent.

There was a distinct tone in Callon's voice when he spoke again. It was a mixture of curiosity and manipulation. "That was quite a kiss back there."

"It was...unexpected." I closed my eyes again. I didn't want to look at him. I continued to run the ring and strap through my fingers. Callon was taking great pleasure in torturing me.

"Colt certainly seemed to sweep you off your feet back there."

"Yes."

"He also made you somewhat breathless?"

"Yes, he was holding me too tight, and I was having a hard time getting air into my lungs." Callon wasn't going to get the better of me this time.

"Did you like that?" he asked, sounding like he was merely curious.

"I like to breathe," I snapped.

"That's not what I asked."

I knew what he was asking, but I didn't want to answer him. I was becoming angry, and when I got angry, I said things I didn't want to say.

I glowered as I replied, "Then what are you asking? Did I like the way Colt grabbed me and pulled me in his arms? When he pushed his body against mine and kissed me? The way I felt totally and completely under his control and helpless to stop him?"

"You're getting closer, but that's still not what I asked."

Now I was really pissed. What did he want me to say? Why was he making me say this?

"Yes!" I screamed. "Is that what you want to hear? I also sometimes like tender moments, a gentle caress, and a soft kiss. At other times I want romance. I want to feel my heart flutter, anticipate the unknown. I don't always know what I want; I'm not the most experienced woman when it comes to men, if you haven't noticed. I've only been kissed once, and you witnessed it."

"You may have only been kissed once, but you've kissed before. You kissed Colt when he was helpless on the sofa and you kissed me—both in the same afternoon. I'd say that you have experience." He was gloating.

"Your kiss was an accident! Are you purposely trying to drive me insane?" I was screaming, completely out of control.

"Maybe a little. It's only fair. I'm trying to figure out what you want. You like the comfort that Colt brings you; he's safe and you can be yourself with him. You like being wrapped in his arms, but you don't have the same passion for him that he has for you. You love him, but not like he does you. You weren't passionately responding to his kiss earlier; you were actually trying to stop him.

"He misread your reaction as something else. You're hesitant to accept his full love because you don't feel like you can reciprocate it.

And you don't want to hurt him because it would hurt you to see him suffer."

My demeanor went from angry to grudging acceptance in a flash. He was right on, and I knew it. How did he figure this out? Then it dawned on me...they'd been watching me for years. They knew me better than I knew myself. Tears streamed down my cheeks. Callon continued to speak, holding my gaze.

"You become uncomfortable when I come into the room; your heart starts to race when I look at you. You don't like to make eye contact because you're afraid to show your emotions."

"You scare the crap out of me," I blurted out, but I knew he was somewhere close to the truth. There were moments when his look was warm and inviting.

"You tremble when I touch you; you were trembling when you touched me today—when you kissed me. You don't know why you did what you did, the way you caressed my arms.

"You held your hand to my face and whispered into my ear. You enjoyed the fact that you had momentary power over me. You were in control, and you could do what you wanted. You taunted me to come after you and find you; you don't want to be alone. You're afraid to let go because you don't know where your feelings may take you."

I didn't know what to say. I had no appropriate response. Callon started to smirk.

"I knew I was right. I can see it in your face."

The blood began to grow cold in my veins, icy cold as the realization set in. I stuttered, "Y-y-you tricked me? You really didn't know so you tricked me into showing my feelings, to lie them right out in front of you? So you could have control and get what you wanted? You twisted my thoughts and feeling around until I was confused?"

I was angry now, livid! I needed to clear my head. I'd picked the worse day to wear a dress and sandals; I wanted to get up and run away from him. I wanted the safety of Colt's arms. I wanted him to protect me right now and to make Callon go away. I wanted him to kiss me again, to make me forget all my problems.

I jumped up from the log and started to dash back into the forest. I didn't know where I was going and kept tripping and falling to the rocky floor below. I didn't get very far before Callon grabbed my arm, spinning me around. He had a self-satisfied gloat across his face.

"So it's okay for you to trick me, but when I do it back it's a problem?" he asked.

"I only tricked you into eating something so I could leave and get the book. I didn't trick you emotionally." I said, my hands shaking.

"What do you call kissing me then? Just tasting the food to make sure it went down the gullet well?"

"Yes, that's it exactly," I hissed.

He let out a big chuckle, "Oh, I see. Just remember, Cheyenne, two can play your game."

I sighed. I was still irritated and angry, but I knew he was right.

"I'm cold and want to go back now." My arms were freezing, and my legs were cut up and scratched.

"I guess, since you're done being in trouble for the moment. I think this was punishment enough. I meant it when I said I wouldn't underestimate you again. I will constantly watch you at all times." His words were laced with threat, and I swallowed. No getting away from him now.

He led me out of the forest, pulling the branches back so I didn't get any more scratches. I clutched the book in my left hand. The ring was slid on my index finger, still tied to the leather strap.

Colt was waiting on the porch. He rose from the chair as we neared the stairs. He raised his eyebrows at my appearance. I was sure I looked a mess. My white shirt was torn and dirty; my legs were covered in bumps, dirt, and bloody scratches, and I had tearstains on my cheeks.

He flashed Callon an angry glare, and I was secretly glad. I was hoping he might come down off the porch and pummel him. I wasn't as heated as before, since the walk back had calmed me, but I still wasn't very happy, and he could see it.

They exchanged glances. Then Colt grinned at me and Callon. I frowned. Why did they keep doing that? Could they read minds or something?

I glared at Colt, "What?"

Chuckling, he leaped down the stairs, wrapping me up in his arms and kissed me on my head. This time his arms were gentler; however, the damage had already been done earlier and it still hurt.

"Ouch!"

Colt pulled back immediately and spoke, although the comment was meant for Callon, "You must have been in more trouble than I thought. I didn't realize you would come back so dirty and ragged. Next time I won't let you go alone."

"Promise?"

He smiled and took my hand as we headed into the cabin, Callon trailing behind. "Let's get you cleaned up, honey. You look good in a skirt, but not with all the dirt and blood attached."

I grinned. I was in my safe, happy place now, and there was nothing that Callon could do about it. Colt two, Callon zero.

CHAPTER 9

I was completely worn out by the emotional trauma of the day. As curious as I was, I would have to wait until tomorrow to inspect the book from the bank. It was no use wrapping myself up in whatever was in there when my brain was in a fuzz. I needed to be fresh and have my mind working at its best.

After showering, Colt helped me bandage the cuts on my legs and arms. He kept fussing, checking and rechecking that he hadn't missed anything, until I snapped at him to cut it out. With a playful grin, he led me into the great room to sit on the sofa. The others were watching TV, catching up on what they had missed the day before because of my little escapade. Callon was watching me just like he said he would, complete with a scowl. I longed to say something nasty, but in the end I curled up closer to Colt and fixed my best "don't mess with me" glare on my face. Colt saw the look directed at Callon and chuckled.

It had been a long and trying day. I should have felt bad, but I didn't. I'd needed to get to the bank to find the notebook and ring my parents had left. Hopefully the answers I needed would soon follow.

I was somewhat surprised Colt wasn't angrier. He had shown me his feelings in other ways—the kiss said more than I realized. I still wasn't sure what I felt for him, and Callon made me uncomfortable. He could switch from caring and concerned to downright enraged in the blink of an eye, without any warning. I hated not being able to gauge his thoughts, especially when he seemed to read mine so freely. But sometimes—and maybe it was just my imagination—it seemed as if he was holding back. He knew more about me than he was letting on, and the thought chilled me to the bone.

When I first arrived, he had refused to tell me anything and was cool and aloof. He warmed slightly when I started to resist less, but when I returned with the ring and journal, his cold and distant demeanor came back with a vengeance. What was the deep secret he was keeping from me? And why did I feel so drawn to him? He was the polar opposite of Colt.

I sighed. The pair of them knew my heart held something there for them both. I'd kissed them without thinking of the repercussions, accident or not. My eyes were becoming heavier, and a yawn revealed my tired state. I rose from the couch. Colt began to follow, but I motioned for him to stay. "I'm just going to bed." I felt the need to add, "Don't worry. I won't try to escape out the windows or anything."

My eyes shifted to Callon. "Colt will be close, and he won't let me go anywhere. Besides, if you thought what happened to you this afternoon was bad, you haven't seen anything yet."

I flashed a cunning smile and left the room. Colt guffawed as I walked toward the bedroom, and I heard Daniel ask, "She's not going to cook for us again, is she?"

Something flew across the room and hit the wall with a soft thud.

Was it Callon who threw the pillow? I smiled as I crawled into bed.

I grabbed the book from the nightstand and laid it next to me on the bed. I stroked the ring with my index finger, admiring the icy blue stone. It was about the size of a one-carat diamond; the craftsmanship was astonishing. Even in the dark, it sparkled in the moonlight. This was meant for me. It would tell me who I was, I was sure of it. Maybe it would confirm what Callon had said earlier, that I was always supposed to be with them. What had he meant by that anyway? My eyes grew heavy, and the last thing I remember was gazing at the ring in my fingers.

I slept well. Colt must have come into the room, as when I woke, the book had been moved to the nightstand and I was under the covers, not on them. He wasn't with me now, and the sun was up. Streams of light were gliding through the windows.

I gave a big stretch, suddenly feeling the ache in my body. I would have to take something today if I was going to be able to move around. I slowly pulled my legs over the edge of the bed and stood up, looking at the closet.

Colt had hung my clothes, making it clear I wasn't going to be leaving anytime soon. Well, it wasn't like I had a better alternative. I threw on a pair of off-white walking shorts, a cream colored tank and a form-fitting turquoise button down blouse. I always loved turquoise, along with the lighter and brighter blues. When I wore a shirt that color, it made my complexion brighter and brought out the color of my eyes.

I headed to the bathroom and finished cleaning myself up. I made my way down the hall and into the great room with the book in hand. No one was there; that was odd. I thought I wasn't to be left alone? I glanced up the stairs, still no one. When I came down the hallway, the other two bedroom doors were open, and they were empty. Should I be uneasy? I shook my head. No, I knew they had to be close by. Probably out securing the area because of the great danger I was in. I smirked. I'd find out soon enough. I'd go look out front while I ate breakfast.

I grabbed something from the kitchen to snack on. I found a small bottle of orange juice in the fridge and reached into the pantry for the granola bars. As I walked by the trash to throw the wrapper away, I saw the pie and tin lying in it. I let out a small laugh and headed for the front door. I had a feeling they wouldn't let me cook for them for a long while.

The large porch was inviting. It had a number of seating areas available, and it made me think of Mom. The way the furniture was arranged, the fabric on the cushions; this would have been something she would have done, and she would have approved. I smiled at the thought. I didn't need to cry anymore.

There were a couple of large chairs with an ottoman, and an oversized loveseat at the far end of the porch just outside the kitchen area. I chose the loveseat. I set down my juice and what was left of my granola bar on the side table, and placed the book in the open seat next to me. I still didn't see or hear any of the boys, but I wasn't too worried yet. I knew I couldn't go anywhere; I didn't need to or have the desire now that I had gotten what I came for in the first place. I had the book now, and this is what my parents wanted me to find. Besides, I had no place else to be...

I finished eating and drank the remaining juice while I looked out into the forest. My gaze travelled down the road and followed as far as it could before the road curved. I glanced at the outbuilding. Both the Jeep and truck were parked there, so they couldn't have gone too far.

I settled into my seat and pulled the book into my lap, untying the leather strap holding the ring and letting it fall to the side. The ring rolled into my palm. It was just as remarkable as I remembered last night. I put it on the ring finger of my right hand and arranged the stone so it was facing my palm. This way I could look at it without flipping my hand over as I turned the pages.

I drew my attention back to the book and removed the cloth wrapped over it. It wasn't a regular book; it was a worn leather journal with unique symbols engraved on its cover. It was cracked on the spine from being held open so many times, and the edges were worn.

I opened the first page. It had darkened with age, and in the center of the page were more strange symbols. Different from the ones on the front of the cover, these were entwined together in a single strip that ran across the page. It was strangely familiar. I looked over at my right hand to the ring my parents had given me as a small child, the ring I had always worn. My eyes widened; the symbols were identical. I'd thought it was just an intricate design, the curves looping and weaving in and out of each other.

I flipped through a couple of pages, examining the symbols. They were always in the center and always in a straight row across. At first glance they appeared similar, but then they would be in a different order, or new glyphs would crop up. Some resembled clovers and squiggly lines connected together.

There were five pages in total with the symbols. I continued to flip through the journal; the following pages held more writing. It looked like a foreign language I had never seen before, but I wasn't quite sure. It was some sort of ancient script.

I frowned. This made no sense. Why would my parents give me a book written in a language I didn't understand? I didn't remember them ever talking about it, or seeing anything with this type of writing on it. But I was sure this is what they wanted me to find. Somehow, they must have believed I would understand.

I pursed my lips. I needed to do some research.

I set the journal down and ran back into the cabin. I didn't recall seeing my laptop in the bedroom, but maybe Colt had brought it in for me. Why hadn't I wanted it earlier? I looked in the closet. It wasn't there. I quickly strode into the great room and glanced around. Empty. I thought back. The last time I used it was at the coffee shop in town. I had done some research on the cathedral and, when I finished, I had tossed it in the case and put it in the back of the Jeep. Of course! It must still be sitting there.

I marched out to the Jeep and tried the handle. Unsurprisingly, it was locked. Peering through the tinted glass in the back, I saw the computer, still in its case on the floor. Great, now what was I going to do? I was sure they hadn't left the key lying around for me to casually pick up, and I was one hundred percent positive Callon had it in his front pocket. Thinking about how I'd acquired it last time brought a blush to my cheeks. No, I wasn't going to try that stunt again, at least not this soon. I also wasn't in the mood to wait for them to return and then kindly ask for it, especially Callon. More than likely he'd refuse just to rile me. I'd have to break in.

I ran inside and grabbed a wire hanger from the closet. How hard could it be? I just had to slide it between the glass and the door. I bent the hanger and worked it down in the crack. It was harder than it seemed. Nothing was catching or moving. Did this only work on older cars? I jigged the hanger back and forth and suddenly, it broke through. My hand slid down, and scratched against the wire.

"Ouch!" I cried. I lifted it to find that I was bleeding from a thin scratch across my palm.

This definitely wasn't going to work.

I searched the area for a stone. I found a decent sized rock, one I could easily handle, and wound up like a pitcher getting a better aim. I felt fairly confident; I didn't have too bad of an arm for a girl. Launching the rock with everything I had, it hit the back window. Success!

However, my triumph was short-lived, as a split second later the rock bounced off the window and ricocheted into my lower lip. Pain tore through my face, and I moaned. I had forgotten the back windows were made from polycarbonate, not glass. I fell to my knees and grabbed the right side of my face. *What the heck was the matter with me? Was I trying to kill myself?*

I forced myself up off the gravel driveway, feeling both stunned and embarrassed. The safest thing for me to do right now was not to throw any more missiles. So what could I use instead?

I scanned the wooded area for a fallen branch I could use to smash the front window. A hefty one was sitting by the road, so I grabbed it and dragged it over to the car. It was heavier than I thought. I wrapped both hands around it, twisting my body so I could get some good momentum into the swing, then let it fly.

It was more difficult to control than I imagined. Instead of breaking the glass, it bounced off the bumper, returning to hit me in my right eye. I fell to the ground. *Crap!*

Clutching my eye in my hands, I tried to work through the pain. So what if the branch was a little unwieldy? I was on a mission. I needed my computer.

I got back up, and pulled my hand away from my face. There was blood on it. Ouch. I came to the conclusion it would be safer if I took my rings off and placed them in my shorts pocket.

Perhaps another approach would be more prudent.

As I looked around the driveway again, my eyes came to rest on the outbuilding. Racing toward it, I flung the doors open. It was more of a horse tack barn, but in the far corner sat a workbench with some tools hanging above it. I glanced through the selection until I came across what I was looking for—a sledgehammer! If this didn't work, nothing would.

Running back to the Jeep, my eyes narrowed in determination. I was going to have the last laugh with this pile of scrap metal and wheels. I planted my feet firmly and placed both of my hands on the long narrow handle of the sledgehammer. I pulled my arms back, then swung with all my might. The window shattered as the hammer fell to the ground.

Precisely on the top of my right foot.

Swearing, I fell to the ground for the third time, grasping my leg. My right foot was throbbing; actually my entire right side was reeling in pain. Rage burned through my veins. I was not going down without a fight! I pushed through the hurt and picked the sledgehammer up. With a yell I swung it repeatedly, beating the window into a glassy pulp.

The car alarm went off, screeching in my ears. That was the last straw. I wasn't as careful as I could have been as I leaned into the broken window to unlock the door. I scratched my forearms. I unlocked the doors and reached across the seat to get the laptop case only to drop it. A piece of glass ripped through my shorts. Pain blazed up my leg, and I looked down to see a deep gash across my upper thigh that was oozing blood. *Could this get any worse?*

Crawling out, I ran around the front of the Jeep to release the hood latches to stop the auto alarm screaming. Stepping up on the front bumper, I found the electrical box and pulled the lid off. It took a few minutes, but I found the fuse for the alarm and pulled it out. The squealing ceased, replaced by blissful silence.

But the Jeep hadn't finished its fun with me yet. As I was about to climb back down, I banged my head against the hood. On instinct I flinched, only to lose my balance and fall to the gravel on my hands.

For a long while I sat on the ground, my head between my knees. *For all that is holy!* How did car thieves make it look so easy?

I wrenched myself up, walked to the driver's door and unlocked it. I headed to the back hatch, pulled it open, grabbed my laptop in its case and put it under my arm. I turned, bloody and battered, then staggered up the stairs to the porch.

I let myself fall into the seat. Everything hurt, and I was probably still bleeding, but all my struggles had only made my desire for answers stronger. I put my laptop case on the small table in front of me, my arm caked with dried blood. I'd clean it off later.

I unzipped the bag, pulled out the laptop, and turned it on. Nothing happened. I wanted to scream to the sky. The battery was dead! I dug into the bottom of my case and found the power cord. I took the laptop and the power cord with me as I entered the cabin, and proceeded to the kitchen table where I could let it charge while I was using it. I then realized that I had left the journal out on the porch.

I stumbled back out the door to grab it. As I entered the doorway, I heard Daniel's voice.

"What the heck happened to the Jeep?"

He was coming up the drive, inspecting the damage as he approached.

Callon and Colt were right behind him, staring at the log, stone, and sledgehammer. Blood coated all three items from where they'd hit me or where I'd grabbed them. The side window was smeared with it, as well as the backseat, driver's door, and grille.

In an instant both of them were sprinting towards the cabin. They stopped dead in their tracks when they saw me. I must've been quite a sight. I was covered in blood from head to toe, my right eye was swollen shut, and my lower lip was turning into a balloon. My arms were scratched, my right thigh was bleeding, and my shorts were torn. To top it all off, my head began throbbing.

Looking at all three of them for a brief moment, I hobbled to the loveseat on the porch to grab the journal. Their eyes were glued to me as I picked up the journal and slowly retreated into the cabin.

Colt burst out laughing, Daniel following with a mixture of snorting and hooting. Even Callon was laughing. Ha, maybe *he who must be obeyed* does have a sense of humor, after all.

I sat down at the kitchen table and turned my laptop on. It was pointless to wash up now; they'd already seen me and most of the scratches and bumps looked worse than they were. It probably would have done little good to prevent the harassing I was about to endure. Did they have wireless internet this far out of town?

The laughing trio walked into the cabin and came towards me. I couldn't look at them; I was far too embarrassed. Colt stepped forward and gently turned my chin toward them. I winced; my jaw and lower lip were throbbing with pain. I peered into his smiling eyes and knew exactly what was coming.

"I guess we know the answer to who won the fight with the Jeep."

They all burst into laughter with Daniel doubled up holding his side. I got up and started to limp out of the room. Both Callon and Colt came to my side and redirected me to the couch in the great room, the laugher momentarily dying down.

They sat me down to assess the damage, but they just couldn't remove the grins from their faces. Colt spoke again, but this time with more sincerity, "So what was in the Jeep you couldn't wait for?"

I tried to answer, but my mouth didn't move quite right since it was so swollen. "Waptop."

The snorting started again from behind the couch; Daniel was having a hard time controlling himself.

"Oh I see," Colt said. "Do you think you could tell us exactly what happened? Since we already know the extent of your injuries."

Colt was trying to keep a straight face, though his mouth continued to twitch into a mocking smile. Callon, however, seemed more concerned. My face flushed. What did it matter? They were never going to let me live this down. If they got it out of their system now, maybe it would be better later. *Dream on, Cheyenne, like that's going to happen...*

I looked at them with my one good eye, and started to explain. The only problem was that while I was trying to talk most of my words came out slurred. This made it even more amusing to them. Eventually, though, they got the majority of their laugher out of their system, and started to tend my wounds. They lay me down on the couch as they cleaned the blood from my face. Luckily the cuts above my eyes were just minor scratches.

Callon brought in a couple of bags of ice for the right side of my face. They moved down to my arms, hands, and thigh, cleaning and bandaging as they went. Callon checked my foot to make sure I hadn't broken it. I was fortunate the sledgehammer hadn't hit in the right spot and that I had a decent pair of hiking shoes on.

So much for researching the journal today. I didn't think I could do it even if I tried. Callon was back in doctor-mode, wanting to know when was the last time I ate. I couldn't be sure, but I thought it was about five hours ago. He made me a small protein shake and handed it to me with a straw. Colt helped me sit up, and I tried to drink as much as I could. Callon wanted me to take some painkillers, and I didn't fight him on this one. Without my irritation over the Jeep's cunning plan to foil me at every turn, I was really starting to feel the hurt.

Next time, I think I'll wait and ask, I told myself.

CHAPTER 10

The medicine Callon dispensed helped; I slept fairly well. I only remembered waking once when Colt shifted his legs from under my head. Low voices were talking in the kitchen—they were looking at the journal. It didn't really bother me they were reading it. I didn't know what it said, so any insight would be helpful.

I remembered I had placed the rings securely in my pocket and pulled them out, putting them back on my fingers. My face was still puffy, and I was sure I had at least one black eye. I thought now was as good a time as any to assess the damages.

I had a hard time trying to pull myself out of the couch; my head was starting to throb again. This was a different kind of throb, not like the headaches I had been getting. This was just your regular "bump on the noggin" type of bothersome headache. I could handle it. I sat up first and then used the arm of the couch for support to help raise myself up onto my legs. In an instant Colt was at my side, tenderly supporting my arm.

"How's my little Jeep assaulter today? Are you going to take on the truck because it said something to make you mad?" he asked in a teasing tone. "You know we wouldn't have laughed if we thought it was more serious, right?"

He loved to tease me; actually just about anyone I met loved to. I was beginning to think I had a permanent tattoo on my forehead that read *"tease me please."* I tried to smile back, but my lips and eyes wouldn't move. This just caused Colt to chuckle more to himself. I responded the best I could, trying to throw some sassiness back at him.

"If you think the Jeep was bad, just don't get me angry enough to do something to you."

He chuckled again and then helped me down the hall to the bedroom. I sat on the bed while he went to find me some clean clothes. He was being thoughtful.

I let out a sigh and was staring down at my hand admiring the blue ring again. When he came back, I placed my folded hands into my lap. Colt stopped and was silent; I could hear his even breathing. He looked at my hands. The ring was wrapped under my fingers now, and I realized I was clutching it harder than necessary. He reached over, and loosened my clasp to reveal the ring. He rolled it over so he could see the stone. His hand froze, and his breath paused. He pulled his hand away and balled it into a fist.

I was confused. He handed me my clothes and walked me to the bathroom in silence. I turned to try and look at him through my one good eye, and he gave a shallow smile as he strode away. I decided the best thing I could do right now was get clean. I went to the mirror only to gasp at what I saw. I was a mess; the right side of my face was a covered in bluish green bruises, mingled with scratches and dried blood. My eye was swollen, and I had a fat lip. I shook my head at my own impatient stupidity, but that hurt.

The cuts and scrapes stung a little when the water hit them. I tried to wash the cuts and bruises as best I could, cleaning off the remaining dried blood. I was pretty stiff and sore too; no more crazy activities for at least a couple of days.

I was a little confused by Colt's reaction over the blue-stoned ring. Both he and Callon saw it in the truck the other day, but said nothing. This time it seemed worse. Maybe he didn't really get a good look at it before? I was going to have to find out why. I glanced in the mirror again and sighed. This was as good as it was going to get. I needed time to heal.

I toddled to the kitchen where they were sitting. They turned as I approached. It was odd—the trio seemed to have blank expressions on their faces. Colt pulled the chair between Callon and himself out for me to sit on. I sat down, and my gaze wandered to each of their faces. Something was up, and it had to do with me.

Colt slowly reached over and took my hand in his, turning it to reveal the rings. He and Callon seemed more concerned than Daniel. Callon stretched out his hand and asked, "May I?"

I moved my hand toward his fingers. He gently grasped my wrist and started to caress my fingers with his other hand. He was rubbing his thumb over the rings. I peered into his warm eyes and saw something I didn't expect.

It was as if he was looking at me in awe. It was hard to imagine how he could in the condition I was in. My half bloody and battered face didn't change his expression. I stared back, not in awe, but something close to that.

He was so stunningly beautiful, his tanned skin highlighting his hazel eyes, the dark brown wavy curls falling onto his forehead. The way he held his jaw taut, the rough growth of whiskers peering out from his chin. I lowered my head; I didn't need to get caught up in him. Colt was who I needed. Callon drove me nuts; Colt made me smile. Callon analyzed everything. They were like night and day. Colt was my sunshine, Callon the dark of night that caused shivers to run down my back.

I allowed Callon to keep my hand in his, but turned slightly so I could lean toward Colt. Colt put his arm around my waist, slid closer, and I gave a weak grin. "Are these rings special?" I asked quietly. I directed my question to Callon since he was the one who usually spoke for the group on these kinds of topics, and he was the one holding my hand.

"Yes, they are—the blue stoned one especially. There were only three of the blue rings in existence. Yours belonged to an extinct clan. The other two were destroyed, and the third was thought to have been lost with the clan line. It is a ring of royalty and power."

He was still holding my hand, tracing the rings with his fingers, his eyes following the movements. Maybe I was wrong previously about my assumption of his moods. He was speaking of the rings; however, I knew it involved information about me, and he had warmth—awe.

"What about the other ring? Is this special as well?" I was referring to the ring on my index finger. The ring my parents had given me as a child, the ring that had the same symbols as the journal.

"Yes, it represents another clan."

"What do you mean a clan?"

He seemed to ignore me, as he was deep in thought.

"Why did I receive them? Why do I have both?"

Callon's gaze met mine and this time he was sincere when he

127

spoke, answering me just above a whisper, "That's a good question."

Okay, now what? No one knew why I had these rings, one of which was exceptionally rare. I asked again. "Callon, what do you mean by 'represents a clan'? What does that have to do with me?"

He still did not release my hand, but turned his chair to face me, reaching out to grasp my other hand in his. Colt slid a little closer. His hand was still wrapped around my waist, but Callon was now semi-straddling the chair I sat on. Daniel sat silently in the chair across the table. I could hear him breathing nervously and sensed his eyes on me as well. This couldn't be good. It was as if they knew I would react badly.

Callon started speaking passionately, all the while intently searching my face for my reaction, "Cheyenne, you need to brace yourself. You don't live in the world you think you do. There's a lot we need to talk about. I'll try to give you as much as I can, but I'll hold some back. It's going to be hard to take it all in at once."

He paused, waiting for a response before he proceeded. I knew I wanted to hear; however, with their reactions as they were now I wasn't sure it would be good. I couldn't speak, so I just nodded, taking in small even breaths. Callon started out slowly in a controlled tone, as if to tell a story.

"Long ago there were many clans roaming this world, each unique in its own way. We lived in harmony and peace for a long time. Some of the main clans were the Sarac, Silloquize, Kvech, Consilador, Coltooro, Laundess and Servak. Many centuries ago, an evil uprising began.

"A leader arose from the Sarac clan, Makhi. He was greedy and lusted for power, hungered to have ultimate control. He ruled his people with an iron fist. He claimed he was the only righteous heir to the throne, that the Kvech clan was no longer royalty, no longer worthy to control the power of our world."

I interrupted him briefly, "What do you mean by power of our world?" He didn't respond, but continued.

"When word of Makhi reached Adalmund, the Kvech clan leader, the ruler of all the clans, he decided action was to be taken. Makhi's evil lies were spreading, his strength was growing, and he was becoming a threat to all the clans and the control of the sacred world.

"Adalmund was the guardian of the power. He was a peaceable man, not a warrior. Adalmund went to Makhi looking for a resolution. As was the custom, Adalmund brought his wife Josalyn and son Qaysean with him. They were ambushed along the way, with only Qaysean surviving."

"Sacred world? I still don't understand," I questioned again. Callon once more ignored me; he was completely focused on his story.

"Seeing that Makhi had killed the only guardians to our world, the Servak clan joined the Sarac in their quest. The Servak's ruler Jorelle was evil as well, only second to Makhi in strength and power. Jorelle brought with him his daughter Sahara. Makhi and Jorelle arranged a marriage between Sahara and Makhi's son Marcus."

"Guardians to our world?" I spit out. Why wasn't he answering my questions? What the heck was he talking about?

"They began slaughtering and decimating the world of all the clans that opposed them. The merging of the Servak clan with the Sarac clan gave them great power, and a marriage of the clans would provide even greater power.

"Many battles took place, and we saw many lives lost. What was left of the remaining clans scattered the face of the earth, hiding, waiting and hoping. There are few of us left now."

He said something at the end that made me stop and think..."many battles...many lives lost."

"You said *we saw*? Did you mean that?" I asked.

"Yes," he replied.

I shot out my next questions quickly as the story he told began to sink in. I was trying to sort it all out, and get him to reveal the whole truth.

"How old are you?" I demanded.

He hesitated again, looking deep within, trying to assess if I would be able to accept it. "Three hundred years old, give or take a decade."

I didn't look away, but directed my next question to Colt. "Colt, how old are you?"

He calmly responded, "Two hundred and twenty-five." At least that would explain why I thought he was always more mature and the deep conversations he had with my parents.

"Daniel?"

Callon responded for Daniel, "One hundred and fifty-three."

I continued my questioning. "How can you live such a long life? None of you look older than your early twenties. Are you human?" Unease draped over me like a cold, dark cloak as I awaited his reply. I fidgeted. Callon had already told me to brace myself, and that the world I lived in wasn't what it seemed. I shifted in my seat and tried to dislodge Colt's arms. He didn't budge.

Callon took a deep breath.

"We age slower, about one year to one hundred in human years, but we are more or less human." Callon replied cautiously.

"So you do age?" At least I knew they were human, more or less—

if that was the truth.

"Yes. Our metabolism is quite a bit slower than normal humans, along with other things that make us different."

"How have you lived all these years? Don't people notice that you don't seem to change?" I asked, my unease still present.

Callon replied calmly, "We move around a lot, typically only staying in one location for about five to seven years."

"What about drivers' license and birth certificates?"

"We can work around that. Forging documents isn't really that difficult when you know what you're doing," Daniel quickly responded.

The floor seemed to be a good place to stare as I took in all this new information, formulating more questions. Was this for real? Were they telling me a lie, a story to keep me here? There was so much they were hiding from me, and it seemed now that some of it was information about themselves too. I had the two rings and the journal, but without their help, I couldn't hope to decipher their secrets. There was still more I needed to know.

"Callon, how long have you been a doctor?" I slowly raised my head up again.

"A few hundred years." He was steady, no wavering. Either he was an excellent liar, or he was telling the truth. It would make sense since he was around three hundred years old. I repeated again some of his words in my head...*Makhi, Sarac.*

"Is this Makhi of the Sarac clan still living?" It could be a possibility if Callon was over three hundred years old. I kept my focus on Callon as now only he responded.

"No, but his son is."

I was slowly piecing this puzzle together. "What clan do you come

312

from?"

"Colt, Daniel and I come from the Consilador clan."

"What clan did my parents come from?" If they knew each other, and died protecting me, they would be a part of this clan thing also.

"They came from the Coltooro clan."

Okay, since Callon was from a clan and my parents were from a clan, somehow I was a part of this mix. Could I be? Even though I was their adoptive child? I looked at the ring on my finger, already knowing the answer before I asked it, or so I thought. Was this for real?

"I was adopted..." I started.

"Yes."

"But I'm a part of this?"

"Yes."

I hesitated. "What clan do *I* come from?"

"The blue ring on your ring finger came from the Kvech clan; the one on your index finger comes from the Servak clan. The Kvech clan is the ruling clan, royalty, the protectors. The Consilador's are second in line."

I stiffened in the chair and paused in my breathing. I turned away to stare at the floor again. The Kvech clan was royalty; they were the ruling clan, he said. The protectors, and I was wearing the one remaining ring. I was also wearing a ring from the Servak clan. I was the secret they were trying to protect—could it be? They couldn't be lying to me...could they? How could they come up with all of this on their own? Callon said they moved around a lot—my parents and I did also. I never knew my dad or mom to have a job, but somehow we never had any money issues.

My parents were always protective of me...and now that I thought of it, they always looked the same. It was as if they never really aged in over eighteen years. My mom was still as beautiful before she died as she was in pictures when I was a small child. Before she died, she had said there were things they wanted to talk to me about, things I was old enough to understand. This was it; I felt it in my heart. Who was I? What I thought I knew, once again, wasn't real.

Colt grasped me firmly and shook my shoulders as I snapped my head around to look at him. He grabbed my face in his hands as I stared into his eyes and spoke forcibly, "Cheyenne, I'll protect you. I won't let any harm come to you. I would give my life for you. I love you. Do you understand me?"

I was still stunned. This was why they were so protective of me—at least that part was making sense now. I nodded my head slowly in agreement. Colt continued to hold my face, searching for something. I closed my eyes, taking in a deep breath, and he released me. Callon let go of my hands, and I crumbled into Colt's arms. He locked them around me and pulled me onto his lap. I just sat there absorbing it all. I released a large sigh, and Colt held me tighter. I sat in his arms for a long time. He was my protector, my comforter when I needed him. He was all I had...

CHAPTER 11

I forced myself away from the table. Suddenly, I didn't feel so well. A bomb had just been dropped on my lap. I needed some fresh air. Colt rose with me, but I put my hand on his shoulder to reassure him so he would stay. I just needed to be alone to think. To come to grips with what was now thrust before me...who I was.

I headed for the front door and went out onto the porch. In the far corner, away from the kitchen hung a hammock. I started for it. The air was warm as it drifted past; it ruffled a few strands of my hair. I sat sideways, gently swaying back and forth, the rhythm soothing. Listening to the birds chirp, I watched the squirrels scamper across the forest floor. A large wasp buzzed by my face while I looked at the flecks of sunshine breaking through the trees, throwing pieces of warmth my way. I began contemplating what had transpired over the last few weeks.

My life was changed; the life I knew was gone. The life I thought was true was different; I was a part of something I never knew about. What the three men had told me was the truth; I felt it deep within. I started pondering what had been said to me, what I was a part of now. The life I thought I had was now spinning in a different direction...and I couldn't stop it. I was a part of something bigger, bigger than I thought my world was—I belonged to something. I was a part of *something*, though I wasn't quite sure where I fit in.

I had two rings, one from the Kvech and one from the Servak. I had no clarity on what either of them meant, and Callon didn't even know which one I was from for sure. He never answered my questions with much lucidity. The Kvech had a surviving son; the Servak had a daughter who was supposed to marry Marcus from the Sarac clan. Could it be? Did the surviving son of the Kvech line marry the Servak daughter?

Footsteps sounded on the porch behind me. I didn't move. I knew it wasn't Colt; his were much heavier. The hammock moved, and I watched as Callon sat next to me, causing me to roll in his direction. He lifted his arms so they rested behind his head as he lay back and placed his feet on the rail, using them to sway us gently back and forth.

I had so many more questions I needed answers to, but where to start? Did I really want to know what part I was to play in all of this? Maybe I was better off not knowing the truth about my adoptive parents or my birth parents, if in fact, they were the ones in the story he told me. I mulled these thoughts over for a long time before I came to the conclusion that I did, in fact, want to know—I needed to know everything. This was my life.

"Callon?" I said softly.

"Yes?"

"You said something about the powers of our world, sacred guardians. What did all that mean?"

"We are all protectors of the powers within this world. We can co-

135

exist with the human world because we are able to keep our presence a secret. We have a responsibility to protect the human world from the evil darkness. If others knew about us, it could swiftly run out of control. Those among us who are evil would overtake the world and rule it as their own."

"So we protect our secret identity?"

"Yes."

A secret to protect, but I was also a secret. I didn't really know or understand what that meant yet. "Do you have a pretty good idea who my parents are?" I had a theory, but I wanted to hear it from him.

He sighed before he replied, "Yes."

I decided to answer my own question. "They were Qaysean of the Kvech and Sahara of the Servak, weren't they? That's why I have both rings?"

"Yes."

"Did you know my birth parents?"

"No."

"Did Gene and Alexis know who my birth parents were?"

"Yes. They purposely didn't tell us; it was for your own protection."

"But you said I was a secret. If you didn't know, then how was I a secret and from whom?"

"We knew you were a secret simply because you're one of us. We were trying to keep your identity hidden from those that would harm you."

"There's more to this story that you haven't told me, isn't there?" Why did he constantly hide things from me?

"Yes."

"Will you tell me about my birth parents?"

He hesitated, carefully wording each sentence. "Makhi thought he had killed the entire blood line of the Kvech clan. He sent his Trackers out to ambush Adalmund, Jasalyn, Qaysean, and the party that accompanied them. The Trackers brought back the two rings as proof they had killed them."

"But you said there were three, right?"

"Yes, but Makhi didn't know Qaysean had already been given a ring, a new ring, more powerful than the previous two. Qaysean had escaped. His bodyguard, who looked very similar in appearance, took his place in death to save his life. Because Makhi thought he was dead, he would not be hunted and could live in secrecy."

"So how did he meet my mother if she was promised to Marcus and Marcus is Sarac?"

"Qaysean lived many long years in hiding, plotting and planning an attack on the Sarac clan. A conflict arose within the Servak and Sarac clans. The arranged marriage between Marcus and Sahara had not taken place. Your mother protested the marriage because she was nothing like her father Jorelle. She didn't want any part of her father's plan. She ran from her old life, and her father lost his life because of it."

"But how did they meet?"

"She eventually found Qaysean and convinced him that she left of her own will and did not want any part of what Makhi and Marcus were seeking. She fought side by side with your father for many years. Makhi eventually found out that she'd joined him. The powers that should have been united with the Sarac were now with Qaysean. This made Marcus ravenous with rage."

"So they fought together and then what?"

"During one of the great battles of the time, your father killed Makhi, enraging Marcus more. Qaysean had not only taken his father's life, but he had taken Sahara. Marcus would not stop until both Qaysean and Sahara were destroyed."

"He hunted them down, didn't he?" I pinched my brow tight.

"Eventually Marcus found Qaysean and Sahara and killed them. He thought he had destroyed his enemy, the only enemy strong enough to destroy him. The Kvech clan was the ruling clan, the protector, and the guardians.

"Marcus has continued to hunt the remaining clans and destroys them unless they join him. I am sure Marcus doesn't know you exist. I didn't know who you truly were until today."

"What about Gene and Alexis? How did they become a part of all of this? Was it Marcus who murdered them?" I asked in a faint whisper.

"They must have known. Sahara and Qaysean must have asked them to be your guardians, to protect and watch over you. They never told us who you were, but we knew you were special. Not many of our kind are born, and most do not live to the age of twenty. Gene and Alexis were killed trying to protect you, trying to keep your existence from being known to the Sarac. It was Marcus who killed them."

I now knew who killed both my birth and adoptive parents. Would he be coming for me as well? The trio obviously thought this to be true because they were protecting me.

More thoughts came to the forefront. "Most of your children don't live to twenty? They're killed?"

"Yes."

"Why? They're just children. What kind of threat are children?" It made no sense.

"When they're born, they're human, but around the age of twenty they become *Timeless*. Any new addition to the clans is considered a threat to Marcus."

"So I will become Timeless?"

"Yes."

"You're Timeless, right?"

"Yes."

"I don't fully understand," I confessed. "What is Timeless?"

"It's a form of immortality. We don't age quickly, but we do age eventually. We are born with a unique gene allowing us to have longer lives than what would be considered normal. It's not a name we came up with, but it stuck over the years."

This was becoming confusing. I was going to be nineteen soon. "So I'm essentially human now, but when I turn twenty, something happens and I will become Timeless...but I can still die? I thought immortality meant you couldn't die—ever. I really don't understand."

"Yes, you'll become Timeless around the age of twenty. You can die, just not by normal human circumstances."

"So if you were to fall from a cliff or be shot by a gun, you wouldn't die?"

"Most likely not. However, we can still feel pain. Our bodies are able to recover quickly, in minutes or hours, instead of weeks. It just really depends on how bad the injury is."

Another puzzle piece fell into place. That would explain a lot, if they had a quick recovery time. If I had delayed leaving for the bank, my plan wouldn't have worked at all. I tensed for a moment, and Callon shifted a little, anticipating my response.

"So that's why the berries' effects didn't last as long on you...how long after I left did the paralysis wear off?"

"About fifteen minutes."

I propped myself up on my elbow as best I could since I was in the hammock. I wanted to look him in the eyes for this question, though I knew I probably wouldn't appreciate the smirk that came with his answer.

"So you were right behind me and saw me go into the bank?"

"Yes."

He did have a smirk on his face. I scowled at him. "Why didn't you stop me then?"

The smirk was gone, and he was sincere when he answered, "We did try. Daniel was about to pull you back, but we decided it was too dangerous right then. We knew you were going to get the journal. It was probably safer for you to go alone than with us. The Sarac know who we are."

"You knew about the journal?" I said in surprise.

"Yes."

So, if they knew about the journal, why didn't they just go get it? Or better yet, why didn't they already have it since they were obviously in cahoots with my parents? I was fuming now. Callon started to reach out, but I pushed him away.

"It was for your own protection," he answered my unspoken questions.

I didn't care if it was for my own protection; I was tired of being deceived. Everyone else knew what was going on except me. I had been constantly in the dark, for years! I pulled myself up from the hammock away from him, swinging my feet to the floor. He wrapped his hand around my wrist and pulled so that my back was now firmly planted across his chest, and his arms wrapped across mine, preventing me from getting up. I kept my face forward. This was way too close.

His face was only inches from my ear as he spoke gently, "I'm sorry. I didn't mean to make you mad. Don't go."

I was too irritated; I just needed to clear my head. I needed to go for a walk, run, do something physical. I managed to push myself away again. This time, Callon relented, and I headed for the front door. I had no shoes on so I went to my room and slid them on. I had to leave for a little while; I would come back when I was calm. When I could focus more clearly and demand answers. I was having a difficult time coming to grips with this whole set of circumstances.

Colt and Daniel were in the great room. I didn't look at them when I entered, but I did as I left. They both glanced at me, and Callon trailed close behind. Colt was distressed, probably because I was. Turning my gaze away, I went for the front door with Callon's footsteps following.

I stopped briefly on the porch, realizing I didn't know where I was going. In the next second it came to me. I would go where Daniel had taken me, to the meadow. It was calming, and that was just what I needed. I was fairly sure I could find my way again.

Callon didn't say a word as he followed a few steps behind. I allowed my mind to wander a little to the forest surrounding me. I liked it here; the ground didn't have a lot of undergrowth like in other areas. I could walk fairly quickly without stumbling over some unforeseen object. The sunshine fell through the trees in specks, creating the sunshine smiles my mom loved.

My dad had taught me to be aware of my surroundings in the forest. He had told me I needed to be aware of any hidden dangers. I missed him so much right now that my heart ached, and I sighed.

Callon heard my sigh and stepped up alongside me. I didn't glance his way. I continued until I thought I was fairly close to the meadow, but I wasn't quite sure. I stopped in an opening between the trees and located the sun's position. It seemed to be in the same spot as when Daniel took me, so I knew I had to be close.

Trudging on, we made our way up a small hill. Once at the top, I knew I had found it. The small opening in the forest revealed the same lovely view. I had just come in at different angle. I stepped into the meadow, allowing the sun to fully absorb into my skin as I tilted my chin up. This was what I needed, the tranquility.

I didn't hear Callon's footsteps any longer. He was waiting at the opening, I was sure of it, although I didn't glance back. I walked forward, lingering as my outstretched hands caressed the grasses and wildflowers. My touch stirred the exquisite scent into the air as I focused on the creek before me. I paused at the water's edge and sat on a boulder, carefully untying my boots and setting them to the side. I moved my feet into the icy-cold water, and a chill swept over me.

My eyes followed the creek as it meandered into the forest. The water licked over a fallen tree and then made a slight descent into a pile of insignificant boulders. It disappeared from sight as it wound further and further into the trees. Standing, I stared for a long time, until my feet began to ache from the cold—the water was numbing them and my irritation.

I glanced around and saw soft matted grass a few feet away. I took the few steps and lay on my back, legs crossed at my ankles and arms behind my head. Closing my eyes, I just listened to the sound of the water, birds chirping...and the rustling of someone sitting down next to me. Callon didn't say a word; I only heard his rhythmic breathing. I didn't need to open my eyes to know he was staring at me. I could sense it. I could see in my mind those mesmerizing hazel eyes. I didn't need to be consumed by them.

A warm breeze blew strands of hair across my face, tickling as they touched my lashes, causing them to flutter. I opened them into slits as I watched his fingers gently brush the hair aside. He was lying on his side with his hand propping his head up as his elbow rested on the ground. He was closer than I thought, and my heart started beating faster. I opened my eyes fully and stared back into his. I couldn't stop myself. Those eyes seemed to peer deep into my innermost being. I could get lost in them, especially when the sun brought out the variations of brown, green, and amber. I had to look away, and get a hold of myself and quit acting so witless! If I didn't, I wouldn't remember why I was so mad. I wouldn't remember I needed answers to my questions.

"Cheyenne, I'm sorry. I didn't mean to upset you. I don't want you angry with me. I understand that you feel you've been deceived all these years. It was always for your own protection."

His words reminded me why I was so angry. I had been lied to for years, information purposely being withheld. But who decided it was for my protection? I couldn't deny that sometimes I did need to be safeguarded, mostly from my own stupidity, like what happened with my Jeep. "Will you promise not to deceive me anymore? I really don't like being kept in the dark."

Callon's voice was smooth and sincere, "I will not deceive you, and I will tell you what I can. Will that work for now?"

I was hastily coming to the conclusion that I wasn't going to get a better offer. He said he wouldn't deceive me, but he wouldn't promise to tell me everything. I really didn't see the difference.

"Did you know what was in the pie?" I asked.

"I suspected something, but I saw you eating and was more concerned about not hurting your feelings than my instincts."

He was concerned about my feelings? My mouth moved without my consent. "You looked irritated afterwards, when you were lying there, and then your irritation changed. It was as if you could have, you would have jumped up and..." I wasn't able to finish my sentence.

His face was just inches from mine. His upper body suddenly hovered over top of me. His lips brushed mine as they made their way to my ear where he tightly whispered, "I would have jumped up and pulled you into my arms to prevent you from leaving. I would have kissed you senseless and made you forget who you were and what you were about to do." My stomach did a back flip, and my pulse increased tenfold.

I was breathless in my quick response. "You're a little full of yourself if you thought you could make me forget." What was wrong with me? Why would I say something like that? This wasn't me; I was just egging him on. I wanted him to kiss me that way. I wanted to feel his arms around me. I wanted to feel alive. Would he make me feel that way? Would it be different than Colt's kiss?

Callon said nothing more; only his warm breath on my neck remained. It was calm and steady. He knew what he was doing and was totally and completely in control of his emotions, while I was the one reacting emotionally. It wasn't fair. He lingered a moment longer and then relaxed back to his previous position.

I turned to see him grinning from ear to ear. He knew he could make me forget, and I knew it too. I didn't smile; I averted my eyes and began the questions again, this time staying under control.

"What do you know about the journal?"

"Not much," he confessed. "We had never seen it before you brought it back with you."

"But you knew about it?"

"Yes."

"You've looked at it?"

"Yes."

"Do you understand it?" I was curious.

"No, but I do know that some of the writings are in Servak. We're not sure about the symbols."

I would have to do more research on the journal. Somewhere there must be materials to help us. I just had to find them. Maybe it was in my house, in some of the books I had packed away. I hadn't paid close attention; I was pretty numb at the time, just trying to put memories away.

The idea of being Timeless was weighing heavily on my mind since he had first mentioned it. "So this whole Timeless thing, how does it work? Does it just suddenly appear on my twentieth birthday with balloons and sign in hand?" I asked sarcastically.

He chuckled, "No, no balloons or signs and I said around the age of twenty."

"Okay, then how does it work?"

"Well, it's different for each of us."

I rolled my eyes. "That's helpful."

"Each of us goes through the change differently. For me, the weeks leading up to the transformation were riddled with physical pain."

"I see, and then afterwards you knew you had changed? Did you go and test your theory? Jump off a cliff or something?" Once again I was being cynical. If he was going to drive me crazy and not fully answer questions, then I was going to give it back to him. Two could play at this game. He didn't answer, so I sat up and gave him a slight sneer. He waited calmly as moments passed and I grew angrier.

"You have a little problem with your temper, don't you?" he observed.

Irritation began to flair its ugly head again. How in the world was he able to keep doing this to me? Twisting things around to get me flustered, bring out the worst in me? "I don't have a temper around anyone else but you, *He who must be obeyed!*" I snapped back.

He grinned, apparently amused with his new title. "That's new. So I bring out the worst in you then?"

I leaned in closer, only inches from his face, and he didn't act surprised. He actually appeared to be enjoying it.

I spoke through clenched teeth, "Only my temper!" My jaw was taut, and I was quickly losing all control. I took a deep breath and exhaled loudly. Our eyes still locked, his amused and mine shooting imaginary flames. This was so unfair!

He broke the silence, a smirk spreading. "I'll take temper. It shows passion."

"Argh!" I rolled my eyes and fell back into the grass, exasperated. Dusk was approaching, and we needed to get back. I wasn't sure I could find my way back in the dark. I was so completely confused—utterly and stupidly confused! How could he make my heart race like this one moment and then have me angry the next? He purposely whispered in my ear about kissing me, but didn't. He was going to drive me crazy! Why did I want him? It made no sense—it was illogical. Colt would express his feelings to me openly; Callon used them to torture. This was just some stupid childish infatuation—it had to be.

I sat up and pulled my boots and socks on, taking my time. Callon just patiently waited. He stood when I had finished and extended his hand. I looked up, hesitated, and then he unexpectedly reached down and pulled me up. He began to lead us out of the meadow, back to the cabin. He didn't say a word; he hummed while I scowled. He was intent on making me insane, I was sure of it. I ran my thumb over my Servak ring, thinking about what I now knew it meant.

CHAPTER 12

I forced myself away from the table. Suddenly, I didn't feel so well. A bomb had just been dropped on my lap. I needed some fresh air. Colt rose with me, but I put my hand on his shoulder to reassure him so he would stay. I just needed to be alone to think. To come to grips with what was now thrust before me...who I was.

I headed for the front door and went out onto the porch. In the far corner, away from the kitchen hung a hammock. I started for it. The air was warm as it drifted past; it ruffled a few strands of my hair. I sat sideways, gently swaying back and forth, the rhythm soothing. Listening to the birds chirp, I watched the squirrels scamper across the forest floor. A large wasp buzzed by my face while I looked at the flecks of sunshine breaking through the trees, throwing pieces of warmth my way. I began contemplating what had transpired over the last few weeks.

My life was changed; the life I knew was gone. The life I thought was true was different; I was a part of something I never knew about. What the three men had told me was the truth; I felt it deep within. I started pondering what had been said to me, what I was a part of now. The life I thought I had was now spinning in a different direction...and I couldn't stop it. I was a part of something bigger, bigger than I thought my world was—I belonged to something. I was a part of *something*, though I wasn't quite sure where I fit in.

I had two rings, one from the Kvech and one from the Servak. I had no clarity on what either of them meant, and Callon didn't even know which one I was from for sure. He never answered my questions with much lucidity. The Kvech had a surviving son; the Servak had a daughter who was supposed to marry Marcus from the Sarac clan. Could it be? Did the surviving son of the Kvech line marry the Servak daughter?

Footsteps sounded on the porch behind me. I didn't move. I knew it wasn't Colt; his were much heavier. The hammock moved, and I watched as Callon sat next to me, causing me to roll in his direction. He lifted his arms so they rested behind his head as he lay back and placed his feet on the rail, using them to sway us gently back and forth.

I had so many more questions I needed answers to, but where to start? Did I really want to know what part I was to play in all of this? Maybe I was better off not knowing the truth about my adoptive parents or my birth parents, if in fact, they were the ones in the story he told me. I mulled these thoughts over for a long time before I came to the conclusion that I did, in fact, want to know—I needed to know everything. This was my life.

"Callon?" I said softly.

"Yes?"

"You said something about the powers of our world, sacred guardians. What did all that mean?"

"We are all protectors of the powers within this world. We can coexist with the human world because we are able to keep our presence a secret. We have a responsibility to protect the human world from the evil darkness. If others knew about us, it could swiftly run out of control. Those among us who are evil would overtake the world and rule it as their own."

"So we protect our secret identity?"

"Yes."

A secret to protect, but I was also a secret. I didn't really know or understand what that meant yet. "Do you have a pretty good idea who my parents are?" I had a theory, but I wanted to hear it from him.

He sighed before he replied, "Yes."

I decided to answer my own question. "They were Qaysean of the Kvech and Sahara of the Servak, weren't they? That's why I have both rings?"

"Yes."

"Did you know my birth parents?"

"No."

"Did Gene and Alexis know who my birth parents were?"

"Yes. They purposely didn't tell us; it was for your own protection."

"But you said I was a secret. If you didn't know, then how was I a secret and from whom?"

"We knew you were a secret simply because you're one of us. We were trying to keep your identity hidden from those that would harm you."

"There's more to this story that you haven't told me, isn't there?" Why did he constantly hide things from me?

"Yes."

"Will you tell me about my birth parents?"

He hesitated, carefully wording each sentence. "Makhi thought he had killed the entire blood line of the Kvech clan. He sent his Trackers out to ambush Adalmund, Jasalyn, Qaysean, and the party that accompanied them. The Trackers brought back the two rings as proof they had killed them."

"But you said there were three, right?"

"Yes, but Makhi didn't know Qaysean had already been given a ring, a new ring, more powerful than the previous two. Qaysean had escaped. His bodyguard, who looked very similar in appearance, took his place in death to save his life. Because Makhi thought he was dead, he would not be hunted and could live in secrecy."

"So how did he meet my mother if she was promised to Marcus and Marcus is Sarac?"

"Qaysean lived many long years in hiding, plotting and planning an attack on the Sarac clan. A conflict arose within the Servak and Sarac clans. The arranged marriage between Marcus and Sahara had not taken place. Your mother protested the marriage because she was nothing like her father Jorelle. She didn't want any part of her father's plan. She ran from her old life, and her father lost his life because of it."

"But how did they meet?"

"She eventually found Qaysean and convinced him that she left of her own will and did not want any part of what Makhi and Marcus were seeking. She fought side by side with your father for many years. Makhi eventually found out that she'd joined him. The powers that should have been united with the Sarac were now with Qaysean. This made Marcus ravenous with rage."

"So they fought together and then what?"

"During one of the great battles of the time, your father killed Makhi, enraging Marcus more. Qaysean had not only taken his father's life, but he had taken Sahara. Marcus would not stop until both Qaysean and Sahara were destroyed."

"He hunted them down, didn't he?" I pinched my brow tight.

"Eventually Marcus found Qaysean and Sahara and killed them. He thought he had destroyed his enemy, the only enemy strong enough to destroy him. The Kvech clan was the ruling clan, the protector, and the guardians.

"Marcus has continued to hunt the remaining clans and destroys them unless they join him. I am sure Marcus doesn't know you exist. I didn't know who you truly were until today."

"What about Gene and Alexis? How did they become a part of all of this? Was it Marcus who murdered them?" I asked in a faint whisper.

"They must have known. Sahara and Qaysean must have asked them to be your guardians, to protect and watch over you. They never told us who you were, but we knew you were special. Not many of our kind are born, and most do not live to the age of twenty. Gene and Alexis were killed trying to protect you, trying to keep your existence from being known to the Sarac. It was Marcus who killed them."

I now knew who killed both my birth and adoptive parents. Would he be coming for me as well? The trio obviously thought this to be true because they were protecting me.

More thoughts came to the forefront. "Most of your children don't live to twenty? They're killed?"

"Yes."

"Why? They're just children. What kind of threat are children?" It made no sense.

"When they're born, they're human, but around the age of twenty they become *Timeless*. Any new addition to the clans is considered a threat to Marcus."

"So I will become Timeless?"

"Yes."

"You're Timeless, right?"

"Yes."

"I don't fully understand," I confessed. "What is Timeless?"

"It's a form of immortality. We don't age quickly, but we do age eventually. We are born with a unique gene allowing us to have longer lives than what would be considered normal. It's not a name we came up with, but it stuck over the years."

This was becoming confusing. I was going to be nineteen soon. "So I'm essentially human now, but when I turn twenty, something happens and I will become Timeless...but I can still die? I thought immortality meant you couldn't die—ever. I really don't understand."

"Yes, you'll become Timeless around the age of twenty. You can die, just not by normal human circumstances."

"So if you were to fall from a cliff or be shot by a gun, you wouldn't die?"

"Most likely not. However, we can still feel pain. Our bodies are able to recover quickly, in minutes or hours, instead of weeks. It just really depends on how bad the injury is."

Another puzzle piece fell into place. That would explain a lot, if they had a quick recovery time. If I had delayed leaving for the bank, my plan wouldn't have worked at all. I tensed for a moment, and Callon shifted a little, anticipating my response.

"So that's why the berries' effects didn't last as long on you...how long after I left did the paralysis wear off?"

"About fifteen minutes."

I propped myself up on my elbow as best I could since I was in the hammock. I wanted to look him in the eyes for this question, though I knew I probably wouldn't appreciate the smirk that came with his answer.

"So you were right behind me and saw me go into the bank?"

"Yes."

He did have a smirk on his face. I scowled at him. "Why didn't you stop me then?"

The smirk was gone, and he was sincere when he answered, "We did try. Daniel was about to pull you back, but we decided it was too dangerous right then. We knew you were going to get the journal. It was probably safer for you to go alone than with us. The Sarac know who we are."

"You knew about the journal?" I said in surprise.

"Yes."

So, if they knew about the journal, why didn't they just go get it? Or better yet, why didn't they already have it since they were obviously in cahoots with my parents? I was fuming now. Callon started to reach out, but I pushed him away.

"It was for your own protection," he answered my unspoken questions.

I didn't care if it was for my own protection; I was tired of being deceived. Everyone else knew what was going on except me. I had been constantly in the dark, for years! I pulled myself up from the hammock away from him, swinging my feet to the floor. He wrapped his hand around my wrist and pulled so that my back was now firmly planted across his chest, and his arms wrapped across mine, preventing me from getting up. I kept my face forward. This was way too close.

His face was only inches from my ear as he spoke gently, "I'm sorry. I didn't mean to make you mad. Don't go."

I was too irritated; I just needed to clear my head. I needed to go for a walk, run, do something physical. I managed to push myself away again. This time, Callon relented, and I headed for the front door. I had no shoes on so I went to my room and slid them on. I had to leave for a little while; I would come back when I was calm. When I could focus more clearly and demand answers. I was having a difficult time coming to grips with this whole set of circumstances.

Colt and Daniel were in the great room. I didn't look at them when I entered, but I did as I left. They both glanced at me, and Callon trailed close behind. Colt was distressed, probably because I was. Turning my gaze away, I went for the front door with Callon's footsteps following.

I stopped briefly on the porch, realizing I didn't know where I was going. In the next second it came to me. I would go where Daniel had taken me, to the meadow. It was calming, and that was just what I needed. I was fairly sure I could find my way again.

Callon didn't say a word as he followed a few steps behind. I allowed my mind to wander a little to the forest surrounding me. I liked it here; the ground didn't have a lot of undergrowth like in other areas. I could walk fairly quickly without stumbling over some unforeseen object. The sunshine fell through the trees in specks, creating the sunshine smiles my mom loved.

My dad had taught me to be aware of my surroundings in the forest. He had told me I needed to be aware of any hidden dangers. I missed him so much right now that my heart ached, and I sighed.

Callon heard my sigh and stepped up alongside me. I didn't glance his way. I continued until I thought I was fairly close to the meadow, but I wasn't quite sure. I stopped in an opening between the trees and located the sun's position. It seemed to be in the same spot as when Daniel took me, so I knew I had to be close.

Trudging on, we made our way up a small hill. Once at the top, I knew I had found it. The small opening in the forest revealed the same lovely view. I had just come in at different angle. I stepped into the meadow, allowing the sun to fully absorb into my skin as I tilted my chin up. This was what I needed, the tranquility.

I didn't hear Callon's footsteps any longer. He was waiting at the opening, I was sure of it, although I didn't glance back. I walked forward, lingering as my outstretched hands caressed the grasses and wildflowers. My touch stirred the exquisite scent into the air as I focused on the creek before me. I paused at the water's edge and sat on a boulder, carefully untying my boots and setting them to the side. I moved my feet into the icy-cold water, and a chill swept over me.

My eyes followed the creek as it meandered into the forest. The water licked over a fallen tree and then made a slight descent into a pile of insignificant boulders. It disappeared from sight as it wound further and further into the trees. Standing, I stared for a long time, until my feet began to ache from the cold—the water was numbing them and my irritation.

I glanced around and saw soft matted grass a few feet away. I took the few steps and lay on my back, legs crossed at my ankles and arms behind my head. Closing my eyes, I just listened to the sound of the water, birds chirping...and the rustling of someone sitting down next to me. Callon didn't say a word; I only heard his rhythmic breathing. I didn't need to open my eyes to know he was staring at me. I could sense it. I could see in my mind those mesmerizing hazel eyes. I didn't need to be consumed by them.

A warm breeze blew strands of hair across my face, tickling as they touched my lashes, causing them to flutter. I opened them into slits as I watched his fingers gently brush the hair aside. He was lying on his side with his hand propping his head up as his elbow rested on the ground. He was closer than I thought, and my heart started beating faster. I opened my eyes fully and stared back into his. I couldn't stop myself. Those eyes seemed to peer deep into my innermost being. I could get lost in them, especially when the sun brought out the variations of brown, green, and amber. I had to look away, and get a hold of myself and quit acting so witless! If I didn't, I wouldn't remember why I was so mad. I wouldn't remember I needed answers to my questions.

"Cheyenne, I'm sorry. I didn't mean to upset you. I don't want you angry with me. I understand that you feel you've been deceived all these years. It was always for your own protection."

His words reminded me why I was so angry. I had been lied to for years, information purposely being withheld. But who decided it was for my protection? I couldn't deny that sometimes I did need to be safeguarded, mostly from my own stupidity, like what happened with my Jeep. "Will you promise not to deceive me anymore? I really don't like being kept in the dark."

Callon's voice was smooth and sincere, "I will not deceive you, and I will tell you what I can. Will that work for now?"

I was hastily coming to the conclusion that I wasn't going to get a better offer. He said he wouldn't deceive me, but he wouldn't promise to tell me everything. I really didn't see the difference.

"Did you know what was in the pie?" I asked.

"I suspected something, but I saw you eating and was more concerned about not hurting your feelings than my instincts."

He was concerned about my feelings? My mouth moved without my consent. "You looked irritated afterwards, when you were lying there, and then your irritation changed. It was as if you could have, you would have jumped up and..." I wasn't able to finish my sentence.

His face was just inches from mine. His upper body suddenly hovered over top of me. His lips brushed mine as they made their way to my ear where he tightly whispered, "I would have jumped up and pulled you into my arms to prevent you from leaving. I would have kissed you senseless and made you forget who you were and what you were about to do." My stomach did a back flip, and my pulse increased tenfold.

I was breathless in my quick response. "You're a little full of yourself if you thought you could make me forget." What was wrong with me? Why would I say something like that? This wasn't me; I was just egging him on. I wanted him to kiss me that way. I wanted to feel his arms around me. I wanted to feel alive. Would he make me feel that way? Would it be different than Colt's kiss?

Callon said nothing more; only his warm breath on my neck remained. It was calm and steady. He knew what he was doing and was totally and completely in control of his emotions, while I was the one reacting emotionally. It wasn't fair. He lingered a moment longer and then relaxed back to his previous position.

I turned to see him grinning from ear to ear. He knew he could make me forget, and I knew it too. I didn't smile; I averted my eyes and began the questions again, this time staying under control.

"What do you know about the journal?"

"Not much," he confessed. "We had never seen it before you brought it back with you."

"But you knew about it?"

"Yes."

"You've looked at it?"

"Yes."

"Do you understand it?" I was curious.

"No, but I do know that some of the writings are in Servak. We're not sure about the symbols."

I would have to do more research on the journal. Somewhere there must be materials to help us. I just had to find them. Maybe it was in my house, in some of the books I had packed away. I hadn't paid close attention; I was pretty numb at the time, just trying to put memories away.

The idea of being Timeless was weighing heavily on my mind since he had first mentioned it. "So this whole Timeless thing, how does it work? Does it just suddenly appear on my twentieth birthday with balloons and sign in hand?" I asked sarcastically.

He chuckled, "No, no balloons or signs and I said around the age of twenty."

"Okay, then how does it work?"

"Well, it's different for each of us."

I rolled my eyes. "That's helpful."

"Each of us goes through the change differently. For me, the weeks leading up to the transformation were riddled with physical pain."

"I see, and then afterwards you knew you had changed? Did you go and test your theory? Jump off a cliff or something?" Once again I was being cynical. If he was going to drive me crazy and not fully answer questions, then I was going to give it back to him. Two could play at this game. He didn't answer, so I sat up and gave him a slight sneer. He waited calmly as moments passed and I grew angrier.

"You have a little problem with your temper, don't you?" he observed.

Irritation began to flair its ugly head again. How in the world was he able to keep doing this to me? Twisting things around to get me flustered, bring out the worst in me? "I don't have a temper around anyone else but you, *He who must be obeyed*!" I snapped back.

He grinned, apparently amused with his new title. "That's new. So I bring out the worst in you then?"

I leaned in closer, only inches from his face, and he didn't act surprised. He actually appeared to be enjoying it.

I spoke through clenched teeth, "Only my temper!" My jaw was taut, and I was quickly losing all control. I took a deep breath and exhaled loudly. Our eyes still locked, his amused and mine shooting imaginary flames. This was so unfair!

He broke the silence, a smirk spreading. "I'll take temper. It shows passion."

"Argh!" I rolled my eyes and fell back into the grass, exasperated. Dusk was approaching, and we needed to get back. I wasn't sure I could find my way back in the dark. I was so completely confused—utterly and stupidly confused! How could he make my heart race like this one moment and then have me angry the next? He purposely whispered in my ear about kissing me, but didn't. He was going to drive me crazy! Why did I want him? It made no sense—it was illogical. Colt would express his feelings to me openly; Callon used them to torture. This was just some stupid childish infatuation—it had to be.

I sat up and pulled my boots and socks on, taking my time. Callon just patiently waited. He stood when I had finished and extended his hand. I looked up, hesitated, and then he unexpectedly reached down and pulled me up. He began to lead us out of the meadow, back to the cabin. He didn't say a word; he hummed while I scowled. He was intent on making me insane, I was sure of it. I ran my thumb over my Servak ring, thinking about what I now knew it meant.

CHAPTER 13

I was determined not to hurt Colt anymore. I would make sure everything I did and said was conscientious. I wouldn't allow him to die for me. Somehow I would have to make sure that such a situation would never arise. For now, though, my focus needed to be on the journal. Given the amount of new information I'd taken in, I needed to work out what message my parents had left me.

I hopped out of bed with a new agenda. First on the list was me going for a run.

I threw my running clothes on, pulled my hair into a ponytail, grabbed my iPod, and headed for the front door. I didn't look up as I passed; someone would follow automatically and I didn't care who.

I swung the front door open and bounded off the porch. I heard some scrambling inside and then steps running behind me. I didn't turn to look. I just turned my music up and kept going down the dirt road.

I ran all the way to the highway; it was about five miles before I headed back. The last mile I picked up the pace and really pushed myself. My mind was clear, and I was anxious to get started on the journal research again.

I came to rest on the porch, my side aching and lungs gasping. I remained hunched over for a few moments trying to catch my breath. It felt good to run; it helped me put events into perspective.

I hopped up the stairs and headed for the bathroom. I didn't make eye contact with Callon or Colt as they waited on the porch. Daniel collapsed in the chair beside them, and I smiled.

This turned into my routine. I would rise in the morning and run, and they would each take turns following me. I always ran the same distance, to the highway and back, turning up my music and pushing myself to move faster and harder.

I solely focused on the journal, scouring the internet, searching for anything that would shed light on its contents. Not the easiest of tasks, as before now I'd never heard of the Timeless or any of the clan names, and Google wasn't that well informed, either. Still, I managed to find a few scraps. I was curious about how being Timeless fit into the history of the world.

"What about this?" I said pointing to the computer screen.

Callon glanced over my shoulder and scrolled down. "No, it's different. See the symbols, they're close, but it's not the same."

I released a frustrated sigh.

"What about your friend? You said you might know someone who can help us?"

He picked up his phone and thumbed through it. "I'm working on it."

I hesitated, then opened the notebook full of my notes. I stared at the paper. "There's a lead in North Dakota..."

"No," Callon said.

"But..." I glanced towards Colt for support and watched him

shake his head.

I closed the notebook and shoved it away.

"You two can be so difficult."

"You keep forgetting there is a murderer looking for you, Cheyenne," Callon said without looking up from his phone.

"Right," I mumbled and rolled my eyes.

Once again we were running out of options.

I decided to change tactics.

"Okay, so what about my transformation into a Timeless?"

Colt moved to sit across the table.

"What about it?" Colt replied.

"You said you each suffered, did you have symptoms beforehand to alert you?"

Callon turned towards me closing his phone.

"I think your warning sign is your headaches."

I lifted a brow. "Seriously?"

"Yes. Before Gene and Alexis's deaths, we'd been discussing the possibilities."

"But they never took me to a doctor..."

"Because they'd never been as severe as this past one or I'd have suggested it."

I looked down a bit worried. "So what if another comes?"

"Callon's a doctor, Cheyenne," Colt said. "He'll take care of you."

I nodded.

"I've gone through many transformations, Cheyenne," Callon reassured. "I know what I'm doing. I've already got a plan of action for the next one."

I looked up into Callon's sympathetic eyes. "But when will it come?" Just the thought of losing the ability to help myself frightened me. What if the next one was worse than the last one?

"We don't know."

There was so much I didn't understand, but to be fair, they did mostly tell me what I wanted to know except for Mr. Evasive.

I had been so consumed with the journal that I didn't realize summer was passing. I'd recently found books at the local library I wanted to check out. I was planning to talk to Callon about it tonight. The morning started out routine, except for the fact that both Callon and Colt were gone and the truck was missing. Daniel was on running duty. Usually he ran behind, but today he was alongside. It distracted me, since he kept smiling as we moved along.

It wasn't unusual for him to be smiling like this; it just meant he was up to no good. He was a bit of a trickster, taking great enjoyment jumping out from behind walls and scaring me. Of course, I always screamed, which only encouraged him. His favorite pastime was to remind me of the Jeep incident. And when he learned I was not fond of spiders that only added to his ammunition. I could handle bugs and even snakes, but when it came to spiders...I shuddered at the thought.

I returned to the cabin and cleaned up. As I was about to throw my shoes in the closet, I noticed clothes were set out for me. A pair of jeans and my favorite green cotton shirt. What did someone have planned for me today that I needed to wear jeans?

Daniel was waiting in the great room when I returned. I never understood how he could get cleaned up so fast. His smile unnerved me. He was up to something, and it probably quite heavily involved me. I liked surprises; however, his usually meant trouble.

"You done?" he asked, a little too perkily for my liking.

I replied cautiously, "Sure."

He jumped up and was by my side in a flash. I had to do a double take. How did he *move* like that? There was a trick to it, and I swore I would eventually learn the secret.

Daniel took my hand and pulled me through the front door. The truck was back, but there was a horse trailer behind it. Why did they need a horse trailer? We continued until we stopped at the outbuilding. He let go of my hand only to step behind and cover my eyes.

"Uh, Daniel," I said apprehensively.

I started to protest until another set of footsteps approached and thick fingers took hold of my arm. It was Colt. They led me on, not saying a word. We must have gone about twenty feet and then Daniel removed his hands.

I had to refocus for a brief second. We were on the backside of the main outbuilding, and there was a corral with four horses. Callon was standing beside a Palomino, and she was beautiful. She was light blonde with flecks of white mixed in. Her eyes were the most playful caramel I had ever seen. She wasn't as big as the other three, more slender...but she was perfect.

All three shouted in unison, "Happy Birthday!"

My mouth hung open. I couldn't believe it. I had completely forgotten what day it was! My tongue disconnected from my brain as I tried to stutter out a response.

"Y—you got me a horse for my birthday?"

"Her name is Mandi," Callon replied.

I stood frozen in awe. Colt pulled me forward toward the fence and was about to hoist me over when I stopped him. I touched his arm.

"Thank you," I whispered. He smiled and kissed my cheek. I glided over to Daniel and gave him a hug. "Thank you."

I returned to Colt's side, and he helped me over the corral, as the gate was further away. I landed on my feet on the other side. I cautiously approached Callon, who was still holding Mandi. I kept my eyes locked on her the entire time, before I touched her face. She bent her head so I could scratch her, moving her nose up and down as I did. I was beaming. I leaned around to make eye contact with Callon.

"Thank you."

Callon's lips creased a smile. I was suddenly nervous. Callon really looked so much more dashing when he wasn't brooding. But more than that, there was genuine warmth in his eyes, and it made me nervous. My stomach churned as I realized that a present of horses could only mean one thing.

"You do realize I've never ridden a horse before," I informed them.

Colt replied, "Don't worry. We'll teach you."

I frowned at him, uneasy. Just what were they getting me into?

Callon pulled Mandi alongside, and I took a step back. She was huge, not in comparison to the other three animals, but in comparison to me. She was daunting. He handed me the reins, and we began to walk her around the corral. She followed easily. The other three Appaloosas just watched.

"We'll start you off riding Sam, the chestnut colored one." Callon pointed out the biggest horse. "He's a little calmer than Mandi. He'll be a good one to learn on."

Sam's coat was more of a copper color, speckled with darker and lighter variations of brown. If I wasn't scared before, I was utterly terrified now. Callon called out the others, so I knew their names. The sleek, slivery grey spotted one was Bo, and Charlie was the buckskin. His coat was very interesting. It appeared more like deerskin, but had black points on his mane, tail and lower legs.

Mandi was to be mine, Sam was Colt's, Bo belonged to Callon, and Charlie was Daniel's.

"We're taking you on a packing trip, Cheyenne," Colt called out. "We got the horses now to make sure you were comfortable riding before we departed." At least now I knew the reasoning behind it, although it didn't make me any less antsy.

Callon took Mandi's lead from me, pulled her bridle off, and hung it just inside the door to the outbuilding. He returned with a different bridle and proceeded to Sam. Sam didn't fight him as he slid the leather over his head. He seemed calm enough. Callon disappeared again, and returned with a blanket and saddle. I watched as he saddled the gelding, tightening the girth on his belly.

Adjusting the stirrups, Callon turned to me. I looked to Colt with wide eyes. He nodded, trying to reassure me, and I gathered up the courage to step forward. Once at Callon's side, I hesitated. I didn't know what to do next.

"Here, hold these," Callon said as he handed me Sam's reins. He instructed me on how to mount. I placed my foot in the stirrup and grasped the saddle horn, thrusting myself up and swinging my leg over. I was amazed I was able to do this without much effort.

Callon readjusted the stirrups while I sat to ensure they fitted properly. He then led us around the corral. After a few times around, I was starting to feel more comfortable. Callon led us to the gate that opened to the field and we walked out. I was gaining confidence until he let go of the reins.

"What are you doing?!" I screeched in panic.

"It's alright, Cheyenne. Just do what I tell you and you'll be fine," Callon said. He seemed to know what he was doing, so I relaxed a little. Even *he* wouldn't let me get hurt. Right?

Ignoring my fears, Callon instructed me how to turn Sam. He told me that just because I pulled back on the reins, that didn't mean the horse would stop. I would also have to learn to use my legs to direct my mount. Each horse had its own rhythm to its walk, and understanding that rhythm would help me avoid bouncing in the saddle and learn how to use my legs in the stirrups.

"You're doing good." Callon nodded in approval as I walked in a large circle around him.

All in all, everything seemed to be going smoothly until a dark shadow filtered across my vision. Sam snorted wildly, rearing on his hind legs, and it was all I could do not to fall off. A split second later, we were running into the forest. A strangled scream escaped my lips. Instinct told me to hold tight as the landscape whipped by.

I leaned over and latched my fingers into Sam's mane. My heart was about to burst from my chest, fear filling every ounce of my being. I heard shouting in the distance.

Sam was moving rapidly through the trees, weaving in and out. We were moving at such a high speed that I wasn't sure how much ground we'd covered. I also didn't know which direction we were heading. I kept my head low and tucked close to his neck; I didn't want to get knocked off.

My chest was beginning to ache; the saddle horn was digging into it, and the horse had run for a long time. He wasn't slowing. I frantically searched for the reins, only to slip in the saddle. I glanced

169

up to see another tree nearing. We were going to make direct contact!

I squeeze my eyes shut, when a hand grasped my waist and yanked me into the air. My eyes flew open. I was now in Callon's arms, safe. He was riding Mandi bareback, her mane in one hand and his other arm securing me to his side. He had me twisted sideways, firmly planted between his chest and Mandi's outstretched neck.

I wrapped my arms around him in a death grip. He wasn't letting go, and neither was I.

Mandi slowed, and thundering hoof beats echoed nearby. Colt and Daniel arrived riding Bo and Charlie. "Cheyenne!" Colt's voice was tense and I heard his deep sigh of relief when he saw I was free from harm. All I could do was stare out into the forest. I began shaking.

"Daniel, go find Sam," Callon said firmly. Hoof beats disappeared in the distance. Callon's long fingers moved, and he started rubbing my back, trying to sooth me.

No words were spoken, and we didn't move for quite a while. I was sure they thought I might break out into hysterics. In actuality, I probably wasn't far from that. Eventually the trembling slowed, and my pulse eased. Mandi moved, and my grip tightened again.

"It's alright, Cheyenne. I won't let go. You're not going anywhere," Callon reassured me.

I could do nothing but trust his words; the thought echoed in my mind that I could trust them. The crunching of hooves in the forest told us Daniel was near with Sam in tow. Time to go back.

It was a long, slow descent back to the corral, and I was too terrified to move. Once we stopped, Colt's hands came around my waist, but he had to pry my hands free before he could lift me down.

"Cheyenne, are you alright? Cheyenne!"

I couldn't speak. My legs slid to the ground, and Colt continued to hold my elbows for support. He was holding back, unsure if he should embrace me or not. I was not going to allow this situation to get the best of me. I would learn to ride, and this would never happen again.

I still said nothing as I walked away and stopped at the fence rail. Colt followed, and was waiting for my next move. I longed to wrap myself in his arms, but I knew I couldn't. I needed to face this alone, or else I'd never get close to another horse again.

I turned, and faced the trio.

"Well, not too bad for a first ride, huh?" I couldn't quite remove all the panic in my voice, but I did my best. "I think tomorrow I'll leave out the excitement if you don't mind."

Colt took my hands.

"I think leaving out the excitement would be a good option."

I sighed.

"Come on. Let's go sit on the porch," he offered.

I nodded as Colt hoisted me over the fence rails once again instead of heading for the gate. Daniel was on the other side and we headed up to the house.

We sat silently as we waited for Callon. I had to try again tomorrow before fear set in and took hold. My father's warnings about letting fear overtake me pushed me forward.

Callon's gaze locked with mine as he stepped up on the porch. His expression was strained.

"Cheyenne, I'm so sorry. I didn't expect Sam to bolt like that. How are you feeling now, sweetheart?"

He called me sweetheart? I fought to push down my surprise at the endearment.

"It's not your fault. It's just one of those things. I'll be fine. I need to get back on a horse tomorrow. And I'll probably be scared to death. But unless I do this, I'll never be able to get near a horse again."

Sympathy made a crease in his brow. "We can do that. I'll ride with you until you're comfortable."

I nodded. "Thanks."

"Cheyenne," Colt said, breaking our discussion. "If you're feeling up to it, we have a couple more presents for you."

I blinked. "More? I would have thought the horse was enough. I wasn't expecting anything..."

He cut me off. "We know, but we have more for you."

He glanced at Daniel, who disappeared, literally. I rubbed my eyes. Did he just fade from sight or was I still a wreck from the runaway ride? This wasn't the first time he'd vanished like that, either, now that I thought about it.

Moments later, he was back with a box in hand. I would have to ask about that trick later. Daniel placed the package on my lap and I hesitated.

"Go ahead and open it," he said cheerfully.

I opened the large white box, and gasped. Sitting inside was a black cotton skirt, a button-down blue blouse, and a matching necklace, earrings, and bracelet.

Tears glistened on my lashes. This was my first birthday without my parents, and this was exactly what my mom would have picked out. Colt had to have known.

"This is more than I deserve," I whispered.

"Oh, you deserve it, Cheyenne," Daniel said warmly. "And you get to wear your new outfit tonight because we're taking you out for dinner."

My eyes lit up. They were taking me out?

"Really?" I hadn't been allowed out of the cabin since my failed escape, barring my daily runs. This was going to be a real treat!

"Yes," Callon replied with a small grin.

Colt flashed his always-brilliant smile. "I know you've ruined some of your clothes recently, so I thought you might enjoy something new. Actually, you have a couple of other new items in the bedroom, as well. I hope you don't mind. Callon and I picked them out for you. I looked at your sizes before we left, and the sales clerk was very helpful."

"I don't mind at all. Thank you." I rose with the box in hand and hugged Daniel first. He sighed. Callon looked at me fondly as I bent to hug him as well.

"Thanks, Callon."

He turned and kissed my cheek. I froze, stunned.

"You're welcome."

I shook off my stupor, and stared at him briefly. He must be being nice to me because it was my birthday—otherwise, how could I explain his civil behavior?

Finally, I faced Colt. I bent to kiss him on the cheek, but he turned at the right moment to capture my lips. I drew back and half-heartedly glared. Then I whispered, "Thank you, Colt, even though you seem to be a trouble maker today."

I wasn't given the opportunity to move as he wrapped me in a bear hug, and I squeaked. He chuckled as he set me to my feet. I headed for the front door, stopped and turned slightly. "What time are we leaving for dinner?"

"Five," Callon replied.

Nodding, I proceeded to my room. Laid out on the bed were several new outfits and a new two-piece swimsuit. I shook my head, knowing it was Colt who picked out the swimsuit.

I inspected the clothes as I put them away. They had done a good job, and I was quite impressed, but really I shouldn't have been surprised. Colt had great taste. They were even thoughtful enough to purchase some personal items like bras and panties, which should have embarrassed me, but somehow didn't. Maybe because I knew they'd done it out of necessity rather than anything else. I was very grateful because when I originally packed, it was only for a week or two—not months. Plus I'd managed to destroy a number of items and even with the clothes Colt had picked up from the house, I was constantly running short. I glanced at the clock; I'd only managed to waste a half an hour. I still had a couple of hours to kill before we would leave.

I headed back to the front porch to see what they were up to. They'd disappeared.

I wandered to the corral and found them. I climbed up on the rail and sat. Daniel was working on a water trough in one of the corners. Callon was in the field near the far side repairing some fence rails while Colt was stacking hay bails and feed with his shirt off.

I blinked.

I had seen him shirtless before, but not since he made his confession that he loved me. I drank in the sight of him. I knew he was large and very muscular, but with the sun glistening off his golden skin...my heart beat just a little faster.

He moved effortlessly as he swung two bails at a time—most

humans could only handle one. I couldn't help but watch each muscle flex, trace every defined curve. I stared for a long time.

Without warning, Colt turned his head and flashed a stunning smile. Blood rushed to my cheeks. I was caught, and all I could do was bury my cheeks between my shrugged shoulders.

It was safer to watch the horses; they weren't as distracting. Mandi was a bit of a pistol. She was pestering Sam by nudging her head into his side, wanting to play. She continued until he showed his teeth. Another tactic she tried was to paw the ground with her hooves until he would shift his weight to move away. As a last resort she tried to bite his hind legs; he had enough and lunged at her. She eventually got bored and moved on to the others.

I glanced around for Callon. He was still repairing the fencing. He looked up and managed a smile. We really were getting along much better now; I was actually growing fond of him. He'd been helpful with researching the journal. I was beginning to see a different side to him. I felt like he'd had a softening of sorts towards me. He wasn't as cold, and when he smiled, I actually got the impression he really meant it. Even today's comments and actions were kind. I had been working very hard on not thinking about him in any other way than a friend since his sudden turnaround. It wasn't easy, but I was intent not to hurt Colt.

Being around the trio twenty-four seven had started to wear me down. I was opening my heart, something I hadn't done in a long time. Inside, I knew buying me gifts and celebrating my birthday was just another tactic to win me over, and it was working.

Because I knew they meant it.

As I sat, I realized just how content I'd come to be around them. They'd somehow started to plug the gap in my heart where I'd lost my parents. There was still a lot we had to work through, and I knew that gap would never fully close, but right now I felt I had somewhere to belong. They accepted me for who I was, not what I was. I still didn't understand the latter, but that would come in time. I was sure of it.

I was so lost in my thoughts that I didn't notice Daniel sneak up behind me until he grabbed my waist. I screamed, and he bellowed in laughter. Callon and Colt both turned, ready to run, until they realized it was just Daniel playing another trick on me.

"Daniel!" I scolded with a scowl. "Quit scaring me!"

He still had a hold of my waist as he pulled me down from the fence and placed a brotherly kiss on my cheek.

"But you're so fun to tease. You were sitting there perfectly. I couldn't pass it up." He had that twinkle in his eye, and I couldn't be mad at him.

I wrinkled my nose, pushing him away and walked back inside to get ready. I changed into the new outfit they had purchased. It fit perfectly. The earrings, necklace, and bracelet were wonderful additions. I grabbed my black wedges; grateful I had actually thought to bring them and headed for the bathroom.

My hair looked fairly decent so I opted to leave it down. I ran my fingers through it to dislodge some tangles. I added a little make-up and perfume before I headed for the great room. My mind began to wander. Would Callon think I looked pretty? I shook my head, to dislodge the thought—crazy girl.

All three were waiting. I glanced at my watch, and it was five till five. I was early and they were still waiting on me...great. Colt was holding my denim jacket. I got the impression we would be out later tonight. I was thrilled.

"Do I meet your approval?" I gave a faint grin.

Colt took hold of my hand and placed a soft peck on my cheek. "You always meet my approval, sweetheart."

"Ready?" Callon said.

"Wild horses couldn't keep me away," I replied, which made them all laugh.

Colt kept a hold of my hand as we walked to the truck. I slid to the middle while he tossed my jacket on the back seat next to Daniel. He leaned over and proceeded to buckle me in. I drummed my fingers against my arm. After he was done, he moved his hand behind my back and pulled me a tad closer. His fingers remained locked on my waist.

"Is there a reason why I can't buckle myself in?" I arched a brow.

He replied with a sly smile, "I'm just trying to make sure you're safe. I wouldn't want you to try and jump out or something. Think of it as a little extra insurance."

I rolled my eyes.

"Like I'm going to be able to jump out of a moving car," I replied sarcastically.

He chuckled lightly, "You never know. You did escape once— briefly I might add."

This time I chuckled. He squeezed my waist, and I glanced down at my hands resting on my lap. I twisted my fingers so I could see the blue stone, the Kvech ring. It was truly stunning.

Just as stunning was its mystery, and what it represented about me. Why me? Why was I so special? I hadn't done anything much except live through misery and death. Any joy I had experienced caused others heartache.

I ran my thumb over the Servak ring.

I was one year closer to becoming Timeless...

CHAPTER 14

Soft music was playing in the background of the truck as we drove into town. It was soothing, as my emotions were running rampant through my head. I'd done well keeping a distance from both Colt and Callon, but Colt's nearness was causing me to rethink my decisions.

I leaned into his shoulder, enjoying the warmth his arm around me brought, and stared out the window. The summer landscape was passing by...faster than normal. I glanced at the speedometer—we were going over a hundred and ten miles per hour!

I tensed, and Callon looked over at me. He smiled, but all it did was make me more edgy. Daniel began laughing in the back seat, and I turned to Colt.

Something flickered across his face. What *was* that thing they kept doing?!

"What's so funny?" I huffed.

"You," Colt replied.

"What did I do?"

A devilish grin spread across his lips.

"Just you being you, Cheyenne." He lightly tapped his finger on my nose. I still caught him ever so slyly cast a glance towards Callon. They were up to something, I was sure of it. What it was I didn't know, but I would figure it out soon.

I sighed and let it go for now. It was my birthday and three very handsome men were taking me out to dinner. What girl wouldn't have wanted this? It was in my best interests at the moment not to look at the speedometer as my protest would have fallen on deaf ears, Colt squeezed my hip, and I snuggled into his shoulder.

Cline's Bar and Grill was bigger than they told me. It was a Friday night, and the place was packed. We parked on the street across from the restaurant; I wondered if it was deliberate because Callon parked on the corner facing the direction from which we had just come. I assumed it was a precaution for a quick escape if needed. They'd constantly said I needed protecting, but I still hadn't seen any dangers yet.

Colt exited the truck and gently lifted me down. Callon seemed to be cautiously examining our surroundings, and Daniel had disappeared. Colt, however, was completely at ease. He swallowed up my hand in his as we strolled to the entrance. Callon's fingers accidently touched my elbow, and caused me to shiver. *It was accidental, right?*

The bar was nestled in the historic district of Helena. There was outside dining, and it was buzzing with music as diners enjoyed themselves. The interior was surprisingly larger than what it appeared. The room was encircled with tall tables and booths, forming a ring around the bar and dance floor.

We moved right past the hostess to a table. Daniel was already seated in the far corner, away from the dance floor. I gave a quick glance at Colt, whose eyes shot to Callon before he grinned. I narrowed my eyes, trying to understand what they were doing. I would get an answer later tonight; it had gone on long enough. It seemed to be a game with them, to see who could surprise me the most with their strange abilities.

The atmosphere was pleasant, not too dark, and the music level was perfect. The waitress arrived and took our order. She definitely had eyes for Callon; it made me want to giggle at the way she ogled him, but I had to admit I was no different the first time I saw him. He was looking very good tonight, his shirt snug across his brawny chest.

I sighed.

Colt kept his arm resting on the back of the booth, occasionally touching my hair with his fingers. Callon would lean in from time to time to speak to me; it made me feel special and awkward at the same time. The waitress returned, and we ordered. I was amazed at the amount of food they could consume when they did eat. We had appetizers, plus they each had their own monster-sized steak, not to mention the drink consumption.

Daniel and Colt didn't let up on their teasing.

"You know, Cheyenne." Daniel's eyes sparkled and somehow I knew he was about to zing me good. "Maybe Sam knew you were the Jeep-a-nator and didn't want to be turned into pulp." A devilish grin appeared. "That's why he ran."

"Jeep-a-nator?" I cringed. Great, he'd come up with a new nickname. Now they'd lever let me live it down.

"Jeep-a-nator?" Colt bellowed with laughter. "That's a good one, Daniel." He slapped him on the back. My cheeks burned, and I turned away.

The time flew by, and the crowd was growing, as was the music. I noticed the stares directed to our table. It wasn't just from the females either. It made me feel just a little uncomfortable. Colt's fingers came to rest on my neck, his thumb caressing it as we continued to converse. It sent goose bumps down my spine, the good kind.

After my third iced tea, I needed to use the bathroom. Callon moved to allow me out and was about to follow until I stopped him.

"No." I put my hand up. "I'm just going to the bathroom. I'll be right back."

He hesitated.

"Really, it won't be that long. I think I'll be safe." I smiled. "I don't think I'll get assaulted along the way."

He gave a shallow smile and leaned in to reply since the music was louder. "I'll come look for you if you take too long," he said in my ear. His warm breath drifted down my neck, and he drew back smiling. I gave a faint, nervous nod and walked off.

I had to walk around the now crowded dance floor to get to the bathroom. I was only mildly surprised to see the long line for the ladies room. As I waited, I was aware of three men nearby in the dark, narrow hall trying to capture the attention of those standing in line. They were intent on having a good time and didn't seem likely to give up until they did.

I kept my gaze averted as I waited patiently, wishing Callon had come with me after all. I stepped forward only to be stopped in my tracks. I looked up. A fairly decently built, dark-haired man stood with his arm leaning against the wall directly in front of me. His two friends stood behind with drunken smiles plastered across their faces. His bicep flexed, and his tight shirt strained.

182

"Excuse me," I asked politely. He didn't move. His brown eyes were now intently studying me. I didn't like his stare. It was as if he knew me...and I was sure I'd never seen him in my life before. His white teeth crept out from under a crooked smile.

"Well, hello there, darling." The way he said it made my skin crawl, and I was becoming annoyed. I quickly glanced at his friends. They were off to the side, and I darted under his arm to make my escape. His response time was faster than I thought; he had looked like he had had one too many drinks. His fingers latched on my arm, and I turned slightly as I yanked it back. I did not want to engage in a conversation with them, let alone anything else. The bathroom door opened, and I slid in.

"Oh, she's a feisty one. I like 'em feisty," I heard him say.

Once again, my skin crawled. There was still a line inside the bathroom. I was hoping they would be gone by the time I exited. I thought about texting Colt, but realized my phone was in my jacket at the table. This wasn't a big deal, I told myself. I could handle it.

Cautiously I stepped out of the bathroom and was relieved to find the three men had gone. I picked up my pace down the dark hallway; once again I had to cross the dance floor. As I rounded the corner to the floor, a rough hand latched onto my wrist. I stiffened as I realized they had lain in wait around the corner. I wasn't scared yet, just becoming more irritated.

I was jerked to the dance floor and thrown into the arms of the dark-haired man who had hit on me in the hall, his friends nearby.

"Hey, baby. I just wanted a dance is all," he said with his face a little too close for comfort. I pushed my hands to his chest, trying to break his hold as his arms locked around my waist, but he leaned forward.

"I would have said no," I replied firmly as I tried to keep my distance. The smell of alcohol on his breath was making me ill. He wasn't drunk yet, but I was sure it was impairing his judgment.

"Just one little dance." A sly smile was etched on his face as his hand roamed up my back and began pushing me forward.

"You need to let go of me right now," I said through my teeth. "Or you're going to get hurt."

He chuckled as he continued to press me closer, his lips dangerously close to mine. "And what are you going to do about it?" a threatening low voice echoed in my ears.

"She doesn't need to do anything, because I will," Colt's deep rumbling raised the hair on the back of my neck. Suddenly the expression on my assaulter's face changed, and his two friends stepped up. His hands released their grasp, and I smirked.

"Told you you'd get hurt." Callon pulled me back and twisted me quickly as he moved us away from the impending fight to the dance floor. I glanced back and saw Colt and Daniel towering over my assaulters. They blended into the crowd, not wanting to cause a scene in front of everyone, and Callon was obviously trying to act like nothing was wrong.

"Are you alright?" Callon's voice was anxious as we began to dance. His hand rubbed my back, trying to comfort me. "I knew I shouldn't have let you go alone. I saw him yank you onto the floor." I stared into the warmth of his eyes.

His eyes were warm...they held warmth for me?

"I'm so sorry. This is twice in one day I've let you down." His brow was creased as his strong arms drew me in closer. The music changed and panic set in as a new problem presented itself. "Cheyenne? What's wrong?"

"I don't know how to two-step," I quickly replied, forgetting that his touch made me quiver.

He released a low chuckle as his head lifted slightly. "You ride a runaway horse, get assaulted on the dance floor, and then tell me in a panic you can't two-step? You truly are one of a kind." He tenderly kissed my forehead as his arms tightened. "Don't worry, I'll lead. I won't let you fall."

The heat from his kiss burned my forehead as crazy thoughts came to the forefront. Thoughts of him and me. He danced us around the floor, and I managed to make it through a couple of songs without falling or looking too awkward. He was a graceful dancer; I shouldn't have been surprised, for as old as he was. He would have had plenty of time to learn. Colt tapped him on the shoulder. "May I have this dance?" His eyes locked on mine. I smiled and sighed; he was so stinking gorgeous, it just wasn't fair. He couldn't have had more perfect timing either; I needed to focus on him, not Callon.

His thick fingers intertwined with mine while his other hand curled behind me and landed firmly on my waist. I tightened my fingers on his bicep. I couldn't help but stare up into the icy blue oceans of his eyes. He didn't hide his love. He showed me, and I absorbed it like a sponge.

"Are you okay?" he asked tenderly.

"I'm with you, dancing on my birthday. It's perfect. Thank you." The song slowed, and he drew me even closer. I rested my head into his chest and closed my eyes. I loved being in his arms, the strength and raw power. It almost made me giddy at times, childish. I could have stayed here forever, with my attention solely on him, but the song ended.

"How bout we take you home now?" Colt suggested. I looked up into his soft, caring face and nodded. We headed for the door where Daniel and Callon were waiting with my coat. Daniel helped me into the jacket, which I was grateful for because it had cooled off. As we exited the bar, the trio scanned the surrounding streets. Colt placed his arm around me, and we stopped briefly at the corner. As Daniel led the way, our pace quickened. I hadn't seen anything, but was guessing they had from the pace they were setting. The truck was within view, and Daniel positioned himself so he was strategically in front of me.

As we neared, I now saw what they did. Leaning just in front of the truck, against the brick wall, were the three men from inside the bar. Apparently they didn't agree with the outcome in the restaurant and wanted to discuss it further. They were each holding what appeared to be long, thick crowbars. How did they know which car we drove? Was it just a lucky guess?

We slowed and came to a stop just to the side of the truck; Callon, Colt and Daniel didn't waver in their positions. Callon's hand shifted slightly as he moved it to his pocket, and the truck doors unlocked. Daniel stepped back as Callon stepped forward along with Colt. Daniel's fingers touched my arm, and the next thing I knew we were in the front seat together.

I blinked.

I never felt my feet move, but suddenly we were sitting in the truck. I turned to question Daniel, but he was gone. I twisted my head to Colt only to see Daniel next to him once more. Once again I blinked.

I could do nothing except watch the fight before me from the safety of the truck. All three men had seen what happened with

186

Daniel and me, because one shook his head. He didn't seem all that surprised, just irritated, as he changed his position to cover his friend. I could see they were talking, but it was so low, I couldn't hear the words. Suddenly one of them took a swing at Colt with the crowbar. In the next moment, the man was flying against the brick wall and slumped to the ground.

That was all it took, the other two glanced at each other and decided to help their fallen friend instead of continuing the fight. Daniel turned and got in the back seat, and Callon slid in next to me in the driver's seat. Colt remained outside with his arms crossed, waiting for them to depart. As he got in the truck, Colt's eyes searched mine; a mixture of worry and apprehension filled them. "Sorry, Cheyenne. I didn't mean to scare you."

I didn't know how to respond. All I could do was stare at him blankly. He leaned over, once again buckling me in, sliding his hand behind me on the seat back, his fingers rubbing my shoulder as he looked down. I folded my hands in my lap as I stared down at them.

It was enlightening and frustrating at the same time. I just wasn't sure what to make of it. The way the three of them would seemingly be able to carry on conversations in their heads without me hearing a sound, the nods of understanding without words being spoken. My sudden appearance in the truck with Daniel and then he was gone— all within the blink of an eye...

It remained silent on the drive home. I got the impression they thought what happened outside on the street really upset me. That it somehow scared me. It hadn't; I didn't feel fear at all. I was more amazed at their abilities. I replayed the entire evening in my mind, honing in on specific details.

We arrived home late. Colt assisted me down from the truck and drew me into his arms in a hug.

"Happy Birthday, Cheyenne," he whispered and kissed my head. I faintly smiled up at him as he took my hand and we entered the cabin, Daniel and Callon trailing behind. I took the lead and headed for the couch but I didn't sit.

"Sit please," I said quietly and the trio complied. Unease rolled over them like a wave. Daniel fiddled with his shirt, Colt ran his fingers through his hair, and Callon folded his arms tight across his chest. I moved the coffee table back slightly and took a seat.

Colt was in the middle with Daniel and Callon flanking his sides. I sized up my nemesis, Mr. Evasive. He knew how to play this game; both he and Colt did too well. I was only a student. I went from somewhat serious to grateful in a flash.

"I want to tell each of you thank you so much for a wonderful birthday. It was filled with pleasant surprises all the way around. I can honestly say I've never had anything like it before. I especially enjoyed our dinner and dancing tonight." I let my gaze rake all of them. My eyes narrowed and focused. In the next moment, I saw the affects of the whiplash at my instant mood change.

"I have come to the conclusion that these, let's call them 'incidents,' tend to come in groups of three. First, there was the runaway horse episode that took place this morning, no harm done. Second, the incident at the restaurant involving the unwelcomed dance partner. And third, the situation on the sidewalk outside, when the gentlemen didn't take to being told 'no' too kindly." All three shifted in their seats.

I continued. "In going along with my theory that incidents come in threes, there are the three of you." I locked eyes with Daniel. "One of whom can make an appearance out of thin air and then suddenly reappear across the room. A location he hadn't been in seconds before." He looked away.

I met Callon's unwavering gaze. "Another seems to arrive where he's needed sooner than he should be able to get there and see things that only an eagle would. Like an incident on the dance floor around the corner from where we were sitting."

I crossed my legs and arms as I turned to stare at Colt. "The third is somehow able to lift two or more bails of hay and toss them around with little or no effort. He also can thrust another human up into the air a good ten feet without much exertion." My gaze drifted to each of them again. "Then there are the telepathic powers the three of you seem to have. Always knowing what the other is about to say, the glances, and the silent nods." I waited impatiently for an explanation. "Some enlightenment would be helpful." I added.

Colt shifted in his seat, leaning forward and suddenly yanked the table towards him. I caught my breath, and my hands automatically went to the edge to steady myself, causing me to lean forward and uncross my legs. He quickly took hold of my hands and placed them on my knees. His voice was low and sultry, "You know, sweetheart, I really can't blame those men for hitting on you tonight. You really are beautiful, and the way you look, well..."

"Colt," I snapped. "Don't try to distract me. You know what happened!"

"Well, you're distracting me." A sly grin was spreading across his lips. "Your legs, your steel blue eyes, and the way your hair falls off your shoulder..."

"Colt!" I said in annoyance.

"You're right; he's right," Callon said calmly.

I flipped my head in his direction. "Excuse me?" I raised my brows. Since when was I ever right?

"You're right, Cheyenne. Your incidents tend to come in threes. When you first came, you had your headache, then you made an escape and we had to bring you back, and third you assaulted your Jeep. All three happened close together. I haven't paid attention before, but now that you've brought it to my attention, I can see it.

"Colt's also right. You are a distraction tonight...actually, most of the time. We have tried to be very careful around you, but apparently we haven't done a good job. You are bright, and pay attention to things. You see more than I thought you would."

I was a distraction for him? I shook it off. I wasn't crazy after all. I'd seen things, but I still wanted absolute confirmation.

Callon continued, to my surprise. "Daniel can *jump*; at least, that's what we call it. He can look ahead to where he wants to go, and his body jumps there. He can only go as far as he can see. He can only jump with one person at a time; it's a nice gift to have in a tight spot."

Interesting...

"All three of us can communicate telepathically to each other. We don't read minds; we just carry on conversations in our heads, although with you, it would be most helpful to know what's going on up in your mind.

"Colt does have extraordinary strength, even for being Timeless. And I can see things most humans or Timeless cannot. I'm also fairly quick."

I relaxed slightly at the admission, and Colt released my hands so I could sit upright. His fingers remained on my knees, and he was still leaning forward. They all seemed a little edgy now. It was almost if they thought I would bolt. Colt's fingers firmed slightly.

I returned my gaze to Callon, and the questions rolled out. "Do all Timeless have powers?"

"No."

"Did my adoptive parents have powers?"

"No."

"Did my birth parents have powers?"

"Yes."

"What were they?"

"Your father could move objects and control some of the elements, and your mother had the ability to persuade people to do things she wanted."

"Will I have powers?" I wanted to know.

"We don't know," Callon admitted.

"So it's not hereditary?" I said, not sure if I was disappointed.

He sighed. "No."

"Do the Sarac have powers?"

"Some."

I pondered his replies. He wasn't going to release any more information than needed. Marcus was Sarac...did he?

"Does Marcus have powers?" I tensed before his answer.

"Yes."

"More than one?"

"Yes."

"Will you tell me what they are?"

"Another time."

Ah, Mr. Evasive was back again. My jaw tightened. "There's more to this, isn't there?"

"Yes."

My irritation was rising. "You're not going to tell me are you?"

"Correct." His lips were straight, not an emotion showing on his face or eyes.

"For my own protection, right?" I snapped out.

"Yes."

My eyes narrowed into small slits. "You like to play these mind games, don't you, Callon? What I'm trying to figure out is why. Just for sheer torture? You say it's to protect me, but I think I need to know what I'm up against." I paused, annoyance poised on my lips. "I'm not angry, but I'm determined. You don't fight fair, so neither will I. I'll get the answers, either from you or another source." Without warning I leaned forward, grasped Colt's face, and kissed him firmly. I stopped as suddenly as I'd begun and stood up. Colt blinked.

I left three stunned men sitting on the couch as I departed. I had no explanation as to why I did what I did, but I wanted to kiss Colt. It was probably unwise.

I went straight for the bathroom. Colt was right; my eyes were a steel blue tonight. I wondered if it was because I was irritated or determined. He had told me before my eyes would change color depending on my mood. I guess he was right.

I entered my bedroom to find Colt waiting, leaning against the headboard. A very mischievous smile was perched over his lips. I had created a monster.

"So," he said casually, "I thought I was the one who was supposed to give you the birthday kiss, not the other way around."

I didn't answer while I entered the closet to hang up my jacket and closed the door so I could change. He was still waiting for me to respond when I came out. I had no choice but to stand at the edge of the bed. He was sitting in the middle, essentially blocking both sides.

"I was a little surprised—pleasantly surprised, I might add." He patted the bed for me to sit, and I hesitantly complied. "So now you know our secret. Are you okay with it?" His tone grew serious.

"I'd like to know more."

His long fingers touched my chin as he raised it up slightly. "In time you will learn more. I suggest you allow this to sink in first." His devilish grin returned. In the next instant he yanked me into his arms, pinning me down. "I will, however, show you more right now...I haven't given you a *real* birthday kiss yet."

"Colt!" I tried to protest, but it was pointless. His soft lips brushed over mine, and I lost all the willpower I'd had to stop him. His velvety softness caressed my lips slowly, purposefully, and I thought I'd died and gone to heaven. I wrestled my hand free and lifted it to his neck, pulling it through the hair at the nape of his neck and locking my fingers in the waves as he crushed me further into his massive chest. He used his tongue to part my lips, and my heart soared even more. My breaths became more labored as his remained level and calm.

He broke away, and I tried to catch my breath. I opened my eyes to see the blue of his. "You're not done yet," I said in a low raspy voice and drew him back down as he grinned. He didn't hesitate.

I had behaved myself for so long. If I was the one who was going to break my rules, then I was going to break them good. I loved being in his arms. I also loved the fact he was so willing to stay with me at night. I didn't like being without him—I didn't feel alone anymore. He had succeeded in wearing me down over the last few months, but how could he not? His kiss slowed, and he hovered over my lips.

"I love you, Cheyenne." He hadn't said those words in months, and I still didn't know exactly how I felt in response. He was trying not to push me.

"I know," I replied faintly. He sighed and rolled off the bed as he lifted the covers and I slid under. I closed my eyes and turned on my side.

"I'll be in soon. Get some sleep." I heard his heavy footsteps leave the room, and I drifted off to a peaceful, happy sleep.

CHAPTER 15

My riding lessons began immediately, but this time I didn't ride alone. Colt and Callon took turns instructing me. They taught me to communicate with the horse by using my legs, seat, hands, and voice. My legs were the power while my hands were the guides.

Of course, it was much easier said than done. I learned about tacking up, mounting, adjusting the tack if necessary, and properly dismounting. We rode bareback together, and they taught me how to place my legs so when I used the stirrups they would be effective. I had to sit up straight; if I leaned forward there was a greater chance I could fall off. My hands needed to follow the movement of the horse's head while the reins rested in my hands like delicate flowers.

I had to learn to absorb the movement of the horse by relaxing and allowing myself to move as one with the motion. I worked on the trot and canter, but they didn't allow me to gallop yet. The fear of what took place with Sam was always at the back of my mind.

I'd found out that they did in fact have powers, and I wondered if I would develop them. What would mine be? Would I have more than one? Were those all the powers they had or were some hidden?

We rode daily, and eventually I was on my own. They were trying to teach me so much in a short amount of time. Sometimes it was overwhelming.

I also learned not to react to Callon's touch.

Our packing trip neared. We were going to find Callon's friend who could interpret the journal, and I needed to be fitted with the proper riding gear, boots particularly. They were planning to do this without me, but I protested. I didn't want to miss out on the opportunity to leave the cabin, regardless of what had happened that night at Cline's Bar and Grill.

I managed to convince them that with Daniel's power I would be safe. He would be able to whisk me away to safety if anything should arise, and after a lot of persistent badgering they finally agreed. Besides, no real dangers had presented themselves yet.

The day was planned out; first we would stop at the farm store so we could purchase all the necessary gear. Second would be the grocery store for food, third would be the library. I was surprised at the last destination, but Callon saw the importance of examining the books I had located online. We knew it would be a long shot.

I stood on the porch and waited to depart. I looked up into the cloudless sky; it was going to be a gorgeous day.

Two hands grasped my waist from behind, and I released a small scream.

"Daniel!"

I turned and smacked his arm as he stepped away, chuckling. "One day I'll pay you back for all your jokes, you know," I threatened. I was trying to act annoyed, but nothing could annoy me today. I was going into town.

A wicked grin spread over his face, and a twinkle in his eye told me he wasn't done tormenting me yet. "You'd have to catch me first," he said.

"Oh, you just wait...one day." He suddenly appeared next to me again and made me jump. Since I knew about their powers now, they made no effort to hide them.

He laughed and kissed my cheek. "I look forward to it." He disappeared again, and all I could do was shake my head.

"Ready?" Colt said as he approached. He was unusually subdued today.

"Yup," I replied cheerfully.

I climbed into the front seat. Colt's arm rested on the seat back, and Callon began our drive. Daniel gently tugged at my hair, and I turned around as we began to chat.

I was excited, and Daniel seemed happy too. Callon and Colt were quiet, too quiet for even Callon. Colt's fingers took hold of mine, and he began playing with my rings. I'd catch the two exchanging glances from time to time; they were having a deep conversation in their heads. I ignored them and continued talking with Daniel.

The farm store wasn't crowded, and we made our purchases with speed. Daniel became a little less chatty as he focused on his job—keeping me safe. He was within arm's reach at all times. And I tried to remain alert as well.

We stopped at the grocery store, and it was no different. They knew what I needed, so I let them choose for the most part. To my surprise, I was able to convince them I needed to stop for a coffee. A cool treat would hit the spot and make my day, and it'd been way too long since I'd had one. Daniel and I went in, and I purchased drinks for them as well. I knew they said they didn't want any, but I didn't want to drink alone. I got them iced lattes while I ordered my favorite iced blended drink with extra caramel on top of the whipped cream. When we arrived back at the truck, and I distributed them, Colt began to chuckle.

"What?"

"You love your caramel, don't you?" he teased.

"Yeah." I wasn't sure what he thought was so funny.

"Do you want me to hold the lid while you lick it?"

I lowered my head and took a drink, my cheeks burning. I couldn't believe he knew about that!

"Maybe," I replied sheepishly. Soon the truck erupted in laughter. "Just drive to the library please."

"You make me laugh, Cheyenne," he said as his warm fingers touched my neck in a caress.

"Glad I'm providing you with enough entertainment."

"Plenty," Daniel chimed in. "I haven't had this much fun in years."

I shook my head. We couldn't get to the library soon enough.

"You do realize I'm not exactly sure where the books are located, don't you? They had them listed in several different locations when I checked online," I said while we pulled into the library, which was located at the edge of town backing up to the woods.

"I know," Callon replied. "You just need to move as fast as you can."

All three accompanied me inside as we began our search. I was able to find a couple of the books relatively easily and made copies of what was needed from the ones we couldn't check out. My eyes scanned the sheets as Callon gave me a cold stare to hurry up. I sighed. The two more important books were proving difficult to find. It was growing late; the library would close in five minutes. I followed them downstairs to check out a few additional books. They were becoming uneasy. Daniel's fingers latched on to my elbow.

"We need to go," Callon said. I nodded, but then remembered. My copies were still upstairs.

"Callon, I left some stuff upstairs. I'll just be a minute."

He gave me a restless glance.

"Leave it."

"But I really need them." I pleaded. "The papers are…"

"Quickly."

I nodded.

Colt and Daniel followed me upstairs. I found my missing papers and tossed them in my pack along with the books Callon had checked out.

Daniel and Colt suddenly froze. They exchanged wary glances.

"Daniel, go!" Colt snapped and Daniel disappeared.

I blinked.

"What's going on?"

Colt went for the windows and I followed.

I found several new cars parked nearby…cars that weren't there when we arrived and shouldn't be there since the library was closing. Dusk was falling, if danger lurked it'd be difficult to see.

"We need to go," Colt said. He grabbed my arm, dragging us down the stairs and towards the back of the library.

"Colt, what's going on?"

"Don't leave my side."

A chill ran down my spine, and my breathing hitched. This was not a part of the plan!

We broke through the rear doors to find three men waiting.

Colt shoved me behind him. I pushed against the door to escape back into the library, but it was locked.

"Colt..."

"Stay behind me," he ordered.

I swung my pack on my shoulders. Who these men were didn't matter at the moment, it was what they were after that concerned me more. Their eyes were all focused on me.

In a moment everything changed as they dove towards Colt. I was suddenly slammed up against the doors, Colt's body pinning me in place.

A hand grasped my arm and began yanking as I let out a scream and kicked toward a shin. Colt shifted breaking their hold and groaned as his arms went out and he took the three men to the cement below.

"Run!" he bellowed and I took off in a sprint towards the forest.

"Over here!" Voices shouted and I looked back..

It was the three men who hit on me at the bar. This couldn't be good.

They were moving dangerously close despite my running. My mind skimmed through the options. I had two choices. I could head into the woods or towards the truck. I glanced back again...the only real choice was to escape into the woods. I knew my way around well enough. I could hide—I was sure of it. I just needed to keep ahead of them. I didn't have a choice now.

Through the darkening forest, my gaze caught sight of something flickering at the edge of the trees. It seemed to be moving in random patterns, appearing and then disappearing quickly. It was like the reflection of sunlight on water. I was attempting to keep enough distance between the men and myself, but couldn't help glimpsing at the lights. They were strangely familiar...

I was restricted as to where I could enter the trees, as I didn't want to get too close to the unknown lights, but it was as if they were beckoning to me. I was so caught up in them that I didn't realize I had stopped running until someone grabbed my arm and twisted me around. I wasn't even in the forest yet.

My heart raced; as I searched behind them. My guardians were nowhere in sight. What had I done?

The dark haired one spoke in an agitated tone.

"Where you going, doll? Remember us? We didn't get to have our fun because your boyfriends got in the way." He paused to look at the other two. "They don't seem to be here now, do they?"

Yanking my arm free, I took a step back, still facing them. Shifting, I took a wider stance, lifting my arms to a blocking position, palms out ready to strike. My dad had shown me self-defense moves, but now I wished I'd paid closer attention.

A slimy smile began to grow over his lips. "Oh, she is feisty!"

This wasn't going to be good. I searched one last time for my protectors—nothing. I was on my own; not even a person on the street in the distance to witness the assault. Fear gripped me, but somehow the adrenaline kicked in as the dark-haired man reached out for me. Taking one step forward, I thrust my hand, palm up and knuckles down, with all my strength at his nose. It made contact.

I heard a crack, and my hand immediately started to throb with pain. He stumbled back a few steps, grasping his face as he bent over. The blood raced through my veins, pounding out the rhythm of my heart. I wasn't going down easy. I would scratch, kick, and claw my way out.

Going on the offense stunned the other two briefly, giving me enough time to swing my pack loaded with books at the man on my right. It smashed into the side of his jaw with enough force to send him staggering to the side. The third man looked on in shock, then anger registered in his eyes.

I managed to jerk one knee up, nailing him square in the groin. He fell to the ground in agony. I caught sight of the dark-haired man and saw his rage as I bolted for the shadowy woods. The thundering of his footsteps was not far behind. Could I outrun them, outlast them until help came? I just needed to keep the space between us wide enough so they couldn't catch me. I would find a hiding place and wait it out. I could do this!

The flickering lights were still ahead, bouncing back and forth. It was difficult to keep track of their location. It suddenly registered where I had seen them before, at the cathedral. I had also seen them outside the library windows, but I mistook them for passing headlights.

I entered the woods about thirty feet to the right of the lights with two of the three men in close pursuit. As I continued into the darkness, I was now not so confident in my ability to keep the distance.

What would happen if they caught me? Would Colt, Daniel, and Callon find me? Argh, and the heavy pack wasn't helping. Why didn't I just drop it?

I was in mid-stride when two arms locked around me and I tumbled to the ground, smashing into a small fallen log. The air forcefully exited my lungs, and a piercing pain completely immobilized my left side. A second later my pack was being ripped off and thrown to the side. For a brief second I had the sensation of a weight being lifted from me, and I scrambled to my feet as I ran.

I took two strides before I smashed into a tree, my right elbow hitting with a loud crack. Instant agony shot up my arm to my shoulder. I lay slumped on my side on the cool forest floor. This was the danger my protectors were talking about. How had I not seen it?

"This is my kill!" one of the three men shouted. "I want to have some fun first, see how long she'll last. It's been way too long since I've had an opportunity like this."

Their footsteps closed in. They were going to kill me? Why? I hadn't done anything except defend myself. At the bar, the dark-haired one acted as if he knew me. I didn't understand. I'd never seen him before. All three were close—I had to get away.

I pushed myself to my knees using my left arm and stumbled to my feet, desperate to flee. I barely turned before I saw a hand closing in on my head. His fingers locked in my hair as he dragged me forward. Raising my good elbow, I wheeled it into his side, but he only bent slightly. There was a growl at the back of his throat, and seconds later I was hurling toward the ground. I once again landed on my right side, crippled with pain.

"She won't last if you keep throwing her to the ground!" one snapped.

"Don't tell me what I can and can't do," the dark-haired one said through his teeth. "I plan on making it long and drawn out. She will suffer greatly for what's she's done."

Black spots were flashing before my eyes as I lifted my head. I needed to get up, or they were going to kill me—I had to keep moving. My breaths were labored, every one bringing excruciating misery. Were these the same ones who killed my parents? The ones Colt, Callon and Daniel were trying to protect me from?

One of them was standing over me, but I couldn't tell which one. My face was planted in the ground while the other two argued. I closed my eyes, my head slumping to the forest floor.

"You idiots! Have you seen the rings on her fingers?"

Suddenly an ear-piercing scream echoed through the trees. The voices became muffled. There was shouting, but the words jumbled together in my mind. Forget them, I had to move! I had to get away...

Every inch of my being was in agony, I forced my head up, only to collapse again.

"Cheyenne!" a deep voice yelled near my head. It was somehow familiar. I couldn't pry my lids open...they were so heavy. The voice was louder now. "Cheyenne! Don't go to sleep. Stay with me! Open your eyes!"

Someone gingerly rolled me onto my back, and my lashes flickered. It was Callon, and his face was intense. He was asking me questions, but they didn't make sense. I opened my mouth to speak, taking short shallow breaths.

"Are...they...gone?"

"Yes, sweetheart, they're gone." His jaw was so tight, the muscles in his neck were bulging, and his gaze remained focused.

"They acted like they knew me," I whispered.

"They're gone."

"The lights...the glittering lights. Did you see them? They were the same...the same as the cathedral...at the library...the same as..." Every last ounce of energy left me, and my eyes rolled shut.

Clank, clank, clank. It was the clang of objects hitting metal trays. I was so heavy, weighed down, but I was no longer in pain. I couldn't open my eyelids, no matter how hard I tried. I could only listen.

My right arm was lifted, gently laid on a cold surface and the whirling of what sounded like a medical machine began. A wet cloth touched my temple, and a tugging sensation came next. Warm hands exposed my ribs to the cool air and then lifted my shirt. The hands were gently probing, pushing. They stopped on my left side. I heard heavy footsteps and then something rolling across the floor followed by a hum. A light pressure behind my head brought me some comfort, as it was cradled in a large hand. My shoulders left the table as another set of hands tenderly wrapped a cloth around my chest, and then laid me back down. My right arm moved once again. There was the sound of Velcro being pulled apart and my arm was folded and placed in something. Low voices fill the room, but I couldn't distinguish them.

"Did you find anything else?" a concerned voice asked.

"I think we've found them all. She'll most likely have a concussion. Two of her left ribs are broken, but I didn't see any fragments puncturing her lungs. The brace will help support her elbow for now."

"We need to move her. I've given her enough to keep her sedated for a while." He sighed. "We don't have a choice." A tender touch to my forehead brushed my hair aside, and I drifted back out of consciousness.

I woke, this time to the sound of humming. I listened closely. It was the truck's engine—we were on the move. I was seated in an upright position; the cool air from the vent was blowing across my face. I inhaled deeply only to flinch, and my eyes remained closed.

"Cheyenne, are you in pain?" Colt asked as his arm moved behind me. I was resting against his shoulder.

205

"I'm okay," I whispered. I managed to force my eyes open. He was leaning over, intently studying my face. I was in the backseat. Daniel sat on the opposite side and squeezed my fingers.

"Colt, are you okay?" The last I'd seen him he was being attacked himself.

"I'm fine, sweetheart."

"Daniel," Callon called out, and I watched as Daniel touched his shoulder. Callon was now seated next to me; I blinked in amazement even though I knew he could Jump. Callon was now poised to take action. I couldn't focus clearly and closed my weary lids again. My head and elbow were starting to ache.

Gently taking my wrist in his fingers, Callon took my pulse. "Cheyenne," he said tenderly. "Are you in pain?" He lifted my shirt and touched my ribs, I gasped and he froze. He pulled his hand back slowly. "I can help you. Can you breathe okay? Is there any pain elsewhere?"

I didn't care about the pain; I wanted answers. "What happened, who were they?" I whispered.

His voice was apologetic, broken. "I'm so sorry..." He trailed off.

"The lights—did you see the glittering lights?" I needed them to know. I knew it was important somehow as I'd seen them several times now.

He was filled with agony, remorse. "I didn't—we shouldn't have put in this kind of danger."

"Did you...see...the lights?" It was getting hard to speak.

His fingers touched my cheek. "You need to rest. Don't talk. We're here now, and we're not leaving your side. I promise."

My chest was aching something awful, like it was being crushed. I was hurt, angry, and annoyed. I rose up, twisting to face him, and flipped my eyes open. "Just answer the damn question!" I sucked in a breath and collapsed in agony. My breathing was short and shallow as the pain increased, but I kept my gaze locked on his, blue on hazel. His eyes grew wide, and his lips twitched.

"Yes."

"Does it...have to do." I sucked in more oxygen. " With the...the attack?" I cringed as I endured the pressure on my chest.

"Yes."

"You will tell me about this later!" I closed my eyes again. Colt brushed my hair aside from my cheeks as I collapsed back into his shoulder; his fingers eventually came to rest on my thigh. A rustling sounded nearby.

I peeked from under heavy lids to see Callon had a needle in his fingers.

"No!" I snapped.

"Please, Cheyenne," Callon pleaded. "I can't watch you suffer."

"Cheyenne, listen to Callon. He just wants to help you." I looked up into Colt's sympathetic eyes. "Please. We'll tell you about the lights later."

I closed my eyes and realized they were truly just trying to help me. I nodded and felt the needle plunge into my shoulder as he injected the medicine. Turning my face into Colt's chest, I began to cry. Everything that had taken place, all the pain I had to endure came down to one large emotional overload. I couldn't control it any longer. Colt's long fingers cradled my cheek.

"Shh, it's alright, sweetheart. We're here; no one is going to hurt you now," he said softly.

Callon took my left hand in his and stroked it. "I'm so sorry, Cheyenne. I can't watch you suffer so much when I can help you.

Rest."

Within minutes my mind grew fogged, and the darkness wrapped around me, drowning out everything else.

CHAPTER 16

It was silent—only the sound of my heartbeat broke through the invisible barrier surrounding me. I was in pain; every labored breath felt like stakes piercing my lungs. My chest burned, and I wanted to scream. I realized I was lying down; I needed to sit up, to relieve the pressure.

I attempted to move my right arm, and it felt as if thousands of needles were pricking my elbow. I opened my eyes and looked down. There was a brace on it.

Confusion immediately set in. What happened?

I used my left arm and rose to a sitting position. I was in the back seat of the truck. I moved, and all at once everything began to spin. Closing my lids again in an attempt to stop the nausea, I knew it was no use. I was going to be sick.

I managed to throw the door open, and the screeching of the car alarm sent me even faster to my knees a few steps away. I vomited, which caused excruciating pain in my left side. I was barely balancing on my quivering left arm.

The alarm ceased, and a cool hand pulled my hair back and held it at my neck while another arm wrapped around my waist.

"I'm here, Cheyenne," Callon said warmly.

I was breathing in short, shallow pants, which made the pain more bearable. I remained arched over the ground, waiting for the spinning to stop.

"We're here," he repeated. "I won't leave you."

What was he talking about? Why did he keep saying he was here and wouldn't leave? Why did my side hurt, and why was my arm in a brace? All the confusion and fear was adding up quickly, and I began to cry. I knew who he was, but why was I hurting so much? What had happened? Callon said he'd protect me...but from what? What was so dangerous that I needed protecting from? I fought to remember, but my mind was so muddled.

Something bad had happened, I was sure of it, but I couldn't think what. Callon was here though. That meant it would be alright? Wouldn't it? I was moving towards the point of hyperventilating.

I tried to speak, the words barely forming on my lips. "Where's Colt...Daniel?"

I looked up and saw Callon's face riddled with anxiety as he helped me kneel upright again. I leaned into his shoulder, unable to hold myself up on my own.

"Cheyenne, calm down," he said as he rubbed my back. "It's going to be fine. Daniel and Colt are fine. I'm fine. You had an accident, and you're disoriented. I won't let go of you. Shh, now. Everything is going to be okay. We're all here for you."

A part of me didn't want to believe his kindness, but it was warm here, safe. Callon would never hurt me, and he said he'd protect me. Eventually the tears ceased, and my breathing returned to normal. I stared out into the woods. It looked unfamiliar and different, somehow. Slowly I looked up. Callon wiped the remaining tears from my cheek.

"Where are we?"

Callon sighed. "We had to leave for our packing trip early."

"Where are Colt and Daniel?"

Callon looked at me strangely before he answered.

"They're here. They're preparing the horses."

"Oh," my voice was quiet. "Are we in danger?"

"You don't need to worry about anything right now," Callon said. "We're not leaving you. You're safe. I promise."

He promised...then it couldn't be a lie. Callon never lied. But I still didn't understand. Was I sleeping? Was this some sort of weird dream?

Callon lifted me to my feet, helped me to the truck, and had me sit on the seat. I stared at him blankly.

"We're leaving soon. I need you to stay here in the truck. Don't move. We're right here, and we're not leaving you."

The only response I could give was a numb nod. Callon walked away, and I glanced to the sky. It was clear. The sun was bright as it rested directly above us. Sighing, I stared out into the woods. The pain was subsiding, and I didn't feel nauseous anymore.

Callon returned soon, helping me to the ground. He held onto my left elbow and placed his fingers around my waist as he led me behind the truck and trailer.

Colt and Daniel were waiting, holding the horses. We stopped in front of Colt, his eyes assessing me before he carefully took over as my support as Callon mounted. Then he lifted me up to Callon, hoisting me to sit in front of him. I knew I was in no condition to ride on my own. Colt squeezed my leg and walked off.

I winced slightly as Callon's arms moved around me to grasp the reins.

"I'm sorry," he whispered. I gripped his forearm as I instinctively leaned back. My mind was a swirling whirlwind of thoughts I couldn't grasp as we set out into the woods.

Daniel led while Colt remained at our side, continually glancing at Callon and then me. I knew they were talking. He wanted to make sure I was okay. Each stride Bo took was painful. Callon tried to ease the impact, but I still felt it. There was no way around it.

I closed my eyes as I concentrated on inhaling and exhaling. It was easier to breathe sitting up. My head began to wobble. Callon moved his fingers to my cheek and gently held it into the crook of his neck until the numbness settled in, and the warm blanket of sleep covered me.

When I woke, the position of the sun told me a long time had passed. We were still riding. I glanced to the side to see Colt's worried stare. He rode closer and touched my leg.

"We'll be stopping soon. You can rest more then." All I could do was nod.

Within half an hour we halted. We were deep in the woods. Pine trees stretched as far as the eye could see. Callon shifted, and I flinched. At once Colt was beside us, and he plucked me down into his arms.

My feet didn't touch the ground as he cradled me against his chest. One hand held me while his other cupped my cheek, and he kissed my forehead.

"We're staying here for the night," Colt informed me. "I won't let go of you. No one can harm you."

I stared into his loving eyes blankly. Why did they keep saying I was safe? No one would harm me? I didn't understand, but I felt safe in his arms. He always made me feel loved.

Camp was set up as I remained snuggled in his hold. A fire was built, the tent raised, and the horses tied down for the night. I began to shake as a chill swept over me. Quick glances were exchanged, and Callon appeared next to us with a blanket in hand. He inspected me first and then as he wrapped it around me, I noticed how much of a mess I was. I was still wearing the shorts and shirt from the day at the library, and they were soaked with dirt and blood.

What kind of accident did I have? I realized I hadn't spoken since we left the truck. I was so disoriented. I sighed as I gazed up into the night sky. I could see the stars dancing in the distance, and it made me think about how they twinkled. Everything snapped into place at once—clarity on the events leading up to this moment. I became rigid, and Colt tensed. Callon was at our side in an instant as he turned back.

"I know what happened." I stared at Callon coherently for the first time today.

"What happened, Cheyenne?" Colt asked warily.

"How this happened. The men, the glittering lights. The attack. All the morphine you've been pumping into me to help ease the pain must've numbed my thoughts. But I know what happened."

"We're here now, and no one is leaving. I promise never to leave you again. You're safe now." Colt lowered his cheek to my head.

We sat quietly as I watched Callon and Daniel move about the camp. Colt said he wasn't letting go, and he meant it. Callon brought water and informed me that if I didn't drink, he would put an IV in.

I drank.

Daniel warmed food over the fire. I didn't know how long I had been out of commission, but by the looks of things, it was at least a day and a half. They were all dressed differently, and I was the only one with the bloody clothes on. I could only imagine what the rest of me looked like; I'd have to work on it tomorrow.

Daniel neared. "I've made you some soup, Cheyenne. I know it's not the greatest, but it'll warm you." His dark blue eyes were so gloomy, that they made me feel guilty. I wasn't worth his sadness as they'd tried to protect me.

I touched his hand and squeezed. "Thank you, Daniel." I ate, even though I wasn't that hungry. I didn't want to give Callon the chance to sedate me. I understood his reasoning, but it wasn't worth having my mind trapped in a fog.

Tomorrow I would have to make them clarify the extent of my injuries. Right now, I was too tired to do much else but close my eyes. I leaned into Colt's shoulder. The warmth from the fire touched me, and I slipped into a sleepy abyss.

Warm knuckles were caressing my cheek, and I peered out from under heavy lashes. I was in the tent. I rolled my head slightly to see Colt's cool eyes staring down.

The sun was up, and the tent was filled with shadowed light; they had to be waiting for me to wake.

"How are you feeling today?" Colt asked softly.

I didn't respond right away, as I assessed my soreness.

"Better," I replied weakly. "How long have I been asleep?"

"Not long enough; it's still early. Do you need to rest more? We don't have to move quite yet."

I thought about his words. I wasn't hurting too much at the moment, but I also wasn't moving. I was in his arms, and I was warm and content. Despite my injuries, it wasn't all that bad a place to be, really.

I wanted to snuggle in longer, prolong the moment, but I knew we needed to get going.

"No, I'll be fine." I paused. "I don't think I can get up easily on my own, though. Do you mind?"

The tent wasn't big to begin with and with him standing up, that made it even smaller. Helping me stand, Colt left briefly. "Stay here for a minute, and I'll get your pack."

He returned with my pack and set it on the ground. He hesitated at the entrance. "Do you need help?"

I gave a faint smile. "I'll try to manage. How 'bout I call if I need help?"

Colt hesitated. "I'll be right outside. You can just whisper, and I'll come."

"Alright."

He exited and zipped the tent closed. I looked at the bag on the ground. This was not going to be fun.

I managed to remove my bloodied articles, but getting the clean clothes on was another issue. The jeans went on without a hitch even though I was bandaged across my chest and movement hurt. I managed to slide the cami over my head and knew I couldn't do much more.

"Colt," I called out and the zipper opened.

"You need help?" He glanced at me half dressed and stepped forward.

"Yes, I can't seem to get my shirt, belt, or boots on." His eyes were soft as he reached down and grabbed the cotton blouse in his hands. Gently turning me, he assisted me, placing my arms in the sleeves and then lovingly buttoned it.

I watched his fingers make light work of it, and sighed. I hated feeling so helpless. He reached for the belt, and lifted my shirt slightly as he pulled it through the loops on my jeans. He knelt down and patted his knee.

"Sit here and put your arm around my shoulder. I'll put your riding boots on." I sat, and he tugged my boots on easily. He didn't move right away as we stared at each other. I leaned in and kissed him on the corner of his mouth.

"Thank you," I whispered.

He smiled faintly and helped me stand upright. We exited the tent to find Callon and Daniel sitting by the fire.

Callon immediately approached and commenced with the twenty questions. "How did you sleep last night, Cheyenne?"

"Fine."

"Are you in pain right now?"

"No," I lied.

"I'm going to need to look at you before we leave this morning."

"Okay." I knew even if I said no it wouldn't matter.

"I want you to eat some breakfast first."

I nodded, and they had me sit on the log by the fire. Daniel placed a jacket over my shoulders and stayed close. They all hovered while I ate a granola bar and drank some water. I was grateful they didn't try to make me eat more. I wasn't sure I'd keep it down.

I glanced up at Callon, knowing he was waiting. "Can I wash up first?"

"I'll take you," Colt said. I followed him a few feet away where he held the canteen while I washed and brushed my teeth. He also assisted with pulling my hair back into a ponytail.

Once done, Callon had me sit near the fire again. Colt stood behind me and helped lift my shirts so Callon could look. Carefully, he began unwrapping the bandage. I glanced down to see the black, blue, and green marks. When Callon's fingers gently grazed over them, I flinched. His eyes locked on mine.

"Your hands are cold," I explained somewhat frantically. "I'm fine." I could tell Callon didn't buy it. He rewrapped the bandage, pulling my shirts down.

Colt left me sitting on the log. The trio began to tear down the camp. I could sense this wasn't the planned packing trip we had talked about previously. It seemed to me this was a get-out-of-danger flight.

I had brought this upon us. I was the one who insisted I was safe if they took me into town. I got cocky; overconfident that first, I could defend myself, and second, the danger they kept insisting was present didn't really exist. I was so wrong. It was there, just hidden, and I wasn't capable of protecting myself at all.

It wasn't long before we were ready to move on. The fire was doused, and I was told to go to Colt. Callon gave me a boost and Colt finished lifting me into the saddle.

Both were being as careful as possible, but there was just no way around it. I gasped as Colt's arm grazed my ribs.

Immediately he reacted. "I'm so sorry. Are you okay?"

I nodded. "I'll be fine. Just let me catch my breath." Callon stood at our side, his hand on my leg.

"Cheyenne, I can give you something," he offered again.

I cut him off in desperation. "No, I'll be fine." I watched as he and Colt exchanged thoughts telepathically, but he left without pressing the issue further. It was going to be a long ride today, I thought as I leaned into Colt's chest.

Daniel led the way and Mandi tagged along behind Charlie. It was a great distraction, since she was very mischievous. From time to time, she would get restless and snap at Charlie's hind legs. Every once in a while, he would suddenly turn his head and show his teeth. I could only imagine the antagonistic look in her eyes while she did it. She wanted to play; this was her standard behavior in the corral at the cabin. It made me smile.

It was quiet and peaceful, and everything was fresh and crisp. I wanted inhale the pine and wood scent, but I couldn't. Colt touched my hand, and I leaned my head into his neck. He sighed.

I stared out into the forest as we rode, and let my mind wander. I replayed what happened after I left the library.

"Colt, the men that attacked me, they said they were going to kill me." His arm tightened. "They acted as if they knew me, but I didn't know them." I hesitated. "Were they the same ones who killed my parents?"

He blew out a breath. "They didn't know who you were, at least not right away, but they knew you would become Timeless." He paused. "We don't think they're the ones who killed Gene and Alexis." His voice seemed strained, like he was holding in his anger. "You were an easy target."

"Did they know you?" I asked.

"Yes."

"Is that why they were waiting outside the truck at the bar that night?"

"They thought they could get you then. Since the Consilador clan has been acting in place of the ruling clan, and the three of us are of the Consilador's, we asked them to leave. Obviously they didn't listen."

"So that is part of ruling? Telling them to leave town?"

"Part of it. If they risk exposing our secret to humans, it needs to be dealt with. We can ask for their cooperation, but sometimes we have to resort to other means."

I pondered his words. I really didn't understand. Colt's clan was stepping up because the Kvech line, which I might be a part of, had supposedly ended. What would happen now? Would I be the one to assume rule? That thought didn't sit well with me at all. I barely knew I was different, wasn't even sure I really accepted the idea yet. I knew I couldn't change *what* I was—Timeless—but who was to say I couldn't change *who* I was. Would the journal provide me with the answers I was searching for?

And what did he mean by resorting to other means? I remembered hearing the screams when they came to rescue me. Colt said he would die for me, but...a queasiness rose in my stomach.

"Colt, what happened to them?"

"You don't need to worry anymore," his low voice replied near my ear. "You're safe here in my arms. I won't ever let you go."

"Colt?"

"Yes?"

"What happened?" I hesitated, not sure I really wanted to know his answer. "Did you kill them?" I closed my eyes as his pause became longer. He wasn't answering, and that wasn't a good sign. My stomach churned. I'd caused someone's death.

His lips moved to my ear. His words flowed out, proof of his deep emotions. "Cheyenne, I would never hurt you. You don't need to be afraid of me." His fingers caressed my cheek. "I would never harm you. Do you understand me? I love you."

"I'm not afraid of you. I just need to know if you killed them," I whispered.

A deep growl rose from the back of his throat, and his arms tightened. His anger rumbled in my ear, "I can't bear the thought of anyone harming you. When I saw you lying helpless on the ground, I wanted to kill them. I wanted them to pay for their actions. Callon's the only one who stopped me. They're alive, but not because of me." His arm tightened about me.

I raised my left arm just enough to touch his cheek.

"Thank you," I whispered as a small amount of relief washed over me.

"Don't thank me. I was the one who sent you off. The condition you're in now is because I didn't do what I said. I didn't protect you. I said I would, and yet I...I shouldn't ask, and I don't deserve your forgiveness, but can you ever forgive me?"

"Colt," I said, my voice hoarse. "You did protect me. What happened was just an accident. I was in the wrong place at the wrong time. There is no reason to ask for forgiveness. You came and found me, rescued me again. You have saved me more times than I deserve. I should be marked hazardous materials."

"You've only needed rescuing since you've been with us..." He trailed off.

"And I wouldn't change a thing," I reassured him. His arm remained tight around me, and we continued our ride in silence.

CHAPTER 17

We rode on. I was right; it was a long, long day, even riding in Colt's arms. As the day finally waned, we came upon a small stream running through a field filled with grasses. Callon dismounted and came to help me down. His eyes searched mine once again, watching for something. He'd been examining me all day, but I'd assumed it was because of my injuries. I was starting to feel uncomfortable under his gaze.

"How are you feeling?" he asked, concerned.

I'd gotten my confirmation—he was worried. "I'll live." It wasn't the answer he was looking for, but he didn't argue. He walked away. I neared the stream's edge, and they watered the horses. It felt good to stand; my legs were stiff from riding for so long. My chest wasn't hurting as bad. I was able to take deeper breaths, and my elbow seemed to ache less as well. My recovery seemed to be coming about more rapidly than in the past. Is this the way it would be when I was Timeless?

My mind was clearing, and I could focus. It was time to ask about the lights.

The field looked inviting with the sunshine, the grasses swaying in the light wind. It was as if they were dancing to their own music, a secret song. If I could've heard it, I knew it would be a favorite. I closed my eyes, imagining my hands playing the song over a piano.

Wild snorting brought me back. Mandi was restless. She wanted to run. Callon, Colt, and Daniel were standing to the side, contemplating something. They began removing the saddles. I jumped as Daniel suddenly appeared next to me.

"We're camping here for the night," he said as he chuckled at my reaction.

"Okay." He grinned and disappeared again. I remained where I was and continued to watch them unload the horses. Sam was released first, then Bo and Charlie. If a horse could show irritation, Mandi did. She was stomping her feet and shaking her head as they removed her gear. Once released, she darted out into the field where the others were grazing.

Her enthusiasm was fun to watch; she ran circles around the others, dancing and bucking. As she raced from one side of the field to the other, the others ignored her. Eventually she halted and began grazing.

The gurgling of the stream reminded me I needed to wash up. I could only imagine what my hair looked like. A good shampooing would work wonders. I turned and jumped once again as Colt startled me. He had appeared in front of me, smiling.

"Sorry, did I scare you?" he asked, not sounding sorry.

"Course not," I muttered, though it was obvious he had. He laughed.

"You hungry?" he asked.

"Yeah, but I was wondering if I could clean up first." I looked at the stream. "Is there a larger pool of water I could wash up in?" I glanced back, and spotted a new twinkle in his eye. That could only mean he was planning something.

"Sure. There's a small waterfall, it would take about ten minutes to walk to. How about that?"

"Well, I'd prefer a hot shower, but since there isn't one around, it'll have to do." I looked up. "I'm assuming you packed my swimsuit?"

He nodded with more enthusiasm than was necessary.

"Of course. You do realize that I can't leave you alone?"

Now I was the one smiling. "Yes, I did know that. I was actually counting on it." He arched his brows. "Don't get your hopes too high. I can't lift my arms, and I'll need help washing my hair."

He waggled his brows, and I laughed.

"I can help with that," he sounded positive.

"I'm sure you can."

Colt led me to where Daniel had erected my tent, and left me temporarily as he grabbed my pack from the pile and tossed it to the floor. He stepped out, zipping the tent closed. I knelt and dug through the pack and found the swimsuit along with a few other items I was grateful he'd packed.

Undressing wasn't as hard as dressing had been that morning. The clothes fell to the ground, and I kicked them to the side for now. I was able to get the suit on with shorts and a t-shirt, this was more than I'd done the day before. I grabbed the soap and shampoo from the bag and left the tent to find Colt waiting.

He had changed as well; his long-sleeved shirt was unbuttoned, exposing his chest. I blushed. He had a towel in hand. He took the soap and shampoo from me and slid them into his shorts pockets.

"Ready?"

223

With a flushed face, all I could do was nod. Glancing from the corner of my eyes, I saw his grin. It warmed me inside, putting me at ease. He took hold of my hand, and we started upstream.

We followed the bank, and I was glad I had thrown on my hiking boots. Colt had to help me over a number of fallen branches. I wasn't quite ready to tackle them on my own.

Just as he said, we made it upstream in about ten minutes. I stiffened. The stream back at camp was only a branch off the river. That gushing monster in front of me was part of the main river, not at all the gentle trickle I'd been expecting.

"This is bigger than I thought," I said. "I don't think I'm strong enough right now to hold myself upright for very long."

"That's what you've got me for," Colt beamed.

I hesitated as I sat to remove my boots. All I needed to do was lose my footing, and I would be swept downstream. I was growing tired of being battered and bruised.

Reluctantly, I removed my shirt and shorts, as Colt waited. We'd been around each other plenty, but usually with more clothing. I had seen him shirtless before, as we'd gone swimming plenty of times, but it seemed different now. I still didn't know how I felt—or did I? Did I love him as he loved me? I loved him, but our relationship had always been different...mere friendship was not what I was feeling now.

All my previous doubts were starting to seem insignificant. Was I allowing him to wear me down? I had no one else; was I supposed to be with him? Was his importance in my life part of what my parents wanted to tell me? Could I trust him and all his vows of love as being sincere?

"I can carry you." I snapped my head up, pulled from my

daydreaming. I was about to respond when he removed my arm brace and then gently lifted me from the ground. He was cautious not to touch any bruised areas.

He didn't have any difficulties wading through the waist-deep water as we neared the falls. He placed me on a section of rocks and stood in front of me. The water pressure was perfect; I didn't feel like I was about to get washed away. I leaned back further into the water. It was cold, but invigorating. It ran over my face and hair, and I lifted my neck to ensure my hair was saturated while my hands remained planted on the rock. I tilted my chin down, and met Colt's eyes. The look I found startled me. I wasn't expecting to see such yearning.

I turned away.

"Shampoo?" he asked over the sound of the falls.

I took a shaky breath and leaned forward. His gaze locked on mine as he began washing my hair. His fingers massaged the shampoo into my scalp, and my heart raced. It was weird; uncomfortable and dreamy all at the same time. I closed my eyes, and enjoyed the sensation of getting clean, fighting to remain calm.

Gently, he pushed my head back into the water, rinsing out the soap. He drew me closer and wiped the water from my face. He left his hands on the side of my neck, and the heat from his chest washed over me. My eyes remained closed as his lips caressed my cheek, jaw, and then moved to my lips. He lingered for a long time, planting soft wet kisses before he sighed and drew back. I sighed too.

I reached out and touched his arm.

"Thank you." He was close enough to hear and gave a contented smile.

"You're welcome."

Staring in to his eyes, losing myself in them, I allowed my good hand to move slowly up to his shoulder. My fingers traced the outline of his chest, and then moved down to the ripples of his stomach. They were trembling...I was trembling.

I glanced down. He was so perfect, like a flawless marble statue crafted by a master. I attempted to raise my right hand to his shoulder, but sharp pain caused me to lower it again. He lowered his left hand and placed it on the small of my back, and pulled me forward, sliding my legs to the side until I was fully resting against him. My open palm was on his muscular peck as his lips took mine.

It wasn't gentle, but firm and assured. He pressed harder, forcing my lips apart. There was a longing; it was as if he wanted every part of me right now. I had been so careful over the last few months, not allowing more than simple kisses. The only exception was on my birthday. It was as if he was making up for lost time, letting me know he wanted me in so many more ways than I could imagine. He wasn't giving up or giving in—and I didn't want anyone else. My desire was for him as well. I had been holding back, searching my heart.

I loved him. As much as I'd tried to deny it, I loved him as he loved me. I didn't want this moment, this kiss, to end. But the pain in my side was aching something awful. I had to pull away.

I attempted to draw my face back, but he held it in place firmly with his hand. I pushed on his chest with little effect. My left ribs were starting to really pinch, and it was becoming harder to catch my breath. He withdrew and began kissing my neck as I took smaller breaths, trying to relieve the building pain. His velvety lips moved to my jaw and traced my neck; tilting my head back they followed my collarbone. His fingers drifted from my neck to my side and pressed against the broken ribs.

"Ouch!"

"Oh, Cheyenne," he said with sympathy as he immediately drew back. "I'm so sorry."

I dropped my head to his shoulder, trying to catch my breath, knowing the kiss was worth the pain. "I know. I'm okay."

His fingers brushed my neck. "We should get you back. You need to eat, and it'll be getting dark soon."

"Just hold me," I whispered as I leaned forward again. He pulled me into his arms; the warmth from his touch filled me. I wrapped my left arm around his shoulder and neck as I nuzzled closer. His steamy lips placed kisses on my neck and shoulder as he waited for me to say I was ready to leave.

I didn't want to ever leave. At long last, my doubts were gone. I'd trust him with my life.

"We need to go." He lifted me in his arms and crossed the river. He set me on my feet, wrapped the towel around me and gently began drying me. I managed to slide my shorts on while he held my arm and assisted with the shirt. I sat on his knee and he placed my boots on.

Carefully he reattached the brace, and I watched as he placed his shirt back on, leaving it open, the water glistening on his chest. I blinked. I knew he could see my reaction, and he was making himself extra sexy on purpose.

Taking my hand in his, he led us back. The return trip seemed short, maybe because I wasn't done having time alone with him. I could have sat and stared at him for hours without getting bored. Let him hold me in his arms forever...

I sighed. I needed to let him know how I felt. He needed to hear those words from me. He needed to hear me say, "I love you."

I was so distracted that by the time we neared camp, I hadn't noticed Mandi closing the distance. She snorted in my ear, and I screamed.

Colt burst out laughing and Daniel joined in as he saw what happened. All I could do was smile and shake my head. Crazy Mandi. Even she thought it was funny to tease me.

Colt left me at my tent while I changed into jeans and a long-sleeved shirt. I purposely left the bandages off, it made it more comfortable to breathe. I was sure Callon would wrap me up again later, but he wasn't here now.

I zipped the tent and turned to find them sitting around the fire. Colt had changed into jeans, but his shirt was still unbuttoned. It was a distraction, and he knew it. He gave me a sly wink, and I blushed.

Fish was cooking over the flames; Callon and Daniel had been busy while we were gone. I wasn't much of a fish eater, but I was hungry, and it smelled good. Colt patted the log between him and Daniel, and I sat. Callon glanced up. "You hungry?"

"Famished," I replied eagerly and grinned.

"Good." He flipped a trout on a plate and handed it over. I willingly accepted. He was cooking quite a few. I ate faster than normal, picking bones out along the way. All in all, it was good, considering I typically hid the taste of fish with tartar sauce.

"Thanks," I said as Callon took my plate.

"Did you want another?"

"No, I'm good." Callon took the plates to the stream and washed them. Colt gently rubbed my back. As I waited for Callon to return, my mind mulled over the lights. I had some questions I wanted to ask. Callon came back and squatted near the fire, stoking it. My thumb passed over the etched ring on my index finger. Now was as good a time as any.

"Callon," I began. He didn't look up, but nodded once. "After my accident I told you about the lights I saw. What are they?"

Callon poked his stick a little too hard, and a stack of ash fell close to his foot.

"You need to stay away from them."

"Why?"

"Because they're dangerous." He added another log to the fire. It was growing dark.

"Why? I don't understand." Mr. Evasive had returned from his absence.

"You need to stay away from them, don't look at them."

"Don't look at them?"

He didn't reply.

Oh, no. *He who must be obeyed* was back in full swing too. My lip curled. Why couldn't he just tell me what they were? Annoyance rang through my response loud and clear, "Why do you do this to me?" My voice was beginning to rise. "Do you think I'm stupid? That my little brain can't handle it? You think I'd willingly run to danger because you said I shouldn't?"

He sighed, looking up at me. His lips were pressed in a thin line, and eyes were slightly narrowed, showing his annoyance. "I never said that, Cheyenne."

"You imply it," I hissed.

"If I don't tell you things," Callon replied calmly, "it's because you don't need to know right now. There's a lot going on in the

229

background that you aren't even aware of."

"Then tell me so I'll be aware!"

"It'll frighten you."

I didn't know if I was more vexed that he wasn't telling me, or the fact that he was so calm when he was doing so.

"*When* will I need to know, Callon?" I stood up. "When I accidentally run into the lights and find out what they really are?" My hands flayed in the air about me and a sharp pain rose, but I pushed it aside.

Colt reached out, but I jerked my arm away. I stormed over to the field where the horses were. I just needed to get away from Callon. I didn't understand his reasoning. I wasn't a child. He was acting like a bossy parent again.

If only I could figure out what the journal said. I bet my parents would have put warnings in there for me. They would have told me everything instead of the tiny bits of information I managed to scrounge from the trio.

I found a narrow section of the stream, and jumped across. Mandi saw and headed for me. She lowered her head, and I began scratching it, moving to her neck and brushing her mane back and forth. The rhythm was soothing, relaxing.

I knew I flew off the handle too easily with Callon. He was trying to protect me. He and the others had proved it after my attack. Like Callon said, there probably was a lot going on in the background that I wasn't even aware of. My fingers traced my ring again. I just wanted to understand. It was unfair. Everyone knew what was going on. It was hard being the only one who truly knew nothing. I didn't like relying on them for everything. It made me feel like such a burden.

230

"Cheyenne," a soft voice called out.

I didn't reply as I continued petting Mandi. I was still calming down; coming to grips with what I had to do. It was best if I didn't speak yet.

Callon stopped behind me.

"I know you're angry. I'm sorry. Look, I don't always tell you things because I don't want to scare you. I grew up knowing I was Timeless and even then it was overwhelming. I don't want you to run from us." He stepped closer, his words gentle. "I don't think you're stupid, never have. You figured out more than I thought you would. That's why I have to protect you, sometimes from yourself."

His fingers raked my hair, causing goose bumps to rise on my arms. "The last thing I would ever want to do is cause you more hurt. You've already been through so much in your short life."

He reached out and took my hand, turning me around. I couldn't look him in the eye. There were too many complicated feelings. I had no choice but to accept his explanations. Would my parents have hidden these things from me also? They had in essence—but would they still? Again I wondered how much they had been planning to reveal to me on the camping trip we never got to take.

I inhaled, composing myself once again.

"No, I'm the one who should be apologizing. I haven't been very pleasant tonight. You've cared for me, protected me, and watched over me, and I've been nothing but ungrateful." I lowered my head. "I'm sorry."

I felt like such a basket case. He drew me closer, looking me in the eyes briefly as an understanding seemed to pass between us. He knew I was letting go, trusting them. His arms wrapped around me tightly, but not snug enough to cause me pain. I rested my head into his chest as his fingers rubbed my back. This was his way to comfort me, to show me he could be gentle and understanding.

"There's so much I want to tell you, so much I want to share with you. In time you'll see; in time I'll keep no secrets from you. But I need you to trust me."

"I just want to understand. If I could just read the journal I'm sure I'd be better."

He kissed my head and warmth spread all the way down to my toes. "Just trust me right now," he asked. "We're going to get help on the journal, I promise."

I shivered. He felt it, and eyed me with concern. "We need to get you by the fire. You're cold."

If only he knew that the chill wasn't from the cold.

"Callon?"

"Yes?"

"I know we're running right now. Are we heading someplace special? Are we going to find your friend you talked about?"

"Yes."

"How long?"

"A couple days' ride."

"Are we being followed?"

He sighed.

"We were, but we've lost them for now. I need you to stay real close at all times."

"Is it the Sarac?" I whispered.

Callon didn't say anything, but his eyes told me I was right. We'd left quickly because we were being followed, but they could still find us. I didn't like it one bit.

Callon helped me back across the stream to the fire. Colt's jaw was tight as he rose, his cool blue eyes stressed. He glanced at Callon and nodded. Colt's face relaxed slightly as I neared. I rolled my eyes. They were going to drive me nuts with the telepathy.

"Speak out loud, please," I demanded, crossing my arms. Colt grinned as his arm slid around my shoulder, and we sat down. I sighed and snuggled in. I was becoming sleepy as I listened to them talk about which direction to head tomorrow.

I sank lower into Colt, drifting off as the fire and his touch warmed me. It was easier to breathe, my chest didn't ache anymore, and I could lie down without it being painful.

Soon it became quiet, and I let the heaviness take over, but not before something inside me stirred. For the briefest moment, a slight ache rippled through me, and a horrible dread came over me, but the weariness of sleep soon pushed it back.

CHAPTER 18

A faint rustling woke me, and I opened my eyes to see it was still dark. Colt was lying next to me in the tent, and I was still in his arms, but facing away. Callon was resting in front of me, face to face, but his eyes were closed. The tent was small, but it seemed more than a coincidence that he was this close. A feeling of impending danger swept over me. I elevated my head slightly; Daniel was on the other side of Callon. Something was going on.

The noise outside the tent made me glance toward the opening. It was closer this time. Lights were flickering. Why would they have a fire going if they were in here with me? Who was out there, and why weren't they checking it out?

I was about to ask Colt when his arms tightened, and his long leg shifted over mine. He was bracing for something. What?

My heart began to pound. Callon's eyes popped open. He was focused. I parted my lips to speak, but he pressed a finger to my lips. Movement at the tent door made me glance back again. The lights were getting brighter. They were dancing. Were these the same lights from before? If so, why were we lying here? Why weren't we moving?

Shouldn't we be trying to get away?

Panic set in, and my breathing came in shallow gasps, but Callon's fingers were still over my lips.

"Cheyenne," he mouthed. "Close your eyes. Don't look at the lights. Colt won't let go of you. Just keep your eyes closed." He was trying to reassure me, but it was too late. I understood what he'd said, but I couldn't close my eyes. I didn't know if it was from panic, fear or...

The lights were in the tent now. They were brighter, more beautiful than I could imagine. My body began to tremble. Colt's hold tightened, almost painful.

Callon didn't speak, but his eyes showed me everything. I narrowed mine because of the brightness filling the tent, but instead of closing them, I watched in wonder. I couldn't break my gaze from them. The reflections were dancing off Callon's face. They began to cast shadows on the walls of the tent. It was as if a thousand twinkle lights were dancing in the night just for me.

The lights began to cluster together, becoming more frenzied. With each progression they jerked back and forth, brightening and moving closer.

I wanted to reach out and touch them, experience their sensation on my skin. They were mesmerizing. They fell upon me, and it was soft like whispering kisses. But soon it changed to a pinch, then a sting. In a matter of moments, the stinging sensation was all over my body.

Every inch of my skin was on fire. I was being yanked, tugged in two different directions. I wasn't the one moving. I looked down on my body from above. I was thrashing in Colt's arms! A force was attempting to drag me away, and there was nothing I could do.

Colt was holding on, desperately trying not to crush me. Callon was in full panic. His hands were holding my cheeks. He was screaming at me to close my eyes. My body didn't respond. In sheer desperation, I watched him lunge his lips to mine.

He was kissing me; fervently kissing me, the way he said he'd wanted to that day in the meadow.

My eyes closed, and I felt his warm lips on mine, pushing, parting, pressing me closer. My heart burned, and I began to respond.

The moment Callon sensed me, he drew himself away. His fingers moved to my temples, placing his thumbs over my eyes.

"Don't open your eyes."

I stopped thrashing, but then the shaking began. I felt clammy and ill. What had just happened?

Callon let go, and Colt flipped me around so my face was now pressed against his chest. I didn't open my eyes. I was afraid of what I would see. My mind was wildly trying to grasp what had taken place. Fear seized my limbs, and I whimpered.

Callon, however, was not sympathetic. "You stupid girl!" he roared. "I told you to close your eyes! You just don't get it, do you? We work so hard to keep you safe, and you can't follow a simple instruction!"

I went from terror to anger in an instant. What right did he have to yell at me? I pushed with everything I had against Colt's chest to flip around and answer.

"Damn me!?" I screeched. "I asked you about the lights. I practically begged you to tell me about them, but all you could say was that it wasn't important for me to know!" I was shaking, this time with fury. "Do you not trust me? Is that it? You think I'm just going to run off to the Sarac?"

Colt suddenly spoke up.

"Cheyenne, Callon's right. You need to start listening to us. I almost crushed you..."

"Shut up, Colt!"

I attempted to get up, but he was holding tight. He grasped my wrists and pinned them to my side. If fire could have been thrown from my stare, Callon would have burned before me, and I wouldn't have felt the slightest bit of remorse.

"Cheyenne, calm down!" Colt snapped, his deep voice rumbling in my ears. He shoved me harshly against his chest. "We don't have time to argue with you. You're not going to win this one. We need to get moving before they come back. It's only a matter of time before they find us again."

He paused, inhaling deeply. In a softer tone he added, "I can't have you wandering off. You need to stay put so we can pack. Are you going to listen to me?"

I didn't reply, too angry to form words. Callon looked over my shoulder at Colt. In the next second Colt was on his feet, taking me with him. I was like a rag doll under his grasp as he ripped through the tent opening; my feet didn't touch the ground.

"Colt, let GO!"

In response he pinned my arms down with one hand as he thrust me to his side. I couldn't move, his vice-like grip hurt my ribs, but my anger numbed the pain. Damn him if he thought he could handle me this way!

In no time, the horses were saddled and camp torn down. The tension was thick between us, but I didn't care. I wanted nothing more to do with them.

When Callon and Daniel were finished, Colt gruffly hauled me to Sam. He shoved me into Callon's waiting hands. I stumbled into him, while Colt mounted. Callon was no gentler as he threw me up to Colt. Colt caught me mid-air and set me in the saddle before him. He jerked his arm around the front to grab the reins and hit my injured ribs. A bolt of pain lanced up my side, and I gasped. He said nothing.

It was still dark, but they lost no time and entered into a full gallop, weaving in and out of the trees.

How dare they treat me like this! Like I would run away. Where would I go? We were out in the middle of nowhere. They constantly lectured me to trust them, but they wouldn't even try to do the same! They only gave me information when it suited them.

I truly was a prisoner.

I sat in the saddle as rigid as possible; I wanted to keep my distance from Colt. Colt raised his arm higher and pushed me back into his chest. I knew it was easier to ride sitting back in the saddle, but I didn't care. I wasn't about to make anything easy for him right now. I sat forward again only to have his arm pin me back down.

"Damn it, Cheyenne. Knock it off! I don't want to hurt you."

"You should have thought of that earlier, Colt," I snapped back.

"If you would learn to control your temper, it would make it easier," he said through gritted teeth.

"If you would tell me of the dangers instead of leaving me in the dark, I wouldn't lose my temper!"

He didn't reply, and I said nothing more. I eyed Callon's pack. I wasn't even allowed to carry the journal myself. Were they afraid I'd run off with the one document I couldn't even read? I remained against his chest, stewing about what just took place, the friction from the movement gnawing at my nerves. I didn't think I was asking for much.

Instead of just saying, "Don't go near the lights, or don't look at them," he could have said, "Don't go near the lights. They'll try and rip your soul apart! It'll scare the crap out of you, and we may not be able to stop them!"

That wasn't hard. I would've got the message...I think.

Then again, I wasn't fond of being told what to do by *he who must be obeyed*. That day he'd warned me not to try to leave, I still did it. I placed myself in danger by leaving for the bank. I also couldn't be patient for their return to get into my Jeep.

Would I have been any different about this? Would I have believed what they told me, or would I have dared to try and find out on my own?

No, it didn't matter. If they'd been honest from the beginning, I could've gone to the bank with them, and they would've trusted me with the keys to the Jeep. I wasn't the one to blame here.

We had been riding for hours when we finally began to slow. We were on a ravine overlooking a river, carefully making our way down. We stopped at the water's edge to allow the horses to rest and drink before crossing.

Colt hoisted me from the saddle and I slipped, dropping to the ground and smacking my backside in the process. Dismounting himself, he reached out and jolted me to my feet. There was no tenderness, and his jaw was tight and brow furrowed as he walked away. He wouldn't even make eye contact with me.

I rubbed my side. I knew he had been scared and was reacting with anger. But it spooked me. I'd never seen him like this before. I expected it from Callon, but not Colt. He had always been loving, caring, and gentle.

He walked to Daniel, spoke a few words, and grabbed a canteen. Neither of us had spoken since the incident. Was he really mad at me? I honestly wasn't trying to be a problem. I didn't like it when we were like this—the quietness was unnerving.

My words had been angry, had flowed from my mouth without thought to the consequences. I never wanted anything to come between us. Over the last few months, I had been very careful about my words and actions, but last night at the waterfall something changed. I had been fighting it, but knew deep down I loved him. He needed to know. I had promised myself I would never have regrets as I did with my parents. I would tell the people I loved how I felt about them and often. I could never live with that crushing blow again— ever.

I was going to have to speak first. I knew he saw the solemn look in my eyes as he neared with the canteen. From his expression, I wasn't sure if he was going to throw it or hand it to me. He was upset, the cool distance of his gaze told me—somehow I'd crossed the line.

I hesitated as he stretched out his hand. He turned to leave, but I quickly latched my fingers around his wrist. He didn't pull away, but he didn't turn to face me either.

"Colt," I said his name. He didn't respond. "Colt, I'm sorry. I had no excuse to act the way I did. You risked your life to keep me safe. I'll trust you." This was the first time I'd said it out loud—I'd finally come to the point that I needed to. The library incident wouldn't have happened if I'd just listened to Callon in the first place and not begged to go into town. I would have to accept his judgments more readily.

I hesitated and my voice cracked. I wanted to say it. My lower lip trembled, and my pulse began to race.

"I—I love you." I inhaled a shaky breath. I'd done it; I'd declared my love for him, the love that he wanted in return. I was offering it to him, and praying he would accept it.

We stood in silence; he didn't move. He said nothing. I felt the tears welling up. I lowered my head, dropped his hand, and closed my eyes. I had created this mess; I would have to deal with the consequences. I buried my face in my hands, ashamed.

"Did you mean that?" he suddenly asked.

Startled, I looked up into his face. His jaw was still tight.

"Yes."

"Did you mean what you said?"

"Yes, I love you."

"You love me the way I love you?" he said in an accusing tone.

"Yes," I whispered. "With every breath I take."

"What about Callon?"

"I love you, Colt."

I couldn't hold back the tears any longer. Still inches in front of me, he didn't move, didn't raise a hand, didn't say anything more. I lowered my head and turned, walking away. I was crushed. I hadn't expected this reaction. He didn't try and stop me as I went to the river's edge.

I stared out into the water. It wasn't quiet or peaceful. It seemed annoyed that the rocks were blocking its path downstream. It would rise and fall and crash with rage against the boulders, sending a fury of water upwards.

My body began to ache; a feverish chill traced my spine. What was happening to me? Why had Colt's feelings suddenly changed?

241

After everything we'd been through, two years of pining for me, and all it took was a few words in anger to end it all?

One of them called my name, and I turned to see they were waiting on me to leave. I forced myself to focus, but found it difficult. Colt had always been my strength; my security. Who could I turn to now that he wasn't there for me?

I needed to get a grip. I could do this—I had to do this.

I kept my eyes down and headed straight for Mandi. I wasn't about to ride with anyone. I knew they were staring at me, contemplating, but they kept quiet.

I mounted and dug my heel into Mandi's side. We began moving toward the water. I was to cross first. Mandi was eager; she'd been waiting to be let loose.

Wading through the water, my legs soon became drenched. I didn't care; nothing seemed to matter right now. Mandi was strong; it took little effort for her to move. We crossed the steep embankment, and I kept her moving. I knew Daniel would pass to lead. I looked at no one; it was too painful.

I wallowed in my sorrows as we rode. Colt had rejected me. I opened my heart like he wanted, and he rejected me. The night before was so different...he was so different. I saw the longing; I thought I saw what he wanted. But I gave him my heart, and he threw it aside. He left it at the riverbank...alone.

Alone like when my parents died—but he'd been the one to bring me through. If he hadn't been there... Too many memories began to flood my mind, and I choked back a sob.

Dusk was arriving, and no one had spoken a word since we left the river. Every muscle in my body was begging for us to halt, but we didn't. I was not going to be the reason for stopping; I would keep going as long as they did. The chill from the darkening sky raked me, especially since my pants had never fully dried from the river.

The cooling breeze sent goose bumps across my neck. I had long sleeves on, but it wasn't enough. The packs were on the other three horses, and my jacket was in one of them, but there was no way I was going to ask for anything. They'd hear it in my voice, the uncertainty, the trembling. My stomach growled. I hadn't eaten or drank since the night before. We left in a hurry this morning and no one, not even myself, thought about food until now. I realized how much had I come to rely on them for everything. I would have to do more to take care of myself.

We rode in a tighter formation; Callon and Colt flanked my sides as darkness enveloped the forest around us. Colt was close, but seemed so far away. Hours passed, and I kept my head low, staring at Mandi's mane. Soon I began to shiver. It was more than the night that was chilling me. I wasn't feeling well. Callon touched my shoulder as he drew a jacket over me. I couldn't make it much longer.

I knew it had to be the wee hours of the morning when I finally broke.

"I'm done," I croaked. "If you wanted to defeat me, you've won. If you wanted me broken, I'm broken in more ways than you know." I grimaced, trying to hold back the tears. "If you want my blind trust, you have it. I will no longer be a problem. I'm truly sorry for any trouble I've caused...for the burden you've had to bear because I'm with you."

I'm not sure what I expected to happen with my confession. I had hoped Colt would draw me into his arms and tell me that all was forgiven and that he loved me too. That he was still my rock, my strength. But of course, nothing happened. Nothing had changed.

I shook my head. This wasn't just because of my temper. It was more like Colt was repulsed by the thought of me. But why?

It didn't matter anymore. The damage had been done. There was another slash, another piece of my heart breaking off. This was far worse than when my parents died. Maybe because this time I had no one else to turn to. Shards had ruptured when I found out I wasn't who I thought I was, that my whole life had been a lie. When I thought Colt was only there to protect me, not because he loved me. Those had slowly healed, but this cut so much deeper. I placed my heart out in the open, and he rejected it...he rejected me.

It was Callon who came, wrapped his arms around me, and slid me off Mandi onto his saddle. I didn't bother to swing my legs over. He just held me as we rode. Somehow his touch didn't reach me like before. I was so numb from the day's events that I couldn't focus clearly.

We didn't speak; he kept his arm just firm enough that I didn't fall. My head was already lowered; I lay it into his shoulder and closed my eyes. I was finished, done. I continued to shiver. I tried to sleep, but sleep wouldn't find me. Callon didn't rub my back as he'd done in the past to comfort me. Did he feel I was beyond comforting? Or did he just not care anymore? Maybe I'd imagined all those feelings I'd thought I'd seen...

Hours passed, and the sun started to appear over the horizon. Through my lashes I saw Colt riding nearby, staring straight ahead. After all these years together, now I was seeing a different man. A part of him he'd never shown to me. I really didn't know him after all.

I opened my eyes further, and noticed that we were nearing the edge of the forest. As we crested the ridge, a large valley emerged. It was expansive, with a large river running through it. Hundreds of acres of pasture lay before us. We stopped at the edge, and the others surveyed it before continuing on.

In the distance, I saw a small billowing pillar of smoke. This had to be what they were searching for, the friend Callon said we needed to find.

Callon lowered his head, and his eyes met mine in concern. I was sure I looked horrendous. I hadn't slept in over thirty-six hours, and I felt weak and sick. I attempted to return the smile, but my lips refused to cooperate. I couldn't blame them; I didn't feel like smiling myself. He adjusted me so I was upright, and we rode on, his long fingers holding the reins.

I was beyond hungry, and dehydration was setting in. The familiar pain in my skull was becoming overwhelming, and I groaned. The awful headache was returning. The last one was when I'd first met Callon at the cathedral. Even after all this time, he was just the same as that day; handsome, with brown locks and mesmerizing eyes. I had been avoiding the latter, trying not to hurt Colt. Obviously, I was no longer what Colt wanted.

The distance between the horses was growing. Daniel and Colt were riding ahead, but the valley had also opened up. At least if danger was near, they would see it approaching.

"Callon," I said weakly.

"Yes." The warmth in his voice told me he wasn't angry. Not anymore.

"What happened in the tent with the lights? What were they?"

His arms tensed.

"Sarac scouts."

"How did they do that with the lights? They're so beautiful, mesmerizing, almost hypnotic. I really did try, but I couldn't look away. Why didn't they affect you in the same way?"

Callon sighed.

"They were ghosting. The Sarac can physically separate from their bodies. They use their powers to transport their spirit to another location. It makes them extremely dangerous."

"But how were you able to look at them and not be affected?"

"Because I'm Timeless. It doesn't affect us in the same way."

I rubbed my hand over my arms, recalling the horrible sensation in the tent.

"It was awful," I said, "like I was being stung and pulled away. I was watching you from above my body. How could they do that?"

"Cheyenne, because you're still human, it's easy for them to enter your mind by seducing you with the lights. They ghost you to their physical body, and when you're there your body follows. This is why they're so dangerous. Your body and soul cannot be separated for long, but as Timeless they have learned to defy this rule."

"So because I looked at the lights, they were able to seduce me?"

"Yes."

"Why couldn't you have just told me this before?"

He cleared his throat.

"I told you, I didn't want to scare you. You've barely recovered from your attack, and I was concerned about your health. We would have protected you, Cheyenne. This is why I keep asking you to trust me."

I understood now, but why couldn't he have said this before? Had he planned this to push me away from Colt? It brought up another thought.

"So, why did they stop when you kissed me?" There was no hiding the fact that he had in fact kissed me.

He kept a level gaze, not a trace of embarrassment or self-consciousness on his face.

"It brought you back to the moment. You shut your eyes and concentrated on what was happening right then."

This was slowly making sense, as much sense as my aching head would allow. "So if I had just kept my eyes closed, then what would have happened?"

"Colt had you firmly in his grasp. You probably would have experienced some tugging or pulling, but they wouldn't have been able to take you the way they tried."

"But why can't they do this to you?" I knew I had already asked a similar question, but Mr. Evasive was in a talking mood, and I wanted to push him as far as I could.

"We've trained our minds over the years not to allow them to take hold. From time to time, they do succeed, but only the strongest of their kind can make it happen." He paused. "But they didn't want us, Cheyenne. They wanted you. I don't think they know who you are yet, or they wouldn't have stopped until they accomplished it."

"Then why didn't we run? Why were we just waiting for them?"

He sighed heavily.

"You were sleeping, and they were too close by the time they were spotted. It was safer to just surround you rather than run."

My chest tightened. If they wanted me, what would they have done to me? Kill me like those men had threatened? Or something worse? If Callon's kiss hadn't brought me back...

His kiss. It hadn't been a simple one to bring me back to the moment. It was something more, and Colt witnessed it. That one

247

kiss—it changed everything. I was sure of it. Was he telling Colt to stay away?

"Callon," I hesitated. "Why is Colt so angry with me?"

"He's not angry with you, sweetheart."

Sweetheart? This was twice now he'd called me that.

"Then why is he acting like this?" My voice quivered. "He hasn't even looked at me since the river." The tears were building, and I lowered my head. I couldn't cry right now. It would only cause my head to hurt more. "I feel like I'm not whole anymore. I don't know what else I can give him."

His arm tightened slightly, and his head lowered.

"I'm sorry, Cheyenne. Your heart can heal in other ways..."

I didn't catch the rest of what he was saying. All of a sudden, the pain in my head increased. Then I was very hot, as if a fire were raging from within.

"Callon?" I listened for his response, but all I heard was silence. I could see his hands on the reins; I could feel his chest on my back, but my ears caught no sound. Droplets of sweat began to roll down my neck, and the pressure in my chest and head doubled. "Callon? Callon! What's happening?"

I glanced up, Daniel and Colt were galloping back to us; they were further away than I remembered. Blurry spots began to form in my vision. I frantically twisted my head. Callon's mouth was moving; alarm was on his face, but nothing...I could hear nothing.

I turned back. Colt was in front of me, but I could barely make out his silhouette. A silvery cloud was forming over my eyes as the perspiration dripped from my forehead. I couldn't hide my fear. I screamed.

"Callon!"

Frantically I grasped for my jacket, I was roasting. I needed it off now. They ripped it off me as my fingers grasped the side of my temples. I could only imagine how frantic I looked.

Two strong hands lifted me from the saddle, resting me like a small child against a broad chest. I knew it was Colt. One arm secured my back and shoulders as he pressed me forward. His lips were near my ear; his chest rose and fell with each tense breath.

Hoof beats pounding the ground vibrated up my spine into my skull. With each gallop, a new lightning bolt of pain struck through me. As much as I was trying to keep control, the horror of the situation was taking its toll. Each breath was labored, and each lungful of air I sucked in burned. I began to shake violently.

Colt's fingers moved to my neck, attempting to brace me further. I was shaking too hard. I closed my eyes. I wanted to be back in his arms, but not this way. Not because I was in pain. I didn't want his pity; I wanted his love. Now I would never know what the anger was about. He would never tell me.

Numbness filled my being, and I no longer knew what was happening. Was I dreaming?

Reality flooded back when we abruptly halted. I was plastered to Colt's chest, but we weren't riding anymore. With my legs flung to the side, he was running. We stopped, and I was laid on a cold, hard surface. A multitude of hands were touching me. I didn't know whose. My pulse was taken, another hand touched my forehead, and my eyelids were pried open only to fall shut again.

I was floating, floating in Colt's arms, and the scent of pine was in the air. Sweat was rolling off me; my clothing was soaked with it. I tensed and let out a small screech as a blast of icy-cold water covered me. I reacted in fear, flailing my arms, trying to reach the surface.

Two large hands grasped my wrists as we came out of the water, and I gasped for air. I began coughing and hacking, removing the water from my mouth and nose—it burned. Thrust up against Colt's chest, he held me tightly, keeping me submerged up to my neck. I eventually stopped struggling and felt the chilly water wash over me.

Opening my eyes, the silvery cloud once more obscured my vision. At least it wasn't black anymore. Lifting my hands, I touched Colt's face. I knew I couldn't see him, but I was looking at his image in my mind. I pictured him smiling, happy, and not angry. I wanted to see the longing in his eyes again, but what kept coming up was the last picture of rage...his steely stare cutting through me. I knew I couldn't hear him, but I began to mumble, over and over again.

"Colt, I'm sorry. I'm so sorry. Please forgive me, I can't have you angry with me. I'm sorry."

I couldn't say "I love you"; I couldn't handle the rejection again. A tender warm kiss touched my forehead. A violent tremor raked my body, and I fell limp. He pushed me through the water; it dripped off as he was running again. He halted abruptly, and a cold hard surface was beneath me again. Smaller, delicate fingers brushed my cheek; it was gentle—a woman.

A tugging sensation was at my feet. She was removing my boots and socks. She was changing me into dry clothes. Once her task was complete, various hands worked over my body again. My arm was extended, and I felt a small prick. I was sure it was an IV. I was floating once more, but the movement was slower, deliberate.

I landed on something soft and warm, a sheet was draped over. Heaviness began to press me down, deeper and deeper until I felt nothing more. No more shaking, no more pain, no more sight, and no more sounds. Darkness surrounded me, but I was too exhausted to fight anymore, so I let it wrap me up and dropped into slumber.

CHAPTER 19

A cool hand touched my cheek; small slender fingers brushed the hair from my forehead, tucking it behind my ear. My eyes fluttered open. I was still surrounded by darkness, but it wasn't the same. My vision adjusted, and I could make out a petite silhouette sitting on the bed as the moonlight drifted over her face. She raised her hand, dabbing the wet cloth across my forehead.

She smiled.

"Cheyenne," her voice was soft, sweet, and angelic. I could hear it; I could hear again! I smiled in return.

"Boys!" Her gaze remained focused on mine. "Cheyenne, I'm Lilly. We're here to help you, honey. You don't need to be afraid." She pushed her hair behind her ear. "You gave us a good scare when you arrived. I can't say I've ever seen anyone look quite as bad." Her smile deepened as we heard the heavy footsteps thunder down the hall. "You're going to be just fine. Your friends are here—they wouldn't go very far. I had to all but kick them out several times. You were so restless."

Callon, Colt, Daniel, and a short, stocky man I hadn't seen before entered the small room. The man flicked the light on in the corner as they neared. My eyelids were still heavy, and I squinted as the light broke the darkness. Colt sat on the edge of the bed. Callon hovered behind him as Daniel stood to the side.

Lilly's steel blue eyes remained locked on mine. I listened to her voice—almost like a melody in its own right. "Her fever is down, and I know she can see because she smiled." Her fingers touched my forehead. "She can hear also; her head turned when you came down the hall. You sounded like a herd of elephants."

Shifting slightly, her coal black hair cascaded down her tiny frame as she extended her hand.

"Dex, why don't you come over here so she can meet you?" The man I didn't recognize slowly approached, grasping her hand. His weathered skin and brown hair immediately made him seem enduring. He smiled and his brown eyes twinkled as he turned his attention to me.

"Cheyenne, honey, this is my husband, Dex. We're friends of the boys. Dex is going to try and help you out with your journal."

He was definitely older than Callon, maybe in his late thirties, which meant he had to have been around a long time, if the one hundred to one theory was anything to go by.

"Hello, Cheyenne." His deep voice was friendly. His gaze met mine; he seemed genuine, knowledgeable. Stepping closer, his rough fingers touched my arm. I recognized his touch; he was the one who had placed the IV.

"You helped them," I said with a cracked voice.

"Yes, I did." He sighed. "I'm sorry I didn't get to meet you differently."

I blinked, and my vision started to sharpen. I glanced back at

253

Lilly; she was so beautiful. Her features were so fine and perfect. Everything about her screamed feminine. It would be nice to have a woman other than myself around.

Colt moved, and I turned to him. It was different now; his face cold, unresponsive. What had I done that was so awful to have him reject me like this? My heart ached. I blinked slowly. My eyelids were becoming weighed down again. I was fighting to keep them open.

"Let her get some sleep." Lilly chased them out. "She's been through a lot in the last week. You need to take better care of her." Her tone turned reprimanding. "She can't keep up with you yet; she's not Timeless. I saw all those bruises on her ribs. If you break her, we may not be able to put her back together. You just keep that in mind. There is something much bigger at stake here."

My blinks were longer, closer together. I was trying to make sense of the conversation, but the words were fading to a dull buzzing. Daniel nodded, though he still looked unsure as he departed. Callon hesitated. He crossed his arms as his warm eyes filled with worry. Lilly touched his arm.

"Callon," she said. "You need to leave. She's not going anywhere. I'll be right here with her. You have other things to work on right now."

He still didn't move.

"You can come back later. I'll call if anything changes." Callon shifted in his stance, wavering, and then reluctantly left the room.

Colt didn't move, a flicker of turmoil rolled over his face.

"Colt," Lilly said. "I'll be here. I won't leave. I'll call you back when she's stirring."

I tried to speak, but the sound just wouldn't emerge.

"I'm sorry," I mouthed silently. He turned away.

What was going on with us? Why was he still pushing me away? My eyes could remain open no longer. I slipped into the restless darkness.

When I woke again, deep voices were talking nearby. I could hear them, but I couldn't open my weighted lids. A chair squeaked, and fingers touched my arm, stroking it.

"She seems to be doing better." Callon said.

Callon was touching me.

"Yes. We should be able to stop the medication tonight," Dex replied. There was a long pause before he spoke again. "There is a lot we need to discuss, the journal being one of them."

"I know," Callon replied.

"You've heard about the disturbances up north?" Dex's voice held concern.

"I know about them."

"You can't leave now. You need to stay here with her."

"I know that, but I have a responsibility as a ruler. We both know what I have to do." I heard him shift in his seat.

"You have a responsibility as head of the Consilador clan, but your first duty is with her." Dex hesitated. "I saw her rings, Callon."

"I know." Callon sighed. "Brogan is still up north?"

"Yes. I was going to suggest you contact him. The Laundess clan would be a wise choice to handle this. There are others who are willing to step up and assist as necessary. You know this."

Callon grasped my fingers and cupped my palm to his cheek. His skin was rough; he hadn't shaved in a while.

"I've wanted to keep her identity secret. If others discovered that the Kvech line wasn't gone, I'm not sure what would happen. I just don't want word to get out to the wrong parties. You know we have traitors among us, some not yet revealed. I'm not sure it's worth the risk yet."

"You know what you need to do," Dex replied. His tone was somehow different.

Callon's jaw tightened under my palm.

"Don't lecture me about what I already know, Dex." His voice was rough. "It's not that simple."

"I can see that. Just don't delay it much longer. It will only make it worse. Lilly hasn't said anything yet, but you and I know she'll corner you. This is bigger than all of us."

Callon lowered my hand and squeezed it. "I know, Dex. Believe me, I know," he whispered.

There were no more responses, so I drifted off.

Light was barely creeping through the windows when I opened my weary lids again. The room was small and bright. The pale blue paint on the walls was soothing. A large chest of drawers was nestled in the corner, along with the armchair Callon must have sat in. I was snuggled in a bed in the center of the room.

Turning my head towards the sunshine, I saw two large picture windows. They were overlooking an awakening forest; large pine trees dotted the landscape. Birds chirped outside my cracked window. It made me realize just how much I'd taken for granted. My sight, my hearing, Colt's feelings about me...

I stretched my arms above my head. Something pulled on my arm, and I looked to my elbow. The IV was still attached. I could leave it in, but I did hear them say they would end the medication. I pulled it out, wincing.

Surprisingly, only a small trickle of blood dripped from the vein. In the past it'd dribble down my arm. It didn't hurt either, and I could flex my arm almost instantly. Was I transforming already?

I pushed up to a sitting position; my right elbow didn't hurt anymore, either. I drew the covers aside, swung my feet to the cold wood flooring and stood up. I waited for the pain to come, but it didn't. No dizziness, either. My recovery time was improving rapidly, which was the only good thing about today. My eyes watered at the thought of Colt.

I kept my chin down as I assessed what I was wearing, a cotton tank and shorts. I was decent and could walk around. It was a good thing; I quickly realized just how badly I had to pee. I forced my weak legs to move. It was hard to keep my balance at first—I must've been asleep for a long while.

The door was open, and I stepped into the hall. I was relieved to see the bathroom a few steps away. I made a quick retreat and closed the door.

The tiles were cool beneath my toes; the apparent luxury of the fixtures was a surprise. I wouldn't have expected the opulence in such a remote location. I moved forward, and my fingers glided across the granite countertops. I glanced at the shower and realized it could fit at least three people in at once, and spray nozzles were everywhere. Even the toilet appeared to be imported from France.

I sighed as I saw a bench outside the shower entrance, and clothing neatly folded—my clothing, a pair of jeans and a black shirt.

Avoidance of the mirror was in my best interest. I went straight for the shower after using the toilet. I just hoped I didn't look as bad as I had felt. The warm water was soothing to my aching body. I knew it would take a little while before I wasn't so exhausted. Time to heal was what I needed.

I reluctantly peered up into the mirror. My injuries didn't appear to be as bad as I thought. My face was a little swollen, but overall it seemed close to normal. I definitely wasn't feeling the same. My heart was still aching, and Colt's last expression was still locked in my memory.

Walking for the door, I hesitated. Someone would be waiting on the other side. I just didn't know who that someone would be.

I grasped the handle and turned the knob; Callon was there, leaning against the wall, arms crossed. I couldn't smile; I wanted to cry. His hazel eyes were searching mine, his soul-piercing gaze trying to assess my mood and condition.

I bowed my head and stepped out. He followed as I went back into the bedroom, stopping in the doorway as I placed my dirty clothes on the chair. I sighed and walked to the windows. I wasn't ready to face everyone yet—face Colt. I needed time to wrestle my emotions back into place. My heart was as cold as the hardwood beneath my bare feet.

Folding my arms across my chest, I stared into the wooded forest before me. I was convincing myself I could do this, that I could deal with Colt's rejection, accept that it was his choice and move on. Even though I would have to see him day in and day out. My throat grew tight.

Callon's boots scraped over the floor as he stood behind me. He was waiting for me to acknowledge him. I would, when I was ready.

When I regained my composure, I spoke quietly.

"What happened to me?"

Callon murmured, "What do you remember?"

I began playing with the ring on my index finger.

"I couldn't hear you." It all flashed before my eyes again. "I watched Daniel and Colt ride back, and then everything went black as night." A shiver ran down my spine. "I was terr—." I was going to say terrified, but they probably already knew. "Do you think this might happen again? Is this a part of the change?"

Stepping closer, his fingers glided over my hair. His touch was electric once more. I stepped away to break the connection.

"We don't know exactly, Cheyenne," Callon said. "I've never seen anything like this before. Both Dex and I are stumped."

"Is Dex a doctor, too?"

"For the most part, yes. I have the formal training, whereas his is based more on experience. Although treating a Timeless and human are different." He stepped forward, staring out the window. "What's most puzzling is the way the change comes on—each time it's a little different. With this episode, you had your hearing and sight diminish, and you ran an extremely high fever."

"How high?"

"Most normal humans can run a temperature around one hundred and two or so and are fine. When it starts reaching higher, say around one hundred and four or five, their organs start to shut down. You were at one hundred and five and still climbing when you passed out. The only thing we were able to do was submerge you in the cold river to bring it back down."

"I see. I didn't think we were randomly taking up cliff diving." Memories of falling came back, and I looked to Callon. "Wait, how did I end up in the river?"

He let out a deep sigh.

"Colt jumped with you. I wasn't happy with him; he could have climbed down. I can't even imagine how terrifying that must have been for you." Callon stepped closer, and I took a shaky breath. There wasn't much room for me to withdraw as I was practically leaning against the window.

"It was an experience I don't care to repeat anytime soon," I said dryly. The thought of it sent a chill down me. "How long have I been asleep for this time?"

"Not as long as your last one. You seemed to have recovered quicker, from your previous accident as well." He cleared his throat. "Lilly has given us a lot of grief because of the condition you arrived in, and I would rather not get her upset again."

I nodded and waited until I could ask the real question on my heart.

"Is Colt still angry with me?" My voice became choked. "Is that why he didn't come to see me?" I could feel the tears again. Why were they coming so easily? What was wrong with me?

"Cheyenne," Callon said, his gaze soft. "He's not angry with you."

"Then why isn't he here right now? What did I do that was so awful?" I sobbed. "I told him I was broken. What more does he want?"

Callon gently touched my shoulders and turned me around, wrapping me in a warm embrace. Resting his chin on my head, his hand rubbed my back. He was trying to comfort again, his gentle side rising to the surface. His words were soft, sincere.

"I don't want you defeated or broken. I love your spirit and charisma. I love the fight you have within. You don't give up or give in." His arms tightened slightly. "Give it some time, sweetheart. It will all work out."

"Callon, I..."

I was cut off by Lilly's entrance.

"Oh," she said in surprise. "I was just checking on you. Is everything okay, honey?"

Lifting my head from Callon's chest, I took a step back. "I'm fine, Lilly. Thank you for asking."

Walking with her hand outstretched, she smiled. They were still worried about me.

"How about we get you something to eat? You've only had an IV in. I'm sure you must be famished." I took her hand, and as we passed Callon, she looked at him out of the corner of her eye. "You can't leave these things up to the boys, you know. They tend to forget." I glanced back to Callon; he had a small grin tugging at the corners of his mouth.

She led us down a narrow hall, and we passed three additional bedrooms. The layout thus far resembled the boys' cabin. We entered the great room; it was the same. How interesting. The furniture was different, and the fireplace made of river rock, but everything else matched.

Daniel and Dex were sitting in the far corner playing chess. They raised their heads as we entered and both earnestly smiled. Daniel appeared at my side in the next second, startling me, and gripped me in a bear hug.

"Glad to see you're doing better. I've missed you," he said sweetly. As suddenly as he appeared, he was gone, and I was left feeling empty. He seemed to have a way to make me feel content.

Lilly's voice drew my attention back to her.

"Cheyenne, what can I fix for you? Would you like some eggs and toast?"

"That would be great. Thank you," I replied as I headed to the kitchen table to sit down. I looked around the room. "Lilly?"

"Yes, dear?" she replied, clanking pans.

"How do you have electricity out here? Are you running on

generators?"

"Well." She cracked an egg into the frying pan. "We have solar panels. We get most of the energy we need from them and then store it under the house until we need it. The fireplace provides warmth through the winter; Dex insulated the cabin well when he built it."

The toast popped up, and she tossed the pieces on a plate while the eggs continued to cook. Callon stood to the side with his arms crossed, leaning against a wall. It was almost if as if he was willing me to stay put with his stare. It wasn't cold, but it wasn't warm either.

My stomach began to growl. I was hungrier than I thought. The smell was enticing. It had been days since I had eaten last. Lilly placed a plate before me, and I ate hastily.

"Would you like more?" she asked as I pushed the plate back.

"No. I'm good. Thank you."

Her smile warmed as she sat next to me, taking my hands in hers.

"Cheyenne, I want you to know up front that we will not be talking to you about the journal just yet. We're working on the translations, but it will take some time. We don't want to tell you anything until we're sure that what we think we're reading is accurate. I don't want you upset that we're not answering your questions, but with the recent event of almost losing you, we decided you needed time to recover before we dive into it. You're still weak," she said with concern. "Let's get you well first."

"Thank you, Lilly." I squeezed her fingers. "The trio tend to just leave me in the dark." I gathered my thoughts, not wanting to blurt out my true feelings about the way they'd treated me in the last week. "I appreciate you letting me know we'll talk about it soon."

Her eyes showed me the warmth in her heart.

"You're welcome," she said. "There's so much you need to know; so much I want to tell you. I genuinely look forward to our time together."

Just knowing I would find out more was helpful, as I'd come to the conclusion that no matter how much I pestered, my guardians would only tell me what they thought I needed to know when they were ready. I had so many questions, so much I wanted to know about my past and what the journal held for me. I'd have to grow some patience.

Lilly leaned forward.

"Colt is sitting on the front porch," she whispered. "He's been distraught about you. I think you should go to him." She gave my hand a squeeze and went back to cleaning up the kitchen.

I glanced to the screen door toward the porch. Colt was waiting—I needed to go. I couldn't handle this distance between us anymore.

I rose slowly, and headed for the door. Callon's eyes locked with mine as I neared. He looked like he was going to stop me. But he didn't. He shifted his gaze slightly behind me, and suddenly moved out of my way as I walked out the door.

I glanced up. Dark storm clouds were brooding on the horizon. I was glad I had jeans and long sleeves on.

I turned to see Colt leaning against the rail in the far corner. My heart fluttered—I longed to be with him.

He was staring out into the valley. He didn't turn, but I knew he heard me. I wanted to jump into his arms and never let go. How or why things had gotten so out of control between us made no sense. I knew I'd felt out of sorts, but something had changed between us, too. I hoped it wasn't too late to change it back.

263

I took slow, deliberate steps. I wasn't going to give him the opportunity to speak. I needed him to understand my feelings. He was the one I wanted, always and forever. If he still chose after that to reject me, I would have to deal with it. But at least I deserved to know why.

His tall frame remained still as I approached. I touched his arm and moved it so I could wrap my arms around his waist. I needed his touch; I needed him next to me. Slowly his arms moved around me in a gentle embrace, and he rested his chin on my head. I tightened my arms. I wanted him to know I never wanted to let go—I wanted him with me forever. I wanted him to want me in the same way, and it drove me to pull back.

His eyes were filled with so much sorrow and despair. What was going on? I touched his cheek, searching to find my Colt. I attempted to draw his face near. I just wanted to kiss him—to tell him it was okay—we would work through this. He wouldn't yield—he held strong.

"Colt, why are you doing this?" I asked in a shaky voice. "I'm sorry for whatever it is I've done to make you like this." His expression didn't change as he looked away out into the valley.

The crack in my heart grew. "Please," I whispered. "Please say you'll forgive me. I can't take much more." My lips trembled. "You left me at the river. You didn't say anything. I need to know you still love me."

I gripped his hands, and if I hadn't needed to be so close to him, I would've been on my knees.

"Please, I'm begging you, just tell me you love me." He wouldn't look at me, and his arms loosened. I lowered my head and stepped away. "Why?" I said through the tears. "I don't understand..." My heart was hanging by a thread as I wiped a tear from my cheek.

I exhaled, closing my eyes, and I was about to move away when his hands grasped my face and his lips covered mine. I conceded immediately. His hands left my face and wrapped around me like a vice, lifting me from the ground and pulling me to his chest. Vigorously his mouth sought out mine, parting, heaving more of himself into me. I gasped for air each time he relented a little. Pressing his hand to the back of my neck, he continued his pursuit. His lips lingered down to my jaw, continuing to my neck and then back up, tracing my jaw line. Desperately inhaling oxygen, my eyes remained closed. He came back for more.

My heart was working overtime. Every ounce of me screamed my love for him. He had to love me; he wouldn't kiss me like this if he didn't.

He backed away, enough to whisper in my ear.

"Cheyenne, I'm so in love with you. I would forever and always choose you. There will never be anyone else for me." His lips touched my ear in a soft caress. "You are the only one who has ever stolen my heart. Only you have the key. Take it and do with it as you please."

His arms tightened. "You are the love of my life. I cannot live without you. No matter what happens, don't ever forget this—ever. I will always be yours, forever."

Now I was the one who frantically sought after his lips, my hands locking into the hair at the back of his neck and encouraging him onward. Eventually our kisses slowed, and gently we caressed each other's mouths in warm, sultry touches.

We drew back, and I saw the Colt who had been missing, the love in his eyes. He was back.

He kissed my forehead and set my feet to the floor. Our gaze still locked together, he led me to a chair where I curled up on his lap. I whispered, "I love you." And I meant it from the bottom of my heart. A contented smile spread over his face. His arms came around, and I lay my head on his shoulder as he brushed the hair from my cheek.

Dark clouds began to circle. The wind began kicking up and the temperature dropped—the storm was closing in. I didn't want to move from his arms. I wanted to stay here forever. There was still something he was holding back—something he didn't want to tell me, but I let it slip by. He'd said the words I wanted to hear, and that was enough for now.

The rain started, but only a few sprinkles touched me. My mind began to wander back to the conversation Lilly and I had earlier.

"Colt, Lilly said something earlier. She said you almost lost me. I didn't feel like I was dying. What happened?"

His voice was uneasy.

"Your fever was dangerously high; I held you in the river as long as I could. You went completely limp in my arms. It was as if your body was shutting down. We rushed you back." He hesitated and his hold firmed. "I didn't know if you would be able to make it." His eyes shut, trying to block out the memory. "This is twice in a short period of time I've looked upon your lifeless body. I felt so helpless. It broke my heart not being able to protect you, to make you strong."

"I'm strong because of you, Colt. You give me all the strength I need."

His blue eyes drove into me.

"Cheyenne, I can't give you enough. I need you so much more than you need me..."

"I am here and alive," I reassured him. "I'm not going anywhere.

We can make it one more year, and then I'll be a little more durable."
I leaned up and kissed him on the chin. He sighed, and a crooked grin appeared. My heart fluttered as it always did when he grinned like that.

The cold wind raked over us, and I shivered. Reluctantly, we both rose and entered the cabin. Callon was standing off to the side in the kitchen; he and Colt's gaze met. Callon's expression seemed to be a mixture of disappointment and uncertainty.

Something was up. I was sure of it. Daniel laughed, and I turned my attention to him. He was still playing chess with Dex. They smiled as we passed. Lilly was reading a book in the far corner, and she glanced up. Colt sat on the couch as I moved towards her. I sat on the hearth nearby.

"Lilly?"

"Yes, dear?"

"The case behind you, does it hold a guitar?"

"Why, yes." She seemed surprised at my interest.

"May I see it?"

Her smiled deepened.

"Of course."

She pulled the case from behind the chair and handed it to me. It was tattered around the edges. Carefully, I unsnapped the latches to reveal one of the most beautiful guitars I'd ever seen.

The sheen was gone, the color fading, and there were indentations from years of play and travel, but I could tell it was a well-loved instrument that had created beautiful music. I let my fingers glide across the strings as I pulled it free from the case. I strummed each note separately; it was in perfect pitch. I had not played the guitar more than a handful of times, yet I knew I could. It was no different than the piano. I just instinctively knew what to do.

I wasn't sad, or upset when I played tonight; I was placid, content, and needed to express this to my heart and soul. I wanted to confirm I was still alive, still me. I allowed my fingers to dance over the strings, slowly embracing each note as it rang through the rain-soaked air. I closed my eyes, carefully stroking and caressing the sound as it filled the room.

I imagined the melody gently cascading over each and every piece of furniture, timing it with the raindrops on the roof, tangling with nature's own melody outside. I forgot about everyone else in the room, and saw myself sitting next to a lazy river. I played the sounds of the water licking the tips of the stones, just as a dandelion blew its seeds in the wind. A ballet of moves, rising and falling with the breeze.

The guitar sang to my heart with words it understood. Each song morphed into another until it finally ended, when my heart was full and I could finish.

Opening my eyes, I gazed at my fingers. Five pairs of eyes were watching me. I hadn't played for an audience. Carefully placing the guitar in its case, I closed the latches and set it down.

"Sorry," I said self-consciously.

I glanced around the room. Lilly was still seated in the chair, tears brimming on her lashes. Dex and Daniel sat with arms crossed and backs slouched in chairs. Callon was leaning against the wall, nonchalantly watching, and Colt was overflowing with adoration.

I lowered my head, and moved to sit next to him. His arm welcomed me in as he whispered in my ear.

"Just when I think I can't love you anymore than I already do." A tender kiss touched my cheek, and he leaned back in his seat. I blushed.

"Cheyenne," Lilly asked. "How long have you been playing?"

I lifted my head up, and saw the softness and love in her face. "Not very long."

"Who taught you?"

"I never had formal lessons. I just picked it up. I hear the notes in my head, and they come together by themselves."

"Callon told us you play the piano also?" she asked.

I nodded.

"No one has played this guitar in a long time," she murmured, deep in thought. Her blue eyes locked on mine. "Thank you for bringing music back into this house again."

CHAPTER 20

Rain continued its descent from the skies above. The persistent wind howled, and the afternoon soon turned into evening. Lilly paced the room, apprehensive about the storm. Dex saw my concern and came to speak to me privately.

"There was an incident a long time ago. When we get the howling rain storms, it makes her uneasy," he said as he touched my arm. "She'll be fine. Don't worry."

"Cheyenne!" Lilly's voice rang with alarm, and I flinched. "You must be starving. You haven't eaten since breakfast." She grasped my hands. "I said the boys were bad about not remembering, but I am the one who's forgotten."

Surprised at her reaction, I tagged along to the kitchen with Colt. I didn't realize I was hungry until she said something. "I'm not starving, but I could eat something small if it's not too much trouble."

She gave a quick reply, "It's never any trouble." She began pulling items out from the fridge and pantry. "Give me a few minutes, and I'll whip up something."

I sat at the kitchen table, and Colt drew his chair up next to mine. As we watched Lilly work, I could see out of the corner of my eye that he was gazing at me. I tilted my head down slightly, and peeked at him, just enough to glimpse his gorgeous face.

Having some normality back with Colt was a relief. A quick wink from his blue eyes sent my heart into overdrive. I blushed and turned away.

Lilly made enough food to feed an army. Having something to focus on and keep her hands busy seemed to calm her. She placed a plate before me. I wasn't sure how much I could plough through, but was willing to give it a fair shot. I ate more than I thought and took my plate to the sink before returning to the great room for the evening. A chill was in the air, and Dex lit a fire to warm us. I loved the crackling and popping of the fire, the flames dancing in the air, licking the wood with its consuming desire.

I snuggled in closer to Colt, and Callon sat down beside us. Daniel was apparently bored, and he announced that we would all be playing poker. I glanced up warily.

"You do realize I've never played before, don't you?"

"We'll teach you," Colt offered.

"This should be interesting," I said faintly.

Daniel pushed the coffee table closer, and I slid to the floor, crossing my legs so I could reach the table. Lilly assured me the boys would be nice since I was just learning to play. Somehow I didn't believe it. I was an easy target, and they knew it.

I watched first, and tried to get the hang of the game. It was amusing to see them laugh and joke with each other. They truly enjoyed each other's company. They had a special bond with one another. Though there was a large age difference, it didn't seem to matter.

Finally they convinced me to join them, promising to let me in easy. I received assistance for the first couple of hands from Callon and Colt, mainly due to the fact I was sitting right between them with exposed cards.

Looking directly at me, Daniel shoved the cards over across the small table. "Your turn."

"Uh, Daniel," I said. "I don't know how to shuffle."

"You've been watching. You can do it."

"Yes, but you look like a casino dealer...I can't do it like that."

"Just try." He produced a wickedly charming smile, and I sighed.

"You're going to laugh," I said in exasperation.

"Probably, but that's the fun part."

I took the cards between my fingers, and what happened next was a comedy of errors. I attempted to fan the cards, and they went flying. They landed on the floor, on Callon's lap, and across the table. Everyone broke out in hysterics.

Face flushed, I scooped up the cards from the table and decided it best to hand the task over to someone more experienced.

"Oh, no," Callon said, holding up his hands. "You can't give up after one try, sweetheart."

My nose wrinkled. There was the sweetheart thing again. What irked me, though, was that I didn't know whether he said to tease me or because he really meant it.

Daniel demonstrated on the small table again. I watched closely, took back the cards, and tried to follow his lead. You'd have thought with the ability to play the piano and guitar, I would have some sort of dexterity.

The cards exploded in a funnel of spades, aces, and jacks. Daniel and Colt were cracking up in the background.

Callon rolled his eyes. He smiled as he leaned over, taking my hands in his and showing me how to shuffle properly. He repeated the steps a couple times. Each time he turned to instruct me, his lips brushed my cheek—the heat of his touch burned.

The laughter ceased, and I became self-conscious about what was taking place. I drew back, but it didn't seem to bother him at all; he was still grinning.

Why was he acting like this? From the beginning I'd gotten the impression that I was just a job, and now it was as if he was barely holding back his attraction. I'd been getting along better with him recently, but I was with Colt. Callon was confusing me.

I shook it off. Forget about him.

I played a few more hands, and beginner's luck allowed me to win a few. I was finally feeling like I was getting the hang of it.

"So if I have a royal flush..." I glanced down at my cards. "That means I win the hand?" I raised my brows as they all began tossing down their cards. "What?"

They started laughing. Colt lifted me from the ground, taking the cards from my hands.

"I thought you said you had a royal flush?"

"I never said that. I was merely asking you what it consisted of. You..." I pointed around the room, "took it the wrong way. It's not my fault you jumped to conclusions."

He squeezed my sides. "And you said you didn't know how to play poker! I won't be so nice next time." He kissed my cheek and gave Callon a sideways glance as he seated me right between his legs on the floor.

I blinked. Something was going on with Colt and Callon. Nobody else seemed to pick up on it, though, and we carried on playing.

We played several more hands, but I was growing tired. I'd been drained from my reunion with Colt, and it was becoming harder to stay awake. Slouching against Colt's leg, my head quickly found its home in his lap. But I didn't want to go to bed. I wanted to continue to enjoy this day—these moments. To forget about the danger awaiting me.

I closed my eyes and listened to the crackling fire; the conversation continued until I could hear no more.

An ear-splitting crack of lightning hit a tree right outside the window, accompanied by a deep roll of thunder. I sat straight up, trembling. I was in my bedroom, alone. My heart was pounding in my chest, like a flapping bird trying to escape. The room lit for half a second more—but that was all it took.

I was staring out the window and saw a shadowy figure in the trees. The room darkened, and I didn't blink. Another flash of light, another half a second, and the mysterious shadow vanished.

A thunderous boom pierced the air again, and a hand touched my shoulder. I screamed as I leaped off the bed, only to find two hands pulling me close.

"LET GO!"

"Cheyenne! It's me, Callon." It took a few moments to realize who the hands belonged to, and I immediately stopped fighting him. "Shh, it's okay. It's just a thunderstorm."

I allowed him to draw me in. "Lightning hit outside your window." He began stroking my back. "You don't need to be frightened. I'm right here."

"W-where's C-Colt?" I stuttered.

"He and Daniel went outside to secure the horses and make sure the lightning didn't cause a fire."

"They went to make sure a fire didn't start?"

"Yes, it's been a dry summer up here. We don't need a forest fire right now."

The shadowy figure stood out in my mind; maybe it was Dex. I knew it wasn't Colt or Daniel—it wasn't the right shape.

"What time is it?" I moved back, pulling my arms away.

"It's around three a.m. You need to get some more rest; you've only been sleeping for a couple of hours."

"I don't think I can sleep now."

At that exact moment another burst of lightning lit up the room, followed by a deafening crash of thunder. I buried myself into Callon's chest again. I was such a baby.

Or was it that I enjoyed being in his arms?

"Come on. Let's go out in the great room. We can sit on the couch, ok?" he suggested.

I nodded. The remaining light from the fire provided the only illumination. The lightning flashes started to decrease, and the thunder grew more distant. My eyes caught sight of the journal setting nearby on a table. A pen and paper to the side, at least I knew what Lilly said was true. Dex was working on deciphering it for me.

Eventually I relaxed, pulling my legs into my chest. I leaned my head onto Callon's shoulder, and my sleepiness returned. His arm moved around me, and he began to gently brush his fingers across my arm. It was softest of touches, as if he was afraid I'd shy from the intimate contact. I slouched more and soon found my head resting

275

on his lap. He pulled a blanket from a basket nearby and placed it over me. Eyes closed, I soon was resting peaceably again.

Sunshine streamed through the windows, and I sluggishly opened my lashes to see Colt sitting on the coffee table. His face was placid, and I very quickly became aware of the fact my head was lying across Callon's lap. I sat up immediately and glanced at both. They were talking. I needed to butt in before something happened.

"So, did you have fun in the lightning storm last night, Colt?" I stretched my hand out, taking hold of his to ensure he would look at me. "Callon said you had to get the horses. Is everything okay?"

"Everything is fine now. They were spooked when the lightning struck so close; Mandi ran off, but we managed to bring her back."

"How far did she run?" I asked, concerned.

"Pretty far. She's fast, you know. Faster than Bo or Charlie; Sam is the only one she would let come close. We just got back."

My gaze traced over him.

"I see you decided to take a mud bath on the way back," I giggled.

A very devious grin spread over his lips. "Yes, as a matter of fact I did." He inched closer. "I thought you might enjoy it too, so I saved some for you."

"You wouldn't dare!"

It was an empty threat. Colt yanked me forward into his lap, making sure to spread the mud across me while he kissed my cheeks. We were both laughing.

"You know." I smirked. "The last time you did something like this, I had to pay you back...it could be worse this time." I winked. He squeezed me tight until I said, "Ouch." Seconds later, I was over his shoulder, and we were heading out of the great room.

"You're a mess, sweetheart. You need a shower," he said playfully.

"Colt!" I screeched. "Cut it out!"

Lilly, Dex, and Daniel were laughing, too. Callon remained subdued, though. He didn't seem happy to have Colt handle me like this.

We stopped in front of the bathroom door. He set me to my feet, grasped my face in his hands, and kissed me firmly. "Stay here, I'll be right back."

I was too stunned to argue.

He returned with clothing rolled into a towel and placed it in my hands. A very crafty smile was plastered across his face. "You know, Colt," I said. "I'm quite capable of picking out my own clothing."

"Oh, I know," he said lightly. "But this is more fun. Before you jump in the shower, hand me your clothes." I gave him a look.

"So I can wash them with mine," he explained innocently.

"Oh," I examined his face, trying to figure out his motive, but finally determined he was just being particularly mischievous today. "Okay, give me a minute."

In the bathroom I undressed and wrapped a towel around myself. I barely opened the door and stuck my arm out with dirty clothes in hand. His fingers firmly grasped mine as he pulled the clothes free and kissed my knuckles.

I showered, and took the time to shave my legs. I finished up and wrapped a towel around me. As I unrolled the towel Colt gave me, two small items fell out. Oh geez, what was he thinking?

On the floor before me were two items, a top and bottom piece for a bikini. He was playing a game with me while all I wanted to know was what the journal said. I shook my head. Lilly did say it would take a while...I decided to play along since I knew he would be holding my other clothes hostage. He was especially rambunctious today for some reason.

I purposely took my time in the bathroom. He may have cornered me, but if he wanted to see the end result, I was going to make him wait for it.

I eventually headed for the door, and peeked around the corner. There he was, a huge grin on his face.

"What's taking so long, Cheyenne? You don't need my help, do you?"

I narrowed my eyes. "You, mister, are in so much trouble right now. What were you thinking?"

"I was thinking that before I give you your remaining items I should inspect what I've already given you."

"Colt!" I snarled. With his arms folded, leaning against the wall, he gave no response. I was going to hold my ground. "I guess I won't be coming out of the bathroom today."

I started to close the door, but a large arm pushed through, pinning me behind the door itself. Colt's head popped around, and he chuckled.

"You need to do better than that, sweetheart. I can scowl better than you." His large fingers grasped my wrist and pulled me out as the door closed. He gawked at me, like I was some kind of exotic zoo exhibit.

"Are you happy now?" I sneered.

"Not quite." He took my hand and twirled me around while I rolled my eyes. "Now I am."

"May I please have some other clothes now?" My irritation had no effect on him. He tossed me a pair of jeans, and I replied, "Is this all I get?"

"No, but I'll give you more when I'm ready. Put them on please," he instructed as he leaned against the vanity with his arms crossed.

"Are you going to tell me why I have to wear a swimsuit today?" I grumbled.

"Sure, you're going swimming in the river with me."

"You could have just told me that instead of playing this little game, you know."

"Oh, I know, but this is way more fun. Put the jeans on."

Rolling my eyes, I slowly pulled them on. "Now can I please have more?"

"For a price." That devilish twinkle in his eyes appeared again.

"Excuse me?" I arched my brows and crossed my arms. "What's the going rate for my freedom today, then?"

"Oh, it's pretty simple actually. Just a kiss."

"Just a kiss?" I asked.

"Yup, just a kiss."

I looked him square in the face. "Nope."

His eyes widened. He stood upright, towering over me.

"No?"

"Can't afford that, sorry," I said. "I already have the jeans. I'll just walk out with what I have and ask Lilly for a shirt." I stared up at him, defiant. "I might also mentioned to her your calculating, devious scheme and see what she thinks about it."

"Hmm," he replied. A cunning grin spread over his lips as he stepped closer. I backed away. "I guess you could do that. However, you would still have to get to the door and I really don't see that happening."

I took a step back, dropping my hands to my sides. "I could scream—somebody would come running to help."

He took another large step towards me. I was now up against the wall. "You could, but I'm faster than you. I would be able to stop you before you even let out a peep."

I quickly side-stepped, but he cornered me as his arm came to rest on the wall next to my shoulder. He lifted his other hand to the wall, caging me in. My heart began to race.

"You're awfully sure of yourself, aren't you?" I asked.

Those imposing blue eyes were peering down at me.

"Yes," he said in a whisper as his lips touched mine, hesitating for a brief moment before he drew back. "Now that wasn't so bad was it?"

"No," I replied breathlessly. "It was awful!" I dove under his arm, grabbing the t-shirt from the floor as I dashed for the door. I turned the corner for the bedroom. Colt was grinning, and in hot pursuit. I pulled the shirt on, and hurriedly jumped to the bed, crossed my legs and folded my arms. I attempted to look impatient. "What took you so long?"

"Now that wasn't nice," he said as he entered the room.

"Never said I was nice; come to think of it, I don't ever remember anyone ever calling me nice." I winked.

He stood there for a moment. I could see he was contemplating something. Within a second he was over me, tickling me.

"Colt!" I screamed out as the laughter took over. Seconds later Daniel came to the rescue. It only lasted briefly before everyone else arrived to see what was causing us to make so much noise. With Colt's attention diverted, I bolted to the other room with Lilly's assistance.

"Colt!" Lilly called out sternly. "You had better treat her right. I've already warned you..." I ran around the corner and didn't hear the rest of her scolding as I chuckled.

I plopped into the couch, and waited for the rest to follow. Colt emerged from the hall first with Lilly still yelling in his ear; he rolled his eyes as he tossed me my shoes and socks. The rest were smirking as I caught their glances.

"So, Colt said something about swimming in the river?" I asked.

"Yup. We're taking you up the mountain to see the waterfalls. It's really beautiful. I think you would really enjoy it," Callon said thoughtfully.

"Are you sure it's safe?" I was thinking back to my recent attack. A few weeks ago I'd have jumped at the chance to get out, but now I really wasn't so sure. Who knew what was waiting out there for me.

"There are five of us. You'll be fine." Sympathy rolled through Callon's eyes. "You've been locked up with us for a while. I thought some freedom to explore would be welcomed."

I smiled. He was right. I couldn't cower in fear about what could happen. Besides, I was going to obey Callon now, no matter what. If I was careful, everything would work out.

"Is the weather going to be nicer today?" I fiddled with my laces as I tied them.

"It's supposed to be warm this afternoon."

"When are we leaving?"

"As soon as you eat some breakfast. We'll be gone all day. We may spend the night if you'd like. Lilly has already packed food for the trip."

I glanced at Lilly who was now in the kitchen. "Thanks, Lilly."

She smiled. "You're welcome."

I followed Colt to the kitchen. He proceeded to scour the fridge. "I'll just take a granola bar if you have one," I spoke up. "You don't need to go through much effort this morning."

Colt went to the pantry. He returned with his prize in hand and a warm grin just for me.

"Anything for you," he said lovingly.

I swiftly kissed him. "Paid in full then." We both chuckled, and Lilly tilted her head at us. As I ate my granola bar, Colt brought me a glass of orange juice. I guzzled it, and we headed for the front door.

Callon was absolutely correct about the weather. The sun was beaming in the sky and its rays warmed my skin. Birds were singing, butterflies flying, and squirrels scampering. The horses were saddled and ready. Seeing Mandi, I knew why Colt was covered in mud. She still had it caked all over her. She was in the corral, but upon seeing me, she immediately came to the fence.

I hopped on the lower rung, and began rubbing her mane. "Hey there, girl. I see you had some fun last night." She moved her head up and down as if in response...odd how human her response was. "You're a little muddy now aren't you?" She nodded again. I raised an eyebrow.

Removing my hand from her mane, I set it on the rail as I stared into her caramel eyes. "Did the lightning scare you?" For the third time, she replied with a nod. I was watching her closely. Could she understand me? I needed to test this theory out.

"Mandi," I said firmly. "If you understand me, stomp your right foot." Still staring into my eyes, she stomped her right foot. I blinked. This wasn't any coincidence...

I turned to Colt and Callon.

"Hey, come over here a second."

"Cheyenne?" Callon left Bo and hurried towards me. "What's the matter? Is everything okay?"

I nodded to Mandi.

"I'm not sure." I furrowed my brows. "This is going to sound crazy, but I think Mandi understands me. I was talking with her, and she nodded her head in response."

The moment the words left my mouth, I regretted them immediately. The look in their eyes said it all.

"But she stomped her foot when I asked." They were barely holding back their laughter.

"Uh, honey," Colt said. "Horses do nod their heads from time to time." His grin grew larger.

"She stomped her foot too," I said earnestly, trying to save myself from complete humiliation.

"They stomp their hooves sometimes too, sweetheart," Callon added, barely containing his laughter.

Rolling my eyes, I turned to Mandi. "Watch this. Mandi, if you understand me, stomp your foot." I watched for her response, but none came.

Shaking my head, I stepped away from the corral. They burst out into a bellowing laugh, and I shook my head.

"Just what I need, to give the two of you more ammunition! Good thing Daniel's not..." I turned my head to see Daniel. He had been behind me. "Oh, forget it!"

I stormed away, leaving the three to chortle.

"Damn stupid horse," I mumbled under my breath. "Thanks a lot, Mandi!" I could have sworn she was snorting at me in laughter, shaking her head.

Daniel's voice echo in the background, "This is just about as good as the whole Jeep incident..."

I cringed. Wonderful, now he had more things to tease me about.

Humiliated, I sat on the porch and waited. The trio kept glancing at me from time to time, laughing on and off. One of these days I was going to have to learn to keep these things to myself. I was a glutton for punishment.

Eventually we were ready to leave; Daniel was holding Mandi's reins while he called out, "Hey, Cheyenne, Mandi asked me to tell you she's ready to go."

Rolling my eyes, I had no other choice but to walk over. Colt stopped me before I mounted.

"You know we love to tease you. You come up with some pretty funny stuff." He wrapped his arms around me.

"Yeah," I replied. "It's my job to provide the entertainment around here. Good thing I take it so well. You know, I could be one of those girls who cry over everything." I looked up into his mischievous eyes.

"You could," he paused as he kissed my head. "But you don't, and that's why we love you."

CHAPTER 21

We were in no immediate hurry as we rode northwest towards the mountains, casually chatting and taking in the scenery. Dex rode alongside me and talked about the mountain ranges, pointing out specific formations. Wildlife was plentiful and the ground fertile. He said not many people traveled this far out; it was rare to see anyone pass through unless they were Timeless, thus giving me a little sense of security. Between the five of them, they thought it would be safe for me to be out and about.

Making it to the base of the mountain, we followed the river upstream to the waterfalls. I could hear it before I saw it. A musty damp odor combined with the scent of pine trees, wildflowers, and grasses filling the air. As we drew closer, the thunderous claps of water hitting the rocks below echoed in my ears. The volume was startling. At the tips of the falls, the green water splashed, running downward to three levels.

A sparkling rainbow rose up from the rainy mist. It danced in the wind, rising and falling, kissing the surrounding mountains and swallowing the sparrows as they dove in and out. The mist touched my cheeks and eyelids in the gentle breeze, caressing my face so delicately it seemed to memorize me, as it did the cliffs in its soft embrace.

As we rode closer, Colt reached out and touched my arm. I had no words to express what was flooding my mind; I could only mouth "thank you" and smile. He was absolutely right in thinking I would love it here—I did. He always knew what I needed and when. I sighed. He was so perfect for me, and he was mine. Why had I waited so long? It didn't matter any longer. He loved me, and I loved him. With love, all things were possible. I wasn't alone anymore.

We continued our ride and returned to the meadow we passed. We dismounted and removed the tack. We allowed the horses to roam freely. From past experiences, I knew they never ventured far away. Colt dug through one of the packs and tossed a pair of shorts at me. "You'll want to change before we hike back to the falls."

I nodded and changed. I had my swimsuit on so it wasn't a big deal. As I turned around, all three of my protectors were waiting—shirtless. It was a distracting sight, all of them in their male glory. I glanced at Lilly, and she smiled.

"Have fun! Dex and I will be in the meadow."

Once again, I nodded and followed. Colt led us and thankfully, Daniel and Callon walked behind. I stumbled a couple of times, mostly because I couldn't take my eyes off Colt. His broad shoulders and narrow waist, my eyes trailed down to his strong legs. I actually contemplated pinching his backside. I just wanted to see what his reaction would be. It would be my chance to catch him off guard, as he always seemed to do to me. If we had been alone I would have, I think. Well, probably not. I was a big chicken at heart.

We chatted lightly along the hike. I came to the conclusion that they were excited to show me the falls up close. We stopped at the base, and I could clearly see the three levels. Each level was about twenty-five feet high, dropping into the next until it ended at the bottom in a deep pool of water. The water seemed calmer at the bottom.

"It's not as calm as it looks," Daniel said as he stood beside me. "It's very deceiving. Get too close to the falls, and the pressure could suck you under. Even for the best of swimmers, it's difficult to get out. When the water levels are higher, it's even worse."

I turned, smiling. "Guess I won't be swimming there then, huh?"

"Not there," he replied.

Colt tugged my hand, and we began our hike up the first and second tier. The path was narrow and rocky, twisting and turning. The misty water made the rocks slick. Colt kept a firm grip on my hand. Callon also stuck close, and his hand skimmed my side a number of times to ensure I didn't fall as my footing slipped. It was just enough to make my skin tingle. Stopping briefly, Colt pointed to the caverns carved out on the far cliff walls. The only way I was able to see them was because the season had been dry; the water levels were down considerably. We continued up the path, and made our final approach to the third level, stopping at a rock wall. Colt turned and smiled.

"Uh, Colt?" I looked at him warily. "I've never been rock climbing before, and I'm not sure if this is the best time to take it up." His fingers remained locked over mine.

"We're not going to let you fall. This will be an easy climb for you."

"How can it be an easy climb if I've never climbed before?" I asked nervously as I drew my hand away and stepped back. He didn't move, and I stepped back again, tripping over my own foot. Callon caught me by my elbows before I fell on the narrow ledge.

"Colt's right, Cheyenne. All three of us are here. We're not going to let you fall."

Firmly I replied, "No." They reached out. Colt took hold of one arm and Callon held the other and pulled me forward. Panic was quickly setting in.

"No!" I said again. "I don't think you understand me. I am not fond of heights, and this is an experience I would rather live without if you don't mind."

"Cheyenne, it will be worth it," Callon said, and they all joined in trying to convince me. I could see it didn't matter what I said. I wasn't going to win. They would eventually wear me down.

"Just put your hands and feet where we tell you to. I'll be on one side and Callon will be on the other," Colt promised calmly.

"Why can't Daniel just jump me up there?" I shot out quickly in what I thought was a brilliant argument.

Colt moved closer, his fingers tightened around my elbow. "Because this is something you need to experience firsthand." He placed my hand into a crevice of the rock and pulled me forward. Callon followed suit. "You need to know how to climb if you're ever in a situation that requires it."

"I'm not liking any of you at the moment," I said in a shaky voice. "Just thought you should know."

"Good to know," Colt replied in a low chuckle.

"Promise you won't let me fall," I begged.

"I think you know us better than that," Callon said in a reproving tone.

I reminded myself that I trusted them. "Ok," I said shakily.

They hovered over me and slowly drove us upwards. My heart

was beating as fast as a racehorse, and my palms were sweaty, which made me think I would slip and fall, which made my heart beat even faster. I hated heights, almost as bad as I hated spiders. They were fairly equal in my mind, both things I despised. I really wanted to rip the three men up and down to let them know my displeasure, but speaking the words aloud was too much of a distraction. Each time I slipped, someone's hand would graze my back or waist. I knew they were just trying to ensure I didn't fall, but it was sensory overload.

How they managed to climb next to me with one hand was a mystery. My heart went into overdrive as the rock footing passed under my boot, and I was unable to right myself. The sensation of falling almost overwhelmed me. I closed my eyes only briefly. Colt's fingers locked into my belt loop as the palm of his hand spread out further on my back. It did nothing to calm my crazy pulse. It only worsened it. My breaths were erratic, and I narrowed my eyes as I stared at him, my cheek firmly planted on the rocks as I hugged the cliff wall.

"You're fine. I have you," he said calmly, and that was even more frustrating.

Eventually, we neared the top. Colt thankfully pushed me up and over into a secure location. I rolled to my back, and closed my eyes, trying to put my heart back into my chest. Moments passed before I was able to speak.

"You are in so much trouble," I said in a low, deep voice. "All three of you. Just wait until I tell Lilly what you made me do." I looked up. Colt was perched right next to me.

"If we're going to get into trouble with Lilly, then we should probably make it worth our while," he said slyly.

Glaring, I wasn't sure what he meant. A gorgeous smile flashed over his lips—it made me wary about what they had planned next. I shook my head, and he helped me to my feet. He had me stand with him closer to the edge. He stood behind while I made sure I remained pressed up against his chest.

The view of the valley from this elevation allowed me to see the stunning beauty unfold below. The majestic rolling hills, the river weaving in and out in the vale below—it was as if the grasses swayed to the music on the breeze. We stood silent, all four of us, for a long time, admiring the view and enjoying the moment.

Daniel smiled. I watched wide-eyed as he simply walked over the ledge and disappeared. I turned to Colt horror-stricken, and quickly saw the devious smile spread over his mouth. Jerking my head towards Callon, I saw the same thing. A second later it dawned on me how we were getting down!

"No!" I said firmly as I side-stepped them and put my hand out. "No! I climbed the rock like you asked, but I am not jumping off it!" Without a word, they each took a step closer. "No!" I screamed out in panic and began backing up further. "I told you I was afraid of heights...I told you I never wanted to cliff dive! No!"

In the blink of an eye, Callon lunged. Half a second later, he was tossing me into Colt's arms as he ran towards the edge. Colt spun me around so I was facing him, and I locked my arms around his neck in a death grip. I let out a scream and buried my head into his chest as we fell. Callon was laughing as he jumped next to us. Fifteen seconds later, we hit the water with enough force to knock the air from my lungs. I was latched on tightly, but still felt the pull of the current as Colt swam us to the surface. As I gasped and coughed for air, Colt turned me around and wrapped his arm around my waist as he began our swim to shore. Callon was smiling as he followed.

Colt deposited me on the shore, and I lay on the river rocks, attempting to catch my breath, eyes pinched closed.

"Don't ever, and I mean *ever*, do that to me again!" I said through my teeth. Colt's hand touched me, and I immediately slapped it away. "Don't touch me! You are in so much trouble!"

"Awe, it wasn't that bad." Colt was chuckling. I knew I couldn't admit that a small part of me had found it exhilarating or I would lose the edge of my anger at them.

I looked up, and all three were hovering above me. I produced the best possible glare I could manage. They knew I wasn't really mad anymore and burst into a bellowing laugh, and soon I couldn't help but laugh with them. I staggered to my feet and attempted to walk away. Each time I took a step, they would block my path. I pointed my still-shaking finger at them. "You just wait until I talk to Lilly!"

Colt raised a brow as he replied, "You have to get to her first."

I flashed a cunning smile and faked to the right as I ran to the left, straight for the water. I took them by surprise and leaped up on a large boulder and I dove into the river. I swam downstream towards the meadow. Seconds later, the water was splashing behind me, and a few seconds more passed before Callon had a hold of my leg and was pulling me back. He wrapped his arm around my waist and pulled my back into his chest. He pulled us into a deeper, calmer part of the river and waded, though my feet didn't touch the bottom.

"Cheyenne," Callon said in my ear, causing a chill to run down my spine. "You should know you can't get away from me." I attempted to pry his hands away without any success as his grip tightened. I glanced down and saw he was standing on a large boulder. Even if I wanted to stand on my own I couldn't. The water would be over my head. I was stuck in his arms and couldn't do anything about it. A small amount of panic rose. Would his closeness bother Colt? I glanced at Colt, but he didn't seem upset.

"You're cheaters, you know," I said with fake annoyance as Colt and Daniel grinned. Callon squeezed my waist lightly.

"It's only because you're so much fun!"

"No," I shot back quickly. "It's because I'm the only woman who has stayed around long enough...oh yeah, I remember why now...it's because I'm not allowed to leave!"

Laughter broke out again. From the corner of my eye, I saw a flash of yellow and heard splashing followed by snorting. Callon turned us, and we saw Mandi swimming full speed. She was coming up fast and knocked Callon off his perch, which in turn caused him to release his hold on me. Surprise and panic swept over their faces, until they saw me latching on to her mane and climbing on her back. She swam quickly, and I glanced back, laughing as I left them stunned.

I reached out and hugged her neck. "Thank you, Mandi. You need to bite them when you get a chance. They've behaved badly today," I said through the laughter. She snorted as if in agreement. She swam in the river instead of going ashore; it was as if she was enjoying herself. Looking back, the trio had made it to shore. Mandi and I eventually emerged from the river further downstream. We took our time walking back. We found all of them sitting in the grass waiting. I smiled as I dismounted and went straight for Lilly, sitting down beside her.

"Did you have fun?" she asked cheerfully.

"You should really ask them." I pointed to the trio. "They would be able to explain it better."

She turned her head and called out, "Boys?"

Not one answered or even glanced in her direction; they were apparently deep in conversation. I turned my back to them and my attention to Lilly and was about to speak when Colt swiftly swept me up into his arms.

"Sweetheart," he said with concern. "You're all wet. We need to get you dried off." With those words, he pulled me away from Lilly and carried me further into the meadow.

"Chicken!" I firmly said as he drew me closer and kissed my cheek. He didn't reply as he finally slowed and set me in the soft grass. He helped me untie my boots and pull them off. I slid my wet t-shirt off as well and lay them in the sun to dry. We shifted to our backs, and stared up at the sky and falls in the distance.

The sun warmed my skin as I lounged, bringing sleepiness along with it. It was as if the thunderous roll of the cascading water was singing to me, beckoning me to rest and listen to its lullaby. It was a soothing song, one that took me back to past memories—good, pleasant ones. Memories that would bring back laughter, smiles, and love.

I lay with my hands under my head. The clouds formed into long strips of white mirroring the mist rising in the air, and moving slowly, steadily, evenly toward the horizon. I shifted my vision to the mountain, and could see where the water had torn through it, carving its way into the rocks and creating the caves and indentations. I imagined how it must have been some time ago as the wild waters raced down, meeting their destiny with open arms. They dove off the ridges, elated to meet the rocks below, and then as if in a joyous celebration, reaching up and dancing in the mist. I sighed.

Colt rolled to his side, propping himself up with his elbow and stared at me. "What are you thinking about?" he asked quietly.

I sighed again. I loved looking at him. "Lots of things."

He placed his other hand across my waist and drew me closer. "Like what kinds of things?"

I grinned. "Good things."

"Like?" He raised his brows.

"Like how beautiful it is here." I wasn't referring just to the falls, and I got the impression he knew that too.

"I see. Anything else?"

"Sure."

"And?"

I chuckled as I teased him. "Oh, you want me to tell you?"

"Only if you want to." He grinned.

"I was just thinking how difficult you've been today...from first thing this morning you have been very devious." I tried to look stern without success.

"Difficult, devious?" he asked in surprise.

"Oh yes. To start with, you rubbed mud on me. Second, you wouldn't let out of the bathroom until I modeled the suit for you. Third, you tickled me in the bedroom. Fourth you made fun of me about talking to Mandi. Fifth, you forced me into rock climbing, and sixth, worst of all...you made me jump!" I nodded firmly. "Difficult and devious, yes."

"Wow." He said considering his crimes. "I guess I have been bad today. Am I in trouble?" A sly grin spread across his face.

"Yes, you are." I tried to sit up. "I'll go and talk with Lilly right now." He pushed me back down and wrapped one leg over mine.

"See," I said smiling. "There you go again."

He lowered himself so his lips were just above mine.

"I never claimed to be perfect," he said softly.

I brushed my hand across his cheek.

"Oh, you're perfect, Colt," I whispered. "More than you know."

"So, despite these minor setbacks, did you have a nice day?"

"I wouldn't call any of them setbacks, and no I didn't have a nice day." I paused purposely. "I had a wonderful day because I was able to spend it with the people I love." I leaned forward slightly, and kissed him tenderly. "Thank you for a wonderful day, and thank you for giving me some freedom." He followed me back down, his lips lingering over mine in tender caresses; just enough pressure to make me long for more, but then he stopped.

"You're welcome," his deep husky voice tickled my ears.

Through heavy lashes I watched a grin appear. "You're so bad, Colt. Your day will come." His grin grew.

The day was coming to a close. The sun was setting, and soon darkness would arrive. He helped me to my feet, and we slowly strolled hand in hand back to the rest. Daniel had gathered firewood and had a fire started. My shirt was now dry, and I put it back on. Colt had placed my damp shoes near the fire. I got the impression we were staying the night.

"I'm sure you're starving, honey," Lilly said as she handed me a sandwich.

"Thank you." She smiled, and I ate my dinner. We sat around the crackling fire, and chatted about the day's events. Daniel got a little too detailed.

"You should have seen her face when I walked off the falls," he chuckled. "I waited at the bottom as Colt and Callon ran off the side with her screaming." He had a twinkle in his deep blue eyes. "I don't think I've ever heard anyone scream that loud. I heard you above the falls!"

It was my turn to smile as Lilly let loose.

"You did what?" she said in an elevated motherly tone.

"Uh..." He cringed as he realized what he'd said.

"You had better be nice to this poor girl! I heard about what she did to you before with the berries. I'm sure she can take care of herself if needed," she scolded them.

"You know," Dex chimed in. "I could show Cheyenne some things that would work better than the berries." He winked at me. They stared at him blankly for a few moments, and I began to giggle.

"I look forward to talking with you later, Dex," I said cheerfully. Colt drew his arm around me and snuggled me in closer.

"I think you'll be busy later," he replied.

"Promise?" I whispered, and his warm smile deepened.

"I promise."

I listened to them chat while Colt rubbed my arm. I was still a little chilled. I leaned more into his arm, as my eyes became increasingly heavy. I slouched into his chest, and a delicate hand brushed my cheek as a blanket was laid over me. I knew it was Lilly. Soon I didn't hear their conversations anymore as I drifted off to sleep.

I woke to an eerie silence; it was still dark. The fire was down to glowing embers, and no one was talking. Colt had both arms around me, and I was tight against his chest. The blanket I had over me was now brushed to the side. I surveyed the area. A thick mist had moved in, and everyone else was gone. Colt's arms flexed, and I attempted to look up, only to be stopped when his hand came to rest over my mouth. I was immobile as he held me; all I could do was be completely still.

My heartbeat quickened. He wouldn't act like this unless something was wrong. And this felt like something was very wrong. I stared out into the mist, trying to allow my sight to adjust to the darkness. Something was there, but I couldn't see anything until the fire sparked. Suddenly, through the misty darkness, I saw two black eyes staring at me. A small whimper came from the back of my throat, and Colt's arms stiffened. The creature was low to the ground, in a crouched position, ready for an attack. A shiver raked me as the hair on the back of my neck stood on end.

It crept through the mist, and I began to see its shape. It appeared to be similar to a dog or wolf, but the size was enormous. Even crouched down, it was taller than me. Its upper lips curled as it growled, exposing razor sharp fangs. Just as the hair on my neck rose again, so did the porcupine-like quills it had on its neck.

Colt slowly lowered his head slightly. His deep voice sent a chill down my spine as he spoke, "Don't move."

Another low rumble came from behind. I didn't think my heart could race any faster, but it did. I felt the blood rush from my cheeks as my head began to spin. There were two! He couldn't fight two at once. Cautiously, the gruesome creature in front began to creep closer. Its ears twitched as it listened, and the hair on its neck rose and fell with each snarl. Colt was tense. His arms vibrated with adrenaline, his steely muscles flexing against my skin.

The beast continued its crawl forward. The grisly creature arched itself as it prepared to spring. I shook from fear. Each breath I took was heavier than the last. It only took a fraction of a second, and

Colt was on his feet, wrestling the beast over the top of me. I jerked my head to the right. The second frightful animal was leaping in the air, only to be hurled in a different direction. Callon was positioned on the other side of me. Both revolting creatures began stalking again as they repositioned themselves, ready for the next round.

Almost in unison they leaped again, teeth gnashing, eyes filled with a wild rage. I turned to the side; Colt positioned himself so the beast leaped into his arms, and he snapped its neck. I whipped my head towards Callon. The other monster's leg had been dislocated; it was limping away, howling in bitter anguish through the thick mist. Daniel and Dex's voices rang out warnings and then I heard the echo of cracking and howling.

I lay motionless on the ground, unsure what just took place. Were these the same shadows I used to see at my house? Callon and Colt dragged the hideous beast away into the mist, and I was alone. The crackling of the fire caught my attention, and I froze. A deep menacing growl rang from the back of a third beast's throat, and two black orbs locked on mine. I quickly sprang to my feet; desperately searching for Colt, but the mist was too thick to see him.

It crawled its way forward as our gaze remained locked. I stepped back over the log. I didn't have many options. I could run into the field and quickly be overtaken, or I could head for the trees to my right. The possibility of diving behind trees as protection sounded better than being completely vulnerable. I took another step backwards and stepped on a large branch we hadn't yet thrown on the fire. Lowering myself slowly, I grasped it with my right hand. I wished I had shoes on.

The beast's hair rose and fell with each nasty breath it took. I steadied my nerves. I wasn't going down easily. My eyes grew wide as

I watched it crouch. A second later, it was in the air. I swung the branch with everything I had. I made contact with its head, and it stumbled to the side.

"Cheyenne!" Colt's thunderous voice rolled out. The creature leaped again as I staggered to my feet and ran. Both men were following behind me as I bolted for the trees. I darted behind a tree just as Colt and the beast rolled past. It broke free and came for me again. I took off sprinting. Colt was already to his feet in pursuit.

"Run, Cheyenne, run!" he bellowed.

I was doing my best to weave in and out of the trees when I was knocked to the ground. The monster's snarling teeth were next to my face. I released a blood-curdling scream. A moment later it was gone. Callon had ripped it away. I scrambled to my feet once more and ran. I had no idea where I was heading; I was just trying to stay alive.

The mist was too thick for me to see any great distance. It wasn't until I came upon the top of the ravine that I realized the danger I was in and froze. The hair on the back of my neck stood up as I heard the heavy snorts nearby. Cautiously twisting myself, fear seized my breath. Two additional creatures stood before me, and a third, smaller one was off to the side. I crept back and stood at the edge of the ravine. There was nowhere left to go but down.

"Colt," I called out in a shaky voice. "Anytime you want to help me would be great." I shook and tried to slow my breaths—it was next to impossible. The animals moved a step forward in unison, pink gums exposed, fangs dripping with saliva. They were fanning out slightly, ensuring I wasn't going to get away this time. Their ears twitched and then pointed back. I had no choice but to hold my ground as they made their approach.

"Colt, have I ever told you I don't like mean dogs? These dogs look really mean." I scanned the dark mist in search of him. The dogs' ears twitched again, but their focus remained on me.

"Colt," I called out again with more desperation. "Remember how you said you wouldn't leave me? This would constitute leaving me. I'd rather not be alone."

"You're not alone, Cheyenne." Colt's deep voice reached out and found me. I wasn't out of danger yet, but some relief washed over me. The creatures didn't move, and I kept my gaze locked on them. Callon and Colt were moving closer; the creatures saw them too. In the next second, they both sprang for me. I jumped to the right and landed in Daniel's arms—we disappeared.

"I have you," Daniel said, and I never felt such relief as I did in that moment.

"What took so long?" my quaking voice replied as I latched onto him tightly. He had jumped us closer to the third smaller creature. It just stared at us. It was strange; it looked timid.

"Go home," he said firmly, and the creature ran.

"How did..."

"I'll explain later. We need to leave." He jumped us through the misty shadows until we were back at the campsite. He pried my arms off and said, "Stay here. Dex and Lilly are close." And then he was gone.

A hand gripped my shoulder. I flinched as I tried to fall into a defensive crouch.

"Cheyenne," Lilly's soft voice said. "It's okay, they're gone."

I stared at her blankly for a second, trying to get my bearings straight. "You scared me. Where did you come from? Are you okay?" She was so small and seemed so helpless against these creatures.

"I'm just fine, my dear. Dex and I took care of a couple further out before they got here."

"There were so many..."

"Yes," she replied as she drew her arm around my shoulder. "They travel in packs, mostly threes, but tonight there were more."

"What are they?"

"They are called Tresez. They're very dangerous creatures, especially at night. With their black eyes and fur, they're difficult to see. The mist here made it even more challenging."

I glanced around through the misty darkness as I heard crackling of branches in the distance. "Do they roam the mountains here?" I said, panicking.

"No," she replied. "They were out on a hunt."

"Out on a hunt?" If they were out on a hunt, and they didn't roam the mountains here, then they were searching for something very specific. "What were they hunting, Lilly?" I said slowly, already guessing her answer.

Concern grew in her eyes. She hesitated. "You, Cheyenne. They were hunting you."

"But Colt said we'd be safe..." I trailed off looking at the embers in the fire. My mind repeated Lilly's words. "Because of who I am?" my voice cracked.

"No, because of what you are. They know you're going to be Timeless, but they don't know who you are."

"Who are they?"

"The Sarac are the ones who sent the Tresez." She threaded her arm through mine. "The Tresez are weapons the Sarac use. They send them out randomly to hunt down and destroy the children of the Timeless because you're still human, an easy target. If the Sarac knew who you were, the stronger ones would be here instead."

"They sent weaker ones? They will find out someday, won't they? And then we'll have to face even stronger beasts," I worried. "How did they find us?"

"Yes, I am afraid they will discover the truth someday. As far as finding us, they must have been tracking you and the boys without them knowing. We will be ready if they send more. Of course, there are no guarantees. We can only do our best and pray we overcome."

It hit me at once; I was the cause of all of this. They came because of me. How many other times while I was at my home in Idaho did they come for me? "I'm so sorry," I said in realization. "I didn't mean to drag you, Dex, or anybody into this mess. They're after me, not you."

"Cheyenne, look at me, honey." Lilly's blue eyes were so soft and caring. "You didn't drag anyone into this. We came willingly. There is a greater purpose to all of this than just who you are. We know what you're capable of, we know what your heritage is, and we know what you will become someday. You have something so great deep inside of you, and one day you will understand. We are here because we love you. Each one of us would give our lives for you."

Her words were filled with such compassion and love. I wanted to believe her. *She loved me? Already?* She drew me into her arms in a hug, and I realized just how much I missed my mom. It was so comforting to have Lilly near, even though I had only known her a short time. There was a deeper connection I didn't understand, didn't know how to explain. A tear rolled down my cheek. How did I get so lucky to have people like them around me? People who I hardly knew, but still loved me.

"Thank you, Lilly. I would give my life for you as well." And somehow I knew in my heart I would. We held our hug until we heard footsteps nearing. I turned to have Colt pull me away. My feet left the ground as his massive arms surrounded me. He hastily kissed me.

"Cheyenne, are you okay?" his voice was filled with deep concern.

"I'm fine, Colt." I quivered slightly. "I'm fine because everyone was here for me."

"We will always be here for you, always," he said passionately as his lips touched mine again softly. He gave me a squeeze and set me to the ground as we went back to the fire. Daniel was adding more wood as we sat.

"Thanks, Daniel," I said. His boyish face glowed in the firelight.

"Anything for my favorite horse whisperer," he replied with a faint grin.

Callon and Dex returned to the fire and sat with the rest of us.

"Thanks, Dex," I said softly.

"You're welcome, sweetheart. Can't say things aren't exciting when you're around." He winked as a smile creased his weathered cheeks.

I took Callon's hand in mine, trying to express my true gratitude, my trust. "Thank you. You've done so much for me, and I don't know if I've ever really showed you how much I appreciate it." I paused. "Without you, Colt, and Daniel, I wouldn't be alive today." I leaned closer, and hugged him. His warm embrace meant something more now, a connection that I hadn't felt before. His lips touched my ear and goose bumps rose.

"You're welcome," he whispered.

I sighed and slowly drew back, snuggling up under Colt's arm. It felt strange now when Callon touched me. It was more than just a touch. It went deeper. I didn't understand how it had changed.

We sat by the fire quietly, as they were still on guard. Each sound in the forest was carefully evaluated. I replayed what had taken place, and knew I would not sleep again tonight. I always knew Colt was strong, but to see him break the neck of the massive Tresez caused me to shiver. Callon's strength was different—but both were equally strong. I was very well protected, and loved—and grateful.

CHAPTER 22

For safety reasons, we waited until dawn before we broke camp. Tension was in the air from the night before; I knew it was going to be a long ride back to the cabin. I insisted I could ride on my own, and Lilly finally helped me convince the boys I was fine.

We rode in a tight formation; Daniel led, with Callon and Colt flanking me. Dex and Lilly were close behind. The sun was shining for the moment, but we could see the dark storm clouds on the horizon. The clouds billowed in the distance and turned the sky a grayish black. It seemed a severe storm was on its way, and we were directly in its path. Anxious, Mandi trotted with wild snorts. We all knew the last lightning storm caused her to run; I wasn't sure how she would react this time. I was with her, but did that make a difference?

We were still two to three hours away when the storm hit. The winds began their assault first, blowing dirt and dust high into the air, making visibility low. It came in sudden bursts, screeching, reaching, trying to grasp out in anger, whipping and slapping at us angrily. Even my jeans did nothing to stop the cold and the stinging dirt particles.

The winds continued, and then the torrential rains began. The water pounded against us, cutting as it cuffed our exposed skin. I lowered myself and buried my face closer to Mandi's mane. It did little good, and the driving rain continued its relentless battering. She was becoming restless, prancing her hooves into the ground. Callon attempted to grab her bridle when lightning struck with such magnitude that it shook the earth around us. Mandi reared up on her hind legs and bolted, with me still attached.

The reins fell from my fingers. I thrust myself forward to latch on to her mane. I knew I couldn't control her. I followed her rhythm while she ran. This was the second time I had been on a runaway horse; this time, however, I had a better idea of what to expect and how to react. I could barely make out the sound of pounding hooves behind us over the rushing wind and rain. Mandi was too fast for them to catch her. Rapidly I began to realize I was on my own.

As unpredictable as she had started, Mandi suddenly came to an abrupt halt. I scrambled to right myself quickly so I wasn't tossed from the saddle. Her head flashed from side to side and then she let out a wild series of snorts. The sound made my skin crawl. Something wasn't right. Out of the corner of my eye, I caught sight of what had caused her to halt; three Tresezes were crouched in the deep grasses. I realized she had gained too much distance from the rest. It would take several minutes for them to arrive—minutes I didn't have.

I lunged forward and grabbed the reins. I had no idea what I was about to do, but at least I would have a little more control. I spoke to Mandi while I held her steady; I could only pray she understood.

"You're going to have to help me, Mandi," I said somewhat calmly, trying to prevent them from jumping. "We need to run fast, very fast. I need you to keep me safe. You're the only one who can help me now." As soon as the words were off my lips, she bolted again, and I leaned forward. Something brushed across my back as she took off in a gallop. I didn't dare look back. I knew what had touched me—a Tresez.

Mandi ran like a thoroughbred racehorse, faster than anything I had ever experienced. We were barreling across the valley at such a rapid pace that I had the sensation I was flying. We were one, moving in unison, our bodies twined together in a single motion. The gully we crossed the day before lay ahead. It was wide enough to ride down, but today, we didn't have that luxury. I glanced back; the three creatures were running full speed, each flanking the other. Callon and Colt were in close pursuit. We had no choice; we had to jump the gully, all fifteen to twenty feet.

My heart leaped into my throat. I touched Mandi's neck and tried to reassure her. "We have to jump this, girl. We don't have any other options. You can do this. I believe in you, Mandi."

She showed no hesitation as we leaped out over the gully, landing safely on the other side, with me still in the saddle. My pulse was racing, blood surging through my veins. Rain was pelting my face; each drop that hit stung. I twisted again to locate the creatures, and watched Colt leap from his horse as one ran towards him. Callon was chasing down the second.

My heart skipped a beat. The third remained in pursuit; it had jumped the gully also. It was faster and stronger than the others; and quickly gaining ground. I could barely see Daniel, Dex, and Lilly coming from behind; the blinding storm was too strong. Mandi jumped, and I lost my balance. I tumbled to the ground and rolled to my side, springing to my feet. I had no explanation how I was able to do this so gracefully, other than adrenaline.

My eyes flashed wildly, trying to take in the layout of the land. I spotted a sturdy branch and grabbed it. I swiftly readied myself as I planted my feet. As the creature came into clear view, it slowed its approach. It began stalking, circling, and slowly creeping closer.

It was becoming harder to see. The wind and driving rain were coming down with such force that it was difficult to stand upright. With eyes as black as midnight, only the Tresez's yellow fangs and pink gums had any coloring to them. As it rushed towards me, I gathered enough momentum in my swing to hit it on the skull, causing it to stumble. It only took a few steps and turned quickly again. Panic rose in my chest. This beast seemed larger than the others and had every intention of ending my life.

Its lips rose in a deep rumbling growl. It began circling, looking for my weakness. My fingers ached as I held the wood tightly waiting for the Tresez to make its next move. My breaths came in short, hard bursts, and my eyes blurred as the rain almost blinded me. The creature lunged in a burst of speed, and I rolled to the side, barely escaping as my make-shift weapon once again came down on its skull. A yelp escaped its mouth, and its black eyes focused in on me with death.

I barely had time to scramble to my feet before it attacked again. Anger rose to the surface. I was not going to let this creature get the best of me. He was hunting me, but I would win in the end. It leaped, and I pushed the branch into the ground so it was upright, holding it with all my might. It fell upon the branch, and the end pierced its body. We tumbled to the ground. There was no struggle— the branch had killed my foe.

The weight of the repulsive creature had me pinned to the ground. Its grisly teeth were next to my face, and its hot saliva was running down my neck. It was becoming difficult to breathe with the dead weight upon me. Its smell was horrid, rancid—unlike anything I have ever smelled previously. It was becoming almost impossible to bear its weight.

Daniel's desperate words reached my ears, "Cheyenne! No, Cheyenne!"

He pushed the creature off and pulled me into an upright position. My limbs came back to life with a painful tingle as the blood returned. Breathlessly I replied, "What took you so long?" I paused, waiting for the oxygen to reach my brain. "Do I have to do everything on my own here?"

I attempted to open my eyes, but the pounding rain impaired my vision. Nervously Daniel chuckled as he drew me up into his arms, "Glad I could come and help a little."

"Is everyone okay? Are the remaining Tresez dead?"

"We're just fine. They're gone now. Mandi is fast and covered a lot of ground. The rest will be here soon."

"Where's Mandi?" I asked in a panic. "Is she alright? She's the reason I'm still alive. She protected me like I asked her."

"She's close; she's fine."

"Cheyenne!" Callon's anxious voice called out.

Daniel turned slightly as he replied, "She's fine, Callon. The Tresez fell on her when she killed it." He smiled. "She just needs to catch her breath." Callon kneeled next to us, and began wiping the mud and blood from my face.

"You killed the Tresez?" he asked in surprise.

"I didn't have much choice, since the three of you were off playing with the others."

Colt appeared behind Daniel. He looked relieved as he reached over and touched my hand. "Playing with the dogs are you?"

"I wasn't able to teach this one new tricks, so I got rid of it," I replied quickly. Three apprehensive grins appeared.

Dex and Lilly arrived. "We need to get moving. I don't like this weather," Lilly said with stress radiating in her voice. "Cheyenne is already soaked to the bone. We need to get her back quickly."

The tremors started as I sat. I was soaked like the rest, and the adrenaline was gone. I was becoming cold rapidly, as I was sure they were also. I attempted to rise, but Callon scooped me up into his arms.

"I'm fine," I said through chattering teeth. "I can ride back on my own." He didn't listen as he placed me in Colt's waiting arms.

The rain was unrelenting. Colt tried to shield me. He handed me up to Callon after he mounted his horse. I knew why I rode with Callon. He was performing his doctoral duty and needed to be near me.

The remaining ride back was treacherous. The rain-soaked ground made it slippery going. We were not able to gallop or trot. I kept my head down and eyes closed as the rain slapped at my cheeks. Tremors raked me as my teeth chattered. I pressed my back against Callon's chest, but it did little to provide warmth. It only brought to light the ache in my back that was beginning to grow. The Tresez's weight must have pulled a muscle or something. Callon tried to help shield me to no avail. The storm was unwavering.

As we slowed, I saw Colt reaching for me; he swept me away into the cabin as Lilly opened the door. Once inside, we headed straight for the bathroom to the enormous walk in shower. The water was running; it was already warm. Colt set me to my feet, and helped hold me up. Lilly began prying off my bloody and muddy clothes. She paused briefly at my back before continuing.

I was glad I had my swimsuit on. Colt removed his shirt and pressed his warm chest against me. I realized I was colder than I thought; he had goose bumps on his arms and chest. Lilly was standing behind me rubbing my arms and legs, trying to circulate the blood to warm me. She walked away for a moment and returned with Dex and Callon. Not a word was said as they stood staring at my back.

"W-w-what's wrong?" I managed to say through chattering teeth. "Am I that hideous?" I tried to turn, but Colt held me still.

"Cheyenne," Dex said warily. "Did the Tresez claw you when you were on the ground?"

"No," I replied as I thought back. "At least I don't remember being clawed. I don't have marks on the front of me. Why?" The chattering was slowing as I was warming.

"You have some deep scratches on your back. They look like claw marks." Dex touched my back, his fingers running the length of them. I flinched. I hadn't realized they were there. That would explain the ache.

"Is it that bad?"

"Possibly," he replied with deliberate hesitation.

Great! What more could happen to me? Wrapping myself up in bubble wrap was starting to look like a good idea...at least it might prevent some injuries. At least I could look forward to being more durable when I was Timeless. I could still be injured, and it might hurt, but at least I would heal quickly.

I began replaying in my mind what took place when I came upon the Tresez. Was there anything that happened I could remember clearly to know one of them had scratched me? Then it came to me!

"Dex, when Mandi and I first came upon them, something touched my back as we began to run. It didn't hurt. I just assumed one of them leaped and missed. Apparently that wasn't the case?"

The water stopped.

"We need to get a better look at these. Lilly is going to help you get changed, and then we'll see what needs to be done."

Lilly gingerly wrapped the warm towel around my shoulders, and I moved away from Colt. There was deep worry in his eyes as he turned and walked away. Lilly took me to the bedroom where I changed into jeans and a tank top. We tried to dry my sopping wet hair, but gave up and went to the great room where the others were waiting.

A fire was roaring and everyone except Lilly was already changed and dry. Colt drew me into his arms as we entered and walked to Callon and Dex, who were anxiously waiting in the kitchen.

"I'd like to take a look at your back now." Callon said as he read my response. "This is going to take a few moments. I need you to be patient with us," he said compassionately.

"I understand," I replied quietly. Colt turned me so I was leaning into his chest. His long-sleeved shirt was open, and my cold cheek touched his bare chest for the second time. Warmth filled me. They pulled my hair aside, and Colt cradled my shoulder in one arm and my head in the other. Carefully they pulled up my tank, revealing the deep lacerations. Warm fingers tugged the material aside and moved lightly on my back. It sent goose bumps down my arms.

With the warmth finally touching me, fatigue hit hard. I closed my eyes and soon relaxed in Colt's hold. My arms began sagging at my sides as I slipped down further. He adjusted his hand to support me more.

"Cheyenne," Dex said softly. "We're going to stitch these up. I'm sorry; you've been so patient, just a little bit longer. There are pieces of broken nails we need to remove first." He hesitated. "Cheyenne? Can you hear me?"

I heard his words, but I didn't care anymore. All I wanted to do was sleep. My legs were weak, but Colt held me upright.

"She's falling asleep, Dex. I have her. Go ahead and finish," Colt said quietly.

I never did fall asleep. I was hanging in a semi-comatose state for a long time. They pulled and pricked, but none of it hurt, except for a few dull twinges.

"Did you get it all?" Colt's deep voice rumbled in my ear.

"I think so. There were quite a few nail fragments embedded deep in the wound," Callon replied.

"We'll know soon enough if we didn't," Dex added.

They pulled my shirt down, and Colt gingerly lifted me. "Are we done?" I said groggily.

"Yes, at least for now. You want to lie down?" Colt asked tenderly.

"No, just stay with me please. You're warm. Can we sit by the fire?"

"Sure." He held me in his lap, and I buried myself further into his heat.

Soft small fingers touched my cheek and forehead. "Dex," Lilly said with concern. "She's still so cold." She draped a blanket over me, and I dozed for a long time, never really resting, catching bits and pieces of their conversations.

"They sent out nine Tresezes this time. Daniel said one ran off.

313

They're going to hear about what happened when it returns," Callon stated.

"How much time do you think we have?" Dex's steady voice asked.

"It's hard to say.. We'll need to move soon," Callon replied.

"I don't think you should go alone, Callon." Lilly said firmly. "Dex and I can come. Qaysean and Sahara would have wanted us to be a part of it."

Was I dreaming? Did I hear them say they knew my parents? She said Qaysean and Sahara would have wanted this. Wanted what?

"Lilly," Dex said quickly. "I think we may be needed elsewhere. We have to prepare things. They are more than capable of protecting her."

"I can't leave her now. She needs us," Lilly protested.

"Lilly, I know you want to stay with her. I promise you we'll see her again, but right now we need to prepare the others. We have to organize the clans. It will take months. They love her too much to let anything happen. You need to trust me on this." Dex's voice was filled with such empathy and authority that she hesitated with her response.

"We've waited for so long," her voice crackled. "I just want to be there for her."

"I know," he said with sympathy. "And you will be, in time. We have to be patient just a little longer. She needs to figure out who she is first, what truly lies within herself. Only then will she be able to accomplish what needs to be done. We'll all be together again someday."

What did I need to figure out, and what was I expected to accomplish? Was that in the journal? Silence filled the space again,

314

and only the crackling of the fire remained.

There was a strange sensation, a tingling on my back, on the right side below my shoulder blade. Shivering, I looked up. Colt was staring at me curiously. It happened again, stronger. I twitched my neck and pulled my shoulder up slightly.

"What's wrong?" he asked as his brow furrowed.

It happened again, only this time it was more like a prick. I squinted my eyes and sat upright. His hand tensed on my leg.

"Cheyenne," he said in distress. "What's wrong?"

I didn't know. It came again, a deep pinch. I winched my shoulders back, and pushed my brows together. My right arm began to tingle. I quickly scanned the room. All attention was on me. Wide-eyed, I leaped to my feet and arched my shoulders back for a moment.

"Cheyenne?" Dex said with anxiety. He and Callon were next to me now.

"Give me a minute," I said breathlessly. I relaxed my shoulders, and looked at them with reservations. "You said there were nail fragments. Did you remove them all?" Both hesitated. This wasn't good. Irritation was quickly rising. "You don't know, do you?" Another sharp pain shot to the surface, and I clenched my teeth together to prevent myself from screaming. My eyes began to water. "What should I expect? Is this going to get worse?" There was an edge to my words.

"Yes," Dex replied.

I balled my hands into fists as the stabbing pain returned. It lasted longer this time, like a hot iron was branding me.

"What should I expect?" I bellowed out. "Tell me!"

Lilly stepped closer.

"Lilly," Dex said forcibly. "Step away from her now."

"Why?" I snapped back.

"Cheyenne, you may hurt her."

"I may hurt her?" I said angrily. "I'm not strong enough..." I trailed off as the piercing pain returned. Leaning forward, I grasped my shoulders with my hands. Stepping closer, Callon attempted to reach out. I straightened and swiftly took two steps back. "Don't touch me," I said through clenched teeth.

Colt was still sitting on the hearth. Callon was closest to me with Dex and Daniel just a few steps behind. Lilly had moved back into the kitchen, panic in her eyes, uncertain what would take place next.

"Colt, Daniel, Callon," Dex said calmly. "It's going to take all three of you for this. We don't want to hurt her."

It hit again, the sensation that someone was stabbing me with a knife over and over again. Callon stepped forward, and I took three steps to the side. I was now in the center of the great room. Colt and Daniel were flanking Callon's sides. The pain wasn't subsiding, and deep within, a rage I didn't understand was building. Fury was running through my veins—no one was going to touch me—no one!

"Come closer, and I'll snap your wrists!" I screamed, surprised at my own violent outburst.

Every muscle was tense as I waited for their next move. In unison, all three stepped forward, spreading out further. "I'll scratch out your eyes!" I spit out with venom. "I warned you!"

Callon leaped, his hands grasping at me. I turned and jumped, clearing the couch in one swift movement. I was completely focused as they stared in disbelief. Colt nodded as he moved to the side of the couch while Daniel did the same. Glancing around, I still had plenty of room to make it to the front door.

Callon suddenly sprang over the couch, and I darted to the right, barely avoiding Colt's grasp and headed for the front door. It opened, and I was about to slide through when Callon caught hold of my wrist, yanking me back and throwing me into Colt's arms. Immediately he pinned my wrist to my sides, I was able to squirm enough to make it difficult for him. My legs went out from under me; Daniel was trying to contain them. I was kicking and flailing about, but they moved me to the kitchen table. Dex was waiting, and I was pushed face down.

Colt pinned my shoulders and hands. Daniel was at my legs and Callon was at my waist.

"No!" I screeched. "Just leave me alone!"

Dex pulled up my shirt, and cold fingers began running over the wound, stopping in one location just above my right shoulder blade. Fighting with all my strength, I tried to break free, but they held me firm.

"Cheyenne," Dex said firmly. "This is going to be very painful. I am going to try and remove the fragment; I need you to be very still. Can you do that for me?"

I heard his request, but I couldn't comply. I was groaning, thrashing about, unable to stop. Lilly's fingers brushed my cheek, pulling the hair away, her words were soft, soothing, calming. "Cheyenne, you can do this. Concentrate on something else. Dex needs you to be still. He won't be able to remove the poison if you don't. He doesn't want to hurt you." She paused. "Think about your music. Play the songs in your head. You said it calms you. You've got to try—you've got to try." She kept repeating her words in a calm, reassuring tone.

I concentrated on her voice, her words, and the music began playing in my mind. I imagined my hands drifting over the keyboard, strumming the guitar strings. Eventually I was able to control the rage and became still. Their grips only loosened slightly. Dex was tugging at my back. After a period of time, the pain began to subside. The tension in my body lessened, and I eventually lay limp on the table.

They released their hold only after Dex gave the okay. Colt immediately lifted me into his arms, my legs falling to the floor. He held me for a long time before I was able to compose myself.

"I'm sorry," I said weakly. "I didn't mean to get so angry—it hurt so much. I didn't want anyone to touch me. I'm so sorry." I truly felt awful. I didn't like feeling so out of control.

"Everything's fine now, Cheyenne," Dex's reassuring voice said. "You actually did better than I expected. I've seen others react much worse than what you did. We know you couldn't control yourself. It was the poison from the Tresez starting to work its way through your system. We won't hold it against you."

"I don't know about that," Daniel chimed in, chuckling to ease the tension. "She popped me in the jaw pretty good with her feet a couple of times." Soon the room was filled with light laughter. Daniel had a way of turning things around and seeing the funny side.

"Dex?" I called out as Colt rubbed my arms. "Did Callon tell you about my theory of three? My accidents come in threes."

"Yes, he did, Cheyenne," he replied calmly. "It's very interesting. I think we need to keep it in mind..." he trailed off, deep in thought.

Colt released his hold, and took my hand as we went back to the couch. I hesitated as I glanced around the room. "I don't want to offend anyone, but I'm feeling a little worn out. If you don't mind, I think I've had enough excitement for one day to last a while. I'm going to head to bed." I turned to Colt. "Do you mind?" He didn't reply, but came with me.

"Good night," Lilly called out.

Colt followed me to the bedroom.

"You don't have to stay with me. If you want to talk with everyone, I understand. You've been holding me all afternoon," I said reluctantly. I really did want him to stay, but I wanted him to want it too. He plopped down in the bed, and patted his hand for me to come and sit.

"I'm not going anywhere. You're stuck with me all night." A satisfied grin spread over his lips. Sighing, I continued forward as he drew down the covers, and I slid under. I touched his hand as he was about to pull them back over me.

"I'm still cold. Do you mind?" I didn't need to say another word. He hopped over the side of the bed, and removed his shoes as he crawled in next to me. He pulled me into his arms, and I lay my cheek on his bare chest again. His warmth filled me as I curled up as close as I could.

"Colt," I whispered.

"Umm?"

"Thank you. I feel like I'm even more of a burden. I'm sorry."

"Maybe I want to bear your burden." He kissed my head, as his hand rubbed my lower back, careful to stay away from the wounds.

"It's not fair for me to ask that of you."

"You didn't ask. I took it—just me being selfish again. Besides, if someone weren't out to get you, none of this would be happening. You were never that accident prone."

"Will it ever end?" I wondered out loud. "Will my life ever be normal again?"

He sighed. "You weren't born under normal circumstances. Your life as you knew it will never be the same again. You're forever changed."

I looked up, with my brows creased. "Why me? Why was I chosen?"

"Who knows why things happen to some of us and not others. It's not always our choice. You are special, Cheyenne. You have no idea who you will become someday, the woman you are becoming now." His fingers began to lightly stroke my cheek, our gaze locked together.

I didn't understand my destiny, didn't understand why any of this was happening to me, but at least I had Colt. I had his undying love, his protection, and his strength. I was strong, but somehow with him I felt stronger—more capable. I could do this if he were here with me.

Lifting my chin with his fingers, his lips caressed mine once, twice, three times before he drew back slightly. "I love you," he murmured on my lips.

I closed my eyes. "I love you too," I whispered faintly. I snuggled back into his arms, and drifted off to sleep—warm, secure, and loved.

CHAPTER 23

The morning light was bright and cheery. Colt had kept his word, and I woke up still in his arms. I lifted my chin and saw his dazzling smile.

"Morning, sunshine." He tenderly kissed my forehead. "Did you sleep well?" he asked cheerfully.

Stifling a yawn, I replied, "Yes, actually I did. How late is it?"

"Ten a.m."

My eyes grew wide. "Geez! I slept for over twelve hours? Why didn't you wake me? I'm sorry I made you lay here all that time. You should have told me."

"You were really tired. You barely moved. The only way I could tell you were still alive was your breathing." A grin crept over his lips; I couldn't help but stare at them and think...

"Besides," he continued, "it wasn't so bad for me. I spent the last twelve hours alone with you in my arms. I'm not complaining at all."

I sighed. "You know, I really don't deserve you. There are plenty of other girls out there that wouldn't be this much trouble." I really was lucky.

"Yeah, but what fun would that be?"

I leaned up and kissed him before I climbed out from under his arms. I sat at the edge of the bed facing away and scanned the room. He still hadn't brought my backpack in yet. It was as if he was holding it ransom, for some reason. It didn't make sense. "Colt?"

"Yeah?" he replied as his arm wrapped around my waist and he drew me back against his chest.

"Do you know where my backpack is? I'd like my blue shirt." He squeezed my waist and climbed out of bed as he left the room. Moments later, he returned with clothes in hand, smiling. I glanced up as he handed them to me. "Why can't I have the whole thing?"

"Because if I have your clothes, you can't run off."

"And where would I be going?"

"You've done it before." He arched a brow.

I rolled my eyes. "You're impossible. I could buy new clothes in a number of different places. They're called stores." I took the clothes and went to the bathroom to change. Lilly said they'd wait to talk to me about the journal because of the trauma I'd been through, but I was ready to know more. Callon had mentioned last night we needed to get moving again. We didn't have much time left here.

As I stepped out of the bathroom, Colt was leaning against the wall, arms crossed. He had already showered and changed; somehow he always beat me. I stood still for a few moments just drinking in the sight of him. His jeans were well worn in all the right places, and his snug t-shirt accentuated his brawny muscles. He cleared his throat, and I realized I was ogling him. His smile deepened.

"How do you do that?" I asked.

"Do what?" He tilted his head.

"Get changed, cleaned up so fast? I know I'm not that slow. How can you be so much faster?"

"It's a gift." He smirked.

I knew I wouldn't get very far so I dropped the subject. I followed as he led the way to the great room, admiring the view along the way. As we rounded the corner, Lilly smiled warmly as Colt and I headed for the table. She had made me breakfast.

"Thanks, Lilly. It looks delicious."

"You're welcome, my dear." She touched my shoulder gently. "Are you feeling better today?" she asked sincerely.

"Much better, thank you." I gulped the food quickly, as Colt watched in awe.

"I guess you really were hungry this morning," he said chuckling.

Grinning, I took my plate to the sink to wash it. Once done, we headed for the couch. Dex had the journal in his hands; he appeared to be waiting. I plopped down next to Callon; Colt sat on my other side. Daniel gently tugged my hair as he passed and sat next to Dex; a faint smile appeared on Dex's face.

"We're going to talk about the journal today?" I looked at Dex hopefully. "I'd like to know more about it if you can tell me." I wanted to know more about who I was.

"There is a lot I don't understand, Cheyenne. I'll do my best." He seemed to pause to collect his thoughts before continuing. Lilly moved to sit in the loveseat beside him, and I waited anxiously for him to resume.

He looked down at the journal in his weathered hands, running his thumbs over the spine. "The writings in the back of the book are mostly your family history. It's written in an old, forgotten language, not many know it." He sighed. "I've had difficulties with it and will

323

try and give my best interpretation. However, you must keep in mind it might not be perfect." His hazel eyes were sincere and warm as he studied mine.

"I understand."

"Callon has already shared with you a lot about your parents, where they came from, and how they joined together to fight the Sarac." He waited until I nodded. "When your mother, Sahara, left her father, Jorelle, it caused her great heartache. She loved him very much, but she knew Makhi was just using him to get what he wanted. Makhi convinced her father to betroth her to Marcus, his son. The joining of the two clans was thought to create a powerful, almost undefeatable, alliance. Your mother was very beautiful, and Marcus wanted her not only for her power but also her beauty. She, of course, wanted nothing to do with him—she saw through his mask."

He shifted in his seat, his eyes still locked on mine as his fingers continued to rub the worn leather journal.

"Your mother managed to leave the Sarac, only to hear they had killed her father out of anger and desperation, hoping she would return because of it. She was now driven to destroy them; she knew their hearts' desire was power and greed. She sought out Qaysean after hearing rumors he was alive. She asked for his help, but your father didn't believe her. He thought it was a trick. After many months together, though, he realized she spoke the truth. A relationship developed, and they fell in love. They shared a common goal: to rid the world of the Sarac leaders. Fighting side by side for many years, they grew stronger together—they became a threat to the Sarac."

He hesitated. "I know this is a lot to absorb. Do you want to hear

324

more?"

"Please, Dex," I replied earnestly. "I need to know more." I'd been waiting for so long, and we'd come all this way.

"Marcus was enraged at the thought of your mother with another man, especially Qaysean. When your father killed Makhi, Marcus vowed to destroy them both and end the Kvech family line. Your mother became pregnant with you and everything changed. Their whole life revolved around protecting you, keeping you a secret from Marcus. If he knew about you, you would have been killed with your parents.

"Your parents sought out Gene and Alexis. They didn't know them, but knew of them. They were the most capable amongst us. Your parents could have asked Lilly and me, but it was far too dangerous since we were part of their rebellion. They sought out someone who was not close to them, someone Marcus wouldn't think to look for. Gene and Alexis took you in, knowing someday they would probably lose their lives for you."

The tears began to stream down my cheeks and I ducked my head to hide them. My adoptive parents knew all along they would die for me, yet they still said yes. Why? Why was I worthy of such sacrifices? Colt's bulky fingers began to rub my back gently. I raised my head up again. "It's okay. I'm okay. Please tell me more."

"Your parents had planned on returning to you someday, once Marcus was gone. He still knew nothing of your existence." His voice deepened, and the emotions filling it were almost palpable. "Your parents never had the opportunity to return. Marcus found and killed them. Gene and Alexis became your sole guardians. They loved you as if you were their own, Cheyenne. They protected you over the years so many times and tried to teach you the valuable things that would help you later on. They tried to provide you with the best they could without ever letting you know your true identity.

"Callon, Colt, and Daniel came into your life a number of years ago. They were told nothing of who you were; only that they needed to protect you. They all agreed willingly. Dangers were lurking everywhere—help was needed. You met Colt, but Daniel and Callon were always on the sidelines, watching and waiting, protecting when needed. There was a lot that took place you never knew about. Gene and Alexis kept moving so often because they were searching for a better location, something more secure. They were unable to share their secret with anyone—even you."

It all made sense now, their constant travels, our moves.

"It was just as Callon told you: Gene and Alexis were murdered. Marcus covered his tracks by making it appear to be an auto accident. We've come to the conclusion he knew nothing about you until recently. The way he's been acting would make us believe he just thinks you to be another child of the Timeless."

I stared at my rings. They represented who I was, what I belonged to. All of these people were protecting me from something I didn't understand, something I knew nothing about. They were willing to sacrifice their lives for me; some already had. I kept my head down.

"You knew my parents," I said in a whisper.

There was a moment's pause before he replied, "Yes, we did."

"Did you know of my existence?" I wasn't sure from what he'd already told me.

"No, they hid it from us. They didn't want to put our lives in danger. They knew we would have taken you in without question. We didn't know until Callon told us. It was safer this way."

My lips quivered, and my voice cracked, "What were they like?" I raised my eyes and saw the oceans of sorrow Dex had for me.

"They were the most wonderful, caring people we had ever met," Lilly said tenderly. "They had such a great love for each other and were determined to make things right for everyone. They wanted to ensure we as Timeless were safe from the Sarac clan." She shifted in her seat. I knew she wanted to come to me, but she remained seated. Dex's fingers touched her arm in support.

"You have so much of both of them in you. Your father was musical. The guitar here was his. We could sit and listen to him play for hours. He had a way with the music, just as you do. He was strong and had a deep passion for life."

A tear glistened in her lashes as she smiled. "Your mother had a passion too, but it was different. I see it in you as well. You remind me of her in so many ways...you're just as beautiful. I can see you have the same determination and temperament; you're independent and strong—just like she was. She was a fighter—you're a fighter."

She rose, stopping before me on her knees, taking my hands in hers. "Your parents loved you so much. They gave their lives to protect you. Gene and Alexis gave their lives to protect you, and we would do the same."

I couldn't say a word as I stared into her sincere blue eyes. Every feature about her was loving, caring, and truthful. I had no doubt in my mind she meant everything she said. The tears were building, and I was fighting to hold them back. They had known my parents; I could do what they had done—be brave and help defeat the evil in our world before it passed to the mortal world. I had their characteristics. I belonged to someone—and they loved me.

My younger years had been spent wondering about my birth parents, what had really happened, how they had died. I never knew if they loved me—I had known nothing about them. What I did know was my adoptive parents loved me; they treated me as their own and sacrificed to keep me from harm. They had given up so much for me to live. I never got the opportunity to tell them how I really felt about them. I never told them how much I loved them, as an adult, understanding all the sacrifices they made for me—I would never make that mistake again.

I sighed. There was so much more I wanted to know, but at the moment, I was emotionally overwhelmed and quickly losing control of my tears. I withdrew my hands from Lilly's and rose from the couch. Colt reached for my hand; I squeezed his fingers and let them drop. I headed for the front door and walked out onto the porch, stopping briefly to look out into the valley. I saw movement out of the corner of my eye and knew one of them would be shadowing my every move.

I stepped off the porch and headed for the river Colt had taken me to when we first arrived. I guessed the direction and strained to hear the sounds of rushing water. Footsteps followed at a distance; I knew it wasn't safe for me to be alone. I fought to push the tears down. The fresh air was helping to clear my head. As far back as I could remember, when I was stressed or just needed to think things through, solitude is what I needed.

I walked for a long time; my head running through the last discussion. All the details I had been missing—the pieces of the puzzle were slowly coming together. There was still so much I didn't know or understand. I heard the sound of the water and lifted my head. I stopped at a nearby ledge overlooking the river. A shiver ran down my spine; this had to have been where Colt jumped. A path lay to the right; I followed it to the river's edge. A large boulder sat in a shaft of inviting sunlight, and I climbed down to sit. I closed my eyes and listened to the water as it harmonized with the rocks it splashed over. It was a soothing sound.

Callon sat next to me, but I didn't look up.

"It's a lot to take in, Cheyenne," Callon's empathetic voice said. I didn't answer, but I agreed. We sat in silence for a long time.

"There's so much you need to know, so much I want to tell you," Callon's voice was warm, caring. "In time, we'll be able to talk freely, and you'll understand why I've held back."

I curled my legs to my chest, wrapping my arms around myself. I rested my chin on my knees. I turned and saw Callon was facing me, his eyes searching mine. It was strange the way he was staring; it seemed as if it held a deeper longing. I tried to look away, but my gaze kept drifting back. His eyes were so mesmerizing the way the brown, green, and amber swirled together. There was so much more to him than I knew, so much I didn't understand. It was as if at times he showed me his warmth, and then only a small crack.

I sighed. "Why are you so willing to sacrifice your life for mine, Callon?" I asked. "I don't understand. You don't have to do this...no one does." A warm breeze touched my cheeks.

"You're right, I don't have to do anything." He paused. "I do it out of love and devotion. I do it because of who you are, and what you will become."

I didn't understand. "Love and devotion? How can you? You really don't know me."

"I know you more than you think. You forget I've been with you for a couple of years. You just never knew it."

I averted my eyes, staring down at my hands—at the rings. "You didn't answer my question, Callon," I said calmly as I began running my thumb over the Servak ring, letting my fingers feel the ridges in the symbols.

I kept my focus on the ring, as he continued. "I've watched over you for such a long time, observed you change into the woman you are now. The little things you do. I know when you're upset, you like to be by yourself. You pull yourself inward to deal with your emotions. Sometimes you like to run or walk or you'll play music to calm yourself until you can resolve the issue.

"When you're deep in thought, your eyes tend to turn grey. When you're happy, they're blue. When you're sad, they're a blue green. When you tease or contemplate something, you bite your lower lip." He lifted his hand to mine, stopping me from playing with my ring, and I glanced up. "When you want to be distracted, you play with your ring."

His eyes were such deep pools of emotions, emotions he was holding back. He continued, and I looked down once again. "Most of the time, you're not afraid to show your feelings, and when you're angry, you let it out. You spit out words and regret them later. When you're happy, you spread the happiness to others around you." His fingers began to caress mine. "You're not afraid to be alone, and sometimes you actually prefer it. You have a passion for life. You're not afraid to take chances, except in a relationship. You're scared of heights, and you don't like cliff diving." He let out a soft chuckle at that.

His long fingers lifted my chin, and I was desperately fighting an internal battle. That unknown sensation was rising up from within again. The connection with him I didn't understand.

"I think I know you pretty well," he concluded. "Probably better than you know yourself. This is not sudden for me; it has grown over a couple years." He paused, and I grew panicked. What was he confessing to me?

"There were times I had wanted to tell you who I was, what you meant to me. I couldn't until now. All those nights I watched over you sleeping, all those days protecting you in the shadows. I longed to be the one to comfort you when Gene and Alexis died. How I wanted to hold you in my arms. This is why I can say I watch over you out of love and devotion. I'm devoted to you eternally."

He released my chin, and I stared at the rock. I couldn't believe he was saying he loved me. Why now? He could have told me earlier, but then again I probably would have bolted. He was right about one thing—relationships were hard for me. It took a long time to figure out I loved Colt. I had the hardest time admitting it, even to myself.

"That's not true." At least for my immediate purpose, it wasn't true. His gaze was questioning. "It's not true about taking a chance in a relationship. If you remember correctly, I told Colt I loved him."

"Yes, you did, but I don't think it had the same meaning you thought it did. I don't know if you truly grasp the meaning of love." He sighed. "You've only had a short nineteen years of life, much of which you never really expressed love. You loved Gene and Alexis, but not like you would have if they were your birth parents. You've held a part of yourself back because you were afraid that if your birth parents left you, they might too. You tend to hold your deep feelings back. Until you let them out, you'll never know the true meaning of love."

What was this feeling deep in the pit of my stomach? Was I actually sensing something more for him? "Are you trying to take me from Colt, Callon?"

"I'm just telling you how I see it."

I turned my head down, drew my hand back and began rubbing my ring again. His fingers passed into my vision, and I saw something I hadn't seen before, a ring on his right index finger. I lowered my hand and took his in mine as I studied the ring. I twisted the thick silver band, and it revealed similar symbols to my Servak ring. Two clover-like symbols were the same as mine, but the others were different. I tilted my head in curiosity, and looked up.

"You have a ring too?"

"Yes," he replied quietly.

"Have you been wearing it this whole time?" I could have sworn I had never seen it before now.

"No."

"Why?"

"I didn't fully understand it until recently."

"It means something to you?"

"Yes."

"Does mine mean something for me then? I know it stands for the Servak clan, but is there more?"

"Yes."

He wasn't going to give any more information than simple answers, but for once I didn't want to get worked up about it. "You're not going to tell me are you?"

"No," he sighed. "You need to figure this out for yourself. I'm sorry."

I rolled my eyes. "You say you're sorry, but somehow I think you just like to torture me, drive me crazy on purpose. Keep me guessing all the time." A small smirk crossed my lips.

A slight smile appeared on his face. "You got me; you figured out my plan all along. Now what am I going to do?" he said sarcastically.

He grasped my hand and helped me up. "Shall we?" He gestured back toward the cabin, and I followed. We strolled back lazily.

"Callon, what's your story? All this time I've been obsessed about finding my life story, and I never once asked about yours."

"Pretty normal," he replied.

Stopping, I turned. "Excuse me? Normal? How can you say that? Being Timeless is not a normal thing."

"I had a mother and father. I was raised under fairly normal circumstances, and my parents died a long time ago," he said without emotions.

I could see this wasn't going to be easy. I was going to have to dig deeper to find out. I sighed, and we began walking again. I drilled him with more questions. "Where were you raised?"

"Ireland."

Surprised, I continued to question him. "Where's your accent then?"

He chuckled lightly. "I haven't lived there in over two hundred years. I don't have it anymore."

"Where else have you lived?"

"Around."

I rolled my eyes again. "In the United States or different countries?"

"Both," he calmly replied.

He was being so difficult. I decided to try a different tack. "What's your last name?"

"O'Shea."

I froze in place, narrowing my eyes and turned to face him. "Colt's last name is O'Shea," I said slowly.

"Yes," he replied flatly.

"Are you brothers?"

"Half-brothers."

"What about Daniel? Is he a brother also?"

"Yes."

"Half-brother?" Why had I not seen this before? He nodded and I looked down. "Is this why you can communicate telepathically?"

"Yes."

"Same father, different mothers?" A few pieces fell into place.

"Yes."

I felt his gaze on me as I thought about my next question. "How many wives did your father have?"

"A few," he replied like it was no big deal.

"Are you the oldest?" I stared at his hand as it held mine.

"Among my siblings, yes."

I glanced up. "How many siblings do you have?"

"About ten."

"Where are they now?"

"It's only the three of us now."

Sympathy furrowed my brow. "I'm sorry, Callon," I said with compassion. "I didn't realize you had lost family also."

"It was a long time ago. I don't think much about them anymore."

"How did the three of you survive all these years?"

"When the outbreak of war started, we were older. The Sarac didn't have any power over us."

I glanced back down and ran my fingers over his ring as some understanding came to the surface. "You have the ring like me because you're all that's left of your clan?"

"No," he replied, and I looked up, wondering what the explanation was. "I have the ring because I am the firstborn of the Consilador clan. I am the leader, the next in line to rule."

"I thought you didn't understand what your ring meant?"

"I said I didn't fully understand it, if you remember correctly."

"So it means something more?"

"Yes."

I studied him; there was always something deeper than what lay on the surface. Lately, I felt like I never fully understood anything they told me. It was almost as if Callon was suffering from some inner turmoil, but over what, I couldn't figure. "How long did it take you to figure it out? The meaning, that is."

"A while."

"So you still have part of your clan left? Some who survived?"

"Yes," he replied calmly. Everything about him seemed calm on the surface...what lay beneath?

"Where are they now?"

"Spread out all over the world. It's safer that way."

If he had clan members spread over the world, did I? I knew I was the last of the Kvech, but what about the Servak? Callon tugged my hand slightly, and we continued. I had so many more questions; so much I wanted to know. I sighed and surveyed my surroundings. We were at the cabin, and Lilly was waiting on the front porch.

CHAPTER 24

"Cheyenne," Lilly said, hesitating as she stepped down off the porch.

"I'm fine, Lilly," I replied warmly. "It's a lot to take in all at once. For so long I knew nothing, and now I'm finding out everything at once. A little time and understanding is what I need."

She took my arm, and Callon walked us up the stairs to a seat. Stepping away as Lilly sat, he leaned against the rail watching. It took a few moments for me to realize he was there to make sure she didn't give me too much information. He never revealed too much, always held back...why? I shifted my eyes to her and sighed.

"Callon," I said politely. "I'd like to talk with Lilly alone if you don't mind." He didn't move. As I turned, his posture had tightened. His jaw was locked, and he was suddenly very determined. Mr. Evasive had returned again.

I glanced at Lilly, saw her determination also, and smiled.

"Callon, go inside. We won't leave the porch; we'll be safe," Lilly said firmly. He still didn't move. Out of the corner of my eye, I could see his eyes narrowing, and a smirk began to form on my lips.

"Callon," Lilly said with more authority. "You can watch from inside the window. You'll be able to see anything coming."

He crossed his arms before walking in the cabin. I listened, waiting for the screen door to close before proceeding. *He who must be obeyed* was overridden by *she who must be obeyed.* Interesting. I refocused.

"Lilly, can you tell me more about my parents? There's so much I want to know."

She took my hands in hers. "What do you want to know, honey?"

"My mother, did you know her well?"

"I knew her the last ten years of her life. I knew your father longer."

"Can you tell me more about her? What was she like?"

Lilly's face warmed. "Your mother was special. She had such a passion for life and your father. I have to admit I was skeptical of her when they were first together. She was from the Servak clan, a clan that was united with the Sarac. My immediate response was not good; I thought she was a spy. I thought she was sent to find your father. As I watched her fight alongside him, I knew I was wrong. She wanted to make right the wrong her people had done." Lilly's cool blue eyes held such love. "She had the gift of persuasion, though she never used it on us. She was genuine, didn't want to change people to get her way. She wanted them to choose to make a difference."

"Do I have her gift?"

"From what I can see, and what Callon has told me, you have some. Not enough to persuade Timeless, but enough to use on humans easily."

I hadn't known it was a power. That would explain how I was able to convince the sheriff to leave me home alone, and the bank teller to give me entrance to the safe deposit box. What else could she see?

"So you can see if I have a power now? I thought it wouldn't show up until after I made the change." I wanted to know more.

"It happens differently for each of us. I can see things in you already becoming pronounced. They will become stronger once you are Timeless. Chances are you will probably have more than one power, as it's clear that you are very special indeed."

I'd also healed quicker than in the past and I had a power already. "What other powers do you see? What else can I do?"

Lilly smiled and her light chuckle filled the air. "I know the boys make fun of you, but I do believe that you are able to talk to animals."

So I wasn't crazy after all. "Do you think it's all animals?" I asked, excited.

"I don't know. I've only seen how Mandi acts around you. I don't know if I would come out and tell them yet though. It might cause you to be teased more."

"You're right," I laughed. "No need to give them anything more to tease me about." I smiled as I stared out into the valley, pondering. "You said I looked like my mother. How?"

She hesitated. "Cheyenne," she said with love, "you are just as beautiful as your mother; the shape of your face, the color of your eyes. Sahara's would change colors just like yours, and you have so much of your father's skin and hair coloring." She sighed. "There's so much of them mixed inside of you. You are more beautiful than you realize, and I'm not just referring to what's on the outside." She reached for my hands and held them tightly.

"I can see into your heart. You have compassion for those around you who are hurting, forgiveness for those who have pained you. You're strong when needed; you've been through a lot in your short life but it hasn't made you angry or bitter. Instead, your experiences have built character and determination.

"You have a passion for what you believe in. That's why the boys can't stand to be away from you. They love you deeply. I can see how Callon and Colt react when you are near. They would give their lives for you. You create happiness, and people are drawn to it. We're your family now, Cheyenne. We will always be here for you, no matter what."

I was speechless as a tear rolled down my cheek; she saw the love they both had for me. Love I didn't deserve—love I had been holding back from accepting. Callon was right: I was afraid of relationships, and until I truly opened up, I wouldn't understand. I knew I loved Colt, but why was I having the same feelings for Callon? It wasn't fair. I looked down, shamefully knowing the truth.

"I told Colt I loved him, but down deep, I know I have feelings for Callon, too," I whispered. "I feel so confused; how can I love two people the same and yet differently? They've both sacrificed for me, and I know both would do more if necessary." I wiped the tear from my cheek.

"Callon told me he loved me, though not in so many words. How am I supposed to make a choice? A choice means somebody gets hurt, and I don't want anyone to hurt. I've held back in opening up for so long out of fear of being rejected. I don't know how much more my heart can take, Lilly. I've lost so much. I don't want to be vulnerable again. I don't know what else I can give."

Without saying a word, she leaned forward, drew me into her embrace, and just held me. It was warm, comforting, loving. I didn't understand how my connection with her could already be so strong, but it was so different than what I had expected. She knew so much about me, about my parents. It was as if they anticipated me finding her someday, to have her fill the empty void in my life, to be able to talk to her about everything and anything. With anyone else, I would never have admitted I had feelings for two men. I would never have put myself out there to be critiqued—with her I didn't feel judged. I almost felt complete—whole.

I would never forget her words about love. They were my family now. I had a family, adoptive, but it was mine if I was willing to take it. I could be happy in this moment with Dex and Lilly, happy with Callon, Colt, and Daniel. They wanted me, they loved me—they would always be there. All I had to do was accept it.

Lilly drew back and rubbed my arms. "This is not easy for you. I understand. You're around them twenty-four/seven, and both want to make you happy—both want to protect you. Things will change soon. You'll see." She sighed. "Wait here, honey. I want to show you something."

I nodded as I watched her walk away, wondering what she meant and how she knew what would happen. "Stay put; we're not done talking yet. I'll let you know when you can come out," Lilly's voice echoed inside the cabin.

Her footsteps disappeared momentarily. I didn't turn, but felt eyes staring at me through the windows. She returned with a small well-worn piece of paper, and placed it in my hands. The edges were slightly tattered; opening it, my hands began to tremble. It was a picture of my mother. Tears began to well in my eyes, and I couldn't look up.

"Lilly," I said in a quivering whisper. "How old was I when she died?"

"They've been gone for over thirteen years, why?"

"I know this face. I've seen her before." I took a shallow breath. "I was six. She was across the street from my school. She came to see me on my sixth birthday."

"Oh, Cheyenne," Lilly said passionately. "I didn't know. I shouldn't have brought you this picture." She touched my arm. "I didn't want to cause you anymore heartache, honey."

The tears flowed freely as I closed my eyes and grasped the picture to my chest. My trembling lips moved once more. "No, it's ok. I'm glad she got to see me. I needed this...I needed this closure. Thank you."

The screen door slammed and footsteps neared, stopping directly in front of me. I didn't move as massive arms surrounded me; it was Colt. I couldn't stop the tears as I lay my head on his shoulder. All the feelings I had for my parents, as well as the feelings for my adoptive parents, came pouring out. I had cried when they died, but somehow this was different. I couldn't contain it.

Colt held me for a long time. Lilly went inside, and he adjusted himself so he was sitting on the bench, drawing me onto his lap. Eventually my sobs quieted, but only after every emotion I was harboring was spent. I had nothing more to give. I knew this would be the last time I cried for them. My dad had always told me to be strong, and I would be. He would remind me that situations were only as bad as I allowed them to be, and my situation of being without a family was over. I had everything I needed here with me now. I had a family; I was a part of something.

"I'm sorry," I said quietly. "I've made a mess of your shirt, Colt."

"I don't mind," he said sympathetically. "Are you okay?"

"Yes." I sighed. "How did you know to come out?"

"It's a gift," he said with a light chuckle, trying to lighten the mood.

I popped my tear stained face up. "You were listening weren't you?"

"Yes," he replied with a sheepish smile.

The weariness showed through. I couldn't hide it any longer. "How much of our talk did you listen to?" I swallowed.

"Enough," he said sincerely.

I dropped my head back into his shoulder and replied in a muffled voice, "I'm sorry." He'd heard me tell Lilly I had feelings for both him and Callon.

"I'm not. I told you before I wouldn't make you choose. I will always be here for you—no matter what."

"I don't deserve your love and affection. I don't deserve anyone's..." I trailed off, feeling completely ashamed of my behavior.

Colt's arms tightened. "Cheyenne," he said affectionately. "We are the ones who don't deserve you." He kissed my forehead, and released his tight hold. I kept my head on his shoulder.

"Why didn't you tell me you were brothers?" I questioned.

"You didn't ask."

"I don't want to come between you and Callon; family is always more important."

"You won't," he promised.

"I already did." I sat up, staring into his icy blue eyes. It all made sense now. "You weren't angry with me that night in the tent were you? The night Callon kissed me."

"No, I wasn't." His jaw tightened.

"Then why did you treat me like that? Why did you let me think you were disgusted with me, that you didn't want me...that you didn't love me?"

He sighed, pain radiating through his words, "I'm so sorry. I was angry, but it wasn't directed at you. I worked through it; Callon and I are fine now. You don't need to worry about it anymore."

There was more to this, more than he wanted to let me know. Callon was the oldest, leader of their clan—did that mean Colt had to listen to him? Obey his orders? Deep down I suspected I was right. I was too emotionally spent to think it out further. I would ask more later. I just needed Colt's touch, his love. I wrapped my hands around his neck, and buried my face in his neck. I kissed it lightly. He always smelled so good, and I inhaled deeply. His large hand rubbed my back gently.

The day was spent; I was fragile and needed my music to work through what I'd learned that day. I needed to set all these emotions free, to spill them out over the strings—covering the wounds— healing my heart once again. I needed to find my peace.

I heard another set of footsteps, and I lifted my weary lids to see Callon standing before me with the guitar. He knew what I needed, just as Colt did. This was why I could love him the same and yet differently, things like this.

He placed the guitar in my lap and sat next to us. I adjusted myself and sighed, remembering that this was my father's guitar. Somehow the thought brought me comfort. I ran my fingers down the fret board and gently caressed the strings. I closed my eyes and imagined the notes twisting and turning in the air. They weaved in and out of each other, rising up into the clouds above—taking with them the broken pieces of my heart, cleansing my soul and helping me gain perspective again—closure.

The notes seemed to be endless. I had held in so much for so long. I played until I felt full, filled with the peace I so desperately needed. Keeping my eyes closed, I finished and took it all in. I knew I would have an audience, and I knew they would be watching me.

"How do you do that?" Dex said affectionately.

Opening my weary lids, I replied, "Do what?"

"Play with such passion. The music is so moving, it's as if I can see into your soul." He paused, his hazel eyes warmed. "Your father played, but not like you. It's amazing. It's truly a gift, my dear."

"I don't know, Dex. I see the notes differently than most I guess. It's as if they move across the air, dancing before me." I paused a moment as I replayed it in my mind. "It captures my heart and soul, healing the hurts and reconciling the pain and anger. I can't really explain it—I just do it for me." I glanced around and saw the compassion and affection...from my family—mine. I could show them my heart. It was safe here. They wouldn't hurt it—I had to trust them.

I slid from Colt's lap and took the guitar inside to the case I found on the coffee table. I laid it down carefully and secured the latches. No one had followed; they were still on the porch.

I was worn out, and I needed to rest. I washed and headed for bed. I curled up on the bed and stared out the window. It was quiet, and I was feeling at peace. The bed shifted as Colt slid in next to me, his arm circling around me, his breath touching my neck. He was always so careful with me, always keeping a barrier between us unless I asked otherwise, always on top of the comforter while I snuggled in the warmth underneath. The room slowly darkened.

There were so many things I loved differently about him than Callon. This was one of them.

"I love this about you, Colt," I whispered.

"Love this?" he murmured his reply and his breath tickled my ear.

"I love the fact you don't mind holding me, the whispering in the dark." I sighed. "Your strength surrounding me. I love this about you, and I want you to know."

He caressed his warm lips on my neck. "I love the fact you want me to hold you." His lips touched my earlobe. "I love to whisper in the dark with you," his deep voice sent a shiver down my spine. "And I love the fact you want my strength surrounding you—I want to keep it here with you always." Another sultry kiss touched me as his leg wrapped over mine. I lifted my hand and touched his as I closed my eyes.

"Sleep, Cheyenne," he instructed. "Rest your weary eyes."

I did just as he said, and I rested my weary eyes, falling into a deep sleep.

CHAPTER 25

Mist was rising, and I was alone in a shadowy forest. A dim light flickered in the distance; it was a fire. I crept closer. I was curious who was around the fire. As I neared, I saw many faces—hard, scarred from battles, some youthful, while others were aged beyond their years. Swords were strapped to their sides, dark clothing covered them, sinister riding cloaks. I glanced around. Their horses were just as rugged as they were. A flash of white flickered in the murky night. Snarls and snapping of teeth echoed nearby. A hideous odor drifted past my nose, the same hideous odor from the day of the Tresez attack.

My pulse quickened, and my breath became more intense—the odor was closer than I realized. A snapping branch caused me to twist around. The creatures were stalking me...I had nowhere to run. No one to turn to—I was totally and utterly alone. Trembling, I stood before them. One leaped, but I was able to scramble away. I turned to run, but they quickly encircled my position. I stared into the blackness, searching for an escape when one stepped back, creating an opening. My heart was racing while another crept closer, pushing me into the gap. I had no choice but to proceed forward slowly, cautiously, my eyes flashing back and forth. They led me to a valley.

It was lighter now. In the distance I saw Callon, Daniel, and Colt, and they were fighting. As my vision cleared, I saw they were fighting the men from the fire. My breathing hitched—there were too many of them!

I wanted to run, I wanted to help, but I couldn't. The Tresez wouldn't allow me to move. I watched helplessly as they each fell. They were dying for me!

"No!" I screeched. "No!"

Darkness surrounded me again; I jumped and realized I was in bed. Panting, I sat up, my heart pounding in my chest. It was a dream! I pulled my legs into my chest. I wrapped my arms around them—trying desperately to regain control. It wasn't working—I couldn't catch my breath.

I flung my legs over the side, and ran for the door and bolted down the hall. The great room was empty—the house was vacant. Panic quickly set in—I needed to know they were alive. I dashed through the screen door, stopping briefly on the porch and staring out into the shadows of the dark night. It felt too much like my dream. I was hyperventilating—I couldn't speak, couldn't call out a name.

Callon appeared just to my right; I leaped from the stairs and ran full speed, throwing myself into his arms. I was sobbing uncontrollably now. I still couldn't utter a word.

Alarmed, his arms tightened, and his voice was tense. "Cheyenne, what's wrong?" I couldn't reply. "Are you okay? Tell me what happened."

He attempted to pry me loose; but I buried myself further into his arms, tightening mine around his waist as the sobbing continued. Calmly he rubbed my back as he tried to reassure me. "It's okay. Shh. Everything's okay." Eventually he reached behind his back and pried my arms free, and helped me inside. My crying was slowing. He was alive.

He sat me on the bench in the bathroom and kneeled before me, tenderly wiping the tears. I stared into his warm eyes. "Sweetheart," he said softly. "What's wrong? I can't help if you don't tell me."

Relief set in, as the reality that it was a dream registered—they were alive. Callon was right before me now, he was touching me. I wasn't dreaming any longer. His beautiful face filled with warmth and compassion was right before me—no *he who must be obeyed,* no Mr. Evasive, no Dr. Callon—it was just Callon. Callon who said he loved me, Callon whom I'd told Lilly I had feelings for also. I'm not sure if I really knew what happened, but in the next moment I leaned forward and kissed him. I closed my eyes and tenderly caressed his lips three times, drawing back only slightly as I comprehended the significance of what I'd done. He grasped my face. He held it, and we gazed into each other's eyes, his searching deep within again.

"I'm sorry," I muttered. "I shouldn't have done that." I looked down, ashamed. What was wrong with me?

"Are you going to tell me what this is all about?"

He continued to hold my face, searching for an answer as it all came bubbling out. "I had a dream, but it was so real. You were all dying for me, and I needed to know you were alive." I waited for my breaths to slow. "I don't want anyone to die for me. I want you to live."

"It was just a dream. We're all here. We're all safe, and no one is going to die," he said firmly.

"It was so real," I said desperately. "And then no one was around..." My panic began to rise again. "Where is everyone?"

"They're close by. It was just a dream—it wasn't real, Cheyenne." Callon tried to reassure me.

"Will you stay with me?" I said anxiously. "I don't want to be alone. Please?"

"I won't go anywhere; I'll stay." Callon helped me stand as he took me back to the bedroom. Sitting, I curled up next to him, resting my head on his chest as his arms wrapped me in the security I needed. No words were spoken. I just took comfort in knowing he was there—they were alive. As he rubbed my arm, his touch was enough to allow me to sleep once more.

A warm hand caressed my cheek. My eyes fluttered open, and I realized I was still in Callon's arms. I jerked my head and saw Colt. My heart instantly started to race. Relief washed over me as I flung myself into his arms. I latched onto his neck like there was no tomorrow, pushing myself closer. He was alive. I could feel him—it was just a dream. The bed shifted, and I twisted my head to see Callon leave through the darkness—he didn't turn around. Colt's arms securely held on.

"It's okay, Cheyenne. It was just a bad dream. Callon told me. We're here, and everything's okay. I told you we're not going to leave you. You're safe; we're all safe."

I released my hold and drew back to stare into his cool eyes through the darkness. There was just enough moonlight to see his face. I grasped it firmly, remembering what he promised me weeks ago.

"Colt O'Shea," I said fervently. "You need to promise me you will not die. You need to promise me no matter what, you will live. No matter what!" I rose to my knees, pressed my lips to his, and kissed him with passion and determination. There was no hesitation in his response as his hands moved, one to the small of my back and the other to cradle my head. Our lips moved in unison, vigorously caressing until we had our fill.

I slumped to my knees, my hands falling to my sides, as I once again realized I had just reacted instead of thinking through my actions. His hands moved to support my shoulders, and I lowered my head.

"I'm sorry, Colt," I whispered.

"Why?" he said in surprise.

"I didn't mean to do that."

"I really didn't mind at all. In fact," he chuckled. "You can have bad dreams more often if I get this kind of response each time." I looked up to see him grinning.

I sighed. "You're such a guy sometimes, you know that??"

"Yes," he replied and drew me close again, kissing me as we fell into the bed. We landed on our sides, and I remained locked in his arms. He withdrew only slightly, his warm breath pouring over my face. "I guess if I'm going to live, then I should probably stay here. Who knows what lurks for me outside this room?" He raised his brows as I rolled my eyes. He was just teasing me now. I tried to turn away, but he held firm.

"You're not going to turn away from me now. If you want me to stay with you, you have to let me have what I want," he said slyly.

I arched a brow. "Excuse me? Have what you want?"

"Yes."

I gave him a speculative glance as I replied, "What is it that you want?"

"First," he said with a hint of deviousness. "I don't want you to turn away from me. I want to look at you."

"It's dark," I replied quickly, and he ignored me.

"Second, I want you to stay right here in my arms."

"I already told you I like to do that," I said flatly.

"Third..."

I cut him off. "Third?"

"Yes, third," he said in exasperation. "I want you to spend the day with me tomorrow and do whatever I ask you to do."

"I can do the first and second, but I don't know about the third. Whatever you ask me to do? I just don't know," I replied tauntingly.

"Okay," he said flatly as he pulled away and quickly headed for the door. I sat straight up.

"Colt," I said in panic. "Don't leave me."

He stopped dead in his tracks, turned back with concern and rushed to my side, sitting on the edge of the bed. His hands touched my shoulders. "I won't leave you. I'm here. I was only teasing," he said tenderly.

A very large grin formed on my lips. "I know," I replied cunningly. "Two can play your game."

His eyes narrowed. "You truly are unscrupulous."

"Oh," I said slyly. "I learned from the best—you!" I winked, and in an instant he yanked me closer.

His lips moved to my ear. As he whispered, a shiver ran down my spine. "I still get all three, and now there's nothing you can do about it."

"You're a little controlling, aren't you?" I whispered. He drew back and what I saw in his eyes told me he wasn't teasing as I was.

"Yes, I am," he said confidently. "You belong to me, and there is nothing you can do about it." His lips pressed against mine, compressing them under his firmly. It only lasted a few moments, but it still took my breath away. He shifted on the bed and pushed me back, lying on his side as he propped up his head with his arm. He laid his free arm across my waist. I couldn't say or do anything—I was speechless. I stared into his icy blue eyes, and pondered his last words.

I was at a loss. He was being over-protective and possessive and saw nothing wrong with that. I'd seen hints of it previously, but had chosen to ignore it. Part of me wanted to belong to him, but another part was screaming no. I was the one who had the dream, who ran into their arms. I kissed them both before I truly knew what I was doing. Did Callon tell him? Was this what this was about? We stared until my blinks became longer, and I could no longer keep my eyes open.

Colt's warm breath filled my lungs as his lips lingered above mine. "I love you, Cheyenne," he whispered. "No matter what happens, you'll always belong to me. You're the love of my life, and I'll do whatever it takes to keep you safe." A tender caress sent goose bumps over me as I drifted off to sleep, this time without any dreams to remember.

When I opened my eyes, the sun was up and the window open. I glanced around the room. I was alone. I sat up, dropping my feet to the floor. My mind began replaying what happened the night before, and Colt's words. He said I belonged to him. What did that mean exactly? It was as if I was a possession to have, not a love to receive. I couldn't help but think maybe it was because of Callon—did he know I kissed him? I was such a fool.

Sighing, I opened the door, unsure what to expect today. I glanced down the hall and didn't see or hear anyone. I quickly entered the bathroom. I was still dressed in my clothes from the day before. I looked at the bench; Colt had laid out an outfit for me. Did this have to do with the whole possession thing? Did he feel like he had control over me by doing this? It was going to stop before it got out of control.

Showering, I dressed for whatever it was we were doing today and threw my hair in a ponytail. As I exited the bathroom, I found him waiting, arms crossed and leaning against the wall. He looked intent, on what I wasn't quite sure.

"Good morning," I said hesitantly as I remained in the doorway.

"Morning," he replied as he stepped forward taking my hand, we went to the kitchen. Glancing around, I saw we were alone.

"Where is everyone?" I said warily.

Not turning as he got my breakfast, he replied flatly, "Close by." He twisted himself around and grasped my waist as he lifted me to the counter and handed me a granola bar as he stood in front. "You want some orange juice?"

"Uh, sure," I said, somewhat surprised. He had caught me off guard when he turned and lifted me to the counter. His behavior was concerning. This wasn't normal. He had acted this way before—the day before I left town to go to Montana when he didn't want me to leave. Was I going someplace without him?

He handed me a juice, and stood in front of me, waiting for me to finish. He took my glass and placed it in the sink. I slid off the counter, and he took hold of my hand. He pulled me through the front door, and we paused on the porch.

"So what are we doing today?" I asked.

A grin appeared as Colt replied, "If you remember correctly, you have only fulfilled two of the three conditions from last night. So you are fulfilling the third today."

Ah, that was what was on his mind. Nervously, I thought about what we were going to be doing. I scanned the area before we left the porch. He headed toward the horses and released my hand when he opened the corral gate. He looked guilty of something—I wasn't sure I wanted to find out what it was about. With Sam in tow, he stopped at my side and raised an eyebrow.

"Up you go," he said.

Hesitating, I replied, "I have my own horse, you know."

"I know, but you have to do whatever I want today, remember?"

He was up to something, I was sure of it. I vacillated as I approached slowly. When I was within reach, he grasped my waist and lifted me into the saddle. Quickly, I threw my leg over before he leaped up behind. He moved his arms around to hold the reins, gave Sam a kick, and we were off in a bolt of speed. The sudden burst caused me to fall back into his arms. He leaned down and kissed my cheek. Turning, I glanced back to see Callon standing on the porch, his arms crossed and his posture rigid.

Was this safe? There were five of them when the Tresez attacked...

We rode in the opposite direction from the falls. The valley sloped down before it condensed into a dense forest. Colt slowed Sam to a walk as we entered the trees. The forest was darker; the pines narrowed slightly and then produced two large cavernous walls flanking each other. We rode in silence through the narrow canyon, twisting and turning our way through the various passages. I could imagine how someone could very easily become lost; it was difficult to see the sun beyond the rock walls. It was also eerily familiar.

My eyes explored the canyon, watching the bird's spiral down only to shoot back up to the other side before landing on the other rock wall. I listened to the wind as it whistled past, caressing my skin as it drifted by.

We stopped at a small, trickling creek. Colt dismounted and extended his hand. I swung my leg over and jumped down. Affectionately, he took my hand and led us into an even more compressed section of rocks. We turned to our sides and slid through. What appeared next caught me by surprise. I paused at the dark cave opening, and Colt saw my hesitation. Smiling, he tugged me forward.

I didn't have a flashlight, and I sure didn't see one in his hands. I wasn't fond of cold, dark places. Typically things I didn't like made their homes there. A chill rippled down my spine as I thought about what spiders or creepy creatures might lurk inside.

"Colt, I'm not sure this is a good idea." I said warily. "We don't have any gear to do cave exploration."

A sly grin appeared as he twisted around. "We don't need any gear, sweetheart. You'll be fine. Just don't let go of my hand."

Great! All I needed to do right now was to get lost in a cave. I didn't need to add this to my succession of unfortunate events. I planted my feet and spoke forcibly, "I'm not fond of cold, dark places. If you haven't already figured out, I don't like spiders, and they tend to inhabit places like this."

"I'm sorry, but if you remember correctly, part of the deal last night was that you would do whatever I ask," he replied with a cunning grin.

"I know, Colt, but I'm really nervous about this. I don't want to be lost in a cave. This would be on my top five of the worst places to die," I pleaded.

"You're not going to die. Besides, you'd go to heaven, and I'm sure there aren't spiders there," he chuckled.

"What makes you so sure I would go to heaven?" I shot back. "I could be banished to hell for all you know." The images of kissing both him and Callon came to my mind. That couldn't be a good thing.

"I think I know you pretty well to say you wouldn't be going to hell."

"Pretty well, huh?" I replied sarcastically. "So I still have a chance?"

Colt rolled his eyes and pulled us forward. "Come on. I'll make sure you're safe. I promise I won't let a spider touch you." I unwillingly followed into the darkness. He was true to his word—he didn't let go of my hand. I inched even closer as the shadows surrounded us, and then I reached out and latched onto his shirt.

We walked slowly, deeper into the belly of the cave. The ground below began to slope, and I pushed myself even closer. As he stopped, my grip tightened. I knew I was next to him, but I couldn't see a thing. He removed my hand from his shirt, and turned.

"Cheyenne, you need to stay right here. Don't move. I don't want you to fall and get hurt." As quickly as the words were spoken, he was gone.

Panic instantly set in. My pulse quickened, and a sensation of overwhelming fear was beginning to overtake me. I crouched to my knees and wrapped my arms around them. I strained my ears to hear him. My breath came quicker. It didn't matter whether my eyes were open or closed...it was all the same—darkness.

I didn't hear Colt's return, but then he crouched down and placed both his hands on my shoulders and helped me stand.

"I'm right here," his soft voice said. "You're not alone."

He took my hands in his, and turned them over as he placed a small round object in each palm. They were rough and jagged; it felt like two small rocks.

"Touch them together," he said softly.

Knowing I couldn't see what I was doing, I slowly raised them until the rocks touched in the palms of my hand. A small glowing light started to appear. I watched in amazement; the light grew in brilliance the longer they were touching. I looked at him wide-eyed; his face was filled with delight.

"How is this possible?" I said in amazement. "I've never seen anything so incredible." Just as the words left my mouth, my gaze wandered to my surroundings. The small rocks were amazing; however, what I saw now was spectacular. The cave was filled with beautiful colors. The stalactites that were suspended from the ceiling were breathtaking. I reached out, touched the rock wall, and the light disappeared. Colt chuckled, and I placed the rocks back together again. The illumination grew brighter. This time thinking ahead, I placed both rocks in one hand while I extended my other to experience the beauty unfolding before me.

The texture of the rock was surprising. I was expecting it to be coarse, but it was smooth under my fingertips. The wall was slimy as the water oozed in tiny droplets to the floor. The colors were dazzling—red, orange, and green. It was as if an artist used watercolors to swirl them together, circling the stems of the stalactites. I took a step closer, and Colt touched my hand. He lifted my arm and rested the stones against another larger piece of granite cascading down from the fissure. It began to glow just as the smaller stones did in my hand. The illumination filled the entire cavern. I stopped breathing for a moment. I had never seen anything so exquisite. The cavern was filled with so many colors it was almost blinding.

We were standing near a ledge overlooking a deep crevasse filled with stalactites and stalagmites. I stared out into the distance. The surrounding beauty dazzled me, and a tear formed. I sighed. This was the Colt I knew; this was the man who wanted to share things he found beautiful and amazing with me. This was the man who wanted to share a piece of his heart with me. I forgot once again that I was the one producing the light and moved my hands away from the granite. Only the dim light now remained.

I stared up into his eyes. Deep oceans of love flowed from them, filling me. This was who I loved; the sincere, gentle, caring man who willingly opened his heart and wrapped me up in its embrace. He could capture my heart with the simplest of things, and I would give it freely—without reservations. In that moment, no one else mattered, and no one else existed.

I draped both my arms around his waist and pushed my head into his pulsing chest. The stones dropped from my fingers and fell— it didn't matter now. I didn't need to see his face to know how he felt—how I felt. I could feel the energy that radiated from our bodies in the darkness.

His hands sought out my face, rendering me helpless with his touch. Our lips met and enveloped each other in their passion, wildly searching for more. My hands were racing to his neck, and I tugged him closer. His arms moved, found my waist, and lifted me further into his able-bodied arms. His fingers traced my spine, stopping at my hairline as he gently found his way to my hair band and pulled it out. He locked his fingers in my hair, and drew my neck back. His lips drifted from mine, creeping down my neckline, caressing my collarbone with his warm breath.

My breaths were heavy. I was locked in the moment. There were no heavy breaths from Colt; as always, he was totally and completely in control. I hated being the one out of control all the time, being weak, so run by hormones. With the effect he had on me, I knew I wouldn't stop him if he were to try, but I knew in my heart he never would until I let him know I was ready.

"Colt," I said weakly as his lips moved across my neckline.

"Umm," he replied.

"How do you do it? How can you maintain so much control all the time? You're breathing is normal, calm, and mine is so erratic," I said breathlessly.

"Years of practice, my love," he said calmly.

I thought about what he said as I took longer breaths, slowing my racing heart. "Years of practice?"

"Yes."

Now I was curious. "Exactly how does someone have years of practice? How many other woman have you practiced on before me?"

He paused in his caress. His balmy breath remained on my neck. It was probably a good thing I couldn't see his eyes. I'm sure it would have given something away.

"It's not important," he whispered.

"Maybe not to you, but it might matter to me." His lips began their assault once more, distracting me—he was good at it.

"Colt, how many? You know everything about me, but I know nothing about you. It isn't fair. You're holding all the cards, and I get nothing. You know I've only been with you."

"That's not an accurate statement," he said with slight justification. "You've kissed Callon three times since you've been with me."

I stiffened, and my heart sank. I was going to hell for sure now. He had me—he knew what happened in the bathroom the night before. I felt so foolish; this was why he was acting so possessive. I was right. It was because of Callon, and this time I was the one who caused it.

"I'm sorry, Colt," I said in a hushed tone. "I don't know what came over me last night. I was so panicked, so scared...I—I shouldn't have done it."

"You don't need to be sorry," he said gently. "I know you're struggling. You have so many choices ahead of you. I'm not going to judge you. I told you I wouldn't make you choose. I love you, and that's all you need to know right now."

I felt like such a fool. I didn't deserve him; he was too understanding. It was as if I could do nothing wrong in his eyes. I rested my head into his shoulder, pulling my arms tightly around his neck. He held me securely, and I took in his graciousness.

A tickling sensation touched my neck, I quickly realized both his arms were around me—I stiffened.

"What's wrong?" he said quickly.

"There's something on my shoulder!" I said in a panic. "Get it off now, please!"

He leaned back and released his hold as he dropped me to the ground and instantaneously swept my shoulder clean, laughing lightly.

"It was just a bat," he chuckled.

"I told you I don't like creepy, crawling creatures," I said with trembling lips. "Especially those that can fly. Can we go now?" He drew me close again, bent and picked something up before taking my hand. I followed in the same way I had when we came in—as close as possible. One hand in his as the other locked onto his shirt. We walked slowly. He was careful to make sure I didn't stumble or fall. The walk out seemed to take less time. As we neared the entrance I could begin to see daylight. I squinted as we came into the sunshine. It took a few minutes for my eyes to adjust. We stopped briefly, and Colt pried my fingers loose from his shirt.

"You can let go now," he said softly.

"Sorry," I replied sheepishly.

He tilted my chin in his large fingers. "Are you okay?"

I nodded in agreement. I saw his other hand held the two rocks from the cave. He grasped my hand again as we continued through the crevasse to where Sam was waiting. Colt left me by the rock wall as he dropped the two rocks into Sam's pouch and returned with a sandwich. He motioned at a boulder to sit, and handed me the food with a bottle of water.

"Sorry, sweetheart. I know it's a little late for lunch, but the time got away from us."

I smiled, taking the sandwich and water. "I don't mind. Thank you for sharing that with me. You show me so much more than beautiful places—you show me pieces of your heart." He returned the smile and watched me eat. As I finished, he stretched out his hand, and I followed. He lifted me at the waist and helped me into the saddle. A micro-second later, he was directly behind. Extending his arm, he took hold of the reins. Sam proceeded slowly, lingering in the moment with us, winding our way through the dense trees until we came to the opening revealing the valley once more.

Another hour passed before the cabin came into view. It had been a wonderful day; I was beaming from the inside out. Tilting my head up, I saw Colt's satisfied grin also. I lifted my hand to his neck and drew his lips closer. I sighed as they briefly met mine. He placed the reins in one hand, as his arm drew me closer. I didn't want this day to end. I was totally and completely happy—I didn't want that to change.

CHAPTER 26

As we arrived at the gate, Colt hoisted me down with one swift movement while he dismounted. I watched as he and Sam entered the corral, and Colt removed the saddle and bridle. Colt pulled down food for Sam also. He latched the corral closed, and his eyes locked on mine as he leaned down and kissed me. He took my hand as we headed for the porch. Voices filled the air, drifting out towards us. A heated discussion was taking place, and Lilly was irritated.

"You can't keep her in the dark, Callon," Lilly said in frustration. "She has to know. It will only cause her heartache later if you wait."

"I know. Please, Lilly, let me do this in time," Callon replied firmly. "There are many factors involved here."

Colt froze, his body rigid, and his grip tightened around my fingers.

"I know many factors are involved," she said in exasperation. "You should have put a stop to it long ago. You cannot treat her like this. If you won't tell her, I will."

"Lilly," he said with authority. "Let me handle it." His voice trailed off, and the room suddenly became silent. Colt must have telepathically told them we were here.

Colt didn't move, and I glanced up to see desperation in his icy blue eyes. My pulse suddenly quickened. Something was up, and it had to do with me—and from their discussion, it didn't sound good. Was I right earlier? I was going away from Colt? Was this the reason for his behavior? I stepped forward only to be stopped; looking back, I narrowed my eyes at Colt in a question. He didn't want me to move, but reluctantly he released me.

I opened the screen door, and all attention turned on me. Lilly and Callon were facing each other, and Dex's hand was resting on Lilly's shoulder. Daniel was nearby; sympathy filled his dark blue gaze. Colt's hand touched my shoulder, and we stopped just behind the couch.

Warily, I spoke, "What's going on here? What are you keeping from me now?"

Dex stepped forward, the worn journal in his hands. "Cheyenne," he said calmly. "Why don't you have a seat? We need to talk."

I was silent as I stared at him. I didn't want to sit; I wanted to know what was going on. "No, thank you. I'm fine standing." Colt's arms moved and rested across my shoulder and collarbone. I lifted my hand and latched onto his arm for support. If I was leaving, I didn't want to go without him. I stood immobile—waiting for the impact of what was to come.

"We need to talk about the symbols at the front of your journal." Dex hesitated, his hazel eyes searching mine. "They mean more than you know. These are the symbols on the rings each clan carries. Each grouping represents a clan. If you look closely at your ring, you can see the symbols in the drawings are the same." He opened the journal and revealed the marked page. I lifted my right hand and studied the two—they were identical. At least that made sense now.

He continued. "Each symbol represents something of importance to the clans. Your ring has two symbols. One resembles a three-leaf clover in shape. If you look closely," he pointed to it on the page, "your ring begins and ends with this symbol. It represents unity, being bound together."

He was hesitating. "Is there more?" I questioned.

"Yes, there are five pages in the journal, but there are six clans that carry these rings. Each ring contains at least one of the same symbols as yours; unity, being bound together." He leaned forward. "Cheyenne, you bind all these clans together. You are the key to our survival."

I swallowed...the key to their survival? I narrowed my eyes slightly. "Why were you afraid to tell me that?"

He didn't reply immediately.

He glanced at Callon before continuing. "Of the six rings, two are of more importance than the others. These rings each have two of the clover-like symbols—just like yours. Both have the symbols for eternity and love. You are bound to these two equally."

I averted my gaze to my ring, studying the symbols. It began and ended with the same symbol—the clover. I furrowed my brow as I looked up. "I don't understand, Dex. How am I bound to them?"

"You are betrothed to them," he said as his jaw tightened.

"I'm promised in marriage to them?" I said in disbelief.

"Yes."

Colt's arm tightened around me slightly.

"I don't understand," I said. "How? Who promised me, and who am I promised to?"

"You are betrothed to the Sarac clan."

"How? Who made this decision?" I said, slightly irritated that something so important could be decided for me without my input. Who in their right mind does something like that? No matter how old these Timeless were, we weren't living in ancient times.

"Your grandfather, Jorelle, promised your mother to the Sarac clan. She didn't follow through on her marriage so the obligation was passed down to you."

I snorted through my nose. "Well, that's not going to work real well, now, is it? Why were you afraid to tell me? It really doesn't have any relevance if it's never going to happen."

"Cheyenne," he said firmly. "You have to realize that once Marcus figures out who you are, he will do either one of two things—kill you or bring you into his clan. Once you are in his grasp, we will be powerless to help you."

"Okay, so I stay in hiding until I'm Timeless and strong enough to resist." No one replied all attention remained transfixed on me. There was still a tension in the air—and then it clicked. "You said two...who's the other clan?"

Lilly's eyes filled with anxiety as she shot glances around the room. Colt drew me closer, his embrace tightening as his breathing grew heavier. For the first time, I felt his heart beat faster in apprehension.

"It's the Consilador clan," he said faintly.

I stared blankly for a few moments and then turned my head down, staring at my ring. I was promised in marriage to two men, one was a crazy, power-hungry lunatic who would either kill me or marry me for my powers—which were practically nonexistent at this time. The other was from the Consilador clan, Colt's clan. My breathing hitched as understanding set in. I flashed my gaze up at

Callon and then quickly down to his ring. I was promised to Callon! It all fell into place. He hadn't worn the ring until now. My fury was building as I pulled Colt's arm away and stepped forward. Angry tears bubbled to the surface as I turned to face Callon.

"Dex, how long?" I said in a low murmur. No one replied. "How long, Dex? How long has everyone known?" My lips were trembling.

"A while," he remorsefully replied.

"What is your definition of a while? Is it just since I arrived, or when you read the journal? Or has it been from the beginning?"

He carefully phrased his answer. "It's not an unknown fact. We had heard rumors, but until I read the journal, I didn't know for sure. I wasn't sure it could be passed down to you—that you would be required to fulfill your mother's obligation."

"So you're just referring to the marriage with the Sarac clan?" I wanted to make sure he was being completely clear.

"Yes."

"What about the promise to the Consilador clan?"

"We knew of the promise through the Kvech line, but we didn't know of your existence, or the promise through the Servak ring."

"*We* as in you and Lilly?"

"Yes."

I managed to hold it together as my eyes drifted to Callon. "How long, Callon? How long have the three of you known this?"

"It's not easy to answer, Cheyenne," he replied apprehensively.

The irritation, the deep hurt, was rising quickly. "It's not hard," I said through my teeth. "Either you knew all along, or just since Dex told you what the journal said."

Callon's brows creased. "From the beginning I knew of the Kvech betrothal, but you have to understand that I...we didn't even know

367

you fulfilled the other part of the pact until I saw the Kvech and Servak rings. I didn't know of the Servak betrothal until Dex told me."

He knew. He could have stopped this—they could have told me, yet didn't. He admitted he knew of the one promise, the Kvech promise. I'd had the ring for months now. Why hadn't anyone said something?

I faced Colt, tears welling up waiting to burst forth. "This is why you've been acting so strangely, telling me I belonged to you like I was some sort of possession." My hands trembled at my side. "You knew—all along you knew, and yet you led me to believe we could be together? I opened my heart to you—I gave it to you...

"This is why I remain closed off—why Callon says I am fearful in relationships. If I have no feelings, there's no pain—no hurt." I searched Colt's sorrow-filled eyes. "This was just a game all along. The two of you trying to see who would win the prize in the end." I shook my head in disgust. "You knew I would find out soon. That's why you took me out alone—trying to win me over." I sucked in a shaky breath. "Trust me, you said. Trust me, and I did. Look what good it did me."

I lowered my head and lifted my hands to my face. I was fighting to hold back the torrent of tears and anger I wanted to release. "The thing is," I said through trembling lips. "You both had me from the start. I've been such a fool to truly believe you wanted me for who I was, not for what I am." I took a shallow breath. "Fool me once, shame on you...fool me twice, shame on me," I whispered.

Colt took a step closer, his hand touching my arm. "Chey—"

"No!" I growled. "You had your chance. I don't want to hear more lies. Just leave me alone." I jerked my arm back as I glared. "I don't want to suffer any more." I looked at the hardwood floor, my shoulders slumped forward in agony. The weight of it all was so heavy. "I've never lied to any of you," I whispered. "I've been an open book from the beginning. However, the three of you have deceived me from the start." I stood completely still for a few moments and then realized I had to leave—I had to get away from them right now.

I bolted for the front door, slammed through the screen and leaped off the stairs into the field where I halted. Footsteps scrambled behind me and stopped just as suddenly as I did. I wanted to run away from this hurt and sorrow—but I knew it would do me no good. It wasn't safe, and they would just bring me back. I collapsed to my knees, staring out into the distance. My tears were dried up; I was beyond them—beyond words.

Sighing, I looked down at my hands, twisting the rings on my fingers. How could I have been so blind? How did I not see that this was a game for the two of them? Colt being so understanding, saying I didn't have to choose. I had been ashamed, thought I had done something wrong by falling for both of them. It wasn't me; it was them! They had wooed me, and I fell victim to their trap—to their deception. Why was I so trusting? Why had I opened up? It took Colt two and a half years, but with Callon, I willingly caved within a couple of months. Was I that desperate to have love? To want love from someone I could call my own? Someone I thought loved me back?

This was not my destiny. This was something that was forced upon me, and I didn't want anything to do with it. I didn't even know who these people were; they didn't even know I existed until recently. Marcus didn't know who I was. I could just walk away. I could create my own destiny—so far all I'd had was sorrow and pain.

Surely I could construct something better than this, a place where I wasn't constantly deceived for my own so-called protection. What they called safeguarding only caused me more heartache.

My father always told me to be strong, and that strength is measured in character. It doesn't come from others; it comes from within—it's something no one could take away. I wasn't feeling strong—I was suffering, weak, and broken once again. How many times did I need to endure this kind of pain? The cracks in my heart, the wounded pieces falling around me. I was trying to pick them up, put them back together again, only to have more break off.

Dex said the fate of the clans rested on me, only me. Only I was able to free them of this evil. I snorted. I was only nineteen. Why did I have to carry this burden? Shouldn't I have been getting ready for college? Beginning my future with prosperity instead of despair? I didn't have the slightest idea how to rid them of evil. I had a hard enough time trying to keep any sense of a relationship intact and stay alive for another year. And how in the heck did both the Kvech and Servak promise me out to marry someone that I hadn't even met yet? It was like I was doubly doomed. Both clans were out to set my future before I even got the chance to make a decision on my own.

I sat in the field, drew my legs into my chest, and wrapped my arms around them. I did nothing but think about the last six months. Dusk was nearing; the cooler breeze sent a chill over me. I knew I would have to haul myself up and walk inside. I would have to face all of them. The anger was gone, what filled its place was emptiness—hollowness from any emotions.

I rose to my feet. I took those unwanted steps back to the cabin. I kept my gaze locked on the ground, not wanting to see who was waiting. I didn't want to utter a word, but I knew I would have to say something. The distance was short, but the walk was long. I saw Lilly out of the corner of my eye. I attempted to pass her, and was about to pull the screen door open when Callon suddenly appeared. I immediately looked away; I had no choice but to stand on the porch. Lilly's light footsteps neared, and she stopped alongside me.

"Cheyenne," she said tenderly. "I'm sorry you found out this way. I hate seeing you suffer like this. You know this isn't easy on them. They both love you desperately—" I cut her off mid-sentence.

"I don't want to talk about this, Lilly," I said flatly. "What's done is done. I will not be the fool again." I inhaled a shaky breath before continuing. "Do you know where my bag is? Colt has it, and I want it back. He seems to think I'm not capable..."

"I can get it for you," she replied quietly.

"Do you know when we're leaving? I overheard everyone talking the other day about needing to depart soon. I'd really like to know." I released an exasperated breath. "But then again, what does it really matter? I don't get a choice in anything. I'm being held against my will."

She shifted uncomfortably. "Cheyenne, you have—" Once again, I cut her off and turned to face her, eye to eye.

"The first opportunity I get, I will be leaving," I said matter-of-factly. "You can tell them. I don't care. I have no desire to stay; I'm tired of being the one who is constantly hurt. I'm not a possession, and I'm not some trophy to be won. I will not be told whom I shall marry." Lilly saw my firm resolve, and I left her standing alone as I walked into the cabin.

I didn't look up; I swiftly cleared the room and went straight for the bathroom. I washed up quickly, and hesitated at the door. I knew someone would be waiting. I slowly opened it, surprised at who

371

lay in wait. Dex was holding my bag, his knuckles white from his grasp. His jaw was taut, his eyes severe.

"Thank you," I mumbled as I reached for the bag, but he didn't release it.

"Cheyenne," he said firmly. "I need to talk with you, and you need to listen." He gestured for me to head to the bedroom and followed close behind, shutting the door as we entered. "Sit," he said in a fatherly, authoritative tone. I complied as he handed me the bag, I laid it across my lap. He towered over me.

"Lilly just told me you informed her you would be leaving the first opportunity you get. Do you realize how dangerous that is right now?" He crossed his arms over his chest. "I don't agree on how they handled this situation; however, they are here to protect you." His hazel eyes bored through me. "Only you can destroy Marcus. You have to go and talk to the other clans. You need to convince them to join us. They need to know you really exist, that the Kvech line didn't die out. They need to see, touch, feel the passion you have.

"I know this is not what you would have chosen. No one would have chosen this, but this is your destiny. Only you can embrace it. We are here to help with what we can, but you have to allow us to."

I narrowed my eyes, as determination set in. "Dex," I said coolly. "What I told Lilly was true. I will leave the first opportunity I get. I've only needed protection since I've been around them." I paused briefly. I could see his anger rising. "You were also right that I didn't choose this destiny—it chose me. I don't want to embrace it. You said yourself I needed to find out who I really am before I can accomplish anything. Let me find myself. No one has given me the chance to do anything on my own. Every decision has been made for me. How could anyone think that at some point in time I wouldn't revolt?"

Dex's teeth clenched and his annoyance rang clear. "I'll tell them what you're planning, and they'll stop you. You'll go and talk with the other clans and convince them to fight with us. You will fulfill your destiny." His eyes narrowed, brow furrowed. "As for the promise of marriage, you only have two choices—Callon or Marcus—and you know who I would choose. I can make it happen sooner than later—I have the authority."

Was that a threat? The room was darkening, but I saw his rage clearly. We both held strong, staring each other down. I was not backing off this time. He turned and walked out, closing the door behind. How did all these people have such control over my life?

I fiddled with the bag in my lap, calming my anger. Eventually, I dug through it, searching for something to sleep in. My fingers scraped across a jagged object. Stopping, I slowly pulled it out. It was a rock, the rock I had used earlier in the day in the cave with Colt. I stared at it for a few moments, tempted to throw it out the window. Instead I let it fall back in the bag and continued with my search finding the journal in the process as well. Little good it did me...

I found clothes, changed, and crawled into bed. I wanted this day to be over. It was strange. Just hours earlier, I was as happy and content as could be in the arms of the man I loved. Now I wanted nothing to do with any of them. Once again I was completely alone. I cried quietly and waited for sleep to find me and bring me some peace.

There was a soft knock at the door. Disoriented, I didn't move immediately. I blinked a few times; it was morning. I must have slept the entire night.

"Cheyenne, we're leaving in an hour. Get ready," Callon said in a heavy tone. I rolled over to look, but he was already exiting the room. I stared for a few minutes before moving again. I was determined not to cry. They didn't need to see my tears; they didn't need to see how deeply they hurt me. If this was just a game to them, they would never see my sorrow—I would hide my pain.

I was not going to accept this destiny. I would create my own. I crawled out of bed, grabbed some clothes, and headed for the bathroom. I showered quickly, threw on a pair of jeans, a t-shirt, and tied a long sleeved shirt around my waist for later. I returned to my room, and the pack was already gone. I turned and headed for the great room. Dex and Lilly were waiting. I paused at the entry, trying to determine the mood. Last night when Dex left he was angry—and so was I.

I took the first step. "Thank you for your hospitality. I wish I didn't have to leave on a sour note, but I really didn't have a choice."

Lilly's unease showed through as she stepped forward and hugged me. I returned the hug. "We're going to miss you, Cheyenne," her voice cracked. "I wish I had more time with you." She was holding back tears.

"I'll miss you, too," I replied sincerely. I would miss her, although it was probably easier this way. I could keep myself closed off—no hurt. I stepped back only to run into Dex. He drew his arm around me.

"I'm sorry," he said gently, his anger gone. "I'm sorry for so many things, Cheyenne. One day you'll understand." He turned back to see my face. "Lilly packed you some food, enough for about three days. You should be able to make it back by then."

"Thank you, Lilly. I appreciate it," I said as I glanced her way again.

The screen door opened, and Callon walked through. I turned slightly and saw he was ready to go—they were waiting on me. I gave one last look to Dex and Lilly and headed for the door. I kept my eyes averted as we paused on the porch.

Callon grasped my arm as he pulled me back. "Dex told me your plans." He whispered. "We will stop you."

I didn't reply. *He who must be obeyed* was not someone I felt the need to obey any longer. I knew Dex had told them, but I would bide my time, waiting until the right moment arrived. I would leave, and they would be helpless to stop me. I kept my head down, gaze locked to the ground as Callon led me to Mandi. Colt was holding her, waiting for me to look up—I wouldn't. Callon's hands locked around my waist as he helped me mount. I didn't need his assistance, but he helped anyway. I took the reins in hand and stared at my fingers. I stared at the Kvech ring, the Servak ring—the rings that determined my future. Colt's hand grazed my arm as he passed, but instead of warmth a chill passed over my skin.

With a kick to Mandi, I followed behind Daniel. I closed my eyes as we departed. I didn't want to look back. I didn't want to look forward, and I didn't want to shed any more tears. As hard as I tried, the tears streamed down my cheeks.

Tears for what had been, for what was lost and for what would never be. I had opened my heart, allowed them in, and found it broken and torn because of it. I was strong, even stronger than my circumstances—I would prevail. I pushed down the tears as I opened my eyes. Opened them to what lie ahead, what my destiny would be—what I would make it. I squinted from the sunlight. My future would be just as bright. No one was going to tell me which way to go.

Destiny had no hold on me—I would overcome.

Timeless Series Novels Data Sheet

See what lies ahead for Cheyenne in Promises. A sampling of chapters are included for your reading enjoyment.

For more information on the Timeless Series Novels visit:

http://www.lisawiedmeier.com/ or timelessseriesnovels.com /

www.facebook.com/TimelessSeriesNovels /

http://lisawiedmeier.blogspot.com/

A Timeless Series Novel

#1 Cheyenne - Released July 15, 2011

#2 Promises - Release date: May 30, 2012

#3 Daylight - Scheduled release date:

Winter 2012/Early Spring 2013

#4 Awakening - under editing

The original construction of the Timeless Series ended with Awakening, but if the demand is still great I will continue on with the following.

#5 Deceptions - under editing

#6 Revelations - under editing

#7 Resolutions - under editing

Side stories:

#8 Bailee - under editing

#9 Sahara – draft

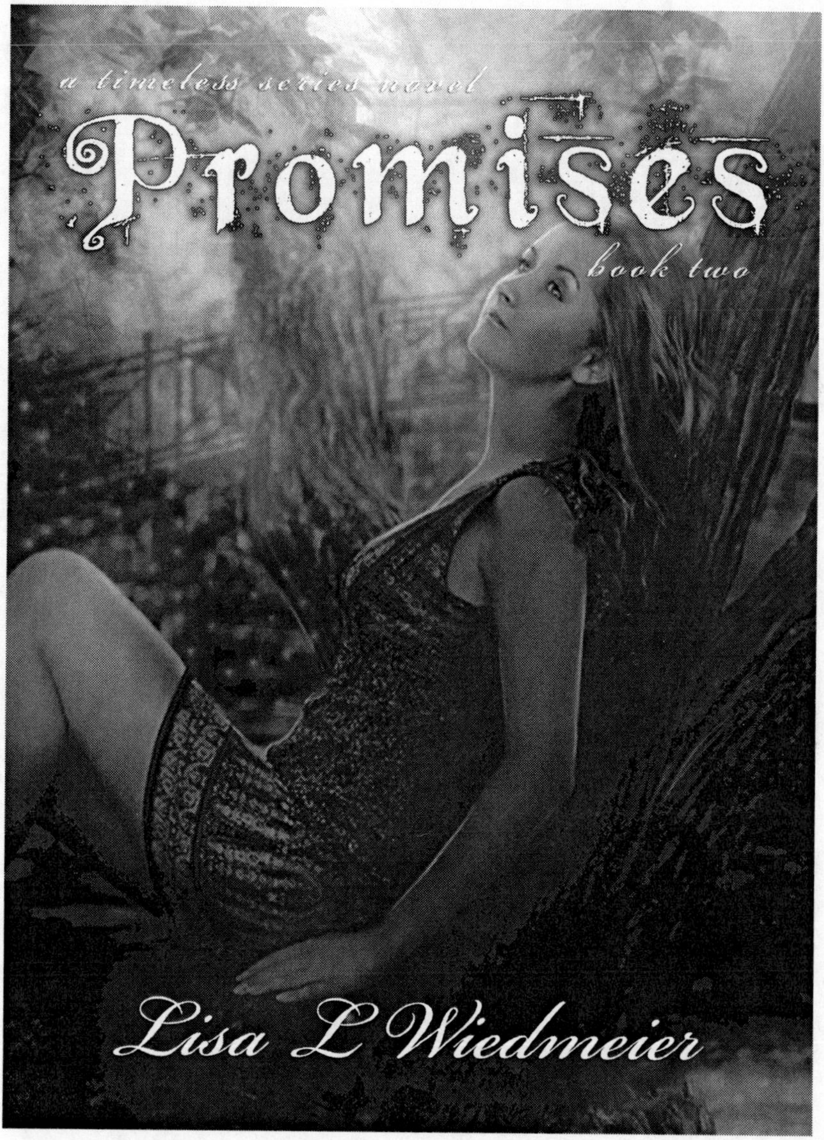
a timeless series novel
Promises
book two
Lisa L Wiedmeier

a timeless series novel

Promises

book two

Lisa L Wiedmeier

Copyright © 2011 by Lisa L. Wiedmeier

Editor: Sam Dogra

Copy Editor: A-1 Editing Services, Jodi Tahsler

Front cover design by Phatpuppy Art

Back cover design by Timeless Productions

Edition I

ISBN: 978-0-9839052-4-0

We promise according to our hopes, and perform according to our fears.

~Francois duc de la Rochefoucauld

Promise is most given when the least is said.

~George Chapman

CHAPTER 1

A gentle wind ruffled my Palomino Mandi's blond mane. She was walking slowly; her head hung low like mine. My heart was heavy, filled with sorrow, and broken beyond measure. As we left Dex and Lilly's cabin earlier this morning, I had tried to hold back the tears—I'd tried to be strong, but without much success.

I sighed. It wasn't their fault I felt like this. They had offered to make me a part of their family, something I'd longed for since my parents' death, but once again, circumstances had turned against me. I couldn't take the pain anymore. The pain of loneliness, the pain of betrayal...I shook my head. I would have to remain distant, close off my heart and not allow the hurt in. If I wasn't attached emotionally, I couldn't feel the wound.

This was hardly anything new for me. We had moved so much when I was young, remaining aloof had been the only way I could deal with the loss of friends. It was only recently I'd learned why we could never stay in the same place for long. It had been for my protection. But even my parents' careful measures, I was sure, hadn't turned out as they'd planned.

1

I sighed. It had already been six months since their death...six long months since the day Sheriff Taylor had arrived on my doorstep to tell me the awful news. I had so many regrets, regrets for not saying three simple words: I love you. I promised myself never to let the opportunity slip by again, but it was much harder said than done. I'd almost lost Colt—the man I loved—because of my insecurities but in the end it really didn't matter. My destiny was already planned out.

The truth that had been hidden from me for so long played on my thoughts, and I raked my fingers in Mandi's mane. I was something different. I was Timeless. Born human until around the age of twenty, then we would transform, aging one year for every one hundred human years. Death would be harder, but not impossible. Our injuries or illnesses would heal more quickly than average—and some Timeless also inherited powers. Like I was supposed to...

I was the last of the Kvech, the ruling clan—the royal clan thought to have been wiped out. I was unexpected, and potentially dangerous. Everyone feared I'd fall into the wrong hands, become influenced under the wrong beliefs, and have my eventual powers used for evil. It had almost happened to my mother, eldest daughter of the Servak clan. Promised against her will to the Sarac's leader, Marcus, she had barely escaped his grasp, stopping his dark plans. As a result, she was forced to give me up to my adoptive parents keep me safe...and she had eventually paid the price.

I sighed and shifted my gaze to my left, then right. Callon and Colt were riding in a tight formation, while Daniel led. They were ready for just about anything, except my broken heart. They were the cause of it, my so-called protectors. I had a personal army of three, who would give their lives for me, who'd sworn their undying love and whom I could depend on. But these same three never thought I deserved to know the truth, and they constantly kept me in the dark, deceiving me. I didn't want to be around them anymore, but I couldn't leave, not yet. I wasn't ready.

"Callon," I said quietly. "Can we please stop? I'm hungry and need to rest."

He rode closer, and his fingers brushed my arm. I didn't look at him, but I kept my eyes forward, forcing back the tingles that raced down my spine. Why did his touches always do this to me?

"Can you wait about half an hour?" Callon replied. "We'll be near a creek and then we can water the horses at the same time."

I nodded and turned to look at Colt. His icy blue eyes—sorrow-filled since we'd left the cabin—locked on mine, and I quickly looked away. I couldn't peer into his face; see those blond locks falling over his tanned brow...it hurt too much.

I was the fool; I should have seen it coming. Colt had posed as my best friend. He had been my only close friend since I was a junior in high school. My parents loved him—now I knew why. He was Timeless himself, had worked his way inside my heart, secretly protecting me all along. He helped me every step of the way through my parents' death, supporting me, allowing me to make some discoveries on my own, before revealing his true identity and the reason he was in my life at all.

I was hurt when I'd found out Colt had only been there as my guardian—I'd thought it was more than that. But when he confessed his love for me, I allowed him back in. I trusted him, loved him, knew he would do anything for me. Like when he ripped a hideous Tresez apart to save me. I felt his love surround me, heard his words of love, and then remembered the pain. I found out I could never be

3

with him—because I'd been promised to someone else from the start.

Callon's horse, Bo, snorted, and I glanced over at the other cause of my broken heart, Callon. I had been naive enough to trust him, too. Even fall for him. How could I have been so stupid? To fall for the two of them...fall for two brothers? That was yet another secret they'd kept from me. At least that explained how they were able to communicate telepathically—Daniel as well. They were probably talking things out right now, plotting their next move.

Despite their blood ties, each looked so different. I tried to locate the resemblance. Colt was larger than life: broad shoulders, hulking arms, and towering frame. Both he and Callon had the same tan skin, probably inherited from their shared father. Callon was pretty toned himself, but nowhere near Colt's size.

I tightened my grip on Mandi's reins. It was Callon's fault I was feeling like this. He had known my identity the instant he spotted my rings; the proof of my Kvech and Servak heritage. He was the leader of the Consilador clan; the clan that had been ruling in my place. I still wasn't sure what kind of authority he had, but one thing was for sure: I was promised to him—both he and Marcus had been forced to bear my mother's broken vows. I could see him shifting in his saddle, his brown wavy hair glistening in the sunshine. His hazel eyes glanced at me, and I looked away.

It probably wouldn't have mattered anyway. Just because my birth mother didn't fulfill her obligation to Marcus, that didn't mean I had to agree to take her place. I accepted neither betrothal; no one was going to tell me who to choose as a husband. I would make my own choice, and it wouldn't be either of them...in fact, it wouldn't be anyone riding with me now.

An hour passed before we finally stopped. Dismounting, I

stretched my legs. Mandi wandered to the creek to drink. Colt neared with an outstretched hand. He was holding a sandwich. I kept my gaze on the ground and accepted it.

"Thank you," I said quietly.

Hesitating, he watched me fiddle with the food. He lifted his hand and touched my cheek. I flinched and walked away, finding a log where I could sit and eat alone.

Our rest was brief, and Callon helped me mount, his fingers locking on my waist. I fought down the urge to growl, to snap at him not to touch me. I knew he was trying to be kind, trying to make amends for his behavior, but I'd never forgive him. Letting things go so far, refusing to tell me what I needed to know...he could reap what he'd sown.

We rode on. The landscape rolled by slowly. The pines moved as the wind touched their tips; an eagle flew overhead, far above the tree line. It was refreshing to notice these things this time around. On the ride in, I had been out of it, attacked by three Timeless men and left broken and disorientated. They had been sent by the Sarac clan to kill children of the Timeless before they transformed. Callon, Colt and Daniel had saved my life—they had saved my life a number of times. But as much as I owed them, I still couldn't forgive their lies.

The day waned, and as night fell, a fresh chill surrounded me. Well, it was late September. I untied my long-sleeved shirt from my waist and slid it on, glad I had thought ahead.

Darkness came, but we didn't stop. There was enough moonlight to guide the way. The pace my guardians had set was as relentless as ever, and I was struggling to keep up. I needed to rest, but I didn't want to slow us down. Callon moved closer, reaching out for my hand. I saw his concern as he checked me over. My lips were parched, and my whole body ached. I needed water.

"Cheyenne, do we need to stop for the night?" Callon asked.

Everything in me wanted to say yes, but I stood firm.

"I'm fine," I replied coolly. "Just..."

I was interrupted as Daniel came to a sudden halt. In seconds, Callon had dismounted and was at my side to lift me down.

"Don't lie to us. You're tired and dehydrated. I don't want you to get one of your nasty headaches before we make it home."

Much as I wanted to argue, I knew he was right. I really didn't want one on top of everything else. They were horrid, part of my transformation. I had suffered one a few weeks ago after we arrived at Dex and Lilly's, right after I had been attacked by three men. It was more than a headache; a fever accompanied it, and I lost my hearing and sight. I had also almost lost Colt, after our fight by the riverside. I sighed. Sometimes I wondered if it would have been better if he had left me there—at least my heart would have remained whole.

Daniel had the tent set up quickly, and Colt began gathering wood for the fire.

"Here, drink this," Callon said, handing me a canteen. "Are you hungry?"

"No." I really wasn't.

"You should eat more. You're not Timeless yet. I don't want you to disappear on us."

"Sorry that my eating habits bother you, Dr. Callon," I said flatly. I'd be glad when I was Timeless. Then I'd only have to eat about once a week. The slower metabolism would mean I didn't have to consume as much food.

"Another ten to fifteen pounds would do you some good." He paused. "And that's from a medical perspective."

I rolled my eyes.

"I'll keep that in mind." Even though I was still angry with him, I couldn't deny that I was thankful he was a doctor. He'd already put me back together a number of times. At the rate I was going, I needed access to twenty-four-hour medical care.

Daniel started the fire, and Callon motioned for me to sit. I sat on the ground, curled my legs into my chest and wrapped my arms tightly around them. I played with the Servak ring on my index finger, feeling each etched symbol. I kept my gaze on the fire. Colt knew what this meant; he knew I would twist my ring when I was deep in thought. He sighed.

No one bothered to sit too close. They kept their distance as they began to talk out loud amongst themselves. For what reason I didn't know—they could talk telepathically and usually did. It was probably just to include me. I was growing more exhausted by the moment. The tent was up nearby; I didn't have anything to prove by staying awake. I stood up and walked inside the canvas, and the conversation stopped. Not bothering to zip it closed, I curled up on the blanket Daniel had laid out for me. I stared at the fire until my lids grew heavy, and I fell asleep.

I was in the misty forest, alone. A dim light was flickering in the distance, and I followed it. I saw men, rugged warriors, gathered. Their clothing was ragged and worn. A branch snapped behind me, and I whipped my head around to see white fangs nearing.

My heart raced. It was the Tresez—and there were a lot of them. That unmistakable rancid smell touched my nostrils; their midnight eyes glowed with rage. They were just as awful as I remembered, just as large, just as hideous. Their appearance was like monstrous dogs with porcupine quills that rose and fell with each breath. Their pink gums exposed razor-sharp fangs. They circled me. They were going to destroy me—their mission was to kill the children of the Timeless.

I had nowhere to go, no one to help me—I was alone—again. One of the creatures stepped back, creating an opening, while another came from behind...leading me forward. They didn't attack. They forced me to follow their path—I had no choice. I blinked, and we were at the edge of the forest. A thick fog still hovered above the ground in the valley, but it was light. I could see clearly—a battle was taking place there. My heart cried out. Callon, Colt and Daniel were fighting! They were paired off against the same men I'd seen earlier. I helplessly watched them fall one by one. They were dying for me—to protect me. No! They would not die for me—I bolted out into the field. I ran with everything within me...I couldn't let them die for me!

"No!" I screamed out.

"Cheyenne!"

I sat straight up, shaking violently. My fingers clawed the ground; I blinked wildly as I oriented myself. It was a dream; the same one from two nights ago. The same terrifying nightmare that had caused me to run into Callon's arms and kiss him...

"Cheyenne!" Callon's rough voice called out from the tent entrance. He came inside and knelt down. His jaw tightened as he saw the fear in my eyes. I could tell he wanted to reach out, but he didn't.

"It was just a dream," I said in a shaky voice. "I'm fine." I forced myself to turn away, to lie back down and face the tent wall, curling into a ball. I wanted Callon to hold me, but I needed to be strong. I could handle this on my own. I stared at the tent wall as he contemplated what to do next. Slowly he drew the blanket over me, and I closed my eyes. His fingers brushed my hair behind my ear as he sighed and rose. I didn't sleep.

My mind kept running over the dream. I couldn't stop thinking about my protectors. It wasn't fair! They had hurt me so badly, and yet I couldn't stop loving them. And even if I didn't love them, I couldn't allow them to die for me. Deep down, I knew I wouldn't stay with them any longer than I had to; however, I would do everything within my power to ensure they weren't harmed.

By the time dawn came, I was even more exhausted than the night before. I rolled over and saw Callon had placed my pack just inside the door. I crawled forward and began to dig through it. The tent door was still open, and I could see the three men were sitting close by. I knew Colt was watching, waiting for me to come out. I looked up to meet his icy blue stare. His shoulders were tense, his whole body ready to leap up at a moment's notice. I took a shaky breath and zipped the tent closed.

I changed and sat silently for a few moments. I wanted to wash up, brush my teeth. The canteen was near the fire, next to Colt. I frowned. I was acting like a child just because I couldn't get my own way. I could face them. I was strong enough—they no longer affected me.

I opened the tent, closing my eyes briefly as I pressed my fingers to my forehead. I forced myself to take the necessary steps, and I paused in front of Colt. He leaned forward and handed me the canteen, purposely touching my hand. I bit my lip. He knew what I wanted without me asking.

"Thanks," I murmured and tried to walk away, but he wouldn't release his hold. Colt's free hand swallowed my cheek as he lifted my chin up. His eyes held such remorse, and a blond wisp of hair fell over his lashes.

"Chey—" he began.

"No, Colt," I whispered. "It's too late." I could hardly keep a level voice. I was on the brink of tears. What was wrong with me? How could I still love him after all he'd done? I clenched my jaw and turned away. Colt released his hold, leaving Daniel to follow me.

Daniel and I stopped a short distance away. He held the canteen while I brushed and washed. The silence was killing him. I finished and glanced up into his deep blue eyes. His silky black hair ruffled in the breeze.

"I'm really sorry, Cheyenne," he said. "We didn't mean to hurt you. I don't want you to go away. I want you to stay around." He hesitated and then touched my hand. Dex had told them I would leave the first chance I got—I had said the words myself the night I found out about the betrothal. "I know we can work this out. Just give us a chance. We can make it right."

I didn't reply. A sudden chill ran down my spine. Seconds later, I winced as a sharp pain flared above my shoulder blade. That was where the Tresez's nail had been embedded in my skin. I pinched my eyes closed and arched my back. When the pain subsided, I opened my eyes to see the anxiety in Daniel's. I grabbed his arm swiftly. "I'm fine, Daniel! I'm fine. Don't you dare say a word!" I stared intently at him, willing him to agree, and waited for him to respond. He nodded, and I released my hold. My gaze shifted to Callon and Colt. They were tearing down camp—they had seen nothing. We walked back.

"Not a word!" I muttered under my breath.

I went straight to Mandi; I felt her unease as she felt mine.

Something wasn't right, but I didn't know what it was. Why did my wound hurt like that? It hadn't been bothering me until right then...

I touched Mandi's neck and whispered softly to her, "It's all right, girl. Everything's all right." I knew she understood me. Lilly had believed my ability to communicate with Mandi was one of my gifts showing itself early. I glanced around. Callon and Colt seemed to be acting normal; only Daniel kept watching me as they packed. He was so much smaller than his brothers, yet I knew he would be willing to protect me if needed. He could disappear and reappear just by looking where he wanted to go, an ability called "jumping." It had often come in handy in the past.

I walked around Mandi's side and was about to mount when Callon approached. I kept my eyes locked on the ground. It was too painful to see the emotion in my guardians' eyes.

He didn't say a word at first; he just stood there, waiting for me to look up. Eventually he lost patience and gently forced my head up. I knew what he was doing—it was time for my daily check-up.

"You don't look so good," he said as his brown curls fell in his eyes in a way I used to find endearing. "Are you feeling all right?"

I sighed. "How many times do I have to tell all of you? I'm fine." I didn't matter that I hadn't actually said the words to Callon yet. I had told Daniel not to worry about me, and that was good enough.

Callon didn't release his hold. He was searching for answers, but I avoided his gaze.

"Will you tell me if you don't feel well enough to continue?"

"Yes," I replied, knowing full well I wouldn't. I'd never tell them. I didn't need his concern—their concern. They would only smother me, and I didn't want smothering—I wanted to be alone.

He withdrew his hand, and I turned to mount. He lifted me with little effort. Colt was even stronger, able to toss me around like a sack of feathers. I wasn't that small, about five foot five, and though I'd lost some weight recently—down to one hundred and ten from one-twenty—I was by no means easy to carry.

It was quiet as we departed. I didn't even hear the birds singing. Callon rode closer and reached into his pack. He withdrew a granola bar and handed it to me.

"You need to eat something." He was using his "he who must be obeyed" voice. "I also want you to drink more today. We still have a two-day ride back to the truck."

I nodded, taking the bar and unwrapping it slowly. I wasn't hungry, but I knew Callon was right. Callon rode closer than yesterday, glancing in my direction more often. For a brief moment, the pain in my shoulder blade returned. I fought down the urge to cry out, telling myself it wasn't as bad as the pain had been before. I managed not to give anything away except a slight hitch in my breathing.

It was enough for Daniel to notice, though, and his head whipped around. His eyes were full of concern. I realized he'd heard my shallow gasp. My teeth clenched. He was going to give me away! Daniel's gaze locked on me for a second, but he turned around. Out of the corner of my eye, I saw Callon and Colt staring harshly at him. They were drilling Daniel telepathically. Then a stray thought hit me. Callon was the leader of the Consilador clan—their clan. Did that mean he had full power over Daniel? Would he force the truth out of him?

I didn't have to worry. As the day wore on, nothing more was said. We rode in silence. The sunlight was trickling through the treetops, and a warm wind caused the tall pines to sway. I pulled my long-sleeved shirt off and tied it to my waist. Raising my arms, I braided my wavy hair at the nap of my neck. It kept the long wisps from tickling my cheeks.

I was beginning to recognize my surroundings as early evening fell. This was the same location we had stopped the second night on our trip in, the same place where the Ghosters—the lights—had tried to take me. The lights I had seen in the cathedral, the lights Callon refused to tell me about...and the lights that had come between me and Colt, driving us apart.

I shook my head. If I'd known there were beings who could separate themselves from their bodies in the form of lights...if I'd known they could steal my soul...I wouldn't have looked. If they had explained to me, I would've kept my eyes closed. I would've held on to Colt, and they wouldn't have had to shout at me after I was so taken in by their beauty that I was almost ripped away.

My emotions bubbled to the surface as we passed a familiar outcrop of trees. Beyond them lay the waterfalls where I first realized I loved Colt. How ironic that with both the cave and waterfalls, he'd shown his heart to me. And both times, circumstances had changed so swiftly. It was as if fate were toying with me. She allowed me to get close enough to knowing real love before she ripped it away— leaving me bleeding and broken.

We stopped to camp for the night, and a single tear streamed down my cheek. I didn't want to be here, and I didn't want to remember those feelings. I knew Callon hadn't chosen this site to cause me misery, but I was finding it hard to ignore the ache in my chest.

As I dismounted, the pain in my shoulder blade came to life. I stumbled, locking my fingers into Mandi's mane to steady myself.

Daniel jumped to my side, his blue eyes full of concern. I flashed him a dark look.

"I'm fine," I practically snarled.

He didn't look convinced. I sought out Colt and Callon; they hadn't noticed anything.

"Not a word, Daniel," I hissed.

Daniel simply smiled sadly before he disappeared.

CHAPTER 2

I stayed close to Mandi as the trio prepared camp. Daniel quickly set up the tent, and Colt went in search of firewood. The distant cracking told me he was splitting wood. Callon tended to the horses, letting them feed in the meadow nearby. I removed Mandi's tack. It was a good distraction for me and I could tell she was glad to be free. Her ears twitched as she stopped grazing to look at me. Both she and I knew something wasn't quite right; we just didn't know what.

Callon was standing next to the tent, waiting for me. Reluctantly, I walked over; my pack was inside the doorway. Callon's fingers grasped mine, and I looked up.

"I know this isn't what you want to do right now, but if you change, I'll take you to the falls to clean up." I shrugged off his hand, then went inside and zipped the tent closed.

Despite the way he had phrased the request, he really hadn't given me a choice. I was going to the falls whether I wanted to or not. I knelt and dug through the pack for my swimsuit, shorts and shirt. Callon was waiting with a towel in hand when I stepped out of the tent. I kept my gaze down as I followed after him. I felt Colt's eyes on

15

my back and wondered if he felt the same misery. I took a shaky breath and kept walking.

The walk seemed much shorter this time, maybe because I was in such deep thought. I remembered how the butterflies churned in my stomach as I'd followed behind Colt. How he'd been so gentle, so loving. How he'd carried me to the falls, and how I knew he was different than anyone else I'd ever met. We stopped at the water's edge, and the sound was almost overwhelming. It wasn't due to the volume; it was due to the memories. Memories rushed forward, wanting to take over, and I had to fight them back down.

I removed my clothes and shoes, then walked forward into the cold water. As I glanced back, I saw Callon perched on a boulder. I grasped the small soap bottle tightly in my hand and dove under. I swam out away from the falls.

The iciness engulfed me, and a chill ran through my body. I saturated my hair with the shampoo as I unbraided it; making sure I was facing away from Callon. I stared out across the river before me. I was in a quiet pool, a few feet from where the current could pull me out. Would it be a bad thing to let it sweep away my memories?

I tucked the bottle in my suit bottom and ducked under to rinse my hair. When I came to the surface, I found I had twisted and was facing the falls again. The cascading water wasn't soothing—it caused too many feelings to bubble up. I saw the rock where Colt and I had sat, where we had kissed. Where I'd discovered deep down that I loved him as he loved me...

Tears welled in my eyes, and the unbearable ache began to beat a rhythm I couldn't stop. I pushed myself under; I wanted the freezing water to make me forget. I wanted it to numb my feelings, deaden my heart, and frost my pain. I pushed myself further down and just floated in the murky, silent solitude.

I stayed there as long as I could, forcing myself to stay under until I thought my lungs would burst. I released one last air bubble from my mouth and swam to the surface, gasping as I came out.

A hand latched on to my arm, and I jumped. I thought I was alone.

"Cheyenne!" Callon's eyes were wide with panic. "Are you okay?"

I yanked my arm away, splashing his face with water.

"I'm fine. Why wouldn't I be?" Callon wasn't satisfied with my answer. He reached forward again and drew me closer.

"But how did you do that?"

I stared at him blankly.

"Do what?"

"Stay under for so long?"

Huh? What was he talking about?

"I wasn't under for that long," I said, irritated. Why did he have to be so overprotective?

"Yes, you were," Callon said. "Why do you think I'm here in the water with you?"

I frowned.

"You overreacted. That's why," I spat. "Treating me like some helpless child..."

"You were under the water for more than seven minutes," Callon said. "I thought the current caught you and took you downstream. After four minutes, I began searching. When I saw your air bubble, I came for you."

"Well, I appreciate your concern, but you didn't need to worried." I tried to pull my arm away again. "Can you please let go? I can swim on my own."

Callon's eyes narrowed, and he wrapped his arm around my waist. He pulled us to shore. I wanted to struggle and make it more difficult, but it was pointless. I wouldn't have won.

Callon didn't release his hold as we came to the bank. Still holding me with one arm, he picked up the towel and to set me down on a large boulder. He wrapped the towel around my shoulders and began to rub me dry.

"Are you going to tell me what's going on?" he asked calmly.

I was still confused. "I don't know what you mean."

"How could you stay under for so long? That isn't normal."

Callon crouched down and dried my legs.

"I don't know," I said, trying to ignore the warmth of his fingers. "I was upset about being here, the whole situation. I wanted to forget, distract myself, so I held my breath until my lungs hurt."

Callon snatched the towel away roughly and stood up.

"Get your shoes on."

I didn't move. He was in a bad mood, but why? I hadn't done anything wrong. Slowly, I crept away from the boulder and pulled my boots on. I drew my hair to the side and began to wring the water out. Callon slinked around me, and pressed just above my shoulder blade. I flinched. He ran his rough fingers down the length of the wounds. I remained still.

"Does this hurt?" His voice had softened again.

"No. I'm fine." I stepped away and grabbed my shirt from the ground, pulling it over my head. I hated myself for still wanting his touch.

"So that's what Daniel wouldn't tell me. I saw him glance back, and you scowled." Callon sighed. "It hurts, and you didn't want me to know. Why?"

I bent again and put my shorts on.

"I don't need your sympathy."

He gripped my shoulders and slowly turned me around to face him. He took my chin in his hand, forcing me to look at him. His hair was wet, which made it curl.

"Cheyenne," Callon said. "I want to help you. Why won't you let me?"

"I can handle the physical pain." I inhaled. "It's the heartache I can't stand."

Callon stepped closer and raised his other hand to my neck, holding me firmly in place.

"I'm sorry we caused you such heartache. I'm the one to blame; I shouldn't have allowed this to go on for so long. I'll make this right. Just give me time." His lips hovered above mine.

Tears formed in my eyes and my voice cracked as I answered, "No, I've had enough. I can't handle you tearing my heart to pieces again. Just let me go."

Callon's face softened.

"I can't. Don't you see? We're bound together eternally, and nothing can change that." He caressed my cheek. "I won't push you. I'll give you time to heal, but I can't let you leave. You're stuck with the three of us, and we'll do everything in our power to protect you. You have a destiny to fulfill, and we're a part of it."

"I didn't choose this!" I snapped. "It's all being forced upon me. I don't know who I am—I don't want any of this!"

"Life's not always about what we want, Cheyenne. Sometimes it's about what we can offer. Sometimes we have to be self-sacrificing for the good of others. One day you'll understand."

My tears were flowing freely now. I lowered my head as Callon drew me into his embrace. His chin brushed my hair as he rubbed my back, like he had after my accident. When would all this heartache end? I'd already lost so much, carried so much on my lonely shoulders. Any happiness, any joy I had was short-lived and soon ripped from my grasp. What did I have to do to make it last?

I didn't move from his arms for a long time. I was exhausted both mentally and physically. I hated the feelings I had for them—for Callon. The way his touch sent a current up and down my spine. I had to resist. I had to fight. Otherwise I'd never leave. I had to keep my distance.

A sudden breeze caused me to shiver. Callon pulled away, his hazel eyes filled with empathy.

"Come on, sweetheart. We need to get you by the fire to warm up." He took hold of my hand, and we headed back to camp.

The day grew darker. By the time we returned, a large fire was roaring. Callon must have forewarned Colt and Daniel that I was cold. I kept my gaze down as I headed straight for the tent. I was trying to hide the fact I'd been crying, although knowing they gossiped worse than old women, I was sure Colt already knew. I changed and contemplated curling up on the blanket, but I could see Callon's shadow in the doorway. If I didn't come out, he'd come in. Reluctantly I stepped out.

I stared at the fire and realized I had few options of where I could go. Callon directed me to sit between him and Colt—their presence around me mimicked the prison around my heart. I pulled my legs into my chest, wrapped my arms around my knees and stared at the flames. They were watching me. All three wanted to make things right, but it was too late. They'd betrayed me, and I was never going to forgive them. I lay my head on my knees, closing my eyes in hopes

20

of maintaining some sort of composure.

Callon departed briefly and then returned. He rested his hand on my shoulder. "You need to eat. You already refused lunch. You can't go for too much longer." I didn't respond. I wasn't hungry, nor did I really care. His grip tightened. "Cheyenne, if you don't eat and drink, it will hurt you later. I need you to keep hydrated. We need you to stay strong."

As much as I didn't want to admit it, I knew he was right. I did need my strength. I didn't know when my opportunity to leave would come, but I needed to be ready. Slowly, I sat up and took the food and water. Callon was clearly distressed; they all were. I ate and drank everything he gave me. When I finished, I went to the tent and curled up on the blanket to sleep. My body trembled in the cold, as I lay still, waiting for dawn to come. I was too afraid to close my eyes. I didn't want to have the same dream—I didn't want to see them die. I was so angry with them, yet I couldn't turn them away. I had no one else, and that's what frightened me the most...I didn't want to be alone. I listened to the fire crackling, knew they were watching, but eventually my tiredness won out, and I drifted off.

Dawn broke, and I forced my weary lids open. Another day and a half, and we would be almost home. It was the brothers' home, not mine. I'd just be grateful for a warm bed, a shower and a door to close them out.

I lay silently, staring at the tent walls, contemplating my life and the mess it had become. It was hard to believe that just a mere twenty-four hours ago, I'd wanted nothing more than to stay in Colt's strong arms as he showed me the beauty inside that cave.

Now, I couldn't be around him—or near Callon—without my heart tearing in two.

I rolled over and glanced out of the tent. They were still sitting around the fire. Colt's gaze was filled with turmoil as he looked at me. His jaw was tight, muscles tensed. He said he would always be there for me—now he couldn't. His promise had been broken because of an older vow that tied me to another; the man who'd killed my parents, Marcus.

Callon, too, had his own part to play in the equation. Quietly siting on the sidelines, letting Colt trick me into believing we could be together, before revealing that I was promised to him as well. Another obligation that dragged on my heart, forcing me to make a choice I didn't want. How could they have done this to me?

Sighing, I sat up and once again slowly zipped the tent closed. The daylight was too bright, and my head was beginning to throb. Digging through my pack, I searched for some pain medication—anything to help ease the pressure. This wasn't like the headaches I'd had in the past. It was normal—well, as normal as normal could be for me. Unfortunately, I couldn't find any painkillers. I'd have to ask Callon for something. Already my dread was mounting, knowing he would pester me with endless questions. I grabbed my toothbrush and slid my boots on, unzipped the tent and stepped out.

The morning air was cool, and the fire was barely flickering. I didn't look up, but I knew Colt's attention was locked on me as I approached Callon, half-guessing what his response would be.

"Callon, do you have any aspirin? I have a headache."

Immediately Callon leapt up so fast that I staggered back to prevent us colliding. My foot caught on a loose rock, and I fell to the ground. Colt and Daniel hovered over me, anxiety ridden.

22

"Where are you hurting, Cheyenne?" Callon's hands were at my temples.

I scowled, pushing myself back to my feet.

"It's just a normal headache. Quit panicking! I need some aspirin or something. I don't want it to get any worse." Callon's fingers latched around my arms. I tried to tug myself free, but he wouldn't let go. "Oh, for crying out loud! I'm not lying! The other headaches come on real fast. This is a slow-building one—it's different." I sighed. "I know the difference between the two. Believe me, I'll tell you if one of the bad ones comes again."

After some hesitation, Callon glanced at Colt and Daniel before he walked away. They moved in closer, making sure I wouldn't escape. I watched Callon reach into the pack that was strapped on Bo and pull out various medical supplies. Apparently, he was more prepared than I had thought. He strode back, dropped two pills in my hand, and extended the canteen.

"Thank you." I swallowed the pills and then attempted to walk away. As I took a step, he blocked my path. My lip curled. Why did he always have to do this? "I just want to brush my teeth and wash my face. I'm not going to wander off." He didn't move, but I wasn't going to back down. "Please, get out of my way."

Finally, Callon backed off. His eyes moved to Daniel, who jumped up to come after me. Taking the canteen from my hands, he helped me wash up.

"Are you sure you're okay, Cheyenne?"

"Don't worry about me!" I snapped. My words came out harsher than I intended, but my pride wouldn't let me apologize.

When we returned, I was surprised to see Callon and Colt had already broken camp. They really wanted to move fast. Maybe they were hoping that if they got me back to the cabin soon, I couldn't run away. I headed for Mandi, but Daniel took my arm and tugged me toward Callon. As he let go, Callon took hold, and I glared at him.

"You're not riding by yourself today," Callon said.

I furrowed my brow in my most impressive scowl. "Why not?"

"I'm not taking any chances with you," Callon answered. "You're riding with me."

"Why? There's nothing wrong with me. It was just a simple headache. I'm feeling better since I took the pills, anyway."

Callon wasn't listening. He seized my arm again, so tight it almost hurt.

"We don't have time to argue."

I stared at him. He who must be obeyed was back in full swing. But there was something in his hazel eyes that hadn't been there before.

"There's a good chance we're being followed, Cheyenne."

He was being honest with me, not withholding information for once.

"A good chance? So you're not sure?"

He didn't reply, so it must not be too serious. Sighing, I shook my head. A little information was better than none at all.

"Fine, but only for the morning. This afternoon I'll ride alone."

"We'll see," Callon replied.

He led me over to Bo, lifted me into the saddle and swung himself up behind me. He reached under my arms and took hold of the reins. I remained rigid; I didn't want to lean into him.

"Relax, or I won't let you ride by yourself later." Callon gently pulled me back into his chest as we set off at a trot.

It was a faster ride this morning. I could tell that the trio were worried I was about to have another episode, another part of my transformation. The last one had been pretty bad; they wanted me home if it were to happen again. I knew that headache wasn't coming; however, the nail wound above my shoulder was burning again. Mandi, too, was restless, and not just because I wasn't riding her. She had only acted like this twice; when there was thunder, or when there were Tresez. And there wasn't a cloud in the sky...

My eyes widened. I looked around, but no one else seemed to notice anything out of the ordinary. Callon said we might be followed. I sighed. Was I imaging things? My worries didn't lessen, even when we stopped for lunch. All three hovered around me. For once I didn't complain as I ate; something was definitely amiss. When I finished, Callon took hold of my elbow and led me to Bo. I dug my heels into the ground and yanked my arm free.

"I said I'd ride with you this morning, but I'm riding by myself this afternoon."

"I don't think that's a good idea," Callon replied. He was casting quick glances around us. Something was definitely amiss.

"Look, my headache's gone, and I ate lunch, too. You don't have to baby me." Riding so close to him again would drive me mad. Danger or not, I couldn't stand it anymore.

Callon hesitated before answering. "You'll tell me if something's wrong?"

"Yes, I promise." I couldn't be petty now; I needed to trust them.

Callon released his hold, and I went to Mandi. Colt was holding her as I prepared to mount. He ever so slyly placed a hand on my waist, pushing me into the saddle. I frowned at him for a few moments, then looked away, but not before I caught his solemn

25

expression.

We trotted out once more, and Callon rode close behind me. A draft touched my neck, and the hairs stood on end. An unusually warm breeze. I'd felt it before...

Suddenly, Daniel disappeared from atop Charlie. Everyone stopped dead. Mandi became restless, prancing and snorting.

I stroked Mandi's neck.

"It's okay. Stay calm, girl. Everything's fine." She stilled almost instantly. I saw the bemused glances from Callon and Colt and couldn't help but feel a little smug. They'd made fun of me before— they didn't believe I could communicate with her.

Daniel reappeared. He was uneasy.

"There's a large party following us, approaching from the south. They've broken into three smaller groups." He looked to Callon. "They've sent the Trackers."

My breath caught. Trackers! Callon was right about us being followed. The Sarac clan must have sent Trackers to kill me. I couldn't believe it. This was exactly the situation I'd seen in my dream.

The brothers exchanged glances; a lengthy period of time passed without external communication. My heart pounded as I waited for directions. Callon moved closer and took my hand.

"Cheyenne, go with Daniel. He'll take you around the Tracking parties and get you to safety. If all else fails, you need to head north and hide. We'll find you." He paused and I saw the unease roll over his face. "You mustn't let them see you, or they'll kill you." He squeezed my fingers. "Do you understand me?"

I nodded, as the details sunk in. Callon quickly removed his pack and tied it on Mandi's back. "There's enough food to last a couple of days. I know you'll be resourceful if needed." All of a sudden, I was reminded of my berry trick, and tears welled in my eyes. I didn't want them to risk themselves for me.

Callon and Colt turned and began to ride off. I couldn't stop myself.

"Callon, Colt!" Both halted to look at me. I swallowed. "Don't...don't think this changes things. But don't make it worse by not coming back. Promise me you'll return!"

Callon said something, but it never reached my ears. The sound was drowned out in the rush of galloping hooves.

LISA L WIEDMEIER

CPSIA information can be obtained at www.ICGtesting.com
Printed in the USA
LVOW131658140613

338654LV00003B/275/P